D0791170

Death in Provence

Death in Provence

A NOVEL

SERENA KENT

HARPER

An Imprint of HarperCollins*Publishers*

DEATH IN PROVENCE. Copyright © 2019 by Deborah Lawrenson and Robert Rees. All rights reserved. Printed in the United States of America. No part of this book may be used or reproduced in any manner whatsoever without written permission except in the case of brief quotations embodied in critical articles and reviews. For information, address HarperCollins Publishers, 195 Broadway, New York, NY 10007.

HarperCollins books may be purchased for educational, business, or sales promotional use. For information, please email the Special Markets Department at SPsales@harpercollins.com.

FIRST EDITION

Designed by Bonni Leon-Berman

Library of Congress Cataloging-in-Publication Data
Names: Kent, Serena, author.
Title: Death in Provence : a novel / Serena Kent.
Description: New York, NY : Harper, 2019. | Series: Penelope Kite ; 1
| Identifiers: LCCN 2018043841 (print) | LCCN 2018049722 (ebook) |
ISBN 9780062869876 (E-book) | ISBN 9780062869852 (hardback)
Subjects: | BISAC: FICTION / Mystery & Detective / Women Sleuths.
| FICTION / Mystery & Detective / Traditional British. | GSAFD:
Mystery fiction.
Classification: LCC PR6111.E594 (ebook) | LCC PR6111.E594 D43 2019
(print) | DDC 823/.92—dc23
LC record available at https://lccn.loc.gov/2018043841

19 20 21 22 23 LSC 10 9 8 7 6 5 4 3 2 1

FOR JOY LAWRENSON AND BRIAN REES,

who would have been much amused.

Death in Provence

The Plunge

PENELOPE KITE STOOD at the door of her dream home and wiped her brow with the back of her hand. The late morning heat had brought the air to a steamy simmer. August was a hot flash that never subsided.

Uncut grass stood waist high in the courtyard, and a thousand cicadas sawed their jittery music. Every so often a large wasp built like a military helicopter would break away from the swarm around the fig tree and enter the kitchen in a show of menace.

She slapped a broken fly swat down onto the thick layer of dust that coated every surface, and missed yet again.

"What have I done?"

The stone-flagged kitchen floor offered no reply.

She sat down on a rickety wooden chair. It creaked ominously. She was definitely going to have to cut back on croissants.

"What *have* I done?" she wailed to the walls. Well, you polished off a whole bottle of cheap rosé last night, they seemed to say. That wasn't clever.

Her head hurt horribly.

She had a sinking feeling that she had taken on more than she could chew in this crumbling wreck of a place, and there was no one to blame but herself.

In the days and weeks afterwards, as she went over and over these crucial hours until they seemed unreal, she would look back on her hot and headachy panic in the kitchen and think that it was nothing compared to what was about to break.

But Penelope was sure of one thing: she had not left the house to brave the searing brightness of the garden until a couple of hours later. So she could not possibly have known what was floating facedown in the swimming pool.

1

IN EARLY SPRING, EVERYTHING HAD been so different.

Penelope had been energized by the cloudless blue skies of the South of France. Following a particularly gruesome family Christmas with her two children and their badly behaved families, she had escaped an Easter that promised more of the same but with added chocolate. Two wonderfully tranquil weeks in April had left her yearning to stay longer.

The Côte d'Azur had long since become Wimbledon-sur-Mer, but the Luberon Valley was charming. Penelope had visited this area of Provence many times during the course of her marriage and had always been able to relax in its sunny friendliness, even when her husband was as distant as the top of the long rippled ridge of mountain that hung like a blue curtain behind the ancient hilltop villages. Churches and crumbling fortresses and narrow streets had the slumbering feel of the warm south, and the orchards and vineyards below promised a land of plenty. The pace of life seemed more relaxed, less full of braying expats, especially English ones from the Home Counties.

By the end of the first week, she had begun to indulge in some delicious daydreams and succumbed to perusing photographs of houses for sale in the estate agency windows. A few days later, after a particularly refreshing carafe of rosé with lunch, she found herself entering the door of an agency in the pretty village of Ménerbes.

The woman behind the desk nodded as Penelope waited for her to conclude her telephone conversation in leisurely fashion. She was the very epitome of an elegant Parisienne in her forties. Her blond hair bounced in all the right places to flatter a beautifully made-up face that no doubt benefited from all the mysteriously effective processes of French dermatology. The tiny navy-blue jacket, nipped in at the waist, looked like real Chanel, too. She made Penelope feel enormous, and very badly dressed.

Finally, she replaced the receiver with a flick of the wrist that set the charms on her large gilt bracelet jangling, and assessed her prospective client. It was the kind of look engineered to deter time-wasters. There must be plenty of them about.

Penelope hoisted her best smile. "Bonjour, madame."

"Bonjour. Comment je peux vous aider?"

A lovely stone house, Penelope told her in faltering French, that was what she was looking for. On a hillside, with a view and a garden—but not too much land. Three bedrooms and two bathrooms. A swimming pool, or space to build one.

Goodness, thought Penelope. Those daydreams were awfully specific.

"I have several properties that might interest you," said the Frenchwoman in perfect English.

Penelope didn't know whether to be relieved or annoyed. "Ah, good," she said.

"My name is Mme Valencourt. Either you can make an appointment for viewing at a later date. Or—you can come with me now." She held up a red lacquered fingernail. "Vous avez de la chance, madame. You are very lucky."

"I am?"

"Mais oui, madame."

Penelope could only guess what this stroke of luck might be as she was ushered straight out of the office and into a shiny red

Mini Cooper that matched the nails. Perhaps she shouldn't have drunk all that delicious rosé. It had made her bold.

"We must hurry," said the estate agent, driving off at speed. With no mercy for other road users, they shot through the narrow streets and out into the countryside, past orchards brimming with snowdrifts of almond blossom. The first acid-green shoots were showing on the gnarled stumps of vineyards. Here and there, men in the fields were bent double in intensive contemplation of crop and soil.

They swerved violently. Penelope clenched her seat belt in one hand and gripped the door handle with the other, her foot instinctively moving to brake as they overtook a Mercedes into the teeth of an oncoming tractor.

Apparently oblivious to the cyclists and tourists who lay scattered in her wake, Mme Valencourt kept up a businesslike conversation in which she established Penelope's credentials as a buyer (clearly satisfactory), history of visits to France, marital status and happiness with the divorce (also apparently satisfactory), and former career (distinct glimmer of respect). The car swept up narrowing roads into the Luberon Mountains, away from the chic villages so beloved of French cabinet ministers, their mistresses, and *Paris Match* photographers and into a landscape of holm oaks and pines.

As the road became emptier, Penelope's heart rate eased slightly.

"La belle Provence!" announced Mme Valencourt, as they swung onto a potholed track that skirted a wood of scrub oak and spiky juniper bushes. Past a rusted tractor standing in an unkempt field, she stopped the car in front of a stone archway and gestured.

"Voilà. Le Chant d'Eau. The name of the property is The Song of the Water. It is an old farm."

Penelope's gaze followed her companion's manicured finger.

The property was decrepit. A couple of substantial outbuildings were suffocating under thick ivy. The two-story farmhouse itself was built of pale stone in the traditional style. The wooden window shutters were flaking lavender-coloured paint. Several were hanging askew. Penelope could just picture the way it could be renovated. A lovely summer sitting room, with a terrace for dining under the stars. No, stop it, she told herself, don't get carried away. Her affected seriousness about buying was only to ensure that she wouldn't be patronised.

But . . . a run-down farmhouse in Provence, she mused, as the door was unlocked with a large iron key. Think what I could do with it!

The dark hall smelled musty and mousy. Penelope caught her breath. Mme Valencourt skittered ahead on her high clacky sandals. Half walking, half feeling her way forward, Penelope followed. In a room that was revealed as a kitchen, the estate agent unlatched the window and pushed open the shutters with a painful creak. Light flooded in, illuminated the dust that dredged every surface.

The house had clearly not been lived in for some time. Penelope tried the light switch, but nothing happened.

Mme Valencourt opened the back door. Penelope caught her breath for a second time. The rear of the house looked out high over the Luberon Valley, which opened in a wide panorama before her. Close by was Saignon, like an enchanted fortress on a cliff. In the valley stood the town of Apt. Farther off, the large red monolith of Roussillon, and beyond it the famously beautiful village of Gordes standing proud on its rocky outcrop. On one side the mountains of the Petit Luberon range stretched away to the Rhône, and on the other, just visible over the hills, stood the bare peak of Mont Ventoux, with its seemingly snow-covered limestone summit.

"See, madame, you are lucky! This is not on the market yet. You are the first to see it."

"It's lovely." Penelope could hardly breathe now. The setting was incredible.

"There are some problems, of course." Mme Valencourt shrugged, as if to imply that it wouldn't be an authentic Provençal house without authentic Provençal problems. "But those can be overcome. Of course, you can buy a perfect new house, but it will not have the atmosphere, the old stones, the views. Those, you cannot fix if they do not exist."

"No. Quite."

"Look around. Take as long as you like."

"Thank you."

The traditional Provençal beams and tiled floors were intact. The bedrooms upstairs—three of them—were all a good size, with high ceilings. The bathroom was a disgrace, but the panorama over the valley from above the stained basin more than made up for that. Penelope wondered whether it would be too decadent to install a wet room so she could enjoy the view while she showered, then slapped herself down. She was only here out of curiosity.

Outside, the grass was green and springy. Plum trees were coming into blossom. What looked like a quince held puffs of delicate rose-pink flowers.

They walked towards a lower terrace where a couple of olive trees offered the silver undersides of their leaves to a pleasant breeze. Mme Valencourt led the way to an ivy-covered wall and what appeared to have once been a door. After some effort, the estate agent pushed open the door against the resistance of a pile of decaying leaves. Penelope peeked inside, and stifled a cry of delight.

A substantial if dilapidated rectangular swimming pool lay

inside a walled garden. Roman steps led down to the bottom of the pool, though this was difficult to make out through the murky leaf-infested water. Cypress trees that must once have been elegant stood brown and lifeless at the four corners of the pool. In the corner was a ramshackle pump house with half a door hanging open on what remained of its hinges. Tall arches in the far end of this enchanting walled space revealed the valley beyond.

It was perfect.

Penelope was so lost in thought on the way back to Ménerbes that she scarcely flinched when Mme Valencourt pulled out to overtake on a blind bend and avoided a mobile pizza van so narrowly that they could have reached out for a slice of margherita.

"What did you think?" asked the agent as they drew up outside her office with a squeal of brakes.

"That I can't possibly buy the first house I've seen," said Penelope. "That would be silly."

Over the next few days, Mme Valencourt managed to combine striding about ancient farmhouses with dress and coiffure so immaculate that Penelope could only gaze in silent envy as she, red-faced and sweating profusely after another death-defying drive, staggered through the old oak door of yet another property perched above the Luberon Valley.

None of them was as lovely as the first.

At last, after another morning of fruitless endeavour, the Frenchwoman turned to her in the white sitting room of a house that had been renovated to suit a die-hard minimalist—the bathroom was a white cube, the walk-in wardrobe held only white clothes, and there was no sign of anything as vulgar as a cooker in the sparkling white kitchen—and declared flatly, "This is not for you."

"No, I agree."

"It is too clean, too chic. Le Chant d'Eau at St Merlot—that's the one for you."

Bit rude. Or was she simply being truthful? Penelope drew herself up, well aware that her Marks & Spencer wrap dress did not cut the mustard. No doubt Mme Valencourt had evaluated its forgiving elastane content with a laser-eyed glance, along with the shortcomings of the comfortable—and very reasonably priced—suedette boots she was wearing.

Penelope had her pride. "I don't know about that."

"It's old and in need of attention."

Now she was definitely being rude. Penelope made an effort to pull in her stomach.

"But it could be brought back to life," went on Mme Valencourt airily.

"That's good to know."

"It has been neglected for many years. The owners lived in Lyon and hardly ever came here after the first few years."

"Why ever not?"

"They were old and now they are both dead, and their children are selling it. I will take you to see it again."

⁂

BY THE time Penelope returned to England, she congratulated herself on having spent an interesting two weeks in the Luberon. She had seen a bit more of local life than just wandering from her rented gîte in Ménerbes to the restaurant to drink rosé. There had been some interesting trips and—now that she had survived to tell the tale—a thrilling amount of danger provided by Mme Valencourt's reckless disregard of other road users.

She had a lot of fun talking up the house hunt, the loveliness of the valley, and her adventures. And it did the family no end of good to think that she just might move abroad and leave them to it. Since she'd taken early retirement, they had taken her too much for granted as an on-call unpaid babysitter, errand runner, chauffeur, and cook.

She did it all willingly and for love—but they might have been a bit more appreciative.

"Typical," said Justin, "always thinking of yourself."

At twenty-nine, he had grown disconcertingly like his father. He was certainly as self-centred, with the same willingness to blame her for everything. No wonder his girlfriend Hannah looked increasingly sour. And their two-year-old son Rory was a holy terror.

"If I *were* only thinking of myself, I would not be looking after Rory this weekend while you and Hannah go away for a break," Penelope reminded him. "Or collecting him from playgroup on Thursdays and giving him his tea while Hannah goes to Pilates."

"I thought grandmothers wanted to be involved. We're doing you a favour."

"Thank you for that."

"We could easily pay someone to do it, no problem."

He had his father's arrogance about money, too, now he looked to be making a success of his job at an investment bank in the City.

His elder sibling Lena was less rude, mainly because she was pregnant again and was counting on Penelope's support. Lena's husband James was trying to get his own adventure holiday business off the ground, and seemed to be away more than he was home, spending large sums in the process. Penelope was often called in to help with Zack and Xerxes, mini dictators of four and three respectively. Xerxes! What would they call the next one, for heaven's sake—Genghis?

"What am I going to do without you? You can't go!" wailed

Lena. "Is this about all the plates the boys smashed because you wouldn't let them play football in your kitchen?"

The rows went on, with a few satisfying results. Lena promised to start disciplining her boys. Justin apologised and assured her that Hannah hadn't meant to be rude when she was overheard calling Penelope "an uptight, mean Home Counties throwback who has no idea about the modern world." That had hurt, at the time. Especially when Penelope thought of all the years of her relative youth she had devoted to being a good mother after she married David, a charming widower with a sad, baffled smile and two small children. On the plus side, it prompted her to book an appointment at an expensive hair salon in London for an overhaul.

She emerged with a choppy bob that showed off the thickness of her natural red-gold hair. Despite the inevitable signs of age in her body since she turned fifty the previous year, Penelope was proud that she had not yet found a strand of grey. Not that any of her friends believed her, but it was true. After that, she embarked on a mission to shop.

This was a rare event these days. Clothes shopping could be so traumatic, what with middle-aged spread and the shock of the initial glimpse in the changing-room mirror. But this time Penelope found it quite empowering. Despite appearances, she felt younger in heart than she had for a long time. After twenty-odd years of trying to be a good wife as well as a good mother despite feeling quite unhappy quite a lot of the time, she had left David five years previously after one affair too many. His affairs, not hers. Until the separation, Penelope had remained utterly faithful.

◈

PENELOPE MET friends for lunch at Café Rouge, tried to get interested in playing bridge, continued to do her bit for Lena and Justin and their families, and experienced all the usual irritations of living in the South of England: the sense that living close to London brought as many disadvantages as advantages; the endless traffic hold-ups and roadworks; the rudeness of young assistants in shops; the grumbling of people who then said, "Mustn't grumble"; the rain and the chill of depressing grey days; the television programmes featuring desperate searches for the few bargain antiques that hadn't yet had their day on-screen.

The unrelenting drizzle had become a deluge on the day the telephone rang from France.

"Allo? Mme Kite?"

"Oui," said Penelope.

"Clémence Valencourt, calling from the Agence Hublot in Ménerbes. I thought you might like to know that Le Chant d'Eau is now available for purchase."

Caught on the hop, Penelope was lost for words. In Esher, the song of the water rattled the guttering as the wind hurled the cloudburst straight at Bolingbroke Drive.

"Madame? Are you there?"

"Yes, yes . . . I'm sorry, I couldn't quite hear you. The property at St Merlot? I thought it was for sale when you took me to see it."

"Yes . . . and no. Technically, it could not be sold as there was a problem because one small parcel of the land had the wrong title attached."

"So . . . what is the situation now, then?"

"The title has been corrected and legally registered. The property can now be sold with no more problems. There are some other people interested in it, but I know that house is right for you. I am never wrong about these matters."

The Frenchwoman had some nerve.

"Yes, tatty and old, just like me," said Penelope sharply. "I understand what you are saying." Even on the phone, this Frenchwoman made her feel huge, though five foot six wasn't exactly Amazonian, and the 5:2 diet, though brutal, seemed at last to be having some small effect.

"Not at all," said Mme Valencourt. "The house has been sadly neglected, but it is very special, with a great beauty that only needs some love and attention to shine."

Penelope pulled her cardigan tighter around her. "I think I see what you mean." In her mind, she could see the vista of the valley, that extraordinary view from above the rocky fortress of Saignon, the rippled mountains and their winding tracks. The blue skies and warm sun. A glass of rosé on a little wrought-iron table on the terrace, perhaps with a painted terra-cotta bowl of black olives flecked with herbes de Provence . . .

"The price is very reasonable. The house, it is solid. And I will be able to assist you with finding builders to renovate it to your taste." The Frenchwoman had lowered her voice to a seductive purr.

Unbidden, more images from Penelope's persuasive day-dreams re-formed . . . long summer days spent finally learning to paint. Wonderful fresh fruit and vegetables to grow and cook. A chance to meet some new and interesting people. That little writing desk in the corner by the open window. And her music, of course. She could start playing her cello again. A new setting would give her the impetus she had lacked in Esher, where she had lost the heart for it. A fresh start . . .

She pulled herself out of her reverie. "Absolutely not. I can't take on a project like that. It's a ridiculous idea!"

2

THE HOUSE, TITLE, AND LAND were duly purchased and transferred, all the knotty legal issues scrutinised by a notary in Avignon. Penelope flew down to the South of France for two days, and spent most of them in the notary's office listening to him read a homeowner's version of *War and Peace* out loud, reciting the history of every aspect of Le Chant d'Eau, including its current status regarding energy consumption, lead paint, and insect infestation. Her house in Esher, which suddenly seemed a model of hassle-free home ownership, was rented out, and most of her possessions sent into storage.

"I am not doing this to spite you!" she said, yet again, to the children. "I am doing it for me, because I have a life too."

They stopped speaking to her, and then came round for more arguments. Justin gave her a lecture on family responsibilities and the name of a private doctor who specialised in HRT and midlife crisis counselling. Lena fumed. Zack and Xerxes wailed and howled and kicked Penelope on the shins when she told them off.

Penelope loved her family very much, but she thought it would do them good to be without her for a while.

꧂

BY THE time she was all set to leave, it was August. The perfect time to move into an old house in Provence. No need to worry about heating it yet, and the days were still long. Penelope took three days driving down through France in a nearly new dark-blue Range Rover she had bought to feel secure on the roads. Nor did she want to worry about navigating the rutted track to the house or getting stuck up a hill in winter weather. It also had plenty of room for the essentials she brought with her. She gave herself treats along the way in the form of spa hotels, and stayed her first night in Provence in a boutique B&B in Avignon. She didn't know when she was next going to be able to sleep in luxury.

First thing the next morning she drove to Ménerbes, where she shook hands with Mme Valencourt at the Agence Hublot and collected the key to the front door of her property. The rest of the keys were in a wooden casket in a kitchen drawer, apparently.

Excitement overcame Penelope's residual fatigue after the long drive on her own. She had made it! She steered the Range Rover due east along the D900, the main valley road, with the imposing rippled backdrop of the Luberon Mountains on her right. Apple and plum orchards, now fruiting, lined the route. Ancient stone mills and farms dotted fields of cut lavender and vineyards. The lower hills were topped with white stone houses and castles and churches like drip icing on cakes. Olive trees waved their silvery welcome in a lazy breeze.

St Merlot was a sleepy village at the unfashionable end of the Luberon Valley, but that was its charm. Hidden in the creases of the ridge, the road ascended through Saignon on its rocky out-crop, and then continued to wind into the high folds of the hills.

Penelope noted the turning for the track to Le Chant d'Eau, marked by a small run-down house, and carried on up into the village. St Merlot was an authentic, unspoilt place, seemingly missing from the tourist itineraries, a sprinkle of sun-gilded stone on a mild hillock surrounded by dry-stone walls and wild-flowers. It boasted no ruined castle or grand church.

The road passed through a small wood and then a cherry or-chard. The oldest part of the village, with its winding streets and hidden alleys, lay to the left. She drew up on the right, close to a large *place* surrounded by plane trees. Behind the trees on two sides of the open space stood pale ochre-plastered houses with brightly painted shutters. One side bordered the road, and the fourth was open to the breathtaking view down the valley.

The square was empty apart from an old man reading *La Provence* on a bench in the shade. Parked up at the far edge was an equally elderly bus painted lavender-mauve, bearing the leg-end "Bibliobus" and the image of a shelf of books. On the far side was a small garage with a petrol pump, where a man in sunglasses and overalls was attending to a car. That was nice to see, she thought—some good old-fashioned service.

The *épicerie-fruiterie* across the street was another welcome sight. On the display outside, peaches and nectarines gave off the evocative sweet scent of properly ripened fruit. Penelope went inside. She was getting a very good feeling about this.

She bought some patties of fresh goats' cheese, *jambon cru*, to-matoes, olives, peaches, an orange-fleshed Cavaillon melon, and a bottle of local rosé. That would do for lunch and supper.

When she asked for bread, the woman at the counter pointed towards the corner of the square. Penelope thanked her and wandered over there, blinking against the brightness. The bou-langerie was a narrow yellow building with a few chairs and tables outside under a vine canopy. She bought a golden-crusted baguette and then, on impulse, added a slice of apricot tart to her purchases. It looked so pretty, it was impossible to resist. Penelope could see she was going to have problems here.

Her spirits sank at the end of the potholed track to Le Chant d'Eau.

The old farm had changed out of all recognition.

Since her last visit, the grass had grown to heights unimaginable in the early spring. As she opened the oak front door, a large lump of plaster detached itself from the ceiling and plunged to the tiled floor beneath, shattering and adding to the fine miasma of dust that hung in the air.

She took a deep breath. *Keep calm.* "This is my adventure," she said to herself. She had to pull herself together and make a go of it.

She went back out to the car to unload bottled water, a primus stove, a camp bed, candles, matches, and cleaning equipment, along with wine and other emergency rations. She flicked switches and turned on taps in hope rather than expectation. Nothing happened.

For the first time in a very long while she found herself wishing she wasn't on her own. That she had someone by her side to share responsibility—and, perhaps, equal blame—for this madness. She picked a piece of plaster out of her hair, now ever so slightly less well styled than when it was first cut but still good enough for Mme Valencourt to have nodded in what seemed like approval when she had gone to pick up the keys.

Her mobile chirruped.

"You have arrived?" It was Mme Valencourt.

"I have." Penelope was absurdly pleased to hear from her, though she hoped that wasn't too obvious. I managed to drive here all the way from England, she thought—I should have been able to make it from Ménerbes to St Merlot.

"Do you need a man, madame?"

"I beg your pardon?"

"A man, to help with the garden. The grass is very tall, is it not?"

Penelope had a sudden welcome vision of a strong man swinging a large scythe. She moved to the window and looked out. The large field of gently waving grass offered a tantalising glimpse of walled garden and pool beyond. "You are quite right, madame. I certainly do need some help. I had no idea the garden would be so out of control."

"I think I know of someone who would be able to help, madame. He also offers other services. Would you like me to introduce him?"

"I think you'd better," said Penelope, weakly. "And quite soon."

"I will bring him tomorrow."

"By the way, I'm going to need some electricity and water, too."

"Of course. I will see to it."

Penelope's spirits rose. She hadn't been expecting this level of after-sales care. She was impressed.

⁂

IT WAS past six o'clock when Penelope finally finished sweeping and dusting and making base camp in the house. She thought about rewarding herself with a cup of tea, but instead went out into the garden, feeling the twinges in her back as she straightened up. An eagle or some other bird of prey wheeled slowly overhead on the thermals. All was quiet, apart from the cicadas.

Penelope took in a deep breath of pine and thyme and allowed herself to relax. The incredible view, as ever, stopped her in her tracks. Le Chant d'Eau was high enough that the hill spurs that sloped down into the great valley appeared one behind the other as if cut out and placed in a Victorian diorama.

It was all going to be fine. One day soon, this hillside garden would be a gorgeous haven of scents and flowers. She and her friends would drift around in white linen clothes, picking sprigs of lavender and sipping glasses of ice-cold rosé. A bit of hard work—quite a lot of hard work—and she would have both a retreat and a social hub when it suited her to invite some guests.

"S-ss-salaud!"

The shout pulled her rudely back to earth.

It was followed by a stream of French swear words that even she could recognise. They seemed to be coming from a large thicket of bamboo nearby. The canes waved about in an agitated fashion, and then released a small, wiry man. He was staggering a little, a soggy roll-up cigarette fixed to his lower lip.

Penelope stared, uncertain what to do. *Get off my land* would surely not have been an appropriate response.

The man stumbled over to her, dropping ash off the tip of his cigarette. She hoped he wouldn't spark a fire in the long dry grass. He fixed Penelope with beady, ratlike eyes.

"C'est à moi!"

Penelope still did not know what to say.

"Ce terrain—c'est à moi!"

This land was his? She felt her face redden and began to prepare a suitable French rebuttal to this ludicrous claim.

The man waved a hand over the garden where they were standing, and had to fight to keep his balance. "Mon terrain!"

"I'm sorry," said Penelope haughtily and in English, to signal that she did not intend to engage with him. She pointed at herself. "Ma maison maintenant."

The news that the house belonged to her now provoked an incomprehensible outburst. The man jabbed his own chest with

a thumb and threw out both arms in a gesture that almost un-
balanced him, such was its fervour.

Penelope stood her ground.

The impasse lasted for several minutes, during which Penelope
took in his rough blue jacket and dirty trousers. His leather shoes
were workers' wear and badly scuffed. His eyes seemed to blur
and then refocus with renewed anger. His hair stuck up in tufts,
as if he had fallen asleep and hadn't combed it afterwards.

No further words were exchanged. They stared at each other.
Then, bristling with Gallic indignation, the man took a threat-
ening step towards her. She started back.

Without another word, he gesticulated and then turned on his
heel. He exited through the bamboo, and she caught glimpses of
him as he made his way back down the track to the main road,
weaving from one side of the path to the other.

Feeling rather shaky, Penelope abandoned further garden ex-
plorations and made for the cool cellar, where she had left her
bottle of rosé. Until she acquired a fridge—and electricity, for
that matter—her evening glass of wine was not going to be ice-
cold as she liked it. But needs must. She poured a large measure
into a plastic glass.

Mon terrain! Ma maison maintenant! The furious exchange echoed
in her head.

She placed a camping chair outside the kitchen door on the
patio, sipping as she let the stunning hillside vista work its magic.

Gradually her nerves calmed and her veins started to fizz
with optimistic anticipation. It was just one odd man. Perhaps
he was some kind of country tramp—did they still have them in
Provence? Perhaps he had been squatting here, and was furious
that she had forced him to move on. After a while, a phrase
welled up from nowhere. *Emotion recollected in tranquillity.*

At first, she couldn't think where it came from. Then she smiled.

It was one of Camrose's quotes. From his beloved Wordsworth, of course.

She could hear Camrose saying it, pathology report in front of him on the mahogany desk. Taking off his glasses and rubbing his right temple. Strain in the cornflower-blue eyes, the cost of revealing the painful truths told by a body after violent death. " 'Emotion recollected in tranquillity,' Penny. That's all I can offer to the dead. Let justice do the rest."

He was probably on a hillside himself right now, rambling down from a long afternoon above Grasmere: book of Wainwright walks in one pocket, poetry in the other; escapee from the new Home Office directives, bureaucracy, and political correctness that were anathema to the eminent and individualistic forensic pathologist Professor Camrose Fletcher. He had chosen retirement, the freedom to speak as he found, and the walking trails of his beloved Lake District.

For ten years he had been a wonderful boss, a loyal friend, and, for the duration of one magical conference in Stockholm, a lover. Not that that had changed anything back in London, and Penelope had continued to work happily as his personal assistant. They were both of that old-fashioned school of thought that decreed that what happened abroad, stayed abroad.

Penelope raised her glass to the north.

He would probably never know how much his integrity and faith in human nature had helped her.

THE BREAD and olives and cheese made a delicious al fresco supper, and tiredness began to overwhelm Penelope. She noticed that the level in the bottle of wine had dropped surprisingly. A fruity little number, she thought, giggling to herself—I must get some more of this! She made a mental note of the producer and, in the spirit of recklessness that had brought her this far, sloshed the remains into her plastic glass.

She was just thinking how wonderfully quiet the location was when the throaty roar of a car engine ripped into the silence, revved up loudly, and took off at speed. A red blur appeared briefly on the bend of the road below and disappeared, trailing a roll of thunder. Penelope frowned. She hoped this was not one of those racetrack roads where daredevil drivers disturbed the peace at night.

But as quickly as it had been disrupted, silence fell once again.

She slept on her narrow camp bed that night less like a log than a felled spruce pine.

3

MME VALENCOURT STEPPED DAINTILY OVER the chunk of
fallen plaster by the front door as she introduced a small old man
straight from the pages of a Pagnol novel. He clutched a beret that
may have once been blue between his nicotine-stained fingers.

"Bonjour, Mme Kite."

Penelope was not at her best. And wailing at the kitchen walls
and diving at wasps in the maddening heat all morning had not
helped. Her headache was a reminder to stick to Perrier for a
while and cross that particular rosé off the shopping list. She
hoped this wasn't the first ominous stage of becoming a cliché:
the wine-soaked middle-aged expat.

"Please, I think you can call me Penny now."

"Of course. Penny. And you can call me Mme Valencourt"—
she paused and smiled—"a little joke, Penny!" Penelope was not
so sure, as the Frenchwoman continued, "I would like you to
meet M. Charpet. He is the gardener who worked for the previous owners."

Penelope gazed at the Provençal stereotype in front of her.
Judging from his walnut complexion and his gnarled hands, he
had clearly lived his life outdoors. His age was difficult to estimate, but he could not have been less than seventy-five, she
thought. A large and droopy moustache gave him a look of
comic melancholy that made him rather endearing. She stood
up and stretched out a hand.

"Bonjour, M. Charpet."

She almost withdrew the hand in shock as he grasped her fingers and swiftly, with a neat bow, kissed the outstretched knuckles.

"Enchanté, madame." He followed with a stream of incomprehensible French patois to Mme Valencourt. Penelope looked questioningly at her estate agent.

"He is saying, Penny, that he did not realise that English women could be so beautiful, even at your time of life."

Ouch. Penelope was not sure how to react to that. Expediency demanded that she take it as a compliment. "Enchantée de faire votre connaissance, M. Charpet."

Another stream of French was directed at Mme Valencourt.

"He wants to know when he should start."

"But I haven't interviewed him—there's the matter of references, pay scales!" Penelope had a view of employment practice honed by the bureaucracy of the Home Office. "And then there's hours, holidays, paperwork, surely?" Like all English expatriates, she was fully resigned to the legendary mountains of French bureaucracy.

Mme Valencourt smiled. "Paperwork?"

"Yes, paperwork—the piles of bureaucratic paperwork before you can do anything that everyone knows is what happens in France! What about the social taxes and employer premiums that the notary in Avignon was so clear about?"

"It is not necessary in this case."

"But the notaire said—always keep the paperwork!"

"Indeed. But not in the case of M. Charpet. A simple handshake will do. He is a man of honour."

The lugubrious face of M. Charpet suddenly brightened in recognition of a word he recognised. He clasped Penelope's hand.

"L'honneur, madame, l'honneur," intoned the new appointee, and broke into a wide and toothless smile.

"Let's go into the garden," said Penelope.

Outside, M. Charpet sniffed the air, then nosed in silence around the garden, managing, in under ten minutes, to find the stopcock for the outside water supply and the electricity meter, hidden behind several years' growth of ivy.

"Il faut tout nettoyer, madame," he remarked, pulling away great branches of vegetation to reveal a stone wall beneath.

He wanted to clean the garden? She supposed he must mean clear it.

In steadily improving French, Penelope enquired about the electricity and water.

"Ah—l'électricité—il faut téléphoner à l'EDF, et pour l'eau, SIVOM."

"How long will it take?" asked Penelope, addressing Mme Valencourt.

M. Charpet contorted his mouth into a clown-like expression of unhappiness. "Beh . . . une semaine, peut-être deux, madame."

Two weeks? Penelope's heart sank. "Et la piscine—the swimming pool? Is it usable?"

They picked their way gingerly past ferocious-looking bramble thorns. Given time, thought Penelope, the swimming pool in the walled garden could be spectacularly beautiful. In her imagination, she placed some old pottery urns and filled them with geraniums. Perhaps some reclaimed stone statues might be found to adorn the four corners of the pool when it was restored to its turquoise glory. The view through the arches was a sheer delight.

She was lost in her garden reverie as they opened the door in the wall to the reality. The old cypresses standing guard looked browner and more lifeless than ever. Penelope surveyed the bare bones of the pool, peering down at the brown rainwater and rotting leaves that nearly filled it. At least that meant it probably wasn't leaking. Getting the house up and running in the searing summer heat was going to be hard work, but it would be bearable if she had a pool to cool off in.

An unpleasant and not entirely encouraging smell rose from the murky water.

She turned to M. Charpet with a questioning look.

The gardener looked grim. He took off his beret again, and shook his head. Then he exchanged some rapid-fire French with Mme Valencourt.

"What does he think?" asked Penelope brightly. Perhaps optimism would sway him.

"There is . . . he is just checking something," said the estate agent guardedly.

Charpet went into the pump house and emerged with a large pole. He plunged it into a clump of sodden leaves and appeared to strike something solid.

"What is it?" asked Penelope.

"It could be a sanglier—a wild boar. Sometimes when there is no cover over a swimming pool, the animals can fall in at night."

Penelope supposed that it must have been very determined to find water, as the only viable entrance to the pool garden for an animal would have been through the arches that opened onto a narrow terrace.

Prodded by Charpet's pole, the mysterious entity seemed to puff up, like fabric filled with air. He pushed the leaves away.

They all made involuntary noises.

"Aye! Mon dieu!"

"Eee!"

"Bloody hell!"

The body was not animal. It was human.

❧

THEY STOOD in stunned silence at the pool's edge. "Mon dieu," repeated M. Charpet, and then again for good measure. The body was facedown in the brackish water. It seemed to be wearing a dark jacket that deflated again and settled on its back, while one arm floated free of last winter's leaves.

Abruptly, Mme Valencourt broke the trance. "La police. Il faut téléphoner aux gendarmes!" She pulled out her mobile and in a moment was speaking in a rapid staccato, too quickly for Penelope to follow.

She felt dreadfully sick again, but was unable to take her eyes off the corpse. A moment of giddiness overcame her, and she stumbled. The estate agent gripped her arm.

"Madame . . . Penny, quelle horreur!"

There were no words to frame what Penelope felt. A dead body, in her swimming pool. It lay in a soup of muddy twigs and leaves, pond weed, a plastic cup, and even an old playing card. The ace of spades floated incongruously just out of reach of the corpse's wrinkled hand, as if it had just been flipped over to win some soggy game. She let herself be guided to the shade of the wall to sit down on the long grass. The estate agent stood over her, tapping a lacquered nail on the screen of her smartphone. M. Charpet stood a little apart from them, still holding the pole that had touched the corpse and muttering to himself.

No one dared leave the scene.

"How long has it been there?" Penelope managed at last.

Mme Valencourt gave her an odd look. "Madame, did you see anything when you arrived yesterday?"

"No, of course not!" Penelope stared at her wildly. All those legal searches on the house that the notary had intoned aloud in his office, all the asbestos checks and insect infestation checks and metal fatigue tests and environmental energy checks on the property . . . not one of them had included a Dead Body Check, had it?

"OK, OK . . . we are calm," said the estate agent.

Penelope didn't feel calm, but she knew she had to keep the lid on her panic. No doubt the police would ask exactly the same question. She thought back carefully. Had she looked at the pool yesterday evening and just not seen anything out of the ordinary?

Her head was pounding.

It was not long before they heard sirens in the distance. The first police officers arrived within twenty minutes. The farm track filled with a mass of blue cars, peaked helmets, and uniforms; an entire police force seemed to have descended on the crime scene. Penelope sat dumbstruck as gendarmes streamed through the door in the wall to the pool garden.

It didn't seem quite real. In all her years working for Professor Fletcher at the Home Office Department of Forensic Pathology and at University College, London, she had worked on detailed photographic reports but had rarely seen a dead victim in the flesh. She certainly had not expected to do so in early retirement in Provence. She sat quietly, knowing that sooner or later she was going to be questioned and trying to marshal her thoughts.

Mme Valencourt was engaged in deep conversation with a beefy uniformed policeman. A dapper man in a dark suit arrived and immediately joined the discussion. They all looked over at Penelope. It was obvious they were discussing her.

Penelope closed her eyes and wished it would all go away. She felt sorry for the man in the pool, whoever he was, and then guilty that she felt even worse that it had to happen in *her* pool.

"Mme Kite?"

Penelope looked up. The estate agent had brought over the man in the suit.

"Mme Kite, I present to you Inspector Paul Gamelin from the headquarters of the Police Municipale in Cavaillon. He will be examining whether a crime has been committed here."

Penelope felt a bit wobbly as she stood up.

Inspector Gamelin shook her hand. He was in his forties, with a tanned, narrow face and greying hair. He looked grave as he spoke to her in excellent English.

"I understand you have only been in this property since yesterday, madame."

"That is correct, yes."

"I will ask you to come to the police station to make an official statement in due course."

Penelope nodded.

"But I ask you now to tell me everything that comes to your mind. What did you hear, what did you see?"

"Nothing. There's nothing I can tell you!"

"Can you confirm that there was no man in the swimming pool yesterday, when you arrived?"

A deep breath. "I'm sorry, I cannot be sure of that."

Gamelin narrowed his eyes. "Why not?"

"Because I didn't go into the pool garden yesterday. I intended to—I came out into the garden after I had done some cleaning in the house and brought my things in from the car. As you can see—as Mme Valencourt will confirm—the house is not in a good state. I spent my time after arriving here trying to make it habitable. Dusting, sweeping. I stopped some time after six o'clock."

And perhaps it was just as well I didn't go into the pool garden, she thought. She didn't know what she would have done if she'd found the body by herself. It would have been thoroughly unpleasant. It was just as well this was the way it had happened.

"I came outside but didn't get any farther than the bamboo over there," she continued, "because there was a man who—"

A series of shouts from the direction of the pool interrupted any further exchange.

They hurried back into the walled garden, where the uniformed policeman who seemed to be in charge was directing operations. The body was already being hauled out by a number of men in white overalls, while another took photos of the scene.

Penelope's first thought was that they couldn't consider this to be a crime, or they would be proceeding much more carefully, to preserve any evidence. They must be sure that the cause of death was an accident.

Half repulsed, half fascinated, Penelope watched as the corpse was lifted from the water.

Muddy drips blotched the stone surround like dried blood.

She gasped.

"What is it?" asked Mme Valencourt. She seemed to be observing Penelope closely.

"The man . . . I think I have seen him before."

Inspector Gamelin was staring at her intently.

"I saw him yesterday evening . . . he came through the bamboo screen from the track and started shouting at me that this was *his* house!"

His tufty hair was now slicked to his head with rotting leaves, but he was wearing the clothes Penelope had noticed and the same shoes. She always noticed men's shoes. The insolent mouth was slack and had lost the roll-up cigarette, but it was him all right.

"Although"—Penelope shook her head—"there's so much puffy bruising around the temples and eyes that it's hard to be absolutely sure."

The discolouration of the face was intensified by a slick of foul-smelling pool debris that dripped from his hairline.

"I'm as sure as I can be that the man I met last night was wearing those clothes. And I think I recognise the face, but I can't be absolutely sure." She had dealt with enough of Professor Fletcher's cases to know that what could not be proved forensically should not be suggested without a caveat.

Mme Valencourt translated as Penelope explained exactly what had happened the previous evening. Gamelin looked more and more serious. They were joined by another officer. Then the estate agent stepped away to call someone on her mobile.

"What's happening? Who is—was—this man?" Penelope asked when Mme Valencourt returned to her side.

"I have spoken to le maire. He is coming down now."

"The mayor?"

"The mayor of the village knows everything that goes on here, and everyone who lives here. He will be able to identify the body." Mme Valencourt shrugged. "You would have had to be introduced to him soon in any case—and it should have been a great pleasure. It is a terrible shame that it has to be now under these circumstances."

"Why should I have had to meet him?" Penelope bristled. Her experience of English mayors was of pompous small-town busybodies with ceremonial regalia clanking around their necks. She had no wish to meet one for a fascinating discussion about traffic management or borough spending priorities. The whole point of coming to France was that she wouldn't have to do anything that was expected of her.

"You must always be introduced to the mayor."

This all seemed rather formal to Penelope. The idea of walking into the *mairie* to introduce herself as the latest foreign newcomer was distinctly Home Counties. And certainly not during the unfolding of a dead-body-shaped crisis at her new house, before she'd even recovered from her moving-in hangover.

"Really?" She gave the word an edge that was apparently lost in translation.

"It must be done."

"But—"

"Le maire de St Merlot . . . you will want to meet him. He is sympa."

"Sympa?"

"Sympathique—nice. And also—" Mme Valencourt widened her eyes.

"Yes?"

"You will see."

—❦—

LESS THAN ten minutes later, a tall man of around forty-five strode towards them, loping through the long grass like Indiana Jones. Penelope immediately understood what the estate agent was trying to say.

In her student years at Durham University, Penelope had joined the French Film Society, a club mainly composed of rather self-satisfied ex-public-school boys rebelling in tight black suits, smoking Gitanes and wearing dark glasses at night. In the dull and fog-ridden streets of the town, the latter frequently led to collisions with bikes, lampposts, or worse. In the figure now standing before her, Penelope recognised the Gallic glamour they had been striving for. This was the real deal. Floppy, sun-streaked hair. Caramel tan. Cheekbones. He was gorgeous.

The mayor kissed Mme Valencourt three times on alternate cheeks and then turned to Penelope and introduced himself in fluent though heavily accented English.

"Mme Keet. What can I say? This must be a terrible shock for you."

Penelope went a bit giddy. She could not frame anything more riveting to say than "Yes."

"You must not be concerned about anything. I am here to help you, and the police. I am going to look at the body to see if I recognise him."

Penelope nodded dumbly.

The mayor went into a huddle with the policemen standing over the body. After a few minutes he returned to where Penelope and Mme Valencourt were waiting by the arches at the far end of the pool garden.

"It is Manuel Avore," he said. "It seems that our M. Avore cannot stop making trouble, even after drowning!"

There was a lightness in the mayor's tone that Penelope found quite disturbing. It sounded as if it carried a hint of relief.

"So you think he drowned?"

"I am not a detective, madame, but when a man who is drunk most of the time finds himself by a swimming pool in the dark, the outcome is certain."

Penelope was less sure. "But . . . what was he doing here, by *my* swimming pool?"

"Clémence has told me that this man came onto your property yesterday and shouted at you that this was *his* house."

"That's right."

The mayor shook his head sadly. "As soon as I heard that, I knew who he was. Manuel Avore lived in this village all his life, which was not a happy one. He was a terrible alcoholic. His family lived on this land, and he was born here. He never wanted to leave it, but it was sold years ago. Hélas, poor Manuel considered that it still belonged to him. He moved into the house on the main road, just by the end of this track here, but it was not the same."

It all sounded very tragic, but Penelope couldn't help feeling that, despite all this unpleasantness, she had dodged a very large bullet. Imagine what it would have been like to have a drunken

Manuel Avore shambling around her lovely house and garden whenever he felt sentimental. It didn't bear thinking about.

She pulled herself together. "Well, I am very sorry for him. It's an awful thing to happen."

"So the question is, Mme Keet, did you hear anything yesterday evening or during the night?"

Inspector Gamelin was now listening intently to their conversation.

"Not a thing. I slept very soundly."

"What did you do last night?"

"I had some supper and went to bed early. It had been a long day."

"You were alone?"

"Yes."

Penelope had to look away from the mayor's stunning eyes. It seemed thoroughly inappropriate that all she could think was how very dark blue they were.

"That is unfortunate," he said.

She bit her lip.

"Did you drink some wine? Maybe you slept a leetle . . . heavily last night?"

That much was true, and Penelope had to admit it. But how dare he! The mayor and Clémence Valencourt exchanged looks. The two of them obviously knew each other quite well.

"If you think that I am a stereotypical middle-aged Englishwoman abroad who glugs wine by the barrel and does nothing but bake herself to a crisp in the sun and look for other expats to talk to, I can assure you that you are very much mistaken," said Penelope, with an attempt at dignity.

A hint of a smile twitched one corner of the mayor's disconcertingly well-formed mouth. "Please forgive me. I am sure this horrible incident is the result of an accident. The death by drowning of a man who was so drunk he was hardly conscious."

"I'm sure he was drunk at around quarter past six when I saw him," said Penelope. "How dreadful."

Other people were gathering on the track from the road now. As an introduction to the locals, it wasn't ideal. Penelope hoped they didn't think it was a bad omen—or that she had anything to do with her neighbour's watery end.

THE MEN in white manoeuvred the cadaver into a body bag. Penelope managed to get a closer look. A loose arm flopped out, and she gave an involuntary shudder. The pale limp hand, gashed and still dripping, trailed along the grass. The back of her neck prickled and she gagged.

She felt a hand on her arm. It was Clémence Valencourt.

"Would you like to come to my house, stay the night there? I would not blame you for not wanting to be here."

Perhaps the estate agent was feeling guilty that she had sold her client a house with a sitting tenant—or rather, a floating tenant. Penelope was fully aware that it wouldn't take much to become hysterical.

The mayor echoed Mme Valencourt. "I think that would be a good idea. The police have much to do here, and it will take many hours for them to finish."

Penelope let herself be guided into the house, where the mayor and Mme Valencourt poured her a glass of cognac from a bottle that appeared from nowhere, and suggested she pack an overnight bag. As she threw items into the case, shivering occasionally when the image of the body came back to her, she wondered again what she had got herself into.

4

"IT WAS HORRIBLE—POOR MAN!" cried Penelope. "What a thing to happen! I feel quite discombobulated."

Her oldest friend Frankie was on the receiving end of the phone rant. Penelope had to talk to someone, and she wasn't about to admit weakness to her children. Not after they had been so disparaging.

"And I know I shouldn't be thinking of myself at a time like this—and I really am trying not to—but honestly, Frank, I haven't even unpacked and now it seems I've never left work. And did he drown, or—well, we just can't know straightaway, can we?"

"How awful," said Frankie.

Penelope put her toothbrush into the open suitcase on her camp bed. "One night! I spend one night here, and this happens. I keep thinking I could have done something to prevent it happening, as it was in my pool—but what could I have done? I'd only just got here."

"Nothing. Of course you couldn't. How awful."

"They won't let me stay here. It's a potential crime scene. My dream house! Well, you know, not perfect as it is, but it was going to be."

"I know."

A pause.

"They don't think you did it, do they?"

Penelope gasped. "Of course not! Why would they? The mayor

says it was probably an accidental death, but the police have to check, don't they. So it could be a crime scene."

"Awful."

"And they fished him out of the pool, and he was all . . . squelchy and—"

"Do you want me to come out?"

"—and this really strange colour because the water . . . What?"

"Do you want me to come out to France, to be with you?"

Penelope pulled up sharply. "What, now?"

"Well, I thought you might need someone."

The thought of Frankie arriving—her oldest and most indiscreet friend—shook some sense into her. "I'm fine. I just wanted to tell someone what was happening, just in case, you know . . ."

In case I get thrown into a police cell in the South of France for weeks without bail, she thought but didn't say. Under suspicion of goodness knows what. Murder while under the influence of irritation with a drunk Frenchman and a reckless amount of rosé on the first night of my new life?

"In that case," said Frankie, "you call me as soon as you know what's happening and where you are. And don't admit anything."

"What do you mean?"

"Joke! Sorry, not appropriate."

"Not funny, Frankie."

"No."

"They think it was an accident, but—isn't that a bit odd? In all the weeks, months, and years that this place has been empty, nothing happened. But then I come along and move in—"

"You just have to calm down, Pen."

"But, you know, working for Camrose all those years—it's given me a suspicious mind. Who knows where this could lead?"

❧

PENELOPE LOOKED over her shoulder at Le Chant d'Eau as she left in Mme Valencourt's red Mini Cooper. She wondered when she would see her new home again.

The mayor had offered soothing platitudes, but the taciturn Inspector Paul Gamelin merely nodded at her with no attempt at sympathy. That was worrying enough in itself. He was obviously keen to keep her out of the way while he got down to a proper investigation. No doubt he would find all sorts of things that had been missed.

Penelope braced herself as the Mini hurtled downhill in the middle of the road, round a blind bend. Down one steep hill and up another.

The police were probably going through her personal possessions right at this moment. Her heart sank as she pictured the French officers seizing upon her bedside reading. Detective novels, mainly. What impression was that going to give? The stockpile of Boots special offer Menopace vitamins. Not to mention the collection of stomach-minimising foundation garments. She could just imagine them being held up to snorts of ridicule. "Qu'est-ce que c'est 'Spanx,' Mme Kite?"

Mme Valencourt swerved round one cyclist, sent another skidding into a ditch, and put her tiny foot down. She too seemed deep in thought. Perhaps it was just as well the estate agent did not live far away.

❧

THE VILLAGE of Viens was set on a rocky promontory. A tall, forbidding clock tower was built into what looked like medieval ramparts, with a gate leading to the mysteries of an old quarter.

Adjacent stood a building with a stone loggia that looked like a set for a tragic opera. Mme Valencourt blasted past this and up the hill for a few seconds before swooping through a narrow stone arch marked with an escutcheon. They pulled up with a lurch in a cobbled courtyard. The estate agent's own very charming property was a magnificent edifice in the heart of the village.

Penelope got out of the car and looked up at a weathered stone loggia and the graceful staircase up to the front door, above which another carved coat of arms reinforced the impression that the Valencourt residence had noble origins.

They hefted her suitcase out of the car and hauled it into the house. The hall was cavernous, with plain walls and a high ceiling. A stylish console table and ornate mirror were the only items of furniture.

"This way," said the estate agent as she turned left into a wide corridor. "Would you like anything to eat?"

"No, thank you."

"I will ask my housekeeper to bring you some water and fruit. Now, here is the guest suite. You don't look very well. Perhaps you should get some rest."

Her room would not have been out of place in an expensive boutique hotel. Penelope couldn't help but be impressed by the combination of austere medieval character and luxurious modern fittings, all with a perfect finish. It was exactly the kind of house in which a woman like Mme Valencourt would live. Was there a M. Valencourt, and if so, what was he like? She inferred there *was* a M. Valencourt from the two rings—a large square-cut diamond and a gold band—on Madame's wedding finger, and the magnificence of the house, the upkeep of which would surely take more than a single estate agent's income. No doubt she would find out soon enough.

As soon as she was alone, Penelope flopped down on the wide, feather-soft bed. She closed her eyes and dozed for a couple of hours, trying and failing to blot out what she had witnessed.

The bathroom provided a pleasurably ruthless power shower that pummelled the breath out of her, gorgeous soaps, gels, and lotions, and fluffy soft towels. Penelope felt herself revive. For a few indulgent moments she allowed herself to forget her predicament.

⚜

AT SIX thirty she went downstairs to find an elderly woman in black busy in the kitchen. A muffled conversation came from another room. Penelope stood awkwardly in the hall for long enough to work out that her hostess was on the phone, then wandered through an open salon to a vine-covered terrace. The view was breathtaking. She went to the balustrade and took in a sweeping vista of hills and a gorge, beyond which mountains rose in the distance.

When Mme Valencourt joined her twenty minutes later, Penelope felt calm enough to face the crisis.

"Any news?"

The Frenchwoman shook her head.

Despite her good intentions, Penelope decided it would be rude not to accept a small glass of rosé. She had had a nasty shock, after all. Then she had another with the delightfully light dinner of fish and braised vegetables, followed by a doll-sized portion of airy lemon mousse. It was all served at a table on the terrace by the diminutive elderly lady, who had apparently cooked it.

Penelope waited for an opening to inquire about her hostess's husband. But Mme Valencourt kept the conversation focused relentlessly on Penelope and what had brought her to the Luberon. Penelope found herself babbling away about her own ex-husband

and his shortcomings. Her children and their scornful certainty that she wouldn't be able to make a success of her move. She didn't seem to be able to stop talking. It was as if the shock had unleashed her tongue and removed all sense of restraint. It was quite horrifying. Even Penelope began to wonder what she was going to say next.

Having refused a cognac—she was relieved to find that she still possessed a shred of common sense—she addressed the elephant lurking on the terrace. "Do you think it was an accident?" she asked.

The Frenchwoman hesitated.

"Mme Valencourt?"

"Please call me Clémence."

That was a small step forward. Penelope wondered who she had been speaking to on the telephone. A terrible thought struck her. Would anything she said to Clémence be reported to the authorities? Could she, even now, be recording their conversation, to be picked over by police detectives?

"The police will not say," said Clémence Valencourt. "I called Laurent to see if he knew—"

"Who's Laurent?"

"Laurent Millais. The mayor."

Penelope shook her head. All that business about having to be introduced to the mayor, and she hadn't actually registered his name.

"But he said the police had told him nothing more either," said Mme Valencourt.

"So you don't know any more than I do?"

"Of course not. Why would I?"

"I don't know. I just wondered. Oh, God, I don't think I'm thinking straight at the moment," burbled Penelope. "They don't think I could have done it, do they?" She suddenly felt exhausted and disconnected.

"I don't think you would be here if they thought that."

Penelope relaxed slightly. But there was another thing. The something that had been nagging at her ever since they left Le Chant d'Eau, making her uneasy. It had taken her a while to work out the logic behind her instinct. Now she couldn't stop herself from blurting it out.

"There was something wrong with that body, Clémence."

"Yes, Penny, it was dead."

Allowing a smile at this attempt at humour—Gallic gallows humour, *peut-être*—Penelope carried on against her better judgement. "The body. It wasn't . . . there is something that I can't help thinking is not quite right."

Clémence Valencourt leant forward, her chin cupped in one hand. Her grey-green eyes fixed on Penelope. For the first time there seemed a glimmer of a real connection between them.

"I thought so too, Penny. Did you not see the terrible bruises on his face?"

"Of course, but my concern was a different one. The problem is . . . the problem is, I just can't quite put my finger on it."

The Frenchwoman waited patiently. Night had fallen, soft as silk, as they ate. Collections of lights sparkled like handfuls of diamonds on the dark hills opposite.

Penelope stared into the distance. "A thought came to me like a jolt, but then it disappeared. It has been bothering me ever since we found him, but it's just out of reach."

They both took a sip of water.

"A blow to the front of the head could have killed him," said Penelope. "Although it looks like death by drowning, we don't know that for certain yet."

"I thought his head was covered with dead leaves, at first. But as he was being moved, some of them fell away, and I saw the dark marks on the side and the front of his head where the hair was thin."

"He could have hit his head as he fell," countered Penelope. "If it happened at the side of the pool, he could easily have clonked his head on the stone surround, knocked himself out so badly he didn't come round in time to stop himself drowning. The water was deep enough to drown in."

"I suppose that could be correct. But what if he had been hit by a person? That is also possible."

Penelope's heart sank again, along with the dreadful picture in her mind's eye of the unfortunate Avore dropping down through the murky water. "It has to be possible," she said. "But all we can do is wait for the police investigation to determine the exact cause of death. There's no point in trying to guess what the sequence of events was. I'm sure they will tell us soon enough."

Clémence Valencourt gave a little pout that seemed to imply that that remained to be seen. "Now, I will ask the housekeeper for some mint tea, and you will try to remember your escaped thought." She rose from the table. "Allow your mind to go back without force."

Alone on the terrace, Penelope closed her eyes. She thought back to the scene at the swimming pool. The still water and the rotting leaves. The dark bulk of the deceased and the billow of his jacket on his back. Then her mind slunk back to the dingy offices of the Home Office Department of Forensic Pathology and Professor Camrose Fletcher's own book-lined study. The detailed reports and lectures she had helped compile. Photographs and reconstructions. Penelope considered other documented deaths, picking carefully through her memories. She replayed Manuel

Avore's removal from the pool, his limp body hanging over the arms of the policeman, the hand falling out of the body bag.

That was it.

She jumped up with a little cry of surprise, as her host returned.

"Penny? Are you all right?"

"Clémence, I know what the problem was now. The thought I couldn't pin down!"

They faced each other.

"It was the limp arm."

Mme Valencourt's arched eyebrows indicated some scepticism.

"No, this is important. The body was limp."

"Is that not normal with dead people, Penny?"

"No, it isn't. For approximately twenty-four hours after death, the body is set hard. That's rigor mortis. The body stiffens two to six hours after death, but nearer two in warm temperatures. It only loosens up at least a full day later."

"So?"

"M. Avore was alive less than twenty-four hours before his body was found in the pool. He came into my garden and started shouting at me. I know almost exactly what the time was when I stopped work. It was past six o'clock, and I had to decide whether to have a cup of tea or if it was too close to wine o'clock."

Clémence Valencourt frowned.

"It's an English thing. Look, the point is, I stopped cleaning, looked at my watch, and decided to go out into the garden for some fresh air. I didn't get to the pool to look at it because M. Avore arrived. He was there in the flesh. We talked for a while—well, it wasn't quite the social call that sounds—and then he stomped off up the track towards the main road. I saw him go. So at half past six yesterday he was alive. His body was found today at about midday. That's not long enough for rigor mortis to have passed."

Clémence was beginning to understand. "And if the death was earlier than that . . ."

"Then M. Avore cannot have been the man I saw." Penelope dropped back into her seat.

The two women fell silent.

Penelope was the first to speak. "When I described the man in my garden, the mayor said immediately, 'Oh, that must have been Manuel Avore"—and then, when the body came out, he was equally sure that it was Manuel Avore. But one of those identifications must be wrong, don't you see?"

She tried to think as clearly and logically as she used to at work, when the dead bodies were not on her doorstep.

"And that also means . . . that either this man was already dead and in the pool when I arrived at Le Chant d'Eau yesterday—or he was killed somewhere else before midday yesterday and placed in the pool later. Which might even have been while I was asleep last night . . . Clémence?"

"Oui, Penny."

"I think I will have that cognac, please."

5

PENELOPE PASSED A LUXURIOUSLY COMFORTABLE but
nevertheless disrupted night. Each time she managed to drop
off, the memory of the macabre discovery prodded her awake.

In the darkness, her thoughts turned to Professor Camrose
Fletcher—her work for him and the chain of events that had led
to her unlikely employment. Penelope's father had been a GP
and police surgeon in South London; a pathologist friend of his
had offered her some secretarial work when her confidence was
at an all-time low. Lena was at university, and Justin was soon
to follow. Penelope had discovered evidence of David's second
affair, and was blaming herself for being dull and too dependent,
still stupidly imagining they could save the marriage.

The pathologist was based at the Home Office in London. After a long career, his role was then mainly administrative, over-
seeing structural changes to the forensic services. A year later, he
retired—but not before recommending Penelope to a maverick
colleague, a forensic pathologist who needed a personal assistant
to type autopsy reports and expert witness statements, and also
to help with his university lecturing commitments at UCL.

Professor Camrose Fletcher was mercurial, dedicated to discovering as much of the truth as humanly possible, scornful of
political correctness yet kindness personified. He was a lateral
thinker who often found answers where no one else could. The
work proved fascinating, if occasionally gruesome. Penelope

blossomed as Fletcher came to value her insights as well as her outstanding office skills. "You have good instincts," he'd say, over a cup of Ceylon tea. "Tell me your thoughts."

And so she would.

Her mind was still whirring at breakfast, and two cups of freshly ground coffee served by the silent housekeeper at a marble table in Clémence Valencourt's vaulted kitchen with a touch of dungeon chic did not help her nerves.

An open floor-to-ceiling glass door ushered in a breeze from the hills. It was a glorious insight into what life in the Luberon could be like: peaceful and relaxing—if only one hadn't found a dead body in one's swimming pool.

Clémence appeared only briefly, to say good morning and drink a small black coffee. She headed out, explaining that she had a viewing nearby but would be back as soon as possible. Her heels ticked like a metronome across the stone floor. She had already started talking on her mobile before she reached the front door.

Penelope absent-mindedly ate three delicious flaky croissants with apricot jam as she tried to make sense of it all.

Through the open door, she could make out notes of music. The heart-stirring rich, sad sound of a cello rose and fell, repeating the same phrase. Someone was practising. Penelope recognised the Brahms sonata and closed her eyes, playing the piece in her mind, feeling the movement in her fingers. If she believed in signs, she thought, this would be one.

She walked to the doorway. The housekeeper was quietly sweeping the terrace.

"La musique?" Penelope asked her.

The housekeeper pointed down to the right. "La répétition pour le concert."

Penelope looked over a jumble of terra-cotta roofs to a church with a tall square tower.

"Dans l'église?"

"Oui, madame."

It was the most perfect venue for an intimate concert. Penelope had a sudden longing to be there, letting the music ease her cares away.

❦

MME VALENCOURT returned around eleven with the news that Penelope had been invited to police headquarters in the nearby town of Apt.

"You make it sound as if a trip to the police station is a social call," said Penelope. Too much coffee and uncertainty had made her feel cross and jumpy.

"It's not the police station. It's the Police Municipale attached to the Hôtel de Ville. The bureaucratic centre of the town. Don't upset yourself. I will drive you there."

"Well, that's another thing," said Penelope. "You driving me. Quite apart from the obvious danger to life and limb, I should be driving myself. I was so shocked yesterday that I just let you drive me away. But that was what the police wanted you to do, wasn't it?"

The Frenchwoman shook her head. "What do you mean?"

"The police wanted to give my Range Rover a going-over."

"A going-over to where?"

"They wanted to check it, run some tests. To see if I had anything to do with the crime."

"But this is not a crime. It is an accident. M. Avore inundated himself."

"Drowned." Penelope supplied the word. "And I thought we'd agreed that was unlikely."

Clémence gave her an odd look.

"We talked about it last night!" Penelope persisted.

"Is that what you are intending to tell to the police?"

"I was rather hoping they had worked out the elementary forensics for themselves."

❧

THE POLICE station was housed in a grand building in the place Gabriel Péri in the centre of Apt, the Hôtel de Ville. This was another name for the town's *mairie*, explained the estate agent.

Mme Valencourt introduced Penelope to an officer on the front desk and waited until someone came down. It was the whippet-faced man in the suit who had attended the discovery of the body.

He greeted her in a distant manner, and they shook hands formally.

"Paul Gamelin. We met yesterday."

"Yes, we did."

"I will introduce you to the chief of police."

He led her up a flight of stairs to a door, on which he gave a half-hearted knock before pushing it open. The office was comfortable, with framed certificates and honours on the walls, along with photographs of sports teams and groups of uniformed gendarmes. Behind a desk was a diminutive man of about fifty with a bulbous stomach. When he stood up and came round the desk, holding a hand to his chest, Penelope couldn't help but think there was more than a touch of the Napoleonic about him. Perhaps it was the square face and the hair, which was obviously dyed.

"Mme Keet," he said with gracious condescension. "Georges Reyssens, chef de police." His hand slithered against hers, and then he flapped it towards a chair by the desk.

Penelope refused to be intimidated. "Enchanted to meet you, monsieur le chef de police," she said in the best French she could muster.

The chief did not sit down. He strutted across a rug on the stark tiled floor, hands behind his back, reminding Penelope of a film she had once seen about the Battle of Waterloo. His red lips quivered in a fashion that she found both unfortunate and fascinating.

"Mme Keet, I am sorry that your introduction to our beautiful region has been spoiled by this terrible accident. Please accept my apologies that you had to leave your property yesterday evening. I am sure you understand why that was the case."

Penelope nodded.

"I regret that I am having to ask you not to return to your house for a few more days."

"Oh? Why? What have you discovered?"

"Discovered? We are making our investigation. All will become clear when the investigation is concluded."

"So it is not yet concluded?" asked Penelope.

"No, it is not."

"Do you not believe it was an accidental drowning, then?"

Out of the corner of her eye she caught Gamelin assessing her in a most disconcerting way. He hadn't said a word since they entered the room.

"I cannot tell you that," said Reyssens.

"Is there anything that you can tell me about your conclusions so far?"

The chief of police pulled his mouth down and gave an expressive shrug. "Let me see . . . *non*."

"But you are sure that the dead man is Manuel Avore?"

Both men stared. Rather unpleasantly, in the case of the chief.

"Why do you say that, Mme Keet?"

"Because . . . because . . ." Penelope began to feel extremely uncomfortable. "That is the obvious question. I thought I saw him the previous evening, and if so—"

"The mayor has identified him. He knows Manuel Avore. He has known him for a long time. Avore was well known in the village of St Merlot. The body," he concluded ponderously, as if he hadn't considered before now that Penelope might be simple of mind, "is that of Manuel Avore."

He paused ominously. "That is a very strange question from a foreigner who has only arrived in the village since twenty-four hours."

"I must be in shock," mumbled Penelope.

"The reason I ask to see you today is to inform you that you may not return to Le Chant d'Eau for a few days, and that a room at the Hôtel St Pierre here in the town has been arranged and is at your disposal. Please wait until we contact you again before you return to your house."

And that was that. The chief wanted her out of the way, and any observations she could offer would clearly not be welcome. She was ushered out by a secretary and given directions to the hotel. Luckily, it was close enough to walk. Which was just as well, as there was no sign of Mme Valencourt.

❧

THE SMALL Hôtel St Pierre overlooked a river embankment and seemed to shimmy a welcome like an old good-time gal dressed to please. The peach ochre façade and purple shutters were the essence of Provence, and a private reassurance to Penelope that the dream was still alive.

Across a wrought-iron bridge, the town's stucco buildings curved into the shape of a Roman amphitheatre, and she spotted other Italianate details in the tiny plant-filled terraces high up under the roofs.

Mme Valencourt screeched up in the Mini Cooper.

"I wondered where you'd got to," said Penelope.

"I went back to Viens to collect your suitcase. You know you are welcome to stay with me, but as the police have suggested you stay here . . ."

"It's wise to do as they ask."

"Yes."

"That's very kind of you."

Privately, Penelope was quite pleased to be independent again, though she would miss the facilities *chez* Valencourt. She doubted that the bed at the Hôtel St Pierre would match up in terms of indulgence.

"If you need any help, please call me," said Clémence. It was hard to know if she was just being polite, but Penelope thanked her and took the suitcase into the hotel foyer. White walls were hung with modern Provençal paintings. A friendly young man on the reception desk told her that he was expecting her.

She was shown to a pretty bedroom with carved wooden furniture and a large window on the first floor. A faint scent of lavender and almond blossom lingered. There were worse places to be billeted.

⁂

"FRANKIE? IT'S me. Just checking in to let you know where I am."

Penelope sat on the window seat and watched the river trickle around clumps of weeds and dry stones. A sign warned that the nearby car park was "submersible," but that was highly unlikely anytime soon.

Frankie was her usual fizzing cocktail of kindness and high

spirits. She listened while Penelope brought her up to speed, and then asked, "So what are you supposed to do now?"

"Well, quite. There's an unplanned police investigation in my moving-in schedule."

"So you're at a loose end, with nothing to do but have a holiday in the South of France."

"When you put it like that . . . well, yes." That was one of the qualities Penelope most loved about Frankie. She could always see the positive. Though even Frankie was hard-pressed to make good news out of a man's death. Penelope was uncomfortably aware that that had rather been pushed aside in the annoyance and confusion.

"And what would make it even better?" asked Frankie, slyly.

"What?"

"You don't have to go through all this on your own. I'm coming out."

I walked right into that one, thought Penelope. And yet, was it such a terrible idea, to accept a friend's offer of support? Even though Frankie could be a liability on occasion, she was a good friend.

"When are you thinking of getting here?" she asked, wavering between gladness and slight dread.

That evening Penelope sauntered out into the warm air, feeling that she shouldn't lose sight of the excitement of arriving here and how much she wanted to make a success of it.

The narrow streets through the centre of the town led to a medieval cathedral. Its stone walls and exterior carvings were pitted with age. Blocked-up ghost entrances offered intriguing glimpses into the past, and the features on the face of a statue were expressionless after years of exposure to the elements. On impulse, she went in and lit a candle for poor Manuel Avore. She did not know how she was going to react upon returning to a swimming pool where a man had died, accidentally or other-wise. She quickly pushed those thoughts away. She would have to come to terms with it, somehow. But not now. One step at a time.

She enjoyed a delicious dinner of lamb and ratatouille on the terrace of the hotel, and long after she had finished the honey and thyme crème brûlée and a final cup of decaf coffee, she was still sitting in the candlelight, replete and lost in contemplation.

She had found a wonderful property. One day, hopefully not too far in the future, she would have a new life here and a lovely place where family and old friends could gather. Lena and Justin and their children would enjoy it, too. Coming to Provence was about turning fifty and wanting to be optimistic about it.

The children were old enough and bound up enough in their own lives not to be upset—or so she had thought. She had lost both parents, and though the sadness would never fade, she no longer had the responsibility for the older generation that pinned down many of her friends.

She had a reasonable pension and some inherited money, along with a handsome divorce settlement—for all his faults, David had at least made money as a City lawyer. Now that legal letters were no longer involved, they were on much friendlier terms. She could remember the good times again, forgive him, and move on.

"And here I am," said Penelope to the candle flame.

By the time she went up to her room just before midnight, she felt sure it wouldn't be long before she could start enjoying all that the South of France had to offer.

6

PENELOPE WAS WOKEN THE NEXT morning by the sound of vans, shouts, and doleful guitar music. In a semiconscious state, she staggered out of bed to the window and opened it.

Her senses were assailed from all quarters. In every available sliver of street space, stalls had been set up. Vegetables and fruit were stacked with artistic geometry. Rolls of jolly Provençal fabric jostled bottles of wine; rows of pastel soaps competed with earthy spices and wide bowls of olives. An all-pervasive aroma of cheese, fish, and lavender hung in the air. Crowds were gathering. It was Saturday, she realised, the day of the world-famous Apt market. Her hair was sticking up unbrushed, her nightie was gaping open, and the guitarist on the other side of the street was staring in a manner that could only be described as lewd. Penelope slammed the windows shut and jumped back into bed to gather her thoughts. They recalibrated around the twin poles of Frankie's arrival and breakfast. Surely a pastry or two would be justified, given the stress of the situation.

Frances Turner-Blake was a force to be reckoned with. She never took no for an answer and could easily make everything worse. Though there was a silver lining to her imminent arrival—once they were allowed back into Le Chant d'Eau, her old school friend was just the person to cast an eye over the house in its raw state. She was Frankie now, and had been ever since marrying Johnny, a distinctly unreconstructed builder. Between them they owned and managed a large property development firm. What Frankie didn't know about bricks and mortar wasn't worth a bag of nails.

In an ideal world Penelope would have waited for a while, and got to know the house before she invited Frankie to see it. But there was no doubt she was the right person to ask for an informed opinion about a building project. And it was probably best to get an honest appraisal sooner rather than later.

Penelope got up and had a shower. Towelling herself down, she avoided looking too closely at her body in the mirror. She was loath to be reminded of all the restoration work required there, too.

She anticipated her friend's reaction to the house. It would follow the tradition common to all builders. A look around, a glum expression, and a sharp intake of breath through pursed lips, followed by an estimate the size of a Greek bank bailout. But at least Frankie would give her a straight answer as to what needed doing and how much it would cost. She was nothing if not uncomfortably honest.

Before Penelope could take a wander out into the market, there was an urgent matter to resolve.

"Clémence, sorry to phone you at the weekend, but I wonder if you could ask the police something for me, please." The request would carry more weight from the redoubtable estate agent, who seemed to know everyone.

"Of course. What is it?"

"My car. It's still at Le Chant d'Eau, and I'm going to need it tomorrow."

"The police haven't brought it down for you?"

"No, they haven't."

Mme Valencourt made an exasperated sound. "OK, I will call them."

She rang back within a few minutes, having obviously got straight through to the right person. Penelope could only marvel at the way she operated.

"Your car has been examined, and you are free to drive it."

"Thank you very much," said Penelope. "Though I'm not exactly thrilled with the idea of owning a suspect vehicle."

"No one suspects your car, Penny."

"I thought you said it had been examined."

"The police took the chance to check that your car is in a good state to drive on the roads here in the Vaucluse. And all is good."

"Well, I should think so." Penelope considered the immense service bill she had paid not two weeks before, supposedly to make sure her trip was trouble-free.

"It was a good thing that they did," said Mme Valencourt. "If you had tried to drive it down the hill yesterday, you would have had a terrible accident."

"What do you mean?"

"The police investigators found that the brake lines were cut."

Penelope's legs weakened. "What? I don't believe it. Why? How?"

"I should let the chief of police explain."

A pause.

"Please tell me now. I would rather hear it from you," pleaded Penelope, not at all sure she wanted to know. And just when she'd begun to feel a bit more optimistic.

The Frenchwoman hesitated. "It seems that Manuel Avore had a history of trying to sabotage whoever displeased him. The ancient owners found their water supply cut. The vegetable garden was sprayed with chemicals to kill weeds. The electric supply was disrupted, and a fire was started close to the house."

"The ancient owners?" It was too much information to process.

"The Girards, who owned the property before you."

Talk about buyer beware! She probably had a cast-iron case

against Mme Valencourt and the Agence Hublot. With an effort, she tried to focus on the worst of it. "Was that why they sold
it, because of this vexatious neighbour?"

"No," said Mme Valencourt. "They died. It was sold by their
children. I told you."

Had she? "Died? How?"

"It was a road accident."

Penelope gulped. "Here in the Luberon?"

"On their way back to Lyon."

"What? Was it caused by mechanical failure, I mean—"

"It had nothing to do with it. Please do not concern yourself."

But Penelope would not be deflected. "So someone cut the
brake lines on my Range Rover. And a neighbour had form for
that kind of thing—Manuel Avore?"

"That is correct."

"And all the time you were so keen on getting me to buy the
property, you didn't think to mention any of these drawbacks?"

"No."

Penelope clenched her teeth. "And will you explain to me why
not, please, Mme Valencourt?"

"Because Manuel Avore was no longer a problem. He was not
here. He was in prison for assault."

"But not forever, surely! In fact, with astonishingly unfortunate timing, his release must have coincided with my arrival in
St Merlot. Brilliant!"

"That is true, but it was not expected. He must have behaved
himself there. Laurent—the mayor—assured me that M. Avore
would be locked up for a long while, and that the village would
try to help him to live a normal, sober life when he returned."

"But did you not think to—"

"Penny, I know this is shocking for you. But do not forget that
Manuel Avore is dead. He cannot harm anyone now."

That at least was indisputable.

Penelope exhaled a long breath. "So, let's just get this straight. My car has been checked over. Possibly as part of a forensic examination to see whether it had any connection to the death of Manuel Avore. But they found the brakes had been tampered with. Which might have been done by Avore himself—and which could have killed me!"

"Penny—"

"Don't 'Penny' me, Mme Valencourt! I am so angry that I could—"

"I am going to the police station to collect your car keys, and I will bring the vehicle to you at the Hôtel St Pierre as soon as I can. I agree. It has been a most unfortunate event."

Penelope looked balefully out of her hotel window. All her enthusiasm for the grand spectacle of the market had drained away. How could she just wander around in the jolly crowds as if nothing had happened? Anything she bought would be tainted with the memory of this shocking turn of events.

She waited in her room, expecting a summons from reception to go down and meet Clémence Valencourt, but it did not come. Eventually she went down to the foyer to find that her car keys were at reception and the Range Rover, newly cleaned, was in the hotel car park.

Because she couldn't think what else to do, she climbed in and checked the interior, which was also in a better state than she had left it after the long drive from Esher.

PERCHED ON its high rocky outcrop, Saignon was the closest place to St Merlot.

From below, the whole village was one vast impregnable castle, but the main street was like an illustration from an old French school textbook. Faded signs and shutters were smothered in displays of flowers in hanging baskets and pots. Penelope strolled past the old *lavoir,* the communal laundry pool. The sound of trickling water came from a fountain topped with a statue of Ceres in front of an old presbytery covered in creeper. It was now a hotel that appeared to have closed down.

On a tourist information board outside the twelfth-century Romanesque church, she read that Saignon had once served as a lookout point for danger in the valley. It was a pity the church bells no longer sounded alarms, she thought. *I could have done with a warning that everything was about to kick off.*

She wanted to go home. But she wasn't supposed to. Though the police hadn't told her directly about her car, and she had got that back. And Clémence Valencourt had spoken to the police on her behalf without passing on any message forbidding her return to Le Chant d'Eau. Perhaps she could just look in on her property, as she was so close. If the police were still there, she would be able to ask them if that was all right, wouldn't she? And it would be safe there now, surely . . .

7

ON THE FIRST STRAIGHT BIT of the road towards St Merlot, a shiny red Ferrari overtook Penelope with a throaty growl. She watched it accelerate away into a sharp bend, changing gear flamboyantly. There was an interesting mix of people here in August, she thought: happy holidaymakers from northern Europe; artists and photographers; walkers and cyclists; the farming community; the butchers and bakers and candlestick makers who gave so much pleasure to everyday life; and some extremely rich people—Parisians and Swiss and Americans—staying at their second homes. Penelope wondered if people would assume she was rich. She didn't feel rich. Comfortably off, perhaps. And, for the first time in her life, adventurous with a lump sum.

Five minutes later, she turned off the main road. There were no police vehicles in sight. As far as she could make out as she took the rutted track at a sensible speed, there was no one there. Penelope parked at the side of the house, where the Range Rover couldn't be seen. She looked around and listened carefully before getting out. There was no police tape, or anything else to denote that an investigation was still taking place.

Inside her house, all seemed as she had left it two days previously. A rustling noise startled her, but it was only a few dry leaves rolling in the breeze on the kitchen patio.

Penelope steadied herself and unlocked the kitchen door. If she wanted to live in this house, she was going to have to face the scene of the accident, or whatever it turned out to be. Best get it over with, and not make a song and dance.

In the stifling heat, the garden seemed to rear up at her. The straw-like grass was more overgrown than ever. After two days away, Penelope was shocked all over again by the immensity of the task she had taken on.

She dug deep into her reserves of British grit. Whoever heard of an Englishwoman scared of a bit of gardening? Everyone knew that what followed was the purchase of a wide-brimmed straw hat, possibly with a veil, and a trowel. Before you could say Sissinghurst, there'd be vistas of roses, boxed beds of white flowers by the olive trees, and an exquisitely placed aubergine for authenticity. In short order, photographers from the Sunday supplements would be fighting for the best shot.

Penelope strode through the grass jungle.

The door to the walled swimming pool garden was ajar. Trying not to think too hard, she gave it a push and stepped inside. Everything looked the same. The pool water was still brown and sludgy, but there was no lingering horror. Had she become heartless? she wondered. Was it the result of being in a foreign country, and what did that say about her?

She stood there for a while, trying to work out what she really thought. Was this some kind of psychological self-preservation? Possibly. Or it might simply be that she was well used to the idea of death in the abstract, thanks to her old job. She decided to leave it at that.

According to all the papers she had signed, the property extended to 1.2 hectares, which translated into a smidgen over two and a half acres. There were parts of it she hadn't seen yet.

The southern boundary was marked by an old orchard. On closer examination the trees were plums, though many were so old they had dried out and toppled over. Penelope walked up a slight slope to a weed-strewn patch of tomato plants that might once have been a vegetable garden. Beyond was overgrown grass and bushes. A large mulberry tree and more olive trees guarded the eastern edge.

By the mulberry, almost hidden by some dog rose bushes, stood a small stone structure that had perhaps once been an animal pen. She made her way over. It would make a wonderful garden shed. Perhaps that was what it had been used for.

The flaking wooden door was padlocked. She rattled it anyway, and pulled at the padlock. It was securely fastened. Undeterred, Penelope marched back to the house and pulled open the kitchen drawer that contained a selection of old keys. She scrabbled through them, scooped up a handful, and put them in the nearest vessel to hand, which happened to be a tea tray bearing the patriotic legend "Keep Calm and Eat Cake."

Back at the locked door, she worked through the keys systematically. The first few she tried were useless, and there was a pile of discarded keys on the ground by the time she pushed a newish one into the padlock. It slid in easily enough, but then refused to turn. Then it wouldn't come out again. Penelope shook it in frustration, and before she knew it, the door had squeaked open. The metal fixing in the doorframe had come away.

After a minute adjusting her eyes to the gloom inside, Penelope could make out rows of pots on a large table, a number of sacks, various plastic jerry cans, and, hanging on the wall opposite, a long line of garden tools, which was a delightful surprise. It was always a bonus to find items left behind in a house, and these discarded implements would come in very handy. They were like a welcome present, and she found herself smiling at the thought.

There seemed little out of the ordinary here. And yet, as she gazed at the tools, she knew that something was not quite right. Along the line of well-worn tools, all showed the dirt, wear, and tear of use, and the rust of being stored in a damp stone out-building. Except one, a large axe. This had either been cleaned thoroughly or was a newer addition.

Penelope took it down from its hook. Maybe it had never been used. She went to put it back on the hook, but in the half dark-ness, she missed and then stared in horror as the tool fell noisily to the stone floor. The metal head flew off the shaft into a dark, spidery corner. She picked up the two parts and took them out-side into the bright sunshine to try to reconnect them.

She turned the implement around to find the right fit. On the neck of the shaft, freshly uncovered by the accident, was an area that had not been cleaned. An area where the wood was stained a deep brown. Exactly, thought Penelope, the colour of dried blood.

"Holy guacamole!" she cried out.

Then she remembered the cut brake cables and started to tremble.

IN THE absence of cake, Penelope lit her primus stove, found the PG Tips and some longlife milk, and made a cup of tea in an attempt to Keep Calm.

There was always the possibility that her imagination was running away with her, she thought. Or this was middle-aged brain fog. Wouldn't be the first time. What was required was logic, not mood swings.

Unfortunately, logic unleashed screaming thoughts that cen-tred on what Clémence Valencourt had said about the heavy wounds on the dead man's head. It followed grimly that these could have been caused by a blow from an axe.

Penelope stirred an emergency teaspoonful of sugar into her

tea. No, that didn't necessarily follow, she tried to tell herself. She didn't even know for sure whether those were bloodstains on the axe shaft. She was just catastrophizing. This was what happened when a person was overwrought. She had to stop this now. The axe shaft—and the head—would have to be submitted for forensic tests before anything could be ascertained, and they probably had nothing whatsoever to do with the body in the pool. She should know better than to go leaping to conclusions.

With the presence of mind that had often been praised by her former boss, she took several photos of the axe, from different angles, on her phone. Then she went upstairs and found some plastic wrapping from a new set of pillows and carefully placed both parts of the axe inside it. She would share her discovery with the police, though she doubted the chief would be thrilled to receive her bearing a strange (and possibly irrelevant) package at four o'clock on a Saturday afternoon. Especially when she wasn't sure she should have been at her property at all.

She was just deciding where she should store it, or whether she should take it out to the car to take with her, when she heard the spitting of stones outside. A vehicle came down the track. Penelope froze. What if it was the police? Had someone seen her coming in and reported her?

There was nothing for it but to face the music. She should open the front door with a big smile on her face, as if nothing was amiss. Then again, no, she shouldn't: that would look calculated. She should sit tight and have a few sips of tea.

No knock on the door came.

After about ten minutes, Penelope went down to the front hall and peeped out of the window. A car had indeed arrived on her property and parked outside. It was a very familiar red Mini Cooper.

For a moment, Penelope thought about staying where she was

and pretending she wasn't there. But then she wouldn't know what the estate agent was doing on her property. It was all getting very silly. She popped on her sunglasses and picked up a book. Armed with that and her cup of tea, she crossed the courtyard and made for a shady spot. No sign of her visitor. She rounded the wall of the courtyard and stopped abruptly.

Ahead of her, by the stone shed, stood the birdlike Mme Valencourt. Another figure emerged from the outbuilding, which Penelope had left open.

"Holy guacamole!" For the second time in an hour the exclamation came unbidden.

Clémence Valencourt was holding the Keep Calm and Eat Cake tray, scrutinising it with a perfectly plucked, raised eyebrow. Penelope couldn't imagine that the Frenchwoman would ever find it necessary to follow its instructions. M. Charpet pointed at the shed, and the two exchanged a few words. Was it her imagination, or did they look worried? What was going on here?

Penelope took a deep breath and called out in what she hoped was a casual tone, "Bonjour!"

They both seemed to jump.

"H-hello, Penny!" Could that be a slight hesitation in Mme Valencourt's voice, a crack in her usual composure?

"Why didn't you let me know you were here?"

"I did not know that you were here, Penny."

"Well, that makes two of us," said Penelope pointedly.

"You remember M. Charpet." A tiny hand waved in his direction.

The extravagantly moustachioed gardener quickly turned around. They all exchanged polite handshakes.

"As M. Charpet's first visit was abandoned due to . . . you

know what . . . he has returned today at my suggestion," said the estate agent. In a nod to weekend attire, she was wearing tight white jeans with a patterned silk batwing blouse, high wedge-heeled sandals, and enormous black sunglasses. Standing in the long grass, she looked like an exotic insect.

"I know that your first days at this property have been very difficult and I wanted to make sure the work to clear the land was achieved as soon as possible. Like that, you will be more comfortable."

Penelope was caught unawares for the second time that afternoon, but this time it was with a strong sense of relief. "That is very kind. Very thoughtful. Thank you."

Mme Valencourt shrugged. "It is nothing. M. Charpet can begin this weekend. We came to decide what should be done first."

"So the police have finished what they needed to do here?"

"Yes, it is done. As soon as I have heard this, I asked M. Charpet to meet me here."

But no one told me, thought Penelope.

"Did you not receive a message from the office of the chief of police?" asked Clémence, as if she was reading Penelope's mind, or possibly the expression on her face.

"No. Well, I haven't actually checked my phone lately. It's running out of power, so . . ." She delved into her bag and switched on her mobile. Sure enough, there was a text from the police, telling her she was cleared to return. It was all so much simpler than she had made it out to be. Another surge of relief coursed through her veins. "So, M. Charpet works at weekends, does he? That's marvellous."

That was another misconception about the French, that no worker would consider putting in more than their thirty-five hours a week, and absolutely never over lunchtime or at weekends.

"Would you both like a cup of coffee?" she asked, in a rush of goodwill and flushed with embarrassment that she could have suspected anything else. "I have some fairly hot water—well, I could heat it up again, and only Nescafé, I'm afraid, but . . ." The look of disgust on the Frenchwoman's face was mirrored on M. Charpet's.

"Non merci, madame," they chorused, a little too quickly for politesse.

They carried on the conversation as they walked around the garden, discussing the priorities as they went. The hip-high grass was top of Penelope's list, and then the clearing and assessment of the swimming pool. There was no black humour in their remarks, as there surely would have been back in England. It was as though each had decided not to mention the last time they were by the pool.

At last, M. Charpet said he was walking home. It turned out he lived on the other side of St Merlot, but there was a path through the woods that he liked to ramble along.

As soon as he had retreated along the track, Penelope turned to Clémence without preamble. "I found something in that stone building."

"Oh?"

"I want to show it to you."

On the kitchen table, Penelope carefully unwrapped the plastic from around the axe. It lay in two pieces, looking rather ordinary on the pillow bag.

"It is an axe, Penny. It is used to chop wood."

"No shit, Sherlock," said Penelope before she could stop herself.

"Pardon?"

"I know that it is an axe. But think of the wound on M. Avore's head. Perhaps it wasn't just bruising. So look at this." Penelope went to her sink and put on a pair of yellow Marigold rubber gloves. It was the best she could do. She picked up the shaft and pointed to the brown stains without touching them.

"I think that's blood."

8

THE SUNDAY-MORNING TRAFFIC ON the autoroute down from Cavaillon was light. Penelope hardly raised her foot from the accelerator. She arrived at the Marseille airport midmorning, ludicrously early. Looking around for a place to wait, she noted with some irritation that the coffee and ice cream shop she remembered from a few years back had been replaced by a Burger King. A sad indictment on contemporary French life, she thought, as she made her way to another abomination, a newly established Starbucks.

By the time Frankie's plane landed, Penelope found herself chewing a croissant, cursing her lack of self-control and justifying it on the grounds of keeping up her strength, both for the whirlwind that was her old friend and for the terrors of the autoroute drive back to the Luberon. The roads always reached peak danger around midday, as the French allowed nothing to get between them and a good lunch.

When a stream of obviously British visitors had begun to emerge blinking out of the customs hall, she wandered over to arrivals.

The shriek resounded.

"PENNY—YOU—ARE—LOOKING—*gorgeous*, YOU OLD TART!"

Frankie was a woman let loose, a thousand sequins glittering under the fluorescent light. She bore down upon Penelope, arms open wide. Every square inch of flesh not covered by shimmering pink was a quite unfeasible shade of orange. From under a hat the size of a café table, there appeared a wide smiling row of perfect teeth. A millisecond later Penelope was swept up, powerless as a rag doll in a bone-crushing embrace. Frankie was a big woman.

"I'm here! No need to worry about anything! So good to see you, darling!"

In spite of a very English mortification at such displays of emotion in public, Penelope could not help smiling, and returned the affection. Frankie might be overdressed, overjewelled, overbearing, and sometimes just plain loud, but there was no doubting the gold of her heart.

"It's good to see you too, Frankie. It really is."

"You know I'll never let you down, Pen. Whatever it takes, eh?"

"I know. Thank you."

"You can stop the misery eating, too."

"What?"

Frankie raised her eyebrows and nodded towards Penelope's mouth. "Croissant crumbs," she hissed. "Dead giveaway."

Penelope hastily brushed away the offending evidence. "You know me too well, Frankie."

"So, off to the new villa—I'm just dying to see it. All the way from Heathrow—which was more appalling than ever, by the way—I've been dreaming of sitting on the terrace of your beautiful house, glass of rosé in one hand, bottle in the other, admiring the view! And trying to get over what's happened," she added hastily as she saw the look on Penelope's face. "Terrible business."

Penelope steeled herself.

"Well, the thing is, Frankie . . ."

"A nice bowl of olives and a beaker of chilled pink, just the tonic to get you back on your feet—"

"Slight change of plan."

"Change of plan?"

"The house isn't quite . . ."

"Quite what?"

"Quite ready for guests—or me, really . . ." Penelope's voice faded away. "It's in no state for visitors. I've booked you into the Hôtel St Pierre with me."

Frankie was having none of it. "Don't worry about me, Pen. I'm used to slumming it. When we did up the manor at Billericay, we only had one bathroom for over a month!"

"There's no water."

"You know me, Pen, love a challenge! Let's get going and show 'em how it's done."

"And no electricity . . ."

"Ah, now that might be a problem, Pen. No electricity—no hair dryer! And no fridge." The full horror dawned. "No fridge, no ice-cold booze!"

"Plus a ceiling that decides to shed its load on various random occasions. A hard hat wouldn't go amiss."

"But the whole point of me coming was to get you used to being there after . . . what's happened. Make it feel comfortable and like yours." Frankie might have registered disappointment, but she was clearly willing to forgo her expectations for the greater good.

"I know, but—"

"The hotel will be fine. Probably for the best."

"We can still go and see the house."

"Course we can! Now, where are we going for lunch?"

Frankie grabbed her arm and propelled her friend and her capacious designer suitcase towards the exit.

IT TOOK a little over an hour to return to Apt from the airport, though the time whistled by, assisted by an excitable monologue from Frankie. The firm was doing well, Johnny was being a pain in the arse, but she still adored him—he was off with his mates at their villa in Marbella, playing golf. The three children were respectively working as an accountant ("very useful when he takes over the firm"), at law school, and at university, studying nursing. The dog was in kennels.

Penelope was glad the dog had not accompanied its mistress. Perky, a Rottweiler, had come close to taking pieces out of her on several occasions, and loved only its master and mistress. Anyone else was viewed as an opportunity for a quick snack.

To Frankie's delight, the terrace restaurant at the Hôtel St Pierre was pleasantly filled with late Sunday lunchers and still serving. They were shown to a corner table overlooking the trickling river. The menu was very promising indeed. The first carafe of rosé disappeared rapidly, to be replaced by a second.

"Well, they are rather small, darling," said Frankie.

Next to Frankie, many things did look small. Her face was wide, her shoulders were wide, and her hands were studded with enormous rings. A vast ruby matched her new red hair.

Penelope laughed. "You seem on terrific form, I must say."

"Fighting fit!" Frankie tapped the side of her nose and leaned in. "HRT. I've been turbocharged."

"Oh lor'! The only thing that's turbocharged with me is my appetite. I seem to be permanently hungry."

Their food arrived.

"Isn't it funny," said Frankie from the other side of a melon and *jambon cru* starter garnished with salad leaves and walnuts.

"How food here tastes of what it's supposed to. This melon is like the most melony melon you can possibly imagine!"

"I know," cried Penelope. "You wait till you have a tomato!" She couldn't help but bask in a certain reflected glory at the quality of the Provençal ingredients.

The salmon dish they both chose was indeed served with a herby stuffed tomato, and they duly pronounced it unparalleled.

Perhaps unwisely, a third carafe of rosé was ordered, which Frankie tackled with aplomb and Penelope approached with caution.

"We might have to have a pud," said Penelope, as if it was a matter of some regret. "Just to soak up all the alcohol."

The crèmes brûlées were simply divine.

"I'm going to be the size of a house if I go on living here much longer," sighed Penelope. "But it is all so lovely."

"You're still finding your feet, Pen. It'll be different when you've settled in. I mean, you don't eat fish and chips every day when you live in England, do you?"

"Suppose not. It's just so hard to lose weight when you turn fifty! You spend weeks eating lettuce to lose a few pounds, then have a few days treating yourself and it's hello to another spare tyre. It's quite depressing."

"You look lovely. And the new hairstyle is a triumph. But what are you going to do with yourself here when all this . . . unfortunate business is over? I mean, you can't just sit around, can you?"

At that point, nothing seemed more appealing than just sitting around in reestablished normality, but Penelope nodded. "I want to take French lessons, obviously. Do up the house— obviously. And I'm going back to my music."

Frankie beamed. "That *is* good news. I'm so pleased. I never really understood why you gave up. It was so much a part of you."

"There are concerts and little recitals going on all over the place, too. We might go to one if you feel like it." Penelope sidestepped her friend's implicit question. It was hard to explain why she had given up her beloved instrument when the children became tricky and she was so unhappy with David. She used to tell herself it was down to lack of space and time as Justin and Lena's lives expanded, but even when they both went off to university, she had still averted her eyes from the black case in the storage room.

"You've brought your cello, then?"

Penelope smiled. "One of the reasons I needed a big car!"

Frankie reached over and squeezed her hand. "Oh, Pen! That's great."

"I'll probably need some music lessons, too, after all this time. So that will be good for getting my French up to scratch as well. And you never know, I might find a group to play with."

Over coffee, they both decided that a nap would be a good idea. In excellent spirits, Frankie was gracious about the adjacent room Penelope had reserved for her. She was used to travelling in style these days.

They retired to their respective beds for a siesta, having agreed to meet at six o'clock for a drive up to Le Chant d'Eau. Penelope lay down in the coolness of the air-conditioned room and drifted off to sleep, lulled by the rhythmic snoring clearly audible through the wall.

9

SHE WAS RUDELY AWOKEN BY a banging on the hotel room door.

"Pen! Pen! You're not still asleep, are you? It's half past five, and I can't wait any longer to see the new place!"

"Gah!" Penelope blinked. She felt liverish and wearier than before the snooze. "Just coming!"

Penelope drove carefully up to St Merlot. "I hope I'm not over the limit," she said.

"This is France, darling."

"You'd be surprised. Things have changed from when no one cared. The drink drive limit is lower here than it is back in the UK."

"Well, it's not far, is it?"

"Luckily not."

Penelope checked the rearview mirror. "There it is again," she said, almost to herself.

"What again?"

"Red Ferrari. Any minute, it'll overtake—on these bends! Why are rich people so impatient?"

Penelope pulled over to the right as far as she could and slowed down. An expensive growl filled the air, and the Ferrari went shooting past and belted up the hill towards the village.

But when they came round the last bend before the track to Le Chant d'Eau, it had stopped on the road, idling a few metres short of the turning. Penelope was forced to overtake and then make a right turn. Through the driver's window she could just make out a man sporting a mop of silvery curls and dark glasses. No sooner had she done so than the Ferrari moved off very slowly, almost as if the driver was making sure he knew where she had gone.

"Plonker," said Frankie.

Penelope didn't relax until she had threaded the Range Rover through the archway and switched off the ignition. Frankie took in the mellow stone farmhouse slumbering benignly in the golden hours before sunset. Pine trees cast long shadows up the hillside. "Come through the garden, and we'll go in the back door," said Penelope.

Rather unexpectedly, someone else was already there.

A woman was speaking, very fast and furiously, in the kitchen.

"Who?" mouthed Frankie.

"Don't know."

Soundlessly, they pushed open the door. Clémence Valencourt was sitting at the table, arguing with someone on her mobile. Penelope suppressed her irritation.

The estate agent stood up, unabashed, and proffered her hand first to Penelope and then to her friend.

"Enchantée, madame . . . ," she said, taking in the sequin dazzle with the kind of facial expression only a Parisian woman can bestow.

Undeterred, Frankie grasped the woman's hand and instantly launched into a conversation in fluent French, whilst Penelope looked on, openmouthed. Mme Valencourt joined in enthusiastically. They jabbered away for some minutes.

"I didn't know you could speak French that well, Frankie!"

"Yes, it is impeccable," agreed Clémence Valencourt. Any lingering sequin-based prejudice seemed to have vanished. She beamed with friendliness as she nodded towards Frankie.

Frankie waved away the compliment. "Don't you remember when I had just left school and I was supposed to be at that secretarial college in London? Well, I got bored with it and went to Paris. I didn't tell my old mum and dad. They thought I was in Kensington bashing out the old quick something fox jumped over the lazy brown whatever-it-was at the typewriter. But I'd always wanted to have a go at dancing, and I was too tall for the ballet, so I blagged my way into working at the Moulin Rouge."

"What, in the box office?"

"No, silly. On the stage. There were lots of us tall English girls."

"Frankie—you never told me that!"

"You never asked. I didn't tell anyone. Johnny doesn't like me mentioning it, now we move in higher circles. But anyway, I did get to meet all sorts of people, and my French came on a treat!"

Frankie had clearly won over Mme Valencourt. She was nodding and smiling with something curiously close to admiration, and they exchanged rapid observations in French. Penelope caught "Paris" and "Champs Élysées" and not much more. That'll teach her to judge by first impressions, thought Penelope. And what *was* the woman doing at her house, yet again?

"Hang on a minute," said Penelope, racing after them as they set off in the direction of the spacious but uninhabitable sitting room, still chatting away in French.

There was no stopping Frankie. She was in her element. Throughout the tour, as they progressed upstairs, Frankie kept up a constant stream of conversation in English and French, laced liberally with bawdy humour. Mme Valencourt, rather unexpectedly, found it hilarious.

"Your friend Penelope, she is so funny! She is always talking about the sex!"

"Yes, Clémence is right, you're desperately in need of a man!" Frankie laughed. So it was Clémence already, was it?

They emerged into the courtyard to find that M. Charpet had also arrived uninvited. Another round of hand shaking and French jokes ensued. With exaggerated courtesy, he solemnly kissed Frankie's hand, setting off another shriek of glee.

"That takes me back. Old-fashioned moustache-tickle! A real French farmer! I wonder if he's organised any good strikes lately."

It was all getting out of hand, like a merry-go-round that was impossible to stop because everyone else on board was enjoying it so much. There wasn't a chance to ask them what the hell they were doing here. Penelope began to feel left out.

"Do behave, Frankie. M. Charpet is my new gardener, and I want to stay on the right side of him!"

"Okeydokey, Pen. From now on, the soul of discretion."

Unlikely, thought Penelope. "What I don't understand," she said, rather too loudly, "is why you are both here today. Again. It's a Sunday evening, and I didn't think gardeners or estate agents worked on Sunday evenings in France." It came out more rudely than she intended.

M. Charpet clutched his hat to his stomach, looking worried.

"Excuse me. I should have explained," said Clémence. "You have had a difficult start to your new life here. We want to do what we can to help, to make everything right for you. M. Charpet has commenced to cut the grass by the orchard, and I needed to check the number on the water meter. As your immobilière, it is my responsibility to arrange the documents for the water company. I am too busy tomorrow, so I came this evening."

"Oh." Penelope felt ashamed of her outburst. "I'm sorry. That's very kind of you."

She did wonder, though, why the estate agent had not done that when M. Charpet uncovered the meter the day before.

◆

UNSURPRISINGLY, FRANKIE wanted to see the scene of the crime. They trooped off to the swimming pool. M. Charpet had already cut the grass beyond the stone surround of the pool. The space looked wider, and the pool had been drained.

"Vous avez connu le décédé?" Frankie asked, and turned to Penelope. "I asked if he knew the dead man."

"Thank you, I do understand, even if I can't speak French as well as you yet."

M. Charpet nodded. With his hands he mimed the universally understood drinking sign. "C'était le pastis, madame."

It didn't take long for Frankie to debrief him to her satisfaction, asking a string of questions that the gardener seemed to relish answering. Mme Valencourt listened without comment.

Suddenly Charpet did a little dance on the spot. Then he wove his way around the pool area, gesticulating and shouting. He picked up an old broom that was propped against the wall and began to swing it alarmingly.

Frankie looked at Penelope. Mme Valencourt widened her eyes.

"What the hell was that?" said Penelope under her breath as M. Charpet recovered himself.

"Your late neighbour, M. Avore," replied Frankie. "Apparently he was a tad unpredictable."

"Unpredictable as in axe-wielding maniac?"

"He was a hopeless drunkard. He was well known in the village. People here used to say that if you sat in the middle of the village for a few hours, sooner or later you would see him fall over."

"But they thought he was harmless, didn't they? Even when

he proved them wrong and was sent to prison. By the way, you didn't say—why exactly was he in prison?"

"He attacked two people," admitted Mme Valencourt.

"What was his problem?" Frankie asked her in English.

"*Bof!* Wine at breakfast, wine in the morning, wine at lunch, and wine afterwards. Gambling, no money, a bad marriage— they said that he was beating his wife—and the unfortunate fantasy that Le Chant d'Eau belonged to him."

"Wait, he had a wife?" said Penelope.

"Ah, yes. Unfortunate woman."

"Hell's bells. How awful for her. What's—I mean, is she all right? How is she coping?" Penelope had not factored in a beaten wife. Why on earth would she have stayed with a drunken fantasist?

"I believe that she is unusually happy for a woman who has recently been widowed," said Mme Valencourt.

"Quite bloody right," said Frankie. "Why did Avore think he was the rightful owner here?"

"It is a very long story, but some years ago, when the previous owners, the Girards, purchased the property, there was an argument over some of the land, which he claimed was his."

"And was it?" said Penelope.

"There was . . . a possibility. A discrepancy before the papers could be prepared. Great care was taken to correct this, as you will remember."

"I certainly do." Penelope recalled the stifling day in Avignon, going through the documents with the notary.

"The difficulty was . . . resolved."

"Well, I do hope it was."

"Do not worry," said Mme Valencourt, "and I am sure that over time you will come to find that your other neighbour, M. Louchard, is charming."

"Over time?"

"Yes. To begin with, he is sometimes a little awkward with . . . with . . ."

Penelope waited glumly for the ending.

"With foreigners."

Drawing a line under discussions about the neighbours, dead or alive, Penelope walked them all back towards the house.

"I could make a cup of tea," she offered. That was just what she needed. "I've got my primus stove, and bottles of mineral water."

"Haven't you got any wine in?"

"I haven't been here long enough to establish a cellar, Frankie."

They all passed on the tea.

As before, M. Charpet said goodbye in the garden, and indicated his intent to walk home after he had tidied away the tools he had used.

"You could really make a killing on this place, Pen—I'm talking gîte—gîte—gîte!" Frankie jingled a multi-braceleted wrist in the air as she pointed out each outbuilding in turn.

"I have rarely heard you talk as much gîte in your life, Frankie. The last thing I want to do here is run a business!"

"But think of the money you could make!"

"I don't need it. This is my time now. I want to play my cello, listen to music, ride horses once in a while perhaps, try my hand at painting—or even, if I feel like living dangerously, do nothing at all. I most certainly do not want to end up managing a B&B for whiny families from Surrey!"

"Well, it's your money, Pen. Just a thought."

Frankie sounded chastened for a moment but quickly recovered as they went through the door into the kitchen. "Anyway, forget that—here's what we are going to do with the main house!

The good news is that the building is fundamentally sound. All these cracks"—Frankie waved her hands in no particular direction—"they're nothing, just a bit of movement in the clay underneath the house. No point worrying about them."

"Well, that's some good news, at least."

"Yes, I'm sure if the walls were going to collapse, they would have done so by now. They're old and they move with the seasons, the wet and the dry weather. It's the modern houses they build on land like this that explode!"

Mme Valencourt waggled one hand to indicate that Frankie knew what she was talking about, more or less.

Hardly a ringing endorsement, thought Penelope, but comforting to a certain degree. "I feel a large 'but' hanging in the air, Frankie."

"But there is an awful lot of renovation to do. The roofs are pretty hopeless, and a lot of the outside walls need serious repointing. And you must get the wiring checked out."

"Le beurrage?" Mme Valencourt jumped in.

"Oui. Repointing. Buttering," said Frankie. "How apt. Yes, large amounts of buttering."

"And the garden?"

"Not my forte, Pen. We always get someone else to do that. I would leave it up to your French retainer—he seems to know what he is doing."

Mme Valencourt nodded her head vigorously.

"M. Charpet, he is one of the best. He knows all there is to know about the village and he used to look after this property. If you let him do what he thinks is right, your garden will be made beautiful again."

"And if I want something particular done?"

"Alas, madame, there is little point in asking him. He will without doubt ignore you!"

There was a lot one could learn about the Provençal psyche from that casual statement, thought Penelope.

"Are we going to tell the police tomorrow about the axe I found?" Penelope reminded her.

"Of course. We will go at ten o'clock. I will collect you from the Hôtel St Pierre."

The Frenchwoman left soon after. Penelope walked her to the front door and watched to see where she went. As she suspected, the red Mini Cooper had been parked all along out of sight in the same place where Penelope had left the Range Rover when she hadn't wanted to be spotted. Interesting.

She answered a toot on the horn with a wave as the Mini Cooper passed.

⁂

THE SUN set behind the mountains in a red ball of fire. The two friends sat out on the terrace, drinking the cup of strong tea that Penelope had been gasping for.

"What do you make of our Mme Valencourt, then? You wouldn't think she was the caring sharing type to look at her, but she's been very good to me. And she really seemed to take to you."

Frankie sipped from a mug of brick-coloured PG Tips. She didn't smile. "What was that about an axe and the police?"

Penelope told her.

"Where is it now?"

"She took it for safekeeping."

"Hmm."

"What do you mean, 'Hmm'?"

"It could mean anything, Pen. But she was talking about an axe on her mobile when we found her in the kitchen."

"What? What was she saying?"

"Well, here's the thing. She was saying that it needed to be managed carefully. I don't know whether whoever it was she was talking to didn't agree with her, because it sounded like they were having a right old ding-dong about it. She was quite worried."

"What about?"

"About what this axe might reveal."

"Hell's bells."

"And do we believe her about the water meter?" Frankie went on mercilessly. "How did she get inside your house, anyway? Is it normal for French estate agents to keep a copy of the keys to the houses they sell?"

Penelope hadn't even thought about that. There had been so many other things coming at her from all directions. "Bloody, bloody hell. Triple hell's bells."

"She needs watching, that one," said Frankie.

"You two seemed to be getting on great guns, though."

"We were sizing each other up."

"What do you think it's all about, then?" Penelope felt exhausted.

"I don't know, but I tell you one thing. I'm glad I'm here, Pen. I have a feeling you're going to need all the help you can get."

They fell silent and finished their tea as one by one the stars began to twinkle in the darkening sky.

"Despite everything, Frankie, all the awfulness—I'm smitten."

"Give yourself another spray with that anti-mozzie stuff, then."

"Not bitten. Smitten. By this place."

They sat for a while longer in companionable silence as the staccato of cicada song began to fill the hot night air. When at last they rose from the table to go back to the hotel, the moon was high in the sky.

10

CLÉMENCE VALENCOURT TURNED UP AT the hotel the next morning an hour earlier than expected. She teetered into the restaurant in a figure-skimming navy linen dress. Stacked heels showed off her slim tanned legs. Penelope stepped away from the buffet table and the further temptations of the continental breakfast.

"The mayor has asked to see us before we go to the police station with the axe," Mme Valencourt said.

"The mayor of Apt?"

"No, of course not. The mayor of St Merlot. We will go there now."

Penelope ran up to her room, cleaned her teeth again, checked her makeup and brushed her hair, made sure all her personal documents were in her bag, texted Frankie—who hadn't yet emerged for breakfast—and soap-scratched a splodge of blackberry jam off her loose white linen trousers.

Mme Valencourt looked her up and down when they met in the foyer. "Is that what you are wearing?" she asked snippily.

"What's wrong with it?"

"No, nothing. It's a little . . . oh, never mind. Let's go."

It was another hot day, and by the time Penelope slid into the Mini Cooper she was already feeling at a sticky disadvantage.

She thought she would have a chance to ask a few probing questions about keys and the axe on the drive up, but swiftly abandoned that idea. Clémence Valencourt was clearly preoccupied and tight-lipped. She took the switchback ascent to St Merlot at full throttle, overtaking dithery tourists and speeding to cut corners rather than easing off the accelerator. An innocuous inquiry about the handsome mayor did not help matters. Clémence only just avoided a nose-to-nose crash with a van being driven with equal insouciance in the opposite direction. She scowled at the driver and cursed.

Penelope clutched the door handle with one hand and her seat belt with the other as the estate agent shot a junction and screeched past the village square, causing the old man with the newspaper to look up in alarm. Even Clémence looked a bit rattled when she got out of the car. They arrived in front of the *mairie* to find a blue police van parked outside.

The *mairie* at St Merlot was a modern building set back from the road on the outskirts of the village. Villagers were chatting by a pretty display of lantana shrubs and olive trees in big galvanised metal planters. A La Poste sign announced the village post office, also housed inside the building.

Mme Valencourt opened the boot of her car and extracted the axe, which was still in the plastic Penelope had put round it. She marched into the *mairie*, and Penelope followed. From behind the counter facing the entrance, a portly young woman with clumsily dyed blond hair looked up from her computer.

"I am sorry, madame, but that item you possess will be too big to post in the normal fashion."

Mme Valencourt was in no mood for pleasantries. "I don't want to post it! I want to show it to monsieur le maire!"

"He is in a meeting with the police—and he has asked not to be disturbed."

The agent ignored her and headed to a door on the right. She rapped a peremptory knock on the door before pushing it open.

The mayor looked up and deployed a devastating smile. Never

could a man have been interrupted to more charming effect. Penelope felt her knees tremble, just a little bit, in the presence of Laurent Millais. The white shirt with two buttons opened brought out his tan and dark blue eyes. He was even more gorgeous than she remembered.

"Bonjour, Clémence! Et Mme Keet, welcome to the mairie of St Merlot!"

He knew how to wear a pair of jeans, too, thought Penelope. She slapped herself down and tried to concentrate. The resurgence of such thoughts, long dormant, was most disconcerting.

Laurent Millais turned to the uniformed policeman with him and introduced him as Daniel Auxois. "He is one of the community police. You will see him often in the village."

Daniel was a pleasant-looking lad, with buzz-cut hair and broad shoulders. Rather excitingly—or not, depending on what you were doing—his black leather belt held a selection of serious weaponry, including a gun.

"First of all, Mme Keet, how is the current situation with your electricity and water?"

Penelope felt heat spread up from her knees. "Some progress but not much." She gulped. "Shocking business. I mean the pool. Not the electricity. Sorry." This was awful. Deep breath. "Mme Valencourt is doing her best to sort it out, thank you for asking."

"C'est normal. If I can be of any assistance, please don't hesitate to ask me. We have a good local electrician here. I can ask him to pass by."

"Here it is," said Mme Valencourt curtly. She put the wrapped axe on the desk.

There was a distinctly frosty edge to her voice. Penelope wondered whether it had been the mayor she was arguing with about the axe on the phone the previous afternoon.

The mayor offered another delightful smile, which had not

the slightest effect on the estate agent. He beckoned Penelope to come closer as he unwrapped the package. She pushed aside various entirely inappropriate thoughts. Was there a hint of mischief about his blue eyes?

The axe—and potential murder weapon—lay on the plastic. The mayor and the young gendarme were careful not to touch it. Penelope gave Mme Valencourt a surreptitious glance. There was no reaction for a few seconds.

"I found it in the small stone building by the mulberry tree," said Penelope. "It was full of old tools and bits and pieces inside that didn't look as if they had been used for years. Except this one with no rust on it. It looks newly cleaned."

They all took a closer look. The axe gleamed in the bright sunshine from the open window.

"But it wasn't cleaned very well. And not at all under the head. Look at that." Penelope pointed, being careful not to touch. "I think that's blood. Dried bloodstains."

Everyone leant in even closer.

"Did you find it like this, or did you remove the axe head?" asked the mayor.

"I dropped it, and the head came off. You see, about the bloodstains . . . I do have a certain professional knowl—"

"You say that you found this in the gardener's hut?"

He was not looking at Penelope, even as he asked her the question. His eyes were locked with Clémence's.

"Yes. Yes, I did."

"Dans la borie d'Henri Charpet?" This, too, was aimed at the Frenchwoman, who shrugged.

"M. Charpet's shed? Mon dieu!" said Penelope. Of course. The gardener would have used it when he worked for the previous owners.

The mayor conferred with the young policeman and then addressed Penelope.

"None of us can believe that M. Charpet could be responsible for this—he is an honourable man. Never! He was a Resistance fighter when he was a boy! Thank you for your help, Mme Keet, but you are mistaken if you suppose that Henri Charpet could have anything to do with the death of Manuel Avore."

"I don't think I said that." A new wave of heat broke. "It did not occur to me that you might think I was accusing M. Charpet. And I wasn't."

"But the evidence is unfortunate. M. Charpet had a key to this store," said Mme Valencourt. She looked crestfallen.

"Hold on a minute," said Penelope. "I couldn't find a key to open it, but when one got stuck, I found the iron catch wasn't attached to the wall properly. It just came away. That could be because someone had broken in, and put the catch back as best he could, so no one would notice."

A palpable wave of relief swept the room.

"*Impeccable!*" said the mayor. "You may take it to the chief of police now. And be sure to tell him about that broken lock. Daniel, make a note of this information, please."

"I don't understand," said Penelope.

"I have to make sure that I have all the facts. I know everyone who lives in this village, and there have been many questions about this tragic death. I need information to protect the innocent."

Penelope sincerely hoped that this included her. "Is that . . . what usually happens here?" she asked.

"The police have kindly allowed me to see the evidence in controlled circumstances." He nodded at the local gendarme.

It seemed most irregular to Penelope. She was sure that this was not the way the Home Office would have done it. France seemed suddenly a lot more foreign.

"I have some news," the mayor went on. He ran a hand through his thick, floppy hair. His hands were lovely and brown. "The results of the postmortem examination have revealed that Manuel Avore did not drown. He was already dead when he was placed in the old swimming pool."

"Well, that's what I said!" blurted out Penelope, looking again at Clémence Valencourt. "I knew it! I have worked on many murder cases."

The mayor looked taken aback. "You were a policewoman, madame?"

"Of course not! I was a senior secretary in forensics at the Home Office, and then became the personal assistant to one of their most eminent pathologists."

"You worked from home on murders?" The mayor was looking increasingly bemused.

"No! The Home Office—you know—the Ministry of the Interior." By this time Penelope was nearly shouting with exasperation.

The mayor assumed an injured pose. "Why did you not say anything to Inspector Gamelin or the chief of police, madame?"

"I tried," she retorted.

Daniel Auxois escorted them back down to Apt, leading the way in the police van. Forced to drive at a relatively normal speed behind him, Clémence tapped her red polished fingernails on the wheel, checked her phone for messages, and touched up her makeup in the rearview mirror.

"Is that normal, having to show the mayor of the village any evidence before the police see it?" asked Penelope, deciding to ignore the strained atmosphere.

"No. It is not normal."

"Oh?"

"He thinks he is God, that Laurent Millais."

"Oh."

"Salaud!"

"Is he not as nice as he looks, then?"

"Please, Penny, I do not want to speak of him."

"But I thought you were friends."

"Pah!"

"If he wanted to see the axe, why didn't he just meet us at the police station?"

"He hates the chief of police, that is why."

"But in that case—"

"Please, Penny! We will go to the police station, we will give the axe, and we will leave. I will go to my work, and you can have some holidays with your friend. Drink too much wine, like all the English. Eat too much. Everybody will be happy again."

The cheek of it.

Mind you, Mme Valencourt sounded anything but happy as both vehicles shot a red light and made a final terrifying turn at speed into the police station car park.

Penelope had been expecting another interview with the chief of police, but the visit was mercifully short. The besuited Paul Gamelin came downstairs to meet them, but Mme Valencourt simply handed over the plastic-packed axe, Penelope signed for it, and that was that.

❧

BACK ON the terrace at the Hôtel St Pierre, Frankie sparkled in a silver lamé tunic. When Penelope arrived, she was jotting down some figures in a notebook, but she straightened up, causing a man at the next table to spill his drink. "You know, Pen, you really could have stumbled on a gold mine here."

"How so?"

"Well, I've been doing a few numbers, and with a bit of renovation, some of that 'buttering,' and a lick of paint, I reckon you'd have three gîtes to sell or rent. And if the prices in the estates agents' windows are anything to go by, that would net you all your money back and more, and you would retain the main house."

"I thought we'd had this conversation."

"So we did, but I know you take a while to warm up to good ideas. How did everything go?"

"All right, I suppose. Now, what do you fancy doing for the rest of the day?"

Two hours and another three ("Quite small, really") carafes of beautifully chilled rosé later, along with justice done to the set lunch menu, Frankie had it all worked out. Penelope, on the other hand, was beginning to get quite confused. The renovation plans had been concentrated into one mighty chart. Expected timelines and delivery schedules blurred in Penelope's brain.

Penelope gazed over at the cobbled, tree-lined place de la Bouquerie, where a statue on a tall, slim column rose from a fountain. A knot of people stood chatting outside a restaurant called Chez Mon Cousin Alphonse.

"You could have it all done in three months, with the right contractors, Pen. Johnny and I have got some fantastic Polish teams, solid workmen and very reliable. I can easily—"

"I'm going to use French builders. A local firm."

"Are you mad, Pen? Half your money will go on three-hour lunch breaks and flash strikes."

"Don't care. I want to live here, Frankie, to feel part of it all. If

I bring in foreign builders when there's so much unemployment here, how will that look to people I want to be friends with?"

"I never had you down as a holier-than-thou *Guardian* reader, Pen. Crikey."

"That's the kind of petty, simplistic thinking that made me want to leave Surrey in the first place. I just want to do the right thing."

They argued a bit more in an amiable kind of way, and were finding common ground on the matter of builders when the tic-tacking of heels that meant business stopped at their table. It was Clémence again. Did the woman never use a phone? She had come to tell Penelope that the documents were at last in order with the water company and EDF, and that M. Charpet would check that supplies of both were flowing later that afternoon.

"Have you got time for a coffee?" Frankie asked her.

The Frenchwoman took in Frankie's silver lamé and failed to suppress a momentary look of horror.

"Sit down and tell me what you think of these plans. And we may need some recommendations for decent local builders," went on Frankie obliviously. She asked a passing waiter for three coffees.

Steamrollered, the estate agent sat down.

"What's the French for *mañana*? Renovation! However . . . we plough on," said Frankie. She pushed a page of drawings across the table towards Clémence.

The estate agent cleared her throat. "I do not know whether you will want to stay at Le Chant d'Eau and renovate it after this unfortunate incident. This may be difficult for you."

"Eh?" Penelope gulped. "Well, it might be a bit weird at first," she admitted. "But I hadn't really moved in. To be quite honest, it feels as if it happened before my time. Everyone knows that old houses have seen their share of deaths. Is there anything so very different about this one? Apart from the suspected foul play, of course."

"Foul play?" said Clémence. "I do not think this is a game."

"Tricherie, acte criminel," Frankie translated.

"Exactly! Why would a woman on her own want to stay in such a place?"

Penelope thought she had explained, but had another go. In spite of the circumstances, she still felt a pang of excitement at the thought of restoring the farm to its former glory.

But it didn't seem as if Clémence Valencourt was listening. She was suddenly preoccupied, just as she had been earlier. Penelope followed the estate agent's gaze over the dribbling river. A red sports car had drawn up at the side of the road, hazard lights flashing. It looked a lot like the Ferrari she kept seeing. Getting out of the passenger side was the mayor. He raised a hand as the car moved off, then sauntered past the painted doorway of a shop selling candied fruits.

"Excuse me. I must go," said Clémence, and she clickety-clacked off at a pace.

"That was weird," said Penelope. "First she was determined that I was going to buy the house, and now it's almost as if she wants to put me off it."

"Perhaps she wants a quick resale. That would be very sneaky, though."

"And why doesn't she just call or text me to say that the utilities should be on stream soon, instead of turning up all the time? And have you noticed how she's alternatively super helpful—and then bloody rude? It's weird," repeated Penelope.

"Don't get stressed. You always repeat things when you're stressed," said Frankie. "And now I'm doing it. Perhaps we should have a drink."

"We really should not. We've had quite enough."

They spent the afternoon walking around Apt, trying new perfumes at the Senteurs et Provence shop, discovering the museum and the labyrinth of underground excavations of the Roman town of Apta Julia, which began under the cathedral and spread out below the present-day pavements. More practically, Penelope ordered two beds for next-day delivery, some linens and towels, a fridge, and a washing machine.

"That's enough white goods," said Frankie. "Now for the pink. Where's that wine shop?"

11

LE CHANT D'EAU CRUMBLED BEGUILINGLY as ever in the sunshine the next morning, quietly reviving Penelope's Provençal dream. She was relieved to note that they seemed to be alone there for once.

"Right. The moment of truth." In the kitchen, Penelope pressed a light switch. Nothing happened. She opened the tap over the sink. It coughed twice, then the pipes juddered and the water gushed out. "Hurray!"

"Halfway there," said Frankie.

A comprehensive stock of food and wine for a picnic lunch was soon unpacked, and then Frankie walked her round the farmhouse again, expanding on where she should start the renovations and what she should expect to pay. She was in her element.

"A centime more, and you put whoever you go with on to me, Pen. I'll talk the talk with them and get you the best deal."

The overgrown garden seemed more manageable somehow in the bracing company of her old friend. Penelope went down to look at the drained pool, relieved that she really didn't feel too bad about it. Almost OK, actually. She stared at the old brown cypresses standing guard and wondered if they would come back to life with some dedicated watering. She eyed up the best spots for some comfortable loungers and a sunshade.

"With all the rainwater it had collected, I'm assuming there are no leaks in the concrete."

"Fair assumption," concurred Frankie. "No obvious cracks that I can see. It may be that you're in luck and all it needs is a good clean and service. I don't mind making the calls to find a pool company for you, if you want. Let's see how much we can get done and then we'll feel we deserve a slap-up dinner this evening."

Frankie took out her mobile, found a spot with a decent signal, and began looking up companies on the Internet.

A noise from the track made them both jump. It was followed by a squeal of brakes.

Mme Valencourt skittered across the garden.

"Back again," muttered Penelope. "Who knew French estate agents worked so hard?"

This time, the after-sales service involved bringing over a man in blue serge, the ubiquitous clothing of the French *paysan*. "Mme Kite, may I introduce your neighbour, M. Pierre Louchard?"

"Enchantée, M. Louchard," said Penelope, her annoyance superseded by delight in the old-fashioned courtesies of social interaction in France.

M. Louchard was a tall man who could have been handsome in his earlier days, before the sun and the farming had taken their toll. Now he walked with a slight limp and hunched shoulders, and his shaven head gave him the appearance of a large bird of prey hovering in the door.

"M. Louchard is a farmer," said Clémence, rather unnecessarily.

Frankie was formally introduced, and the farmer shook each woman's hand in turn, without a trace of a smile. From a large bag, he produced a bottle of wine and a jar of honey. "Pour vous, madame."

"Merci beaucoup, M. Louchard." She turned to Mme Valencourt. "I would offer you both coffee, but as we haven't really got the kitchen sorted yet . . ."

"That is not a problem, madame. M. Louchard would like to

offer you coffee at his farm. It's only a few hundred meters far-ther down the lane."

M. Louchard stood there scowling. And his scowl only deep-ened after Mme Valencourt seemed to prompt him with a sotto voce aside.

Mme Valencourt turned back to Penelope. "You must accept!" she whispered.

"What about my deliveries?"

"I will leave my portable phone number on your door, and if anyone arrives, they will call me."

Unable to see a way out, Penelope nodded. "C'est très gentil, monsieur."

They began to walk down towards the farm.

Frankie whispered out of the corner of her mouth. "Don't know what your agent is up to. He was desperate to get away."

In silence, they went through the gate and into Louchard's farmyard. It had an air of slight neglect, with one exception. In an open garage was a gleaming blue tractor, polished to within an inch of its life.

Louchard showed them to some dusty seats at the front of his house, mumbled something, and disappeared indoors.

"He does not want to see us, Clémence. Why did you make him?" Penelope was half embarrassed and half irritated.

"Because that is what you do with a new neighbour, even if you dislike foreigners. Do not worry about Pierre. He is shy and does not like change. And he can get angry sometimes, but un-derneath he is a good man."

Frankie plopped down into one of the chairs, raising a large cloud of dust. "Let the games commence!"

A few minutes later, the farmer emerged bearing a tray with coffee cups, glasses, and a bottle filled with a deep purple liquid. He poured four glasses. "Prunier."

"Plum liqueur," whispered Frankie.

"Santé," said Louchard.

"Santé," they responded, and then Penelope closed her eyes and knocked the glass back in one. The liquid burned its way down her throat and growled menacingly in her stomach.

They placed their glasses back on the table. They were refilled.

Conversation was halting, due mainly to the fact that Louchard's answer to any question inclined to the monosyllabic. Mme Valencourt tried valiantly to initiate discussion, but like streams in an arid land, sentences would meander slowly and then drain away.

The only positive that Penelope took from this awkward meeting was the drink. The plum brandy, his own recipe from his own trees, seemed to warm up the spirits in a most delightful way as they threw even more of it down their throats. Mme Valencourt's mood in particular was markedly improved. There was even a touch of a thaw in the farmer's demeanour, but his countenance darkened once more when Frankie brought up the subject of their late neighbour.

"Avore!" M. Louchard's knuckles whitened as he gripped his glass. There was a stream of unintelligible French, which Penelope suspected would not have been acceptable in polite company.

Frankie turned to Penelope. "Our friend here didn't like Manuel Avore very much either."

Another torrent of Gallic invective.

Penelope opened her mouth to follow that intriguing lead, but Mme Valencourt attempted to calm M. Louchard down with questions about his lavender crop, and then swerved back to the subject of her favourite mayor, confiding that she was en route to a meeting with him.

"We will speak about your electricity. Le Chant d'Eau is definitely connected now, but sometimes in the country the wires get eaten by the wild animals."

"Naturally," said Penelope, rolling her eyes. She giggled at a sudden vision of bears and wolves nibbling at the cables. "Les petits animaux, I hope?"

"Loirs," said the estate agent. "Like écureuils—squirrels with big eyes."

"Loirs!" The farmer raised his arms, and mimed holding a rifle. "Bang, bang!" he shouted, followed by something unintelligible.

They drank another round of plum brandy.

"Au trésor du Chant d'Eau!" Louchard raised his empty glass.

"Quoi?" said Penelope, rather less than elegantly. "Le trésor—treasure?"

"Oui, madame."

The liquor was definitely warming up the spirits.

Frankie was onto the treasure business in a flash. The two of them were soon yapping away like a pair of terriers. Mme Valencourt maintained a heard-it-all-before dignity.

"This is great, Pen. The village gossip is that this place has buried treasure—not that anyone really believes it, or anything has been found. Tell you what, I'll buy you a metal detector for your next birthday!"

Penelope was starting to think they had better eat something to mop up the alcohol. The overindulgent picnic they had bought would easily stretch to the four of them. Perhaps she should pop back and fetch it. But M. Louchard rose with some effort from his chair, and announced that it was time for them to leave. Another handshake each, and they were dismissed.

The women set off down the track.

"So, it seems that no one in the village cares much for M. Avore," ventured Penelope.

"He was always drrrrunk, from the morning onward," said the estate agent, apparently oblivious to their own current state. She was rolling her *r*'s with vigorous emphasis. "People in the village tried to help him, but they could not. Avorrrrre would not listen to rrrreason. He drrrrank and he drrrrank, and in that state, a man reveals his black heart. And Avorrrre, he had a very black heart. He was 'orrrrrible to many people. They said he beats his wife. No one in the village likes him, but what can one do? Hélas!"

What Penelope wanted to say as they walked back was, *So let me get this right, Clémence. You knew when you sold me this house that I was going to have to deal with a psychopath on one side and a man who hates foreigners on the other?* But she held her tongue. While Clémence was flushed with plum brandy, it was an opportunity to get the answers to a few pressing questions, such as why she was always turning up unexpectedly, what the issues with the house were exactly, whether Manuel Avore could have had anything to do with the fatal accident that killed the previous owners, and what kind of hold she had over this Louchard character.

But the unmistakable sound of a large vehicle on the unmade track announced the arrival of the first of the deliveries.

By the time Penelope had dealt with the fridge and the washing machine, Mme Valencourt was preparing to leave.

"May I use your bathroom first?"

The estate agent emerged ten minutes later with her hair just so and makeup beautifully reapplied.

"I hope she's all right to drive," said Penelope as they watched the Mini Cooper roar down the track. "I bet she didn't have a proper breakfast this morning, and then she golloped down all that plum brandy. I'm not surprised it went to her head."

"French women don't eat croissants," said Frankie. "If they

do crack over at breakfast, they won't even contemplate eating until dinner."

Penelope sucked in her stomach.

"At least she's not going far," said Frankie. "Only to the mairie to see Laurent Millais, and she's hoping they'll have lunch at his house, and she can sleep it off afterwards, if you know what I mean."

"What *do* you mean, Frankie? Clémence and the mayor?"

"Uh-huh. They've been having an affair for months, but she thinks he might be getting cold feet."

"No! How on earth do you know that?"

"She blurted it all out. She's crazy about him, but it's all going off the boil. Crikey, that plum brandy is like a truth serum. She's been fretting for days—and you know what, Pen, I think that may well be the reason she's always turning up, getting involved in all this business. It's an excuse to keep coming back to St Merlot and old dreamboat at the mairie."

Penelope gave a low whistle. "Well, that would make sense. And why she was in a tense mood when we went up there yesterday morning with the axe. Why she charged off when we saw him in Apt yesterday."

"Where's M. Valencourt in all this? Did you meet him when you stayed the night at her house?"

"No, he wasn't there."

"Talking of food," said Frankie.

They went inside to load up on fresh baguettes, creamy Camembert, ham, pâté, salami, tomatoes, celeriac mayonnaise salad, grapes, melons, nectarines, and a large raspberry tart.

"Just a light lunch." Penelope winked.

"Pity the fridge hasn't been on long enough to get the rosé cool," said Frankie.

"We really don't need any," said Penelope. "I don't know what it is about France, but every time I think I'm going to have a sensible dry day—or even just a meal—someone comes along and waves a bottle at me."

"Just the holiday mood, Pen."

"Sorry, I don't mean to spoil your fun. You have some if you want it."

In the end they shared a big bottle of Perrier that was still cold from the supermarket, and Penelope felt much better.

"So what's happening about Avore and the axe, then?" asked Frankie as she helped herself to a massive chunk of baguette.

"Your guess is as good as mine."

"No doubt my estate agent will acquire some information this afternoon behind the mayor's shutters," said Penelope, with a giggle. How exciting and lovely it must be, she thought, to be as slim as Clémence Valencourt and have a gorgeous French lover. She bypassed the bread and cut herself several slices of melon. "He is very attractive, isn't he? The mayor."

"He certainly is. I would."

Penelope smiled to herself. She knew Frankie well enough to know she was all talk these days. It had long been a source of some surprise to Penelope that, despite her friend's flamboyance and apparent appetite for the good things in life (including men), Frankie's marriage to Johnny was rock-solid and had survived longer than most relationships. Hers included.

"Apparently he's one of those men who gets bored easily. He's done all sorts of things, from working in television to setting up a property company. Divorced. Two children who live in Paris with the ex-wife."

Not for the first time, Penelope wondered how Frankie did it. She had found out more in ten minutes than Penelope could ever have done. "But we digress," she said.

"From what we know about Avore, then," recapped Frankie, "the dead man was an unpopular drunk. No one in the village liked him, but even so they tried to help him. He still went to prison for assault. Louchard hated him. Plenty of people, including Avore's wife, are delighted he's dead, by the sound of it."

"Why would a wife stay with him?"

"Women stay for all sorts of reasons, Pen. You of all people know that."

"Did they have children, then?"

"We don't know, do we?"

They ate in silence for a while. Frankie loaded her bread with yet more perfectly ripe Camembert and closed her eyes in bliss as she bit in. Penelope luxuriated in the cloudless blue sky and the monumental ridged hills beyond her own sweet olive grove.

"We could go up to the mairie ourselves," suggested Frankie. "We might even see the mayor and his lady friend."

"Bit stalkerish."

"Not at all," said Frankie with a straight face. "There are all sorts of things you need to get sorted out. Like a postbox at the end of the track, for example. Once you get that done, it'll only be natural for you to get talking to whoever's there. I'll be with you if you need a translator. You never know what we might find out."

12

LUCKILY, THE DELIVERY VAN WITH the beds arrived just after two o'clock. As soon as it left, Penelope and Frankie decided to walk into the village. All was quiet, except for the incessant jittering of the cicadas. They reached the end of the track, stared at the badly maintained Avore house, and turned onto the main road that wound up the hill. The views across to Mont Ventoux and the far side of the valley were truly majestic. It really was a very special place, Clémence was right.

They were approaching a sharp bend opposite the cherry orchard when suddenly the red Mini Cooper scorched past them. Penelope had a second to register the lady driver's pinched expression before she was pushed with some force into the ditch at the side of the road. Frankie fell on top of her, still with her hands on Penelope's back.

"Are you all right?" Penelope said, gasping.

"Yes. Are you?"

"I think so. Not one of our more elegant manoeuvres. Crumbs, Frankie, that was close. I think you just saved my life!"

"I think we can safely assume that lunch with the mayor didn't go too well," said Frankie.

They checked themselves over and dusted themselves off. Below where they stood on the bend, they could still make out a red blur hurtling down the road towards the town.

They walked on cautiously.

The village was still practically deserted, save for the old man reading *La Provence*, who appeared never to move from his seat by the boules pitch under the plane trees. "He was there when I arrived last week," said Penelope.

"Is he dead too?" asked Frankie.

"Not funny. That's today's headline."

Based on this evidence, they refrained from checking a pulse as they passed, and only jumped slightly when he suddenly rustled the newspaper and muttered a guttural "Bonjour, mesdames." They returned the greeting and walked on to the *mairie*.

The post office was closed, they were informed when they presented themselves at the counter. It was always closed in the afternoon, said the cheerful chubby woman behind it. Thanks to Frankie's linguistic skills, though, they established with the help of a woman at an adjoining desk that it was only closed for letters and parcels. A discussion about the process needed to establish a postbox was permissible.

The plump woman introduced herself as Nicole and explained that she would register Penelope's details with the post office, though it was difficult to say when a postbox would actually be forthcoming.

"What is your address?" Nicole started tapping on a computer keyboard.

"Le Chant d'Eau, St Merlot."

The hands froze above the keys. Nicole looked up with the utmost sympathy. "What a terrible thing to happen—and so soon after you arrived."

"Yes, it was."

"You intend to stay at this property?"

"Yes, I do," said Penelope, with more firmness than she felt.

"What are people saying about it in the village?" asked Frankie, drawing a mark of respect for her impeccable French accent.

"Well," began Nicole, "most people think that Manuel Avore was an accident waiting to happen. They are not surprised, to be honest. He was not a nice man, not at all. Though I hate to speak ill of the dead."

Penelope strained to keep up with the woman's outpouring and the twang of her Provençal accent.

"How long had Manuel Avore been out of prison?" Frankie pushed on.

"A couple of weeks."

"And had he upset anyone in St Merlot since his return?"

"So . . . let's say that his wife was not very happy to see him again! She thought he was going to spend longer behind bars. M. Charpet was not pleased either, because Manuel was trouble and had often stolen garden equipment from him. M. Louchard, the same. He found his car tyres slashed after he confronted Manuel and forced him to hand over the stolen goods."

"Don't forget Jacques," said the other woman.

"Who's he?" asked Penelope.

The door to the mayor's office opened, and Laurent Millais strode out. "Yes, thank you Nicole and Marie-Lou, that is quite enough!" He looked so devastatingly handsome in a blue shirt that matched his eyes that Penelope let out an involuntary sigh. The sequin heart across Frankie's chest visibly rippled.

"Bonjour, Mme Keet. Madame . . . ?" He nodded towards Frankie.

"Frankie Turner-Blake. Enchantée, extremely enchantée."

The mayor gave her a havoc-making smile that Penelope suspected was a tried and trusted weapon in his armoury. "Please do not believe all the village gossip. We are all very friendly here."

"I do hope so," said Frankie, with a nauseating simper.

Behave, Penelope mouthed at her. "Have you heard anything more about the police inquiry?" she asked the mayor.

"Unfortunately, no."

"Perhaps we could talk it through," proposed Frankie, bust still glittering. "It would be very helpful to go over everything that has happened."

"I regret that will not be possible. It is now a murder investigation, but we will no doubt remain in contact. On other matters, I have asked the electrician to come and see you as soon as possible. You should wait at your house." The mayor turned to Marie-Lou. "I am going to see the priest now. Would you get the building applications for me to look at when I get back, please?"

He picked up a cream jacket from a peg by the entrance, said goodbye, and walked out to a dark-blue Mercedes convertible in the car park. I bet he bought it to show off his eyes, thought Penelope. What a smooth operator he is.

They watched him drive off, and then began the walk back.

"He can remain in contact with me any time he likes," said Frankie.

"Frankie!"

"What? No wonder old Clémence was upset she wasn't getting any of that today." Frankie gurned lasciviously.

"You look like Danny DeVito when you do that."

Her friend was unabashed. "So is he off to see the priest to salve his conscience with a timely confession? From what Clémence told me this morning, there's a fair bit to atone for."

⁂

THE ELECTRICIAN was waiting for them when they returned. Contrary to Penelope's expectations, service really was excellent in France.

"Didier Picaud," he introduced himself. He was a stocky young chap in his late twenties, wearing a T-shirt and knee-length shorts. His coarse brown hair stuck straight up as if he had just plugged himself into a live socket. He walked jauntily around the house with a full-wattage smile.

As one of the younger generation, he was also keen to practice his English. "There are always problems in these old houses," he said with a slight American twang.

Penelope showed him the fuse box in the kitchen cupboard.

"It is all good, madame. See this?" He pointed to a small sticker she hadn't even noticed, which read "JRM Électriciens." "Our company. My family has a long association with this house, and I will gladly continue the service."

"That's good news, thank you," said Penelope.

He started pulling out fuses and blowing on them.

"So, your family has lived in the village for many years?" said Frankie.

"Maybe even centuries."

"You must like it here, then," said Penelope.

Frankie cut to the chase. "You and your family must have known Manuel Avore—what do you think about what happened to him?"

If Didier Picaud was taken aback by her directness, he didn't show it. "*Bof!* Obviously it was terrible, but . . . it was not surprising that he died. Something was always going to happen to him."

"Why do you say that?" asked Penelope.

"He made difficulties, always. Even after three years in prison, a good long sentence that was supposed to teach him a lesson, he came out ready to steal and drink and fight, same as ever."

"He was in prison for assault—is that right?"

"Yeah, he hit some debt collectors."

"Did you have disagreements with him?" asked Frankie.

"We all did."

"What was yours?" Frankie ploughed on.

"He owed me some money."

"An unpaid bill?"

"He said he could not pay after I fixed an electrical problem at his house. He said I should do it for free, because everyone knew he had no money and he would make trouble for anyone who did not help him."

"That's extortion, then. Like asking for protection money!"

Didier Picaud looked up from a meticulous check of the trip switches. He did not seem to mind digging in for a gossip, which was exactly what Penelope had been hoping for. His lively brown eyes shone. Perhaps he was pleased to have a chance to have a look around and check out the new arrival. Though that worked both ways, Penelope reminded herself. She was sure that she and Frankie would also be the subject of a great deal of village chat.

"It was more for his wife that we helped Manuel Avore," Picaud continued.

"Yes, what about his wife, who stayed with him?" Penelope shook her head. "How could she bear it?"

"Ah, poor Mariette. She is a nice woman. Very religious. She tried to help him to change, and she thought she could do it. She suffered. He hit her, and she allowed it. And nothing changed. It was very sad."

"But she's all right now—at last," said Penelope.

"Yes, she is all right. Though she feels capable of his death."

"Capable? You mean you think she might have done it?"

"No, you mean *coupable*, don't you?" butted in Frankie. "The word in English is 'guilty.' Guilty because she never managed to stop his drinking and destructive behaviour."

"Yes, exactly." He pulled his mouth down in a gesture of sympathy.

"M. Louchard seems very . . . shy, though I am sure he is

delightful when you get to know him," said Penelope, hoping it would get back that she was appreciative of her new neighbour. "And so is M. Charpet. He is going to continue to do the garden as he did for the previous owners. I am very lucky to have them both nearby."

"They are both . . . personalities, that is true! Louchard, he was a military man. Even now, he is the best man with a gun in the village. People have said that the army changed him. He keeps himself apart until he knows people. Maybe he is just, as you say, shy." The electrician raised his eyebrows, however, to signify a lack of faith in this view.

"What do you think?" asked Frankie.

"I think . . . you must be a little bit careful. I think he does not like foreigners. Even French foreigners. There was some trouble, I heard, between him and the former owners of this house."

"Trouble?" Penelope did not like the sound of this.

Picaud took a dramatic glance left and right, and moved closer. "I have heard, madame, that he shot their cat after they had an argument."

"What kind of argument?"

He shrugged. "There are always arguments in village life. This disagreement, that insult . . . in summer the heat rises and tempers explode."

Frankie changed the subject abruptly. "Talking of village life," she said, catching Penelope's eye, "does the village have its own priest?"

"No, we have no church in this village."

Penelope took him upstairs, still chatting about this and that, for an initial assessment of the state of the wiring. He took a light switch off the wall to have a quick look behind, screwed it back in place, and turned it on.

"Voilà!" he said, as a naked bulb dangling from the ceiling lit up.

"Fantastic! Thank you so much!"

"I will come back soon to do a complete check," he said. "It is always necessary to make sure all is in order. But don't worry, you have power, and I think you are safe for now."

They made up the new beds, and decided the best plan would be to spend the night at Le Chant d'Eau.

"I want to make sure you're all right staying here before I go back to England," said Frankie. "Now is that fridge getting properly cold? Ooh, yes, it is." She shoved a couple of bottles of rosé in.

They collected their things from the Hôtel St Pierre and went on to M. Bricolage to buy an outside table and chairs. The flat pack just fitted into the Range Rover's capacious boot.

As expected, Frankie was a dab hand at flat packs, and before they knew it, Penelope had a galvanised metal table and four chairs for the terrace outside the kitchen door. In double-quick time, a chilled bottle and two glasses joined them.

"Cheers, m'dear," said Frankie. "A new start!"

"Perhaps I can pretend this is my first night here," said Penelope. "Cheers! And thanks, Frankie. You've been a complete star."

"Know what, Pen, this place is going to be lovely when you've got it how you want it."

"I can't wait to be able to have the family out. I know that they'll love it, and it will be fantastic for the boys—all this space for running around and exploring, and the pool, of course."

"Absence makes the heart grow fonder, eh?"

"I'm always fond. And Lena and Justin are too, really. They took the divorce worse than I thought they would. They didn't understand why I had to make everything so final."

"You always loved them like your own, Pen."

A pause.

"I did."

"Not having your own . . . and everything."

"No." Penelope hoped Frankie would leave it there, but inevitably she didn't.

"Just wasn't to be."

"A long time ago now. Though sometimes it seems like yesterday."

"Nasty, that last miscarriage."

"Thank God you were there," said Penelope. "Though I can still see that traffic policeman's face. Red light. Canary-yellow drag-race car. Pregnant woman, screaming."

"Two screaming women," Frankie corrected her. "I was yelling at him to get out of the way. We were an emergency. Johnny was not pleased to find his car vanished before the big race, but it showed form in the dash to the hospital."

"Made it to A and E in ten minutes flat. Still a Surrey record, I believe."

Frankie reached out and squeezed Penelope's hand.

"You and David speaking again?"

"Actually, yes. Not a lot, but I saw him at Lena's before I left, and he was remarkably civil. We laughed about the weekend trips to the zoo we used to do when the children were small. I think Zack and Xerxes's naughtiness at teatime reminded him of the chimpanzee house."

"Wasn't all bad, then."

"Of course it wasn't. Just takes time not being angry to remember that."

They charged their glasses and drank to that.

"If you hadn't got angry, you never would have gone to work for the legendary Camrose Fletcher," Frankie reminded her.

"Very true," said Penelope.

She felt a bit wistful as she pictured her interview, which took place over a gin and tonic in Bloomsbury. Camrose couldn't have been more self-effacing. He was tall and broad, with an athletic air that she had not expected in a man who spent his days with the dead. His hair and well-groomed beard were white, but his face was tanned and his startling cornflower-blue eyes seemed permanently amused behind black-framed glasses. They had talked about hill walking and chamber music, and he ended the meeting saying he knew she could do the job, it was just a question of whether they'd get on.

"It was the making of you, Pen."

"You're probably right."

"You still in touch with him?"

"Haven't actually seen him for a while. But, yes."

"He never married, did he?"

"Married to his work," said Penelope.

No matter how hard they tried, though, and despite the distracting loveliness of the views down the valley, where the hills softened in a pink and apricot dusk and the scented pines sent long purple shadows up the garden, they could not avoid talking about the events surrounding the body in the pool.

"Something strange is going on," said Frankie, lighting an oil lamp that Penelope had found in the cellar. "First they were sure it was an accident, and now it's definitely murder. Mr. Gorgeous up at the mairie wants to lock everything down so that no one in the village comes under suspicion. He doesn't get on with the chief of police, he sends his mistress packing just when she was hoping for a bit of afternoon delight and zooms off to 'see the priest.' See the priest, my arse. 'Scuse my French."

"It's all conjecture, though, isn't it?" said Penelope. "We're on the outside looking in. There's always the possibility that we're judging from our culture, not theirs. We think the French are just like us because we travel back and forth so easily these days, but actually they're as foreign as they ever were. In a good way, of course. Vive la différence, and all that. Talking of which, my English constitution can't take all this wine on an empty stomach . . ."

She went inside to fetch the remains of their lunchtime picnic.

"So let's think through what little we found out this afternoon that we didn't already know," said Penelope as she put the baguette, cheese, olives, and fruit on the table. There was still enough to feed an army, and they grazed on it happily. She popped a slice of Camembert into her mouth. "Nicole at the post office confirmed that Avore's wife wasn't exactly thrilled to have him back."

"How long was he in prison for?" asked Frankie.

"Didier Picaud said it was three years. And he was released early."

"Didn't she mention your gardener chap, M. Charpet? Avore used to help himself to his tools and garden equipment, and she said he thought Avore was trouble. And M. Louchard, who we met this morning, he also had the Avore treatment. Hang on, let me just focus . . ."

They both took a deep gulp of wine to help the process. The rosé from Roussillon really was very light and delicious.

"Going down a treat," said Frankie. "Just as well we bought a few of these. All right, what do we know about Charpet and Louchard? They had to deal with Avore being a thief as well as a bad neighbour. Are those strong enough motives to kill him?"

"I would definitely put Louchard in as a suspect. Angers easily, has an army background, and can't stand Avore. But the mayor was fairly indignant that anyone would even put M. Charpet in the frame, what with his past as a boy member of the Resistance. He must be older than he looks, mustn't he?"

"It's the sun and the fantastic food here. Hard physical outdoor work, too—that makes them all live so long and healthily."

"Most of them." Penelope raised an eyebrow.

"Look, I agree, it seems unlikely that Charpet could be responsible, but you never know," said Frankie. "What about the wife?"

"Well, she probably had the strongest motive of all. But if she did do him in, unless she's a giantess, she would have needed help to get the body down the lane and into the pool," Penelope pointed out. "So who could have helped her?"

"Open another bottle, Pen, and we'll have a think."

After another glass, Penelope said: "Who is Jacques?"

"Eh?"

"When we went to the mairie, one of the women said straight-away, 'And there's Jacques'—who presumably had some beef with Avore. Don't you remember?"

"Vaguely . . ."

"The mayor interrupted. So we need to keep an eye out for Jacques. Whoever he is."

13

PENELOPE FELT CONSIDERABLY LESS GUNG ho in the morning. A knock on the door announced a steaming cup of tea and Frankie, dressed for action in khaki silk combat pants and a rather frightening leopard's face peering from her top. The big cat's eyes glittered as the morning light glanced off green and gold sequins.

"Wakey, wakey!"

Penelope groaned and turned over, cursing both her hangover and her friend's resistance to wine-induced headaches. Was that down to the HRT too? The mug of tea was placed, rather too noisily for her liking, on the stone floor.

"See you in half an hour, Pen."

The door closed.

Penelope fumbled for the packet of Anadin Extra and popped two, wondering whether all the drinking in France was going to make her a painkiller addict. Her heart sank. Something else to worry about.

Luckily she felt better fairly quickly after closing her eyes for twenty minutes, drinking the tea, and perking herself up under a cold shower. When she went downstairs, she found a jug of coffee and a pile of warm, buttery *pains au chocolat* and almond croissants waiting for her on the table outside.

"How lovely! Thanks, Frankie."

"No worries. I was up with the lark, so I walked into the village. That boulangerie is phenomenal, isn't it?"

"Unfortunately, yes. I've only let myself go there once. It could be my undoing."

"Nice chap, the baker, too. He's expecting you."

"Eh?"

"We started talking, and I told him it wouldn't be long before you were a regular customer. He asked me if you were the English lady who's had the Regrettable Incident at her pool."

Penelope's spirits soon soared. Surely there was nothing nicer than a summer breakfast outside. The promise of a day exploring the valley showing Frankie some of the stunning hilltop villages energised her. "Perhaps we can do some clothes shopping or visit an art gallery. It'll make a change from dealing with all the things I need to do here."

She sat back in her seat. The latest croissant seemed to have made it under the waistband of her trousers already.

Frankie shrugged and bit into a second *pain au chocolat.*

"Surely you want to go shopping, or walk through a lavender field or see some of the sights?" Penelope persisted. "Shouldn't we go out, do what people normally do on a little holiday in Provence?"

"I'm not here under normal circumstances," Frankie reminded her. "And anyway, we can't stop now."

Penelope sighed. "I'm not saying we're stopping, just that we need a change of scene. Some perspective, maybe."

❧

IT WAS another cloudless day, and the blue sky seemed to extend to infinity. "This is the Provence I want to show you," said Penelope, feeling happier.

They slowed down as they passed the Avore house. It mouldered mournfully, tightly shuttered, with no sign of the elusive merry widow.

At Bonnieux, Penelope parked the Range Rover close to an impressive church on the lower slopes of the village, and they walked up narrow cobbled streets to a vantage point at the summit. Behind them, another church spire reached into the heavens. The Luberon Valley lay before them from a completely different perspective.

"See over there, the ruined castle?" Penelope pointed towards a neighbouring hilltop village. "That's Lacoste. The castle was once the home of the infamous Marquis de Sade."

"The whips, the whips!"

"That's the one. Back in the day, the two villages were always feuding. Sacred and profane. Church versus obscenity."

"And plenty of hypocrites dashing along the road to Lacoste, no doubt."

Penelope laughed. "The castle, or what's left of it, is now owned by the fashion designer Pierre Cardin. He stages an opera festival there every summer, very lavishly."

They wandered down towards the middle of the village, past the open doors of shops that smelt as good as they looked. Every display offered vibrant colour. The shiny black-purple of a pile of ripe aubergines vied with a hundred shades of green and pink and orange and red at the grocery. Bars of perfumed soap: lavender and fig and patchouli and vanilla. Another shop sold patterned Provençal fabrics in yellow and red, and yellow and purple, all contrasting beautifully with the building's faded silver-green shutters.

They lingered outside a chocolate shop, taking in the mouthwatering display of pralines and ganaches and other enticing bonbons. After a few minutes, the cocoa scent overcame their willpower and they went inside to make some carefully considered, though still substantial, purchases.

Frankie then decided she ought to buy some mementos of Provence to take home, including a dog toy containing lavender that was supposed to calm overexcitable pets. "He'll love it," she trilled. Like so many dog owners, she became ridiculously soppy and detached from reality when she talked about the animal she loved.

Penelope privately reckoned the toy would be reduced to its elemental constituents within about a minute by Frankie's hound from hell.

The streets were getting more crowded. Tables outside the restaurants were starting to fill up.

"Fancy a quick drink?" asked Frankie, hopefully.

"Just a quick one, then."

They installed themselves at a table for two at a ravishingly pretty restaurant by a stone fountain in the shade of several plane trees. Crowds strolled by and bottlenecks formed as groups of people were attracted to the large, vibrant paintings on display at an artist's atelier opposite. A carafe of rosé was ordered, and by the time the waiter brought them the lunch menus, there was no going back.

"Rude not to," said Frankie.

And indeed it would have been. Dainty dishes of local vegetables and langoustines and black olive tapenade with croutons were being ferried to other tables. Penelope's stomach gave a rumble.

They were halfway through their exquisite *galette de légumes provençaux avec mozzarella et tapenade* when Frankie put her fork down and nodded towards the crowds wandering past. "Psst!" she hissed.

"What, already? I can't believe that, Frankie. We've only just started the second carafe, even if you are having more than I am because I'm driving."

"No. 'Psst' meaning look over there and don't draw attention to yourself."

Penelope raised her eyes from her plate and looked in the direction Frankie had nodded. She couldn't see anything untoward. "What am I looking for? A person?"

"Yep."

"Someone we know well?"

"Nope."

Penelope shifted her gaze to the street. She was just about to tell Frankie to stop playing silly games and just say it when she saw what her friend had spotted.

Clémence Valencourt was going into another restaurant and being shown to a table. Waiting for her to be seated was Penelope's farmer neighbour M. Louchard, suited and booted for a special occasion.

"Interesting," said Frankie.

"Very."

They both popped their sunglasses back on and took a long look while pretending they were focusing elsewhere. Two glasses of champagne were brought to the table, and Mme Valencourt raised hers in a toast that M. Louchard matched.

"A celebration?" wondered Penelope.

"More like a job well done. Or a business deal."

"Something to do with the hold she seemed to have over him yesterday when we went to drink his plum brandy?"

Try as they might, they couldn't work out whether it was significant, or just one of those coincidences that seems more important than it is.

Penelope giggled. "Perhaps Clémence is hiring him to note down the mayor's movements in and out of the village. She's going to pay M. Louchard to tail him in one of those cars that looks like it's made from corrugated iron."

"Or pull out in his tractor when the mayor tries to zoom off in his open-top Mercedes to meet another woman!"

They both snorted with mirth.

Then Frankie stopped laughing. She grabbed Penelope's arm. "Aye aye . . . maybe not. Guess who has just entered stage left?"

Penelope pretended to look in another direction and swivelled her eyes behind her dark glasses. It was the mayor himself, exuding laid-back charisma. "This is all very cosy," she said. "Wonder what's going on here."

"Perhaps we should go over and say hello."

"And perhaps we shouldn't."

"They might see us anyway," said Frankie. "Does it matter if they do?"

"I'm being paranoid, aren't I?" Penelope shook her head, then fanned herself with her napkin.

"Oh, here we go. That'll be the Mayor Effect," whispered Frankie.

"It most certainly is not," said Penelope.

Frankie wiped her brow with her own napkin as Laurent Millais went over to the table occupied by Mme Valencourt and M. Louchard. "It's either very hot today, or he's having much the same effect on me—and I am not only happily married but subject to the finest hormone replacement therapy money can buy."

"But he's not sitting down with them," said Penelope. "He's pointing down the street and looking at his watch." They watched as nods were exchanged and the mayor wandered off in the direction he had indicated.

They debated what this might mean as they ordered desserts. They were going to have to spin out their meal in order to see what happened next. The white chocolate mousse with black cherry compote was heavenly.

Frankie insisted on paying the bill before they had finished their espressos, and they lingered at the table surrounded by the aroma of strong, rich coffee. When the estate agent and M. Louchard got up and shook hands, the two friends were ready to go.

"You follow Louchard, and I'll take Valencourt," said Frankie. "See you back at the car."

They waited until their quarry moved off, then slipped into the stream of tourists behind them. M. Louchard took the direction the mayor had indicated. Penelope kept him in her sights as he loped down the descending narrow street. He did not stop to look in any of the shops or bars until he came to a café at the very end of the road.

The café was set on the junction opposite the grand church, close to the car park where Penelope had left the Range Rover. The few tables and chairs outside the café were not occupied. As M. Louchard went inside, Penelope ducked into a doorway, wondering what to do next.

She did not have long to wait. Louchard emerged a couple of minutes later with the mayor and another man she recognised. He was sixty, maybe, but well preserved, with silver curls and a beard. He was wearing a beautifully cut charcoal linen suit and pointed Italian shoes. There was a film star quality about him that ran the mayor quite close.

The three of them walked briskly over to the parking spaces beneath the trees in front of the church. They stopped by a car that Penelope also recognised with a shiver of unease.

14

"QUICK!" SQUEAKED PENELOPE. "IT'S THAT red Ferrari again!"

She started the Range Rover as Frankie opened the door. They were off with a scrunch of gravel before she had closed it.

"Clémence has gone, by the way," said Frankie, pulling on her seat belt. "Her Mini was obstructing the pavement just round the corner from the restaurant. She went off like a bat out of hell, with some bloke in a delivery van shaking his fist at her."

Penelope peered round as they reached the spot where the Ferrari had been parked. "Damn it! They were still chatting when I went past on the other side of the road."

"They can't have gone far," said Frankie.

"No, they can't. The parking space is still free. Any space on the road fills up immediately in summer." Penelope accelerated.

They reached the edge of the village and made the first bend in the road leading down into the valley. There was a clear view of the countryside below.

"There they are!" Frankie pointed.

A low red car was speeding away in the direction of the main road to Avignon.

Penelope shot the Range Rover forward like a heat-seeking missile.

"Whoa! Hang on, Pen, what are we doing?"

"Following them, of course!"

"But why?"

It was a good question. "Call it woman's instinct," said Penelope grimly.

"Because you've seen this car a few times? You're not stalking some rich potential husband, are you?"

"Don't be ridiculous."

They lurched round another bend.

"I just want to know what these people are up to," said Penelope. "Call me suspicious, but I don't like the smell of this. I feel as if I'm being set up somehow, and I don't like it. Doesn't it seem like a big coincidence that Mme Valencourt and the mayor, and now my neighbour M. Louchard, all seem to know the silver fox in the red Ferrari that keeps appearing everywhere?"

"Silver fox?"

"The guy who came out of the café with Louchard and the mayor. It's his car. I recognised him from the time he stopped just by the entrance to the track."

"Is tailing him a good idea?"

"Probably not. But I'm doing it anyway."

"Your call. You look at the road, I'll keep them in view."

Penelope gunned the engine and swerved to overtake.

"I don't remember you having this turn of speed behind the wheel, Pen."

"All those years on the school run. You learn base cunning and ruthlessness. I still got it when I need it."

They made up some ground on the Ferrari as it was held up before joining the main road. It turned towards Avignon, and Penelope concentrated on keeping it in sight while not getting too close. Before long, it swooped off, taking the turning to Gordes on the opposite side of the valley.

"Right . . . concentrate, Frankie. We don't want to lose them here."

"You'll need to get a bit closer, then. And get round this Dutch caravan. Now . . . go!"

Penelope pulled out with blind faith, making it back to the right side of the road just before a BMW travelling in the other direction flashed past them.

"That was close," she said.

"Do you want to do this, or not?"

Penelope gripped the wheel tighter.

The village of Gordes was a beauty, no doubt about it. It rose on a rocky hilltop like a highly decorated wedding cake, each layer holding charming stone houses and gardens full of regimented cypress trees, oleander, and geraniums. The castle at the summit was white against the deep blue of the sky.

"I hope we don't lose them here, it's packed with tourists at this time of year," said Penelope.

They continued to climb. The road ahead twisted, and trees obscured the bends. For minutes on end, they lost sight of the Ferrari.

Frankie opened the window

"Don't do that, we need the air-con on."

Frankie ignored her and leaned out. "Right, I can hear that distinctive engine up ahead. It's very easy to recognise, that thundery sound a Ferrari makes. Johnny has a friend who drives one and—"

"Hell's bells!" cried Penelope.

"What's wrong now?"

"The sound of a Ferrari engine. It *is* unmistakable . . . it's what I heard that first night! My first night at Le Chant d'Eau!"

"Er, Pen. Correct me if I'm wrong, but all kinds of cars are allowed on the roads these days. What about it?"

"No . . . OK, you're right. I'm clutching at straws now. It's just that—good God!" Penelope sighed in frustration and overtook a Belgian car that had stopped abruptly in order to admire the view. She pressed on, beginning to wonder what kind of fool's errand she had embarked on.

Frankie craned farther out of the window as they approached the village. "It's turning left. About a hundred metres ahead."

Penelope followed. The road led rapidly away from the village again and out into a landscape of scrubby hill and rocky escarpment. After a while, it narrowed and began to descend into a steep wooded valley.

"If you can stop, do so," said Frankie. "There might be a viewing spot or a lay-by. We'll be able to see where they go without being seen ourselves."

"There's nowhere to stop here."

After another few bends there was still nowhere to stop. The view became more open as they went down the hill. In the crease of the ravine was a stunning ancient building surrounded by striped fields. Through the open window came the most gorgeous smell of lavender.

"I know where we are," said Penelope. "I recognise it from all the postcards. The Abbaye de Sénanque."

"A monastery? Of all the places—"

"There are lots of medieval monasteries and convents in this part of Provence. The Cistercians decided this was the place to worship in poverty and simplicity while working the land. As it worked out, their farms were very successful and they went from self-sufficiency to living the high life."

She slowed down to keep their vantage point, and they watched as the red Ferrari turned in to the entrance to the monastery.

"What do we do now?" asked Frankie.

"Well, we can't stop here. We'll have to go down and park. It's full enough down there that they won't notice us."

The Abbaye de Sénanque was indeed busy. It was a highlight

of the Luberon tourist itinerary. But it was equally obvious why that should be. The grey stones of the medieval abbey exuded peacefulness. The lavender field that reached right up to its portals had been recently cut. The purple blooms were drying in the sun, and wafts of perfume infused the warm air.

Penelope slotted the Range Rover into a space. "Have you got your phone?" she asked.

"Yep."

"Let's just check we can both get a signal and then separate. Pretend to be a tourist and wander around, looking to see where they've gone. First one to see the Ferrari texts, OK?"

"Ten-four," said Frankie.

"What does that mean?"

"No idea. It just sounded right."

"If you're not going to take this seriously—"

"Penny, calm down. Come on, let's do this. I'll take this side of the car park."

They popped wide-brimmed sun hats on and set off.

Penelope walked to the far side of the car park and then along the rows, peering at every vehicle. No sign of the Ferrari.

People in shorts and sandals milled around, taking photographs and posing in front of the lavender garden, but the atmosphere was surprisingly serene. No one let their children shriek and run around, and Penelope felt warmly disposed to these sensible Continental parents. Perhaps she might bring her extended family here one day, to show them how it was done.

She wandered towards the abbey. The scent of lavender intensified. A bell tower rose from a round Romanesque chapel on the oldest section. All was still. No Cistercian monks toiled in the field, and no cars spoiled the scene.

Penelope decided to begin by walking behind the wing that extended the length of the lavender field. It was the only possible place the Ferrari might be. She quickened her pace, wondering what she would say if anyone asked her what she was doing.

The path was shaded by trees, and wide enough to drive a car down. Shaking off a voice in her head that told her this was madness—that she had read far too many detective novels—she squared her shoulders and pushed on.

She saw the nose of the Ferrari just before the movement of a bush and a British expletive alerted her to Frankie's presence. She was hiding behind a Mexican orange blossom, trying and failing to send a text.

Penelope tapped her on the arm.

"Wah!" Frankie jumped.

Penelope put her finger to her lips and joined her round the back of the bush.

After a while she whispered, "Shall we wait here, or should one of us go back to my car?"

"Why don't I stay here and see who comes out, and you go back to the car so we're all ready to follow when they leave?" suggested Frankie.

"Will that work?"

"I'll run to the car park once the Ferrari moves off. When you see it go, be waiting for me at the closest point to the footpath. They can't go very fast back up that narrow road."

"You're getting into the spirit of this, aren't you! OK, that's what we'll do," agreed Penelope.

She extricated herself from the bush, looked around, and hurried back up the path. Her heart was beating fast by the time she reached the Range Rover. She got in, flung the hat off, and rootled in her bag for a tissue to wipe her forehead. Then she stared at the exit, not daring to look away.

Half an hour later, her eyes were smarting. It was a ridiculous mission, and she felt rather ashamed of herself. She should have known better, at her age, than to get carried away with a drama of her own making.

The Ferrari growled past.

Penelope waited until it reached the exit, backed out, and zoomed round to collect Frankie.

Gasping for breath after a jog up the path behind the abbey, Frankie flung herself in. She fanned herself with her hat as Penelope set off in pursuit of their prey.

"What did you see?" asked Penelope.

"Let me get my breath . . . hooo . . . hooo . . . not as fit as I thought . . ."

Penelope gunned the Range Rover up the twisty hill road back towards Gordes, trusting that the Ferrari was ahead.

"Right, hooo . . . Your neighbour Pierre Louchard came out of a back entrance, might have been a delivery door, with a silver-haired and -bearded man. Is that the silver fox? He was wearing a loose dark suit."

"That's him. No mayor?"

"Just the two of them. But think about it, there are only two seats in that Ferrari."

"Did you notice anything else?"

"M. Louchard was carrying a large brown envelope and an old-fashioned medicine bottle."

"He didn't have those when he left Bonnieux."

"Thing is, Pen, does any of this *really* mean anything?"

Penelope grimaced. "Don't you think it's odd that Clémence and the mayor and Louchard are meeting up away from St Merlot? That man in the red Ferrari stopped for a good long look at the track to my house—you were there, Frankie, you saw him. I can understand Louchard the farmer talking to the mayor, but what is he doing with a flash guy in a Ferrari? It just seems rather suspicious. Don't you see, they all have some connection to my house, and they've all been there since the murder! And there's something else."

Even as she said it, she was wondering if she might be overreacting, though. Perhaps she needed to up her dose of Menopace vitamins. And she hadn't yet tried black cohosh, which was supposed to be good. "Look, I just want to see where they're going. Indulge me."

"Up ahead, turning right!" shrieked Frankie.

The Ferrari purred its way past the southern edge of Gordes and took the same road they came up on. It wasn't going nearly as fast as before.

"When we chased them there, they might have been late for whoever they were meeting at the abbey," suggested Frankie.

"Or they might have had a drop of the abbey's honey liqueur, and the silver fox is taking it easy so he doesn't get done for drink driving."

They followed the red Ferrari all the way to St Merlot. It went through the village, then disappeared down a private tree-lined drive.

"Well," said Penelope. "That's that."

"At least we're not miles from home. Slow down a moment."

As she crawled past the entrance, Penelope looked down the long avenue of trees towards the large grey stone building at the end. There was a name carved into the gatepost, but it was obscured by moss and lichen.

THEY HAD a snack supper at home that evening, with Penelope trying not to eat or drink quite as much as on previous nights, and Frankie going for the full Poirot on the facts of the case so far discovered.

"So now we have a xenophobic ex-army guy as a neighbour—who obviously hated Avore. Another suspect?"

"Well, everyone says it can't possibly be M. Charpet—but isn't that suspicious in itself?" said Penelope.

"And who keeps telling us that it can't be Charpet? Your Mme V, who always seems to turn up round every corner. And is she quite on the level with you, Pen? I told you she needs watching."

Penelope felt disinclined to argue. She sat back.

"And what about Mme Avore, then?"

"We need to find out more about her." Frankie chugged rosé into her glass. "But let's think. Mariette Avore is a religious woman, and this priest that the mayor was going off to see . . ."

"We're going round and round in circles," said Penelope. "And I have no idea why you think the mayor going to see the priest has any relevance whatsoever."

"Perhaps it doesn't. It might have been a woman priest that our old Alain Delon of the mairie was interested in." Frankie tapped the side of her head. "We use ze leetle grey cells, non?"

Penelope rolled her eyes.

"And, I zzzort zat you would wan' to know, zis becozz ah haff zeen ze way you look at 'eem, zis mayor!"

"Oh for goodness sake, Frankie! Don't be ridiculous."

"It eezz not zo ridicooolous for anyone 'oo 'as ever seen Penelope Wilmot aged fifteen going crazy over Duran Duran and in particul*aire* zee very pretty-boy John Taylor . . . we can zee ze signs of lurve . . ."

"Give over. And can you stop doing that awful cod Poirot, too."

"You still do that! You get all prim and proper when you don't like being teased. Do you fancy him or something?"

"I think you've had quite enough rosé for one day." Penelope grabbed the bottle and shot the last few inches into her own glass. "Besides, the priest isn't a woman, is he?"

"Doesn't sound like it."

"Didier Picaud told me when we went upstairs that there's no church in St Merlot, not any longer. So no call for a village priest. But he thought the mayor did have a good friend who was attached to a nearby monastery in the wild hills to the east near the village of Reillane."

Penelope pictured him in robes and sandals, walking through a medieval cloister. "Perhaps this is more of a Cadfael case," she mused.

"A what?"

"Cadfael. A series of mysteries solved by a twelfth-century monk. The Cadfael Chronicles by Ellis Peters."

Frankie stared at her. "Now you really are being silly."

15

THE NEXT MORNING, WITH A relatively clear head, Penelope drove her dearest, most infuriating friend back to the Marseille airport.

It took both of them to steady Frankie's suitcase, which was even bulkier and heavier than when she arrived, stuffed as it was with lavender perfumes, soaps, candles, one doomed dog toy, and a large organic air-cured ham.

"You'll never get that ham through customs," said Penelope affectionately as they hauled the case towards check-in.

"Nonsense, Pen—I once made it through with the remains of a Greek lamb that had been spit-roasted for Easter. Perky's treat."

Penelope shook her head. "I find that very hard to believe."

Frankie dealt smoothly with the excess baggage fine, and they embraced one last time outside departures.

"Frankie, thanks again. It's been really good fun having you here, and I feel so much better about everything."

"Same here, Pen. Next time I'll bring Johnny—he can do some gardening while we chat. Don't forget I'm at the end of the phone whenever you need me. And I need to know what happens next."

With that, Frankie slung her enormous shiny pink Dolce & Gabbana bag over her shoulder and disappeared into the throng of waiting passengers for a final assault on the airside retail outlets.

Penelope walked back to the car with a smile.

She decided to drive back from Marseille via Aix-en-Provence and then over the Luberon Mountains, rather than going around them again by autoroute. The road proved to be a switchback in places, and she did not enjoy the moments on a number of blind bends when she rounded the corner only to see a large lorry or car thundering towards her. Then, all of a sudden, she was at the summit. The wide valley of the Luberon lay before her.

Between green fields and forest, intermittent purple and grey squares indicated lavender and olive farms. The air was so clear that she could see the peaks of the pre-Alps in the far distance, though they must have been a hundred kilometres away. The view was breathtaking. She realised that she was already starting to think of the place as home.

The afternoon was almost over as Penelope finally climbed the hill to St Merlot from the eastern side through the hamlet of Les Garrigues. On her right she passed the tree-lined drive where the Ferrari had turned in the day before. Something caught her eye. She slammed on the brakes and reversed quickly. Luckily there were no other cars in sight.

The mossy sign on the stone gatepost was just about legible, now she had stopped. "Le Prieuré des Gentilles Merlotiennes," she read aloud.

She would have to look it up to make sure, but she thought that *prieuré* might mean "priory" in English.

The temptation was to head straight through—there was no actual gate—and down the drive. She hesitated. She really shouldn't. She drove on round a corner, and then swung the Range Rover in to the side of the road. It was invisible from the entrance.

She returned on foot to the gates and peered down the avenue of plane trees towards the dark building at the far end. The trees had evidently not been looked after for some years, and the thick branches met overhead, cutting out most of the light to the road underneath. It gave the scene a sombre and rather sad air, even though the sun was shining brightly overhead. Penelope looked left and right, and then plunged into the gloomy tunnel. All was quiet. The land on either side seemed to be lying fallow, full of meadow wildflowers.

The drive opened out in front of an austere stone building that ended in a chapel, with a wooden door but no windows. If this was a religious foundation, it was on a much more domestic scale than the Abbaye de Sénanque. It did not seem to be open to the public. Were the Gentilles Merlotiennes an order of nuns?

She reached a gravelled turning circle in front of a flight of wide, low stairs leading up to the imposing front door. In fact, Penelope thought, it looked less like a front door and more like a medieval fortification, studded with black iron rivets and the odd fearsome-looking gargoyle.

Penelope hesitated. Set within the larger entrance was a small square door with a bell pull hanging from it.

She mounted the stone stairs and pulled upon the chain. There was no answer or sound from within. She gave it a harder tug and jumped back, hand on mouth, as it came away to hang limply in her hand. Silence. Her breath slowed back to normal.

Penelope examined the welcoming device, then instinctively she pushed at the door. It yielded easily. Aware this could well mean she was not alone, she prepared her excuses. Lost and looking for directions. Historical research. Fascination with ecclesiastical buildings. None of which would have been the least bit convincing.

It was dark and cool within. She tiptoed across a stone floor. As her eyes grew accustomed to the gloom, the walls revealed large portraits of saintly looking old women glaring down at her. A thick layer of dust covered everything, save for a set of fairly new footprints that headed off down a long corridor to the left. Shuttered windows let in thin strands of sunshine where age had eaten away the wood, providing just enough light for Penelope to follow.

Carefully placing her own steps in the footprints, she made her way down the corridor to another large door, which opened on to a library or study of sorts. Bookshelves, mostly empty, covered the walls, and in the middle of the room stood a trestle table and three camping chairs. A stack of papers sat on the table.

Her ex-husband David had more than once told her that her curiosity would get her into trouble. (In fact, her persistent curiosity had been what got *him* into the divorce mire, but she put such thoughts away and concentrated on the here and now.) The trouble was, it was too dark to read by the table, and she didn't want to pick up the papers. What, she wondered, would Camrose have done?

Too risky to open the shuttered windows, even if she were able to unlock them. No torch. Her mobile phone! And even better—the scanning app, downloaded by an irritated Justin some months before she left the UK when he wanted her to send him some documents he needed but had left in his old room at home.

She hovered over the first page with her phone on scan mode, hoping the light it produced would be enough, then cast around for something to use to move the pages. She found a stalk of dried lavender. It would be very hard to get fingerprints from that, and she could take it away with her.

A muffled thump came from deep in the building. Penelope stopped. She tiptoed to the door. Peeped around the edge. In the distant hall, a shaft of light danced from a torch. It was moving towards her.

She stepped quietly back into the room, into its far recesses, and crouched down behind some old boxes. It would not have hidden her for seconds in the normal light, but in the gloom it might just work.

Footsteps outside the door heralded the entrance of a large figure, probably male, Penelope judged from the weight of the footsteps. Or a particularly hefty nun. There was a pause, and then a riffling of papers. She guessed that the documents on the table were being collected—that was why the door was still open. After a moment, the light from the torch swung erratically around the room and then disappeared as the door was closed. Retreating footsteps echoed along the corridor, and finally in the distance a door was slammed shut and bolted.

Heart pounding, Penelope waited for some time before daring to emerge from behind the boxes. It occurred to her that she did not want to be locked in for the night in a place like this. She had to find a way out, unseen.

Hurrying back to the entrance, she found the door was, as she had feared, locked and unmovable. Feeling her way with her hands, she hugged the walls until she found another door at the far end. It opened with a loud creak.

She found herself in a large hall decked with long tables and benches. The refectory, perhaps. On the far side was another door through which light poured more strongly into the room. She scurried over, and found herself in an old kitchen. There were no shutters on the windows here, and several had broken panes of glass.

Beyond the windows lay a jungle. It may have once been a kitchen garden, but now it reminded Penelope of the state of her own garden when she first arrived. The back door looked weak and already had a few windowpanes missing. When Penelope gave it a large kick with her left walking boot, the wood gave way immediately. After a few more blows the door hung drunkenly from one hinge, allowing egress into the back garden.

Pushing through the shoulder-high grass interspersed with old uncut vines and lavender, she followed a high brick wall, until eventually a wooden gate to the outside world presented itself. She breathed a profound sigh of relief. It was as decrepit as everything else, and gave way quick under her weight—rather too quickly, in fact. But she was at least out of the building and could make out a path returning to the road.

❧

A GENTLE breeze ruffled the large plane trees standing over Le Chant d'Eau as Penelope stopped the car. She breathed in deeply and willed herself to relax before pulling out her phone. Had the scan even worked? That was the trouble with apps— they were either too easy to be true, or ridiculously complicated for those who had never played computer games.

The scanned document was fairly hazy, and it was unfortunate that she had not managed to scan more, but the page she had managed to capture gave her a jolt.

PROJET DE CONTRAT

Entre

Investissements Paris-Midi

[BdeR]

[LM]

et

Monsieur Pierre Xavier Louchard

Monsieur Manuel Alain Avore

[Date xx]

A contract—a draft agreement? Between BdeR and LM and her grumpy neighbour and a recently murdered man? LM— Laurent Millais? The plot was most definitely thickening.

16

PENELOPE SLAMMED THE CAR DOOR behind her. Relief at being home was heightened by a new sense of space. The atmosphere at Le Chant d'Eau seemed lighter somehow, despite her pounding heart.

It took a while to work out what it was. When she opened the back door to the terrace, she realised that while she was gone, M. Charpet had finally cut all the grass. There was now a neat park outside the house. The courtyard had been cleared. Some of the ivy had been stripped off the house, revealing gorgeous mellow stone. The place actually looked lived-in. A small tear made its way down Penelope's cheek.

About twenty minutes later M. Charpet appeared over the horizon on a sit-on motorised mower. It was all Penelope could do not to fling herself in its path and jump up to hug him.

The two had not yet reached that stage of familiarity, though. Penelope shook his hand vigorously when he appeared on the kitchen doorstep later to say that he had finished for the day. The hand was hard and scuffed as stone. "Merci, monsieur, merci bien!" she repeated several times, knowing she was overdoing it but unable to stop herself.

She owed a debt to Clémence Valencourt as well. No matter how much of an enigma the woman was, with her kindness alternating with haughtiness, and the way she had of wrong-footing Penelope, her choice of gardener had been an inspired one. There was a dependable stubbornness about the man facing her that mirrored the granite crags of the surrounding mountains, weathered by countless days of mistral and rain. Everything was going to be all right.

"À demain!"

See you tomorrow! That meant more progress! "À demain, M. Charpet," she replied, still shaking his hand. "La transformation—c'est magnifique!"

Was there a scarcely perceptible blush under that olive skin? He extricated himself, took the compliment, and left.

In the evening sun, Penelope gazed around her property with a feeling of immense satisfaction. She made herself a cup of tea and sat outside ruminating about the events of the past few days, losing herself in the view as the lights started to come on across the valley. On the drive back she had wondered whether she would feel lonely now that Frankie had left, but all she felt was tired and curiously happy.

In the corner of the beamed sitting room lay the large carrying case, scuffed and showing its age.

She had once been a good cellist. A very good cellist, in fact. Good enough to reach the stage where constant practice was needed to maintain the standards she had attained. At school and university she had won several prizes for her playing, and at one point thought seriously about it as a career. But when the ruthless world of professional music opened up to her with an audition at the Royal Academy of Music, and she listened to fellow applicants play, she realised that, good as she was, she would never reach the heights required. She decided to remain a talented amateur, and went to secretarial school. The plan was to work in music or concert administration, but that didn't happen either after she met David. Over the years the case was opened less frequently, and eventually she gave up completely.

That was nearly twenty years ago, she mused, as she pulled the case from the corner and unclipped the rusting locks. But she still felt the thrill of anticipation as it opened to reveal the golden-brown cello, resting on its red velvet, as perfect as the day she had been given it by her father on her eighteenth birthday. She sat down on the chair and pulled the instrument to her. Tightening the bow, rubbing the rosin up and down the taut horsehair, tuning the strings, it was all part of an elaborate ritual prior to music making, and had to be done in order. It calmed the temperament, and left her in the right state of mind.

She felt quite nervous as she picked up the bow. She had no idea how far her technique had fallen in the years of lassitude, and silently cursed at the life that had robbed her of the chance to keep it going. She wasn't quite sure whether she would re-member the pieces once known by heart. Eyes closed, she drew the bow across the strings for the first time in decades.

The next hour was punctuated by grunts of dissatisfaction, swearing, and the occasional melody. Her fingers ached from the unaccustomed positions, her attempts made worse by the knowledge of how proficient she had once been. She could still hear in her head how it should sound, but the results emanating from the instrument fell far short. Still, when she paused, she felt a deep sense of pleasure. She vowed to return to a strict practice regime. The magic was still there.

She played on.

Two hours later, she sat in a near trance by the open window, still almost hearing echoes of the well-loved Mendelssohn sonata floating on the night air. As ever, the music had not only soothed her mind but connected her to the best part of her being. She could think clearly. How she had missed this!

Perhaps she shouldn't have been so selfless in her marriage. Perhaps then Lena and Justin wouldn't have taken her so much for granted. Too late for all that now, but it brought it home to her that now Frankie had left, she was on her own. She was going to have to draw on her own inner resources to make a go of living alone in St Merlot.

But it had not been an auspicious start.

What was really going on here? Why did Clémence Valencourt keep turning up? Was it just her affair with the mayor? And if not, were her actions suspect, or was she just complicit—especially if the LM on the draft contract was indeed Laurent Millais? Did the contract have any bearing on Avore's death? Had Clémence played Penelope into buying Le Chant d'Eau because she was a foreigner, and could almost be guaranteed not to understand whatever was going on? Penelope frowned. It remained to be seen if they really were on the same side.

Then there was the alluring mayor. What did he know that he was keeping from her? He had been so sure that it was Manuel Avore who had threatened her on the path her first evening—but what if he was wrong? Or worse, had intentionally misled her? No one, not even the chief of police, seemed interested in the crucial fact that the man on the path and the man in the pool could not possibly both have been Manuel Avore.

Were Laurent Millais and Clémence in it together, whatever *it* was? Where was her elusive husband—and what could possibly involve them that would necessitate bumping off a disagreeable old neighbour?

17

MIST HUNG LOW OVER THE blue hills the next morning, a first intimation that summer would not last forever. Penelope greeted M. Charpet and a young lad called Olivier who arrived with him. Olivier fetched ladders from the roof of his van and immediately resumed work pulling ivy from walls, Charpet directing operations.

Penelope would have liked to ask Charpet some questions about Clémence Valencourt and the mayor, but decided she didn't know him well enough. It could do more harm than good. She left them to it and drove down to Apt to buy a serious amount of cleaning equipment, some Polyfilla and white paint, and a powerful vacuum cleaner. When she returned, the main house and the outbuildings were completely surrounded by tangled piles of ivy.

Stripped bare, the outbuildings were so much prettier than Penelope had ever imagined. The largest comprised what must surely once have been stables or a group of barns, linked, but with roofs of different heights, and lovely arched doorways. She heard Frankie's voice in her head—*Gîte, gîte, gîte!*—and now she could see what she meant. They would make perfect small holiday lets, if she ever decided to go down that road. The other, a small barn, would be ideal as a studio. If the light was right, perhaps for some painting—or even (Penelope felt her heart flutter) a warm and inviting music room. There were more marvels in the garden, too. The orchard already looked twice the size it had when she left.

On the wall of the kitchen terrace sat a little pile of small pink plums. They felt firm, but when she tried one, it was deliciously sweet. She took it as a sign, this thoughtful gift from M. Charpet and the orchard.

The afternoon passed in backbreaking work to remove the layers of dust that had accumulated over the years. The more Penelope looked, the more she noticed the hideous cobwebs, and a large and varied number of insects both alive and dead. But she also saw the rooms from different angles, and appreciated their generous proportions. In the sitting room the ceiling sloped upwards to at least eighteen feet in height. Its beams, inset with traditional lath and plaster, would be stunning when painted white. The red tiles on the floor could be brought back to life with a professional polishing machine.

She was just thinking that the huge stone mantelpiece could preside over a real wood fire in winter when there was a knock at the window. Didier Picaud the electrician beamed his full-wattage smile and waved. He was wearing a T-shirt with the legend "I (heart) London" under a picture of a red double-decker bus. Penelope motioned for him to go to the back door. "Bonjour, M. Picaud," she said, ushering him into the kitchen. "Have you come to start the rewiring?" It seemed a bit late in the day.

"Bonjour, madame. Please call me Didier. No . . . this is not work. I would like to ask you something very important." His alert brown eyes held hers, then looked away, as if he was nervous.

"Of course, what is it?"

"Thank you, madame." He raked a hand through his mad crinkly hair. Despite the big smile, he was a bit awkward and geeky, she realised. "You see, I love to speak English, madame. And you are an English person. The only one in this village."

Penelope was extraordinarily glad to hear it. "You want me to talk to you in English, yes?"

He nodded. "I love all the things English. The Beatles, heavy metal, the Queen." Then he looked deadly serious. "Jams Pond."

"Jams Pond?"

He struck a pose and pointed his fingers at her, as if aiming a pistol. "Pond. Jams Pond. Zero zero seven!"

"Ah! Right you are, James Bond."

"Oui. I watch the movies in English."

"Films."

"Eh?"

"Movies are American. The British watch films."

"Thank you, madame. Already you are helping me. I love the English things. Rrroger Moorrre. Sean Connery. Dark Zide of ze Moon."

"Aaah, Pink Floyd." Penelope thought back to her school days, grimacing at the memories of dark, sweaty parties where the group's albums were invariably played as sound tracks for making out.

"And I have Em."

"Em?"

Didier whistled. A large black Labrador pushed round the kitchen door, tail whirring. She was an adorable creature.

"Isn't she a darling! Look at those melting chocolate eyes!"

Didier gave his dog a stroke. "Her name is Shoo-dee, but I call her Em."

"Shoo-dee . . . Judi! After Judi Dench. M!" Penelope got it, much to Didier's delight.

"She is very intelligent. Bye-bye!" he ordered, looking at his dog. M raised her front paw and waved it in a regal circle.

Penelope giggled.

"I like everything English, dogs including," said Didier.

Penelope acknowledged his good taste, and threw out a true test. "Cup of tea?"

"Delicious."

"I'll put the kettle on, and let's have a chat, then," said Penelope.

There was no stopping him after that. Didier rattled off the titles of Pink Floyd numbers that lurked in the dark recesses of Penelope's memory. He was certainly a great fan. He told her about going to London when he was twenty-one, and a trip to Liverpool to see the Cavern Club where the Beatles used to play. His English was really pretty good.

It was a while before Penelope managed to steer him towards a more fruitful subject. "What were they like, the previous owners of this house?"

"They were nice people. I can't say I saw them very often, as they never spent so much time here. They preferred to stay in Lyon."

"I thought they wanted to retire here. But they obviously never did the renovations the house needed. Why was that?"

Didier shrugged. "Perhaps they did not have the money. Renovations are always more expensive than you expect."

"That's true."

"I felt a bit sorry for them. They were quite old, and maybe they realised too late that this project they had taken on was too serious for them. Jaguar! Aston Martin!" he said, changing the subject abruptly. "Range Rover! Can I look at your car? It is so English! Please to sit inside it?"

"If you like."

Eventually, after a lengthy discussion on the merits of Aston Martin versus Lotus as the seminal Bond vehicle, Didier finished the last of his cold cup of tea and stood up.

"Madame, I must leave now, but I will return to start the re-wiring soon."

Penelope shook him warmly by the hand. "Anytime you want to learn some more English, just call."

"It would be my pleasure. And maybe you would like to prac-tise your French too? If you like, you could come to a pétanque match in the village? I am playing on Sunday evening. St Merlot against Rustrel."

"That would be wonderful." Penelope felt quite touched.

It was still hot and bright when Didier and M departed. The dog gave a queenly wave goodbye.

PENELOPE DUG out some sturdy shoes and wandered outside. A late afternoon walk was just what she needed. She set off down the track in the opposite direction to the main road and saun-tered along, immersed in the smell of wild thyme and the ever-present fidgeting of the cicadas. Birds wheeled overhead, and butterflies fluttered.

In no time at all, she was passing the entrance to Pierre Lou-chard's property. And there he was.

She waved. "Bonjour, monsieur!"

"Bonjour, madame," replied M. Louchard without any no-table enthusiasm. He was carrying a large rifle under one arm, and an oily cloth in his hand.

Trying her best in French, she explained she was taking a walk, just to explore the countryside.

The farmer grimaced. "Pourquoi?"

Why? "Il fait très beau, monsieur."

The weather was indeed fine, he agreed, but he thought it

would rain later. Penelope looked up at the deep cloudless blue above and smiled. She'd noticed that weather forecasts in La Provence often predicted clouds when all that happened was that the sun went in for half an hour. In a place where it shone reliably for so many months of the year, the locals seemed to take clouds as a personal affront.

"Faites attention à la chasse!"

"La chasse?"

He stroked his gleaming rifle, raised it to his shoulder, and mimed firing in the air.

"Hunters! Oui, je comprends." Penelope explained that she was going to stick to the paths. It may not have come out quite as well in French as she'd hoped, but she was sure he got the gist.

M. Louchard rattled off a few phrases that Penelope did her best to interpret. His accent was rough, and she could make out only a part of what he was saying.

"Est-ce qu'il y a un problème, monsieur?"

From what she could understand, the care with which he stalked rock partridge and *bartavelle* was not shared by all other hunters. According to him, many would blunder around the woods shooting anything that moved, animal, vegetable, mineral . . . or human.

"Alors, je vous dis, madame, faites attention! Be care-fool!"

"I will, thank you."

Penelope found it hard to believe that any hunter, unless certifiably blind, could mistake an English woman out on a walk for a wild boar. Or if they did, she would definitely write to L'Oréal and ask for her money back. She walked on, kicking herself for not finding a way to ask Louchard about Le Prieuré des Gentilles Merlotiennes. Another time, when she had had time to think it through. She couldn't just go blundering in.

The track entered the woods. Every so often the holm oaks

and pines would clear to reveal rows of cut lavender, a vineyard groaning under the weight of grapes, or a field lying fallow. In one clearing was a long line of beehives. She neither saw nor heard any evidence of hunters.

After a short while she came across the remains of a stone wall, which on further examination revealed evidence of a more complex structure. She pulled out her large-scale walking map. A little cross indicated a ruined chapel. She stepped off the track and started to nose round the undergrowth. She could just make out the remains of the building, though the walls were probably only half of what had once existed. Was this once the village church? Outlines of old windows punctuated the moss-encrusted stones.

She was gazing up at what was left of the chapel walls when a sudden whoosh of air zipped past her ear, accompanied by a loud crack.

"Holy mackerel!" There could be no doubt about it. That was gunshot.

Instinctively she ducked and pressed herself against a cool, moist exterior wall.

There was another dangerously loud volley of shots.

For a moment Penelope gave in to blind panic. Should she jump up and wave her arms around to show that she wasn't a potential haunch of venison or wild boar *saucisson*? Luckily, just as quickly, her logical forensic mind reasserted itself. She hurled herself into the ruin.

A large holm oak was growing in the middle of what had once been the nave. Penelope crept carefully over the rampant ivy that snaked throughout, trying not to make a sound. She hunkered down inside the chapel walls.

Another loud shot sent her farther in, crouching lower, back against the wall. A fusillade went off, far too close for comfort.

This must be what the First World War was like, thought Penelope, teeth chattering. She closed her eyes. It seemed like an age before the intermittent gunfire gradually died out. Was that the sound of retreating voices, or was she imagining it?

Penelope gazed up at what was left of the chapel walls, trying to gauge the safest place to look out. In the far corner was a large mound of earth and stones underneath a window opening. She picked her way across, as quietly as she could.

She climbed the stones slowly, looking around for something to hold on to. More shaken than she cared to admit, she grabbed an ivy root on the mound. Inside her rib cage, her heart was pounding uncontrollably. Her legs and arms had been scratched by thorns. She made the first of several cautious attempts to stand up, her eyes on the ledge. The aim was to see out, but not to be seen.

The ivy root pulled away from its anchor.

Penelope started to topple forward, and in a reflex action snatched at another hold. This failed too. She looked more closely.

And froze.

She was clutching a large bone, pale and speckled with black mold.

"Holy mackerel!"

Penelope had seen enough photographs of bones to know that this was an example of the radius, the more lateral and slightly shorter of the two forearm bones. The ivy root she had grabbed first to steady herself was no ivy root. It was a finger bone. And she had been holding hands with it.

"Holy *fucking* mackerel!"

She knew not to touch the bones—though she must have disturbed the scene enough already—but she peeled away ivy and weeds until she could see enough to be sure she was not making a terrible mistake.

She was not. From the earthen mound in the corner of the abandoned chapel, close to the wall and the sill of the window space, protruded parts of a large skeletal arm. Woven through the remaining finger bones was a filthy playing card. The ace of spades.

Her head buzzed, as if she might faint. She closed her eyes. All she could see in her head was the card. A lone ace of spades—where else had she seen one recently? A few deep breaths seemed to be in order.

Then she remembered. Its twin had been floating in her swimming pool, as if cast on the murky water by the hand of Manuel Avore.

Despite the shock, her years of professional experience kicked in. From the state of the radius, her first impression was that it had been in the ground for a number of years. None of these bones were dried out and brittle, though. They were well preserved. Years but not decades since burial, then.

All thought of hunters banished, Penelope stood up. She patted the pockets of her loose trousers and could have cried with relief that her phone was still in the pocket. She took some photographs of what she had found, exactly how she had found it. Using a dry twig, she painstakingly bent the playing card back so she could see the reverse side and took a photo of that. Old habits died hard. Or the habit, at least, of knowing how to make the work of a forensic pathologist easier.

She stepped away and tried to be rational. Surely she was mistaken. This was nothing more frightening than a long-buried body that had worked its way to the surface, helped by decades—centuries, even—of winter weather and insect and animal activity. The mound of earth in the far corner could well have been formed by torrential rain and the force of the wind howling the length of the valley. Clay soil cracked in summer, and opened up. Maybe she was letting her imagination run away with her. Penelope exhaled deeply through her mouth, as she had been taught in yoga. *Calm . . . calm . . . calm, still centre*, she repeated the mantra.

By the time she stepped back on the path, the rapidly cooling sun was partially obscured by incoming rain clouds. Then two gunshots cracked the air again. She stopped. Listened. The shots seemed to have come from a bit farther away. She was distinctly shaky as she staggered back the way she had come.

M. Louchard was still outside his house as she ran towards the farm. She must have looked a fright because as soon as he saw her, he rushed to his gate, concern etched on his face, and shepherded her to a chair at the garden table.

He went inside and came out with a bottle of plum brandy. A small glass was placed in front of her and filled. One for himself, too. Penelope downed it in one, almost gagging on the fiery passage of the liquid down her throat. It did the job.

"Mais qu'est-ce qui s'est passé, madame?"

"What happened to me? Les chasseurs! I was shot at, monsieur! Bang bang!" She was all over the place, incapable of speaking French. "It was like they were hunting me! Je suis gibier—I was the prey!"

Louchard looked shocked. "Non!" he exclaimed, shaking his head. Penelope described the situation she had found herself in, and after further gestures of surprise, the farmer seemed to believe her.

"Incroyable! Horrifiant! Les maudits!" he murmured.

"Mais une autre chose . . ." She could hardly bring herself to speak of it.

"Quoi?"

"Un corps—a body. Or rather, the bones!"

Louchard began to look even more worried. "Un corps? Where is zizzz?"

"In the chapel, the ruined chapel. Where I hid after hearing the gunshots. I was trying to get out, and then . . ."

"You are sure?"

"Of course I am sure! I know what bones look like!" Penelope crumpled into the chair, head in hands. Had she made a terrible mistake? She might have disturbed a legal grave. Bodies *were* buried in chapels, long ago.

But Louchard had already brought out his mobile and was gesticulating and shouting into it. Penelope realised he was calling the police. Her heart sank.

The sky had now clouded over. She felt the first spots of rain. The farmer looked at the sky and smiled, as the shower became more insistent. Raindrops bounced off the iron café table and fizzed on the barrel of the rifle that was propped against his chair.

The farmer eventually finished his phone conversation and turned back towards her, looking up at the clouds and shrugging as if to say *I told you so.*

"Madame, we return to the chapel now. The chief of police, he is coming."

18

AS M. LOUCHARD AND PENELOPE walked back to the scene of the latest unfortunate events, he lectured her about the hunting fraternity. The bands of local hunters, he explained, were composed of two types—the responsible ones (amongst whom he clearly counted himself) who obeyed the rules, knew their quarry and its whereabouts, and stalked it with a cunning born of experience; and those who drank too much and staggered about in the undergrowth shooting at anything that moved. Penelope had clearly and unluckily blundered into a group of this second type.

"Les Cro-Magnons avec fusils! You were lucky, madame. Every year there are one or two accidental deaths in the woods." He glanced disdainfully at her dirt-smeared gardening trousers and black top. "Next time you go for a little walk, I advise you to wear something bright. Pink! Turquoise! Yellow!"

As they arrived at the chapel, a car drew up quietly behind them. The vehicle bumped up on the uneven, stony track, and out stepped the chief of police. He glared up at the sky, then at her, as if it was all her fault it was raining as well.

A moment later, the mayor appeared on foot with a large golf umbrella, looking more than usually concerned. How on earth does he always find out about these things so quickly? thought Penelope, brushing the mud from her hair.

"Now, Mme Keet," he said, in a quiet, businesslike tone. "Please will you show us what you have found?"

Penelope nodded, and led him through the overgrown nave. Two young gendarmes, one of whom she recognised as Daniel Auxois, stumbled noisily on loose stones behind them.

"There!" she said, pointing.

They all looked, including the chief of police, who arrived abruptly headfirst, having tripped on what actually was a rope of ivy root. Daniel helped him up. Everyone else pretended not to notice.

The rain intensified.

Penelope stood well back. She was waiting for Chief Reyssens and the mayor to shake their heads pityingly and tell her that buried bodies were quite often to be found in the vicinity of old churches. But no one said anything of the sort. Perhaps they were being kind because they suspected that she might have mental health problems.

The mayor, M. Louchard, and Reyssens talked amongst themselves. The gendarmes went about their business methodically. Penelope sat miserably on a low lump of wall, away from the action.

Within twenty minutes the area had been cordoned off with tape, and a tent was erected in the midst of the ruined chapel walls. Another unmarked van appeared, this time bearing men in white coveralls with masks and various digging implements. Gradually, the rain eased off. Penelope could not help but notice how low-key and quiet this police operation appeared to be, in stark contrast to their previous attendance.

"Are you OK?"

Penelope looked up. It was Laurent Millais.

She nodded, not trusting herself to say anything sensible.

"It is incredible," he said. "What were the chances?"

"Sorry?"

"We should be saying sorry to you. What a start you have had to your new life in France! It is unbelievable!"

There was no chance for him to say any more, as the chief was approaching, pawing at streaks of mud on his uniform. He gave her a look that clearly implied this was her fault, too.

"It seems, madame, you have a talent for finding dead bodies." He sniffed. Clearly, he had been disturbed doing something far preferable to this, and was not in the best of moods.

Penelope bridled at the inferred accusation. "It seems to me, monsieur le chef de police, that the people of St Merlot have a talent for getting themselves killed in suspicious circumstances!"

They all paused to look as the second body bag of the summer was carried past them and towards the tent.

"You have no idea who, I suppose," she said flatly.

"We will make the investigation," said Reyssens, "and I must ask you most seriously not to mention this to anyone in the village for the time being. You may have noticed that we are trying not to draw attention to this find."

Penelope nodded as he continued.

"There is often a local element to cases like these, and we would not want anyone else in the area to find out about it."

She wondered how much progress they were making with the Avore case, but decided against mentioning it. Feeling drained, she answered his questions about what time she had left her house; when exactly she had heard the shots and found the bones; and who could corroborate her version of events.

The chief of police closed his notepad and dismissed her curtly.

"Don't you even want to discuss the dangers posed by out-of-control hunters?" she cried, infuriated. "You seem to have forgotten that I was shot at here! What if this body turns out to be a hunting victim?"

He turned on his heel like a little spinning top. Rather disconcertingly, he gave her a twitching grin. "Ah yes, madame. The hunters." He sounded positively cheerful and friendly.

"I think you will like to know that we have the results from your murder weapon, the axe you have brought to me!" He spoke in English, very clearly, so that there should be no mistake. "The mystery of the axe is now solved."

Gosh, thought Penelope, he seems pleased about this at least. Was the Avore investigation over? For a few heady seconds, she allowed herself to imagine the headlines in *La Provence*: MURDER CASE SOLVED BY SHARP-EYED BRITISH NEWCOMER. MISS MARPLE DE-NOS-JOURS PROVIDES VITAL CLUE.

"Tell us, then," said the mayor.

"Madame," began the chief of police, looking more like Napoleon than ever. "We have had the results from our laboratories."

"So, there *is* blood on the axe?"

"Yes, it is blood. You made an excellent observation, madame. Congratulations."

"Thank you." Penelope felt a swell of pride.

"And as you also told us, it is clear that someone has used this axe recently and cleaned it. The blood was also not very old."

"I knew it!"

Penelope glanced at the mayor. He looked her straight in the eye in a most disconcerting manner. She looked away, feeling like an embarrassed teenager.

"Ah, the blood, madame!" The chief was finding it hard to contain a bubbling undercurrent of mirth, which Penelope thought in rather bad taste, given the circumstances. The mayor said nothing.

"The blood, madame, it solves this riddle for us. We have analysed it with all the modern techniques available, and now know the identity of its source."

"And?" Penelope was getting a little tired of this preening monologue.

"Until recently, this blood was coursing through the veins of . . . of . . ." At this point the chief could contain himself no longer and burst out laughing.

Penelope drew herself up, quite shocked. "I'm sorry, but in England this would be considered most inappropriate. The DPP would hardly be—"

". . . the veins of, how do you English put it, some bunny rabbits!"

"Rabbits?"

The mayor's mouth twitched, suppressing a smile.

"Madame, many of the farmers round here lay rabbit traps, and usually kill the unfortunate creatures that are caught with a short sharp blow from a large instrument—in this case, your axe."

Penelope did not answer. She felt her face redden as she searched for the right words.

"Do not worry, madame. It is an easy mistake to make, and at least the innocent M. Charpet can be removed from our list of suspects." The chief of police released a patronising sneer.

Heat flooded Penelope's body. The mayor stepped forward. "I think, madame, that I should take you home."

Numbly, she agreed.

CONVERSATION WAS awkward as they walked towards Le Chant d'Eau. Penelope felt deflated. She had only been trying to help. She debated whether to mention the ace of spades close to Manuel Avore's body. Surely the coincidence would not have escaped the police; if she had noticed it, they would have, too.

It should be in the photographs taken of the forensic scene by crime officers. She didn't want to give them another opportunity to make her feel stupid.

They walked on in silence.

The mayor placed a friendly hand briefly on hers. She jumped. Don't be ridiculous, Penelope told herself sternly, and risked meeting those incredible blue eyes.

"Madame, do not be upset. The chief may not have said so, but the find was actually most helpful. A useful piece of detective work."

"What, to find out that M. Charpet, unusually for a country man, kills bloody rabbits! Come on!"

"No, madame. Whoever used the axe to kill rabbits, it was not M. Charpet. You see, M. Charpet says he has never used that axe to kill rabbits, or anything else. It is not his. He has never seen it before, and we believe him."

"So someone else must have used it and put it in the borie!"

The mayor inclined his head in tacit agreement.

"The axe could have been used to kill M. Avore and cleaned afterwards—but the killer didn't clean underneath the axe head, which is where most of the rabbit blood was found." Penelope perked up. "So who put it there and why? Even if rabbit blood was found, that doesn't mean it couldn't also have been used as a murder weapon. I mean, what if it was used on Manuel Avore and then cleaned—and *then* used to butcher a rabbit just to con-fuse matters? Or the shaft alone was used?"

He did not dismiss this out of hand.

"Why was the chief of police so mean about it, then?"

"Ach, that's just him. Take no notice. I don't."

"He has an odd sense of humour, doesn't he?" said Penelope. "So, are they any closer to finding out who killed Manuel Avore?"

"I don't think so."

"And what about the hunters? Surely you can't be happy that there are thickheads with guns rampaging around the village."

"No, I am not."

"But do you think it's just a bit of traditional fun, like M. Louchard does—or can you do something about it?"

"I am sorry you had this experience, Penny. If the hunters are from St Merlot, I will speak to them most seriously. They will not want to lose their gun licences."

They said goodbye at her door.

It was only when she looked in the bathroom mirror that she realised she had mad hair, mascara splodged over her cheeks, and a streak of dirt across her chin. She had also missed her chance to ask about the initials LM on the draft contract.

"Oh . . . rats!" cried Penelope.

Under the dribbling shower, she scrubbed her thighs harder and harder with an exfoliating mitt as she tried to make sense of it all.

Would a playing card be placed in the hand of a body prepared for a funeral? Surely that meant it was unlikely the bones had been dislodged from a legitimate grave. No, the presence of the ace of spades indicated foul play. And a strong likelihood that there had been a sinister significance to the one she saw floating in her pool, close to Avore's corpse.

19

ACCORDING TO WIKIPEDIA, THE ACE of spades was a symbol of death. The time had come to call in a favour.

As usual he picked up on the fourth ring. "Camrose Fletcher."

The familiar strident tones of her former boss made her feel homesick for the first time. He still talked far too loudly on the phone.

She held the handset slightly away from her ear. "Cam, it's me, Penny."

The voice at the other end gave a warm laugh and took on a softer tone. "Penny, how wonderful to hear from you! Tell me, how is la belle Provence?"

"Slightly less belle than expected, all things considered, Cam. But still lovely. I need your advice about something."

Without pausing to draw breath, Penelope launched into a potted history of the events since her move. From her mobile, she emailed the sharpest photos of the hand and the playing card, and he opened them on his computer. Her account was punctuated by the odd remark from Camrose, an occasional sympathetic murmur, and one or two exclamations of surprise. When she had finished the tale, there was a moment of silence.

Finally, with the understatement so recognisable in an Englishman of a certain background, he gave his reaction.

"*Two* dead bodies. What a pickle, eh! Almost like being back at work again."

"Well, quite," said Penelope.

Professor Fletcher slipped into professional mode. His powers of concentration were legendary in the Department of Forensic Pathology. With a constant stream of questions, he probed and teased out the minutiae of evidence that would lead him incisively to the truth, though it had to be said that Penelope had always provided meticulous observational backup and vital insight on more than one occasion.

"You're quite right about the Avore body and rigor mortis—you know that as well as I do. He must have been dead for at least twenty-six hours for the rigor to pass, and limpness to manifest. That's the first thing.

"As for the second body, it is almost impossible for me to give a professional opinion without examining the bones, but you know that, too. However, I can give informed guesswork, from what I can see in the photographs."

There was a pause at the other end of the line. Penelope knew that at this moment, in the house he had bought in the Lake District for his retirement, Camrose would be cleaning his spectacles as he let the information flow through his impressive brain. Finally he resumed.

"Given that the body has decomposed, it must have been there for a number of years. What type of soil was it found in?"

"Clay, mainly. Dark, occasionally moist location. Vegetation: ivy, brambles, holm oak."

"As far as I can see, these bones don't look heavily eroded or stained. Best guess, then, around five or six years, maybe a bit longer. No more than ten in the ground."

"That's what I thought."

"From the radius and size of the hand relative to the playing card, male. Fully grown adult, but I can't be more specific on age. . . ."

"That playing card is interesting," said Penelope. "The card of death—right?"

"Quite so. Symbol of ill fortune and ancient mysteries."

A pause. Penelope heard him striking the keys on his computer.

"Hold on a minute," he said. "I'm just running it through high definition. Rather usefully, I managed to walk out with my old Home Office computer."

"I know," said Penelope. "I had to cover for you. Those new HR people believed me when I told them it was practically obsolete. Steam-driven, just like you."

"Ha ha."

Penelope smiled to herself. In her mind's eye she could see the twinkle in his cornflower-blue eyes, the thick white hair, and the weathered tan from the walking he loved so much. "The new brooms had no idea what they were sweeping out," she said. "I just couldn't stick it back in the secretarial pool after you left."

"You were always a gem, Penny. You and your phenomenal memory and eye for detail. I assume they had no idea what a shining star you were."

"Well . . . not exactly."

"I'm enjoying this, though! I may be retired, but that doesn't mean I want to be completely out of the game. It is lovely to hear from you."

Me neither, she thought. I miss this. In so many ways, Camrose Fletcher had been the man in her life since the end of her marriage. Not that he knew that, nor ever would.

"Now . . . that card . . . very interesting indeed," he went on.

"Can you tell how long that has been in the ground? Insect erosion? I checked, and there are a variety of ants, beetles, and woodlice at the location."

"It's a relatively modern plastic-coated playing card. The

plastic doesn't degrade. Where the coating is worn, there is some ingress of mold. But that's not what I'm looking at. There it is . . . a cut on one edge."

"Not beetle nibble?"

"Absolutely not. I can see it quite clearly, and it's a good sharp sliced cut."

"Meaning?"

"It's a marked card, Penny."

"What?"

"My guess is that this is the kind of old-fashioned marked card used by professional tricksters and card sharps."

"The highest-value card in the pack."

"Indeed."

"That *is* interesting."

"What about the other card, the first one? Do you have a close-up photo of that?"

"No. I only saw it. I didn't think anything of it."

"I suppose the police have it now."

"I expect so," said Penelope, not altogether confidently. "What are the chances that they are connected?"

"My professional opinion would have to be that it's impossible to say without examining both cards. But personally, I would strongly suspect a connection between this and your body from the chapel. Though obviously that is only a guess between friends."

A guess born of long experience, thought Penelope. "That's what I thought."

There was a cough at the other end of the line. "Now, to other more important matters."

"More important!" Penelope nearly choked. "What could be more important than two dead bodies?"

"Practically everything, my dear," came the reply. "But to be specific . . . when are you going to ask me over?"

Penelope grinned. "Who says I want to?"

"Well, in that case, an invoice for my consultation fee will be in the post tomorrow morning. It will, I can assure you, be of stupendous proportions. Or you can chalk it on the slate, and I'll take dinner at your place next time I'm in the South of France."

"Deal!" said Penelope.

"Bye, Penny, so good to hear from you. Chin up!"

She replaced the receiver and smiled again. Camrose Fletcher always had the knack of lifting her spirits.

Over the weekend, she kept the doors locked and cleaned like a woman doing penance. She had expected calls from the police—or Clémence, who would surely have heard about what had happened. But she was left to her own devices. The only other person she spoke to was Frankie.

Penelope barely managed to stop her friend from boarding the next flight back to Provence. "I'm fine, honestly. I just wanted to, you know, keep you updated. If anything else kicks off, you will be the first to know."

"Well, whose bones are they? Do you have any idea? Who else has gone missing?"

"I don't know! No one is telling me anything!"

"Is there anything in the paper? How can you find out?"

"No, and I'm not sure yet. Whatever happens, I have to wait until Monday." Penelope was exhausted just having this conversation. Which was terribly unfair, she knew, as Frankie only wanted to help.

"And you're sure you don't want me to come back?"

"Absolutely."

Positive thought and daydreams of how the house would look

eventually and the gatherings it would host spurred Penelope on
to greater efforts with scrubbing brush and scourer.

✦

ON SUNDAY evening at six o'clock Penelope wandered into the
village square. Once more, she thought how very pretty it was,
the pale stucco buildings graceful in the shade behind the plane
trees. She adored the exuberance of the maroon, sky-blue, and
sea-green shutters. When she turned to look back through the
open side of the square, the whole scene seemed to hang high in
the sky. One day, she thought, she would know who lived here
and might even be friends with some of them. Would she look
back in fond nostalgia at this memory of herself, still travelling
hopefully towards her new life?

On the rough, dusty pitch under the trees were gathered two
teams, one in claret, the other in dark blue, old and younger
players alike. The older generation wore berets, and many were
smoking. Pungent plumes rose, the sweet tobacco of unfiltered
cigarettes, so redolent of old France. The old man on the bench
had put down his newspaper and moved fractionally in order
to get a better view of proceedings. A few children ran around,
and wives chatted. This was clearly what passed for prematch
tension in the world of Provençal pétanque.

From the earnest huddle of the team dressed in claret vests
and a peculiar assortment of baggy knee-length shorts, two familiar faces emerged. First Didier and then M. Charpet raised a
hand in greeting. Penelope found herself a spot on the low stone
wall and sat down. A few other spectators had turned out but it
was clearly not a big match.

"Ah, Penny, I am so glad that you have come," said Didier.
"We are just about to start. You know pétanque?"

"It's a form of boules, isn't it?"

Didier was not to be stopped from parading his English in front of his friends. He had clearly been working at the phrases and was aching to try them out.

"This," he started, pointing to the jack, "this little ball is le cochon, the pig. These—big balls, les boules—" Didier hefted out a pair of weighted silver balls.

Penelope bit the inside of her mouth to avoid laughing.

Everyone in the two teams was listening, perhaps wondering who she was, and why Didier Picaud was speaking to her in English.

Didier was now in full flow. "The game! Big ball, throw near little pig." He left a pause for his listeners to agree. "Big ball nearest little pig, you are the winner!"

The game apparently required a combination of skill, ruthlessness, and extreme verbosity. Penelope had never seen a competition where the players would indulge in ten minutes of conversation about angles and velocity, with voices raised and much gesticulation.

Every so often the slow pace of the match would be interrupted by a more aggressive attempt from one side to change the game.

Penelope watched intently as a strongman from Rustrel rocked on his heels, knees bent, and hurled a boule underarm towards the pack. He froze for a few seconds in a strange posture like a crouching ancient Egyptian, one palm raised in front, the other behind. The boule smashed into the middle of the others surrounding the pig, scattering them hither and thither. There was a roar of approval from the visiting side.

Penelope noticed that the boulangerie-bar at the corner of the square was open, the tables outside crowded. The players all had glasses of cloudy pastis, which they placed on the low wall by the pitch when it was their turn to throw. She wondered if it would be rude to leave the field of play and get herself a soft drink. Luckily for her, Didier caught her longing gaze and came over during a lull in the proceedings.

"The news is good, madame. We are up by one, but there is still time for them to win."

Behind him, M. Charpet gave her a thumbs-up. From underneath his droopy moustache emerged a smile. The evening sun glinted on various gold teeth as he replaced his beret and prepared to defend the honour of St Merlot.

"If you would like a drink from the bar, I will get you one," said Didier. "Then it is the second half. It will get exciting!"

Equipped with a cold Orangina, Penelope watched the remainder of the game unfold. As the climax approached, it became clear that things were really very close. Gitanes were being smoked down to the very last nub, voices raised, and on one occasion even the normally placid Didier had to be restrained from poking an opposing team member in the chest.

The end was a tense affair, with St Merlot and the visiting team still neck and neck. M. Charpet had the last throw. If he could edge out an opposing boule, St Merlot would win. Much was riding on his elderly shoulders, perhaps too much. He approached the throwing circle, only to step away, walk down the far end, light another cigarette, and discuss tactics yet again with his colleagues. This gambit was repeated several times.

Eventually, with a few encouraging pats on the back, and a steadying draught of pastis, he went down on one knee in the circle, a picture of concentration. Penelope could see Didier draw in his breath in synchronisation as Charpet drew back his arm. Dropping his wrists to provide backspin, the old man threw. The ball seemed to hang in midair for an instant, then dropped out of the sky into the perfect position, where it landed and came to rest immediately, touching the pig. St Merlot erupted with joy.

Penelope held back, simply watching but feeling immense pleasure. The team clapped each other on the back and were congratulated by the spectators. The wives applauded and called to their children. Man of the match Charpet was borne off to the bar before Penelope had a chance to add her felicitations. On his way to join the others, Didier stopped. He didn't seem to have a wife or girlfriend in the melée.

"Well done! What a game!" she cried.

"It's always good to beat Rustrel!"

"Are they your great rivals?"

"No, we just hate Rustrel. But not as much as we hate Saignon. Though we despise Bonnieux, the arrogant pigs. And we detest Viens and Caseneuve. And don't even mention Gignac and Gordes."

"Goodness," said Penelope. "Do you like anyone?"

"Well, there is St Merlot. But in truth, we don't like many people here either."

Penelope laughed, then saw he was nodding seriously.

"Not until we are sure we can trust them," he added.

"Is everyone going to the bar, then? Perhaps I should come too and start showing my friendly credentials to the St Merlot sporting set."

Didier smiled sadly. "Penny, where is your English reserve? Did you see any of the other women going with the men to the bar? This is still a very traditional village in many ways. Women come to support the men when they play a match, but they do not go to the bar afterwards."

"Gosh, that is quite old-fashioned, isn't it! I thought it would be the perfect time to meet a few people here."

"Me, I don't care. But some of the older ones do. Can I give you some advice, Penny? It would be better if you just let them get used to seeing you in the village for a while. After that you can make an approach. In St Merlot, relationships happen very slowly."

He shook her hand with a formality he had not shown at her house and crossed the road to the bar. Penelope walked back home down the hill, feeling slightly flat. She had been starting to feel at home in St Merlot. Now the lid had been lifted on local life, it seemed to be far more complicated than it had first appeared.

Then again, it was the same in any small country village, anywhere in the world; Didier was simply being honest about it. Only when she reached the Avore house at the end of the track—it was shuttered and looked empty—did it occur to her that at no time had anyone made her feel an object of curiosity. Perhaps she just looked like a tourist. But that was better than being pointed out as the Englishwoman who had found Manuel Avore dead in her swimming pool.

And how many of them knew about the bones in the chapel? Surely word had spread. It always did in small villages.

Perhaps it was just as well that Didier hadn't asked her to join the victory drink in the bar.

⊱

ON MONDAY morning, her long-awaited telephone line with Internet connection was installed, but before she could set to work a shiny van arrived. On its side was a picture of a mermaid and the words "Geret et Fils—Piscines Claires."

Two men got out. The elder shook Penelope warmly by the hand, and said how glad he was that the house was occupied again. His Provençal accent was so broad she could only just understand what he was saying. The younger—presumably the "and Son"—looked sullen and distinctly uninterested in the pro-

ceedings. He was wearing torn leather trousers—in this heat!—
embellished with punky zips and safety pins.

Penelope gestured to the walled garden and was just thinking
she wished she had someone to translate when she heard a familiar scrunch of brakes on the gravel.

Moments later, Mme Valencourt was apologising for being
late and initiating another round of handshakes. M. Geret was
clearly among her wide circle of acquaintances. She took charge
immediately and led the way to the walled garden.

They all surveyed the swimming pool, except for the punk
throwback, who picked at a scab on his hand. Geret *père* peered
at the old pump and then into the dry basin of the pool, pulled
faces and shook his head, walked back and forth, and then said
he thought it was worth trying to clean it up. He gave no indication that he knew of its recent macabre history.

He rattled off a string of French that Penelope rapidly gave
up even trying to follow. She looked despairingly at Mme Valencourt.

"He is overjoyed that you have decided to renovate it," said
the estate agent. "In fact, he says he built the pool there some
twenty years ago. He and Plastic Bertrand here—"

Goodness, thought Penelope, was that a joke from Clémence,
referencing Europe's only successful punk act? She definitely
seemed happier. Perhaps she had got back together with the
mayor.

"—they are going to clean it with the high-pressure water jet
and repair the cracks. Tomorrow they will return to assess if
there are any leaks."

Penelope marvelled at the sense of continuity. Just like when
Didier Picaud the electrician had shown her the sticker bearing
his family firm's name on the fuse box. "I will let you get on with
it then," she said.

The sullen young man was the only one who looked askance at the pool. For the first time, Penelope wondered if she really was going to feel all right about swimming in a pool where a dead body had been found. In truth, she had been trying not to think too hard about that.

She took a deep breath and smiled more brightly.

"Allons-y, mon brave," Geret said to his son. "I try to teach him the business, madame, but he is more interested in his music. Les Sex Pistols!" He shook his head. "Le punk rock was for my generation, and I never like it even then! Terrible . . . but there is no good music for the young these days. They all look to the past."

"I know what you mean," said Penelope. "About punk, I mean. Though the Stranglers were quite good."

"Strangler? What is this?"

Penelope wished she hadn't said anything. It didn't seem right to be discussing any form of murder, in the circumstances. All too easy for a misunderstanding to arise. "Nothing. Forget it."

Geret and his uncommunicative son got cracking with the water tap in the garden and the pressure jet.

❧

PENELOPE NEEDED to decide what to say to Clémence. Naturally, the estate agent hadn't asked whether it was convenient to send the pool men round. Was it really possible that she was in league with the mayor concerning Manuel Avore's death? It seemed less likely than Frankie's theory that her appearances at St Merlot were entirely linked to the chance of seeing Laurent.

As water hissed against the sides of the pool, Penelope visualised how the walled garden would look when she had finished planting it. She could train climbing plants over the walls—

scented climbing plants. Her fantasy grew more ambitious, involving statues of contemplative Greek maidens bearing cornucopias of fruit.

"I've just heard the news about the shots! Why did you not call me?" Clémence broke the spell of Penelope's inner garden designer.

Penelope wheeled round, startled. Clémence was staring at her phone as if she couldn't believe what she had heard or read on it.

"Yes," said Penelope. "Slight cause for concern when I was shot at by hunters and then found human remains. Just an everyday walk in the park around these parts."

"It is unfortunate, yes. But do not worry. The police are in control."

"Of course they are." She wondered whether her estate agent got English sarcasm. "The chief was quite cross that I was making more work for him. Oh, and it turned out that it *was* blood on the axe, but absolutely nothing to do with M. Charpet. Not that anyone thought it was in the first place. Something to do with hunters and rabbits. I didn't really take it in. I just want to let the police get on with their jobs now."

It must have been obvious that Penelope was a terrible liar, but Clémence had something else on her mind.

"Have you spoken to Laurent about this?"

"He was right there when I was receiving my lecture."

Clémence seemed to be thinking hard.

"Even so, you probably know more about it than I do," said Penelope.

The Frenchwoman gave her a withering look.

"Anyone gone missing hereabouts in the past ten years?"

Clémence raised her palms. "Idiot hunters! And there will be an explanation about the bones."

"I'm sure there will," said Penelope, with more heavy sarcasm.

"I have some other news. Penny, the day that you met Pierre Louchard, when we drank his plum brandy, did you notice how he became very angry when we mentioned Manuel Avore?"

"Notice? His hands were clenching into fists—I thought he was going to break his glass!"

"I know why, Penny! Laurent told me." The Frenchwoman's eyes lit up. "It is because M. Louchard is a man in love!"

"A man in love? With whom?"

"He loves Mariette Avore. He has loved her for many, many years."

"So why didn't she marry him in the first place? He seems much nicer than that awful old drunk."

"Hélas, the two families of Louchard and Avore hate each other. There has been bad blood between them for generations. And Mariette was a cousin of the Avores. It could not be allowed."

"Like the Montagues and the Capulets."

"Exactement! Roméo et Juliette!"

"So poor Mariette had to marry her cousin? Marrying a cousin, even a second cousin, is never a good idea."

"It was arranged by the family. She was very young. She had no choice. They wanted a bride for Manuel, and no one else would have him. But think of all the life she has missed!"

"How do you know all this, suddenly?"

"The mayor, he might have whispered it in my ear."

I'll bet he did, thought Penelope.

"Anyway, the two young lovers, Mariette and Pierre, were forbidden by their parents to marry. Pierre Louchard went off to join the foreign legion. A very old-fashioned reaction, but it showed how much he cared. No one heard from him for a long time, not even his parents. He only returned ten years ago when his father died, to take over the farm. His mother passed away last winter, since when he has lived alone. And apparently he is still in love with Mme Avore."

"Well, she's a widow now, so . . . Surely nothing is so bad between the families that they couldn't make up?"

"Around here, there is one thing that *is* that bad. The family of M. Avore were suspected of being collaborators during the war. Most things can be forgiven. But not that. It is the reason why M. Charpet could hardly bring himself to speak to the man. He lost so many friends, many betrayed, and he will never forgive."

"Hang on a minute. I thought everyone in the village tried very hard to support M. Avore, even though he tried their patience again and again?"

"That was the mayor's idea. He thought that if the village showed it had forgiven Manuel Avore, other family feuds would end."

"Is the mayor a very religious man, then?" Penelope remembered the priest. "Forgiveness and all that."

Was there a ghost of a smile on the Frenchwoman's lips? "No, the mayor is not religious."

"So would you say that—"

But Penelope's opening to a trickier conversation about the Avore/Louchard draft contract was interrupted by a shout from the walled garden. The punk youth came running out, belligerence lost to panic.

"For goodness sake, what now?" asked Penelope.

"La piscine! Il y a un—"

The two women looked at each other aghast. They hurried in the direction of the pool.

M. Geret was standing frozen in the empty pool, looking towards the corner of the deep end where some leaves remained. They followed the direction of his outstretched arm.

This time the unwelcome guest was a live one, and it took a while to dispose of it. It was a brown snake, about a metre long. The ensuing palaver gave Penelope no chance to ask Clémence any more about the Louchards and the Avores, and any vested interest of her own in Le Chant d'Eau.

❧

ALONE AT last, Penelope made herself a cup of tea and fired up her laptop. Amazingly, the Internet connection was a lot faster than BT had been in Bolingbroke Drive. It was a matter of seconds before Google came up.

There was no news online about bones being found at St Merlot. Neither was there anything she hadn't already seen in the papers about the death of Manuel Avore.

Penelope turned to her next subject for research. She had no intention of letting herself be ridiculed without fighting back. Pages of axe images came up immediately. She scrolled through them and eventually found what she was looking for. She double-checked it against the picture on her phone.

Then she keyed the make of the axe—Strauss—into the web search. The page loaded. She clicked around the website. Astonishingly, the Germanic name belonged to a firm in Dagenham, England, that exported across Europe. She ran a finger down through the countries listed until she reached France. Another click.

There were only seven shops that stocked Strauss axes and knives. Penelope's excitement grew as she went through the list. Three around Paris, far too distant to be significant. One in Lyon, ditto. One near the German border, which could also be discounted. That left two. There was an outlet in Nice, which was a possibility, albeit a slim one.

"Yesss!" Penelope gave a most unladylike punch to the air. Vaucluse, the last on the list. "Darrieux SARL, Rue des Monts Sauvages, Coustellet, Vaucluse."

Coustellet was a large, flat, almost industrial village on the main road from Avignon. She had driven through it but never stopped there. It seemed too good to be true, but surely it was possible that this was where the axe had been bought.

She allowed herself a single glass of rosé that night. She had work in the morning.

20

PENELOPE JUMPED INTO THE RANGE Rover after a black coffee breakfast. If she could help the police—not catch a murderer all on her own, obviously, but show she was an upstanding citizen—she would be accepted all the sooner in St Merlot. That was how Penelope rationalised her plan. All she wanted was a normal life, but to get that she had to *do* something, especially as she still had a gut feeling that her suspicions about the axe were correct. It was all very well for Chief Reyssens to laugh at her, but that didn't make him right.

Professor Fletcher had always trusted her instincts. Penelope's excellent memory and great grasp of detail had sometimes led to connections that senior professionals had overlooked. She couldn't override her sense that this was yet another example of a busy man, in this case the chief of police, being too quick to seize on what he wanted to believe.

Coustellet announced itself with a hypermarket and a cluster of bakeries, one of which had a lengthy queue outside and a small forecourt that was heaving like a bumper car rink at a fairground. The other was deserted. She turned left at the crossroads and found herself a space in a vast car park.

This large, workaday village where the Petit Luberon mountain ridge came to an end was an odd mix of wine cooperatives, modern streets, and business premises. A butcher's shop stood between a sushi restaurant and a store that seemed to market a combination of organic food and hard bread at eye-wateringly high prices. A computer shop was shuttered.

Penelope consulted the map she'd sketched roughly from the Internet, walked on, and found a road that joined at a right angle: rue des Monts Sauvages. And there, a long yellow sign: Darrieux. An ironmonger's with a display of power tools and a hundred-and-one varieties of hammer. The premises next door had posters of agricultural machinery in the window and an office.

Inside the shop were long rows of shiny new tools, hanging on pegs. And there, halfway along one wall, was a selection of axes. Her heart pounded as she searched for an exact match.

There it was.

She approached the large man at the service counter. "Bonjour, monsieur. I am looking for an axe to use in my garden."

"Oui, madame."

"Could you show me the axes you have, please?"

"Oui, madame." The shopkeeper made no effort to move from behind the counter.

This is not going well, thought Penelope. How am I going to be able to engage him in conversation about the virtues of various makes of axe, if he only knows how to say "Oui, madame"?

"Could you help me select an axe—which do you think is the best make?"

"That depends, madame."

Penelope felt a glimmer of hope at having upped his vocabulary, and launched in, hoping her French was up to the job.

"I have a friend who came in here a while ago and purchased a Strauss axe. For general work in the garden. She lent it to me, and I found it was exactly what I needed. Ivy! Very good for cutting down ivy," embellished Penelope as inspiration struck. "Perhaps you have one of those?"

The man exhaled, rather impertinently in Penelope's opinion, and eased his belly round the side of the counter. He led her over to the wall where the axes hung.

"I think it might be this one," said Penelope casually, pointing at the medium-weight Strauss. "I don't suppose you have a record of everyone who has bought this axe from you—just so I can be absolutely sure it's the correct one?"

He shook his head.

"Ah," said Penelope. "Is it a popular model?"

"Not really."

A man of few words, clearly. He stared, but then said, "Why are you so interested in this Strauss axe?"

Was she acting very suspiciously? However, Penelope had anticipated this and prepared her cover story. "Ah, you are too clever for a Secret Shopper, monsieur! I am from Dagenham in England," she said with graceful self-importance. "I work for the excellent toolmaking company of Strauss. We wish to know the social profile of all the customers who buy our axes in France. This is part of a Europe-wide marketing assessment, most important for future designs!"

The shopkeeper nodded sagely, and Penelope breathed again, until he spoke again.

"Your company is indeed most diligent, madame. One of your agents has already spoken to me this week!"

"What?" Penelope snapped to full attention. "Ah, I must apologise for our . . . overenthusiasm. As you can see, we take our duty to customers—and retailers—very seriously indeed."

"Yes, one of your colleagues came in asking the same questions about the same axe."

Penelope grew flustered.

"One of my colleagues . . . oh . . . yes, of course . . . he was due to come down here . . ."

"*She*, madame."

"Of course, *she*! What was I thinking? *She* was due to come down here to help me—and she must have started early, been passing . . . something like that!" Thinking on her feet, Penelope added, as casually as she could, "She must have been our French agent. I have never met her—what did she look like, madame, madame—"

"Very elegant. I must admit I was surprised that such a petite, elegant woman would have an interest in Strauss tools. Mme Val . . . Valin, something like that I think—blond hair, a typically Parisian look and accent."

Penelope wasn't sure she managed to hide her shock. "Ah, yes. Mme Valencourt. I will talk to her and explain that you can send all the details you find to me, as I am from the parent company."

"I have given her all the help I can."

Penelope felt as excited as she was irritated. So Clémence Valencourt was also on the case, was she? The same busybody who was always telling her to drop it and leave it to the experts was doing her own information gathering on the quiet.

"We shall see about that!" she said as she got into the Range Rover and slammed the door.

21

PENELOPE STARED AT THE HANDSET for her newly installed
landline, working out what she wanted to say to Clémence Valencourt, and whether it might be better just to present herself at
the estate agency in Ménerbes, when it rang in her hand.

"Bonjour, Mme Keet. This is Laurent Millais."

"Oh!" she squeaked. How on earth had the mayor got her
number? "Hello."

"I was wondering if you would like to come to lunch with me.
It is very short notice, I am sorry."

Penelope surveyed her kitchen table, on which was arrayed
a shocking amount of food, purchased on the trip home. She
shook her head once again at her inability to control herself in
the face of French temptation. "Now, you mean?"

"I hope to entice you away from your house. I would be most
pleased if you would have lunch with me today. There are a
number of matters we should discuss. Shall we say, about one
o'clock?"

"Let me consult my diary," Penelope said, and waited a few
seconds as she rustled the pages of *La Provence*. "Yes, monsieur le
maire, I find I am free, and I would be delighted to lunch with
you."

"Excellent. Shall we meet at Le Sanglier Paresseux?"

The lazy boar? "Is that a restaurant or an item on the menu?"

The mayor laughed. Was he buttering her up for something?

"It is a restaurant not far away, in Caseneuve," he said. "It is very good."

"I'll see you there, then. One o'clock?"

"*Impeccable.*"

Penelope moved swiftly. There was major work to be done, not least on her face. This time she was going to meet him with immaculate makeup. She had washed her hair that morning, and for once it had fallen into the style it was supposed to. She selected a burgundy linen dress that showed off her waist and worked well with the red-gold of her hair. Though why she was bothering to make an effort, she really didn't know. Just her own pride, she supposed, as she slipped on a pair of high-heeled sandals. A chunky gold necklace completed the look.

The question was, would it be a good idea to confide in the mayor? Could she trust him, or was he just trying to keep her on-side to protect the villagers in his precious St Merlot? The more she found out about the village, the more its feuds and machinations dismayed her. Or were all small communities the same, the world over?

❧

SHE FOUND Le Sanglier Paresseux easily enough, in the lee of Caseneuve's austere, menacing castle. Laurent Millais was waiting for her at a table outside, under a vine canopy from which hung bunches of purple grapes, close to ripeness. The views from the terrace stretched west over the length of the valley towards Avignon, framed by blue-grey mountains on either side.

He stood to greet her, which was a magnificent view in itself. Penelope noted the surreptitious glances from ladies at other tables. "Is it OK to sit here," he asked, "or do you prefer to be inside?"

"Outside is perfect. I'm British—you have to drag us inside in summer, even if the sun hasn't been spotted through the clouds for days." Oh, lor', thought Penelope, I hope I'm not going to start burbling. "I haven't been here before. It's lovely," she said in a slightly more measured way as she took a seat at a table laid with stiffly laundered linen.

"The village has been, as you say, put on the map by this restaurant. Now—will you join me in an aperitif? They serve an exquisite blackberry kir."

"That sounds wonderful. Yes, please."

The mayor had a twinkle in his eye when he placed the order. Penelope told herself, not for the first time in his presence, to get a grip.

She looked at the menu. "What do you recommend?"

"Take the pork."

Penelope suppressed a giggle. That smile of his was quite saucy, she decided. Surely he wasn't flirting with her. They hadn't even had a drink yet. Far more likely he was laughing at her.

"The pork here is excellent," he reiterated. "The *pata negra*—from acorn-fed pigs."

"I will have pork, then," she said robustly, to show that whatever he was playing at, it wasn't going to affect her. This was business as far as she was concerned. She was being given a chance to find out all kinds of information and she was not going to pass it up.

"M. Millais, I—"

"Laurent, please."

"Laurent—"

"May I call you Penny?"

"Of course. Now, I wanted to ask—"

The sparkling blackberry kirs arrived, along with some delightful *amuses-bouche*. Laurent had a quick chat with the maître d', who obviously knew him well, and then started telling her about the places in England he'd visited. His favourite city was Brighton, and the worst place he'd experienced as a visitor was the Elephant and Castle, on the basis that there was nothing about it that remotely lived up to its name. "I love to go to the theatre in Drury Lane and to the Ritz for dinner!"

"Ooh, yes," said Penelope, rapidly losing her inhibitions as the aperitif hit the spot. "That pink and gilded dining room is to die for!"

"Ah, yes," said Laurent, as if that reminded him. "Penny, you may be wondering why I wished to speak with you."

She came down to earth with a bump. She shouldn't lose sight of the fact that the only reason she was here having lunch with this man was that she had racked up two dead bodies since her arrival, and the mayor was on a damage limitation exercise. "I should think that you have some news for me about the police investigations."

"Well, in a way, I have. It is a matter of some delicacy, and I wanted to be away from St Merlot to discuss it—you never know who is listening at the door to my office!"

"Fire away!" An unfortunate turn of phrase, in the circumstances. She flushed. "I mean, tell me what it is. Do the police know who the bones in the chapel belonged to?"

"They are still working on that."

"Did they lift out the whole skeleton?"

"I can't say."

"If the skull is there, they'll be looking at dental records."

"I am sure the investigators are making progress. Though that reminds me. We have discovered some interesting information about Manuel Avore that we did not know before. It seems that he was a more serious gambler than we thought."

"But I was told he had no money," she said.

"He did not have money. That was the problem. He borrowed heavily from the black market to fund his betting."

"So he borrowed, and then couldn't pay it back, I guess."

"Exactly. He gambled it all away, or spent it on drink."

"How has all this not come out until now? I find it very hard to believe that no one knew. Surely his wife had some idea?"

"Apparently not. Until the enforcers from the gangs who use the casinos came menacing at their door——"

"More than one?"

"Sadly, yes."

"Where is this going?" asked Penelope.

The mayor leaned forward conspiratorially and continued, "Well, from this point we only have theories, but one thing is clear. It is a very unwise move to borrow money to play at the casino, and not to pay it back. Especially when the lenders have links to the Marseille underworld."

"Why Marseille?"

"Most of the organised crime around here is centred in Marseille—you remember, The French Connection, no?" He paused theatrically to look right and left. "Around 'ere it is small frying, but they are still vicious, especially to their debtors."

Penelope felt sorry for the small, bitter man who had shouted at her in her garden that first evening. And even more so for his wife. "Poor man, a gambling addict too. He must have been desperate." She suddenly had a thought. "Did you see the playing card in the pool when his body was being removed?"

"A playing card? No."

"I did. And what's more, I think that it might be a link between the two deaths. Don't you?"

The mayor studied his place setting, then looked up. "If I can give you some advice, madame? I think that you should allow the police to conduct their investigations. I know that you want to help, but there is no advantage in pushing your theories on them. It does no good."

"There's something else, though," said Penelope. "And it's been bothering me. The day we found the body in the pool, I described the man who came into my garden the evening before, and you said straightaway, 'That would have been Manuel Avore.' But if the body was Avore, it can't have been him I saw alive. There just wasn't time for rigor mortis to pass and the body's arm to become limp. Have the police said anything about that?"

There was an awkward pause. "No, not to me. Does it matter? The body was that of Avore. We can be sure of that. Could you be wrong about the time? Or perhaps all the alcohol in the body made a difference."

Penelope frowned. "But—"

"Now, you have met your neighbour Pierre Louchard, I hear."

"I have, yes."

"What kind of liqueur did he give you?"

"How did you know about that?"

Laurent tapped the side of his nose. "Was it plum brandy?"

"It was, actually."

"That is very good news for you. It means he likes you. Or he has decided to like you. It's a kind of village code. Since the days of the Resistance during the war. Plums mean 'a friend.' "

It made M. Charpet's little gift left on the wall all the more touching.

"It's astonishing how often people here still talk about the war and the Resistance. Is everyone's opinion of Manuel Avore still influenced by his family's alleged collaboration back then?"

"Probably, yes."

The food arrived, two very appetising plates of glistening pork, delicately presented, and the conversation moved on from the unfortunate and unmourned man.

A bottle of Vacqueyras was opened and tasted with some ceremony. Against her better judgement—red wine at lunchtime was just asking for trouble, in Penelope's experience—she accepted a glass. It tasted sublime.

Penelope listened to what Laurent was saying about why this wine was typical of the region's terrain and tried to remember the questions she wanted to ask. Two drinks had already made him quite dangerously attractive.

It seemed it really was true that everything stopped for lunch in France, and that included spoiling the taste of the food with talk of murder.

The mayor steered the conversation to her family, and she told him about Justin and Lena, and the ruinous lack of discipline where Lena's sons Zack and Xerxes were concerned.

"You are a grandmother? How can this be possible?" exclaimed the mayor.

Penelope blushed, furious with herself that she had mentioned it. "I married very young . . . practically a child bride. . . . Actually, Justin and Lena are my stepchildren."

She knew from what Frankie had passed on from Clémence that Laurent was divorced, with an ex-wife in Paris. She wondered in passing whether he had a new partner now, in addition to his dalliance with Clémence. Best not to ask. But she was determined to take the chance to find out a bit more about what he had been doing in Bonnieux with Louchard and the silver fox in the red Ferrari. She seized on the subject of marriage, tenuous though it was.

"I visited the Abbaye de Sénanque for the first time the other day," she said, "Do they do weddings there?"

The mayor's eyes twinkled. "Weddings? No."

"Oh."

"Are you considering getting married again?"

"Me? No! Absolutely not. No, I just wondered. It would be a very lovely place to get married in, that's all."

"Ah."

"There's a priory just outside St Merlot, isn't there?"

"Yes. Le Prieuré des Gentilles Merlotiennes."

"Are they nuns—the Kind Ladies of Merlot?"

"Sadly, the sisters are no longer there. They had to leave in the fifteenth century due to decadent behaviour."

"Oh, my. The building is still standing?"

"It is."

"What is it used for these days?"

"Nothing, currently. Though some interesting possibilities are being investigated."

"Sounds intriguing. Tell me more."

The mayor grinned, but did not elaborate.

She put down her knife and fork for an elegant pause, hoping he would fill the silence with some details.

"So, Penny, apart from the obvious recent problems, how are you enjoying your new life in Provence?"

Disappointing. "I love it here. Despite what has happened, I am very pleased to have come to St Merlot. I just hope that once everything has calmed down after, you know, we can all move on from it."

Laurent smiled. "And we are pleased that you have joined us as well. There are some who would prefer no one from outside ever to own properties here, but without the foreign money, there would be many empty houses."

Penelope thought for a moment. "So you only tolerate us for the money we bring in, then?"

"No, that is not true. Well, maybe some people think that, but not all. You add colour and interest!"

"That doesn't make me feel as bad as it might. I've already

worked out that I will always be a foreigner here—but the definition of a foreigner starts very few kilometres away. The chief of police, for example. He's a foreigner, and he only comes from Apt!"

"Very true!" The mayor saluted her perception with a raised glass.

"Why don't you like him?" she asked, pressing home her momentary advantage.

"Because he is the worst kind of foreigner. He makes no effort to understand us!"

They both laughed.

"It's the same the world over in country places," said Penelope.

He drained the bottle of red wine into their glasses—how on earth had they finished it?—and then insisted they order a dessert entitled "Le Tout Chocolat."

"Oh, all right, then. If we must," said Penelope, hoping he understood the ironic tone in her voice. There again, he probably just thought she was greedy, which—sadly—was fair enough.

Over coffee and some strange local liqueur that came in a bottle shaped like a large aubergine (refused by Penelope), she tried to find out a bit more about him.

"How long have you been mayor of St Merlot?"

"Almost four years."

"Is it a full-time job?"

"Not really, not for me."

"Do you have another job?" She remembered what Frankie had found out about him having all kinds of strings to his bow. She was hoping he would tell her more, perhaps about working in television.

Laurent sat back in his seat and gave her a grin. "This has been an unexpected pleasure," he said.

It certainly had. Penelope felt neither too full nor too tipsy, but just right.

"Are you going to see Clémence Valencourt anytime soon, by the way?" she asked, as innocently as she could.

"I expect so. She is often in the area, always here, there, everywhere."

"You're telling me," said Penelope. "She's very . . . busy. Always popping up in the most unexpected places."

"That is true."

"You and she know each other quite well, don't you?"

He raised his palms in a gesture of admission that could have meant everything, or nothing at all.

"Her house is beautiful. What does M. Valencourt do that allows them to live in such splendour?"

"Mon dieu! Is that the time? I am sorry, I must get back to St Merlot!"

He called for the bill, which he insisted on paying, waving away her protests and joking with the waiter about getting back to his office, where the administration of his village would be missing him. They left together, and she looked around for his flashy Mercedes, but there was no sign of it.

"Would you mind giving me a ride back?" he asked.

He must have had a lift there. So he hadn't been quite as reckless with his lunchtime drinking as she had supposed. Just as well she hadn't gone mad.

He climbed into the Range Rover, after going automatically to the wrong side first. "It is so strange, having the steering wheel on the right side of the car! It is very hard to drive on our roads, no?"

"It's fine if you go carefully. Actually, it's quite useful when you have to pull right over to the side of the road to pass another vehicle—you can see exactly how far you are from the sheer drop on some of your hillside roads!"

She drove extra cautiously back to St Merlot along the steep, winding shortcut he showed her.

The only car they met came bucketing out of nowhere towards them in the middle of the road.

"Oh là là—the lunchtime drivers are always a danger."

"But it's getting on for four o'clock!" said Penelope.

"Yes, now they are returning to work."

Penelope slowed to a nervy crawl as they approached the next bend.

"Ah, look! Did you see that sign there? The lane leads to the best goats' cheese in the region."

For the rest of the journey, until she dropped him off at the *mairie*, he held forth on the best restaurants in the area and the recommended back routes for drivers to take after they had wined and dined well.

So she never did ask his opinion on why the estate agent was making her own inquiries about the provenance of the axe. Or get any traction on the papers she found. Nor really understand why he had asked her to lunch in the first place.

She pulled into the drive, and immediately all thought vanished. The door to her house was hanging drunkenly upon its hinges. It had been broken open.

22

SHE KNEW SHE SHOULD TELEPHONE the police, but the thought of Reyssens's curling lip was too much for her. Maybe she could telephone Clémence. But could she trust her? Why exactly had her estate agent been asking about the axe at the shop in Coustellet?

Penelope put the kettle on for a cup of tea to give herself some thinking time, then switched it off again. She looked closely around the kitchen. Had her papers been disturbed? Hard to tell—she had left them in a bit of a mess. Had she left her computer on when she left the house? She might have done, given that she had rushed upstairs to get tarted up. Could an intruder have been checking her Internet searches? She would need to be sure.

Then she felt sick to her stomach. Had Laurent Millais deliberately lured her away in order to give that intruder a few hours when the coast was clear? *I hope to entice you away from your house.* Hadn't he actually said that?

She called the police.

The conversation with Laurent replayed on a loop in her head. Was he the LM on the draft contract she stumbled across at the priory? And what would it mean if he were? What about the Marseille mafia theory? Was he serious, or was that just a bum steer to frighten her off?

One thing she had noticed was the way he spoke English.

When he'd first appeared in her garden the day Avore was fished out of the pool, the mayor had sounded like a Frenchman straight from central casting. The same when they were discussing M. Charpet at the *mairie*, the old man's Resistance record and how he could not possibly be implicated in any crime. But during their conversation over lunch, his accent had been much lighter. Perhaps high emotion affected his linguistic skills.

He too had warned her off getting under the police investigators' feet. Perhaps that was why he told her about their current line of inquiry—so that she'd feel she was being kept in the loop with no need for any more input from her.

Any other middle-aged woman newly arrived in the South of France might have taken the hint. But Penelope Kite had form in picking up details that some of the best Home Office forensic pathology experts had somehow missed.

As Professor Fletcher's PA, Penelope had helped prepare his autopsy reports for the police and the courts but rarely went into an autopsy room or to crime scenes. But she saw all the photographs. Her first intervention came when an ex-convict, who had taken up knitting while in prison, was arrested for murder shortly after he was released. His fingerprints were found on knitting needles and a half-finished scarf.

It was a homely detail that most women would have registered—though clearly those working on this case did not. Nor indeed, did the real killer. "That scarf is not being knitted," Penelope informed her boss. "That's crochet work."

Eventually, detectives proved that the knitting needles had been stolen from the prison craft room and used to frame the suspect by another ex-prisoner.

As her confidence grew, Penelope became bolder.

She saved the day after a vital clue was lost in a case involving the murder of a young woman. When car upholstery samples recovered from the vehicle used to abduct the victim went missing, Penelope doggedly worked out that the samples had been sent to the wrong lab for analysis, allowing the prosecution to go ahead.

Another time, a fingerprint expert reported a negative result, but Penelope's intuition told her that something was wrong. The scientist had difficulty concentrating when she called him. Over tea and cake at a café opposite the Home Office labs, she offered the young scientist a sympathic ear as he told her about the problems with his unfaithful girlfriend. Then she quietly got a second opinion on the fingerprint. It was a positive match. The scientist was given compassionate leave and several cold cases were re-opened, resulting in the conviction of a serial killer.

Back off now? The heck she would.

So Avore had been a serious gambler. Was it significant? When she considered the bones in the chapel, the body in the pool, and the most puzzling aspect—the ace of spades at both scenes—she decided it had to be.

Penelope sat tight for the rest of the day, waiting for the police to arrive, which they finally did around teatime. A very youthful officer surveyed the damage, dusted for fingerprints, called a locksmith for her, took diligent notes, and asked questions she could not answer. Who could have wanted to get into her house? She had no idea. Had anything been taken? Nothing that she could see. Could they have been looking for something? Possibly. But what? The murder of Manuel Avore and the skeleton were not even mentioned.

The locksmith arrived while the officer was still with her, and between them the door was fixed in double-quick time. It was as if they wanted to make sure she could cause no more trouble.

Penelope's concerns were swatted away.

"If nothing has been perturbed," said the young policeman in English, "then it was probably the wind that attacked the door."

"Seriously?"

"Very great winds come up this hill. Violent! There is no breaking of the wood in this door. See? Maybe you did not shut it properly when you leave?"

She was certain she had, but there was little to be gained by arguing.

❧

NEXT MORNING, Penelope went up to the village square. If she was going to turn detective—and let's face it, that decision already seemed to have been made almost without any conscious will, her natural reluctance to get involved having been well and truly overtaken by events—she needed to meet some more of the locals in normal circumstances.

At eight o'clock, the boulangerie-bar was crowded. Penelope felt honour-bound to support local businesses, but she feared for her waistline in the presence of this baker's sublime *pain tradition* with its thin crispy crust and soft interior, his sugar-dusted twists of *sacristan*, his round, custard-filled *tartes Tropéziennes*, cinnamon-flavoured palmier biscuits, *religieuses* made of choux pastry, filled with *crème pâtissière* and dripping with chocolate, delicate macarons, mille-feuilles, and madeleines in decadent flavours of violet and wild strawberry. Discovering sweet treats she had never even known existed was going to be a severe test of willpower.

Penelope joined the queue with a nodded greeting to all. She breathed in the heavenly aroma of newly baked loaves and caramelised sugar, vanilla, and coffee. Was she imagining it, or were there a few sidelong glances, as if the locals knew exactly who she was, but were not inclined to introduce themselves? She pulled her shoulders back and half smiled before returning her gaze, as any normal person would, to the glories on display at the counter.

A large woman wrapped bread in paper and put cakes and tarts in white card boxes, while the baker himself—so Penelope assumed from his white hat and apron—kept up a repartee with the customers. The name Jacques Correa was embroidered on the apron, just as a renowned chef would have on his breast. Jacques! Penelope did a double take.

So much had happened, she had almost forgotten her quest to find a Jacques in the village with a motive to kill Avore. It was a common name, wasn't it? This one seemed an unlikely candidate. He was fortyish and stocky, with strong forearms from kneading and hefting trays of dough, but he moved around like a dancer on his small feet, darting here and there, a wide grin on a wide face, pointing out specialities and new recipes, a cup of espresso coffee in hand.

Then it was Penelope's turn. "Bonjour, monsieur, madame, une baguette et un croissant, s'il vous plaît."

The woman, doughy around the middle herself, hair in a bun like a cottage loaf, reached round for the bread.

"La dame anglaise? Le Chant d'Eau?" said the baker. "On vous attendait—we are waiting for you! You are going to be a good customer. Don't you like pâtisseries? Your friend, she say you love pâtisseries!"

"Oh, I do." Penelope sighed, aware of the other customers earwigging. "Very much. A bit too much."

"But you must try my puits d'amour—the little well of love, yes? The jelly of redcurrant inside the cake, a surface of caramel."

How could she refuse? She purchased one, and the generously sized croissant, along with the baguette, a copy of *La Provence*, and a cup of coffee with milk to drink at one of the tables outside. Morning coffee while improving her French with the newspaper was quickly becoming a pleasurable habit.

She scanned a few pages, taking in a dull summary of the lack of progress in the Avore murder at St Merlot. If there was any new information, the police were certainly not releasing it. A flick of another page, however, revealed something intriguing.

"Penny!"

The interruption came tilting across the gravel on high heels towards her. Almost as if I've been followed, thought Penelope. She wouldn't put it past her.

"Mme Valencourt." She nodded, stiffly.

The Frenchwoman clearly noted the formality of the greeting. She asked, with a haughty froideur in return, if she could join Penelope.

"Please do."

"I'm glad I saw you. There is something I need to talk to you about, Penny."

"Why, what's the matter?"

"I was phoned last night by Laurent."

"Laurent the mayor?"

"Who other? Yes, the mayor."

Penelope raised an eyebrow as the other woman, just for a split second, showed some discomposure and the merest hint of a blush.

"Oh, Penny, do not leap to the conclusions! In fact, that is what Laurent wanted to talk to me about. He thinks that you are getting too involved in the investigation, that you are asking too many questions."

"Really?" Penelope was not overjoyed at the thought of being discussed like this.

"You must understand, it is very embarrassing for him—a murder in his village, and now the mysterious bones! Such things have not happened around here for years, and it is important that St Merlot is seen as a calm and peaceful village. He is worried that it will affect his chances of reelection next month. And perhaps he does not want one of the big families in the village to be suspected. There are many votes at stake."

"So just hush everything up, then."

"I am glad you understand, Penny."

"But Clémence, here's the thing. When I had lunch with Laurent yesterday—"

The estate agent did an almost imperceptible double take.

"He rang up out of the blue and asked me—and he was the one who did all the talking about the Avore case. All I did was listen. Well, I may have asked a few questions, but only conversationally. And you're right"—Penelope put up her hand to show she would not be stopped—"I do want answers to plenty of questions. How can I not be curious when St Merlot is turning up corpses under every stone! Something is going on around here, and we can't just hush everything up."

Clémence looked startled as Penelope unleashed her pent-up frustrations, but let her go on.

Penelope lowered her voice, hoping that no one nearby had understood what she had said. "This man Avore, horrible as he was, was murdered," she hissed. "Whoever did it seems to have tried, not very well, to frame M. Charpet for it, and to have chosen to do the deed just as I was moving into a property that had been empty for years. Why do it *then*? To scare me off? To make life difficult for me? To implicate me in the crime? I don't understand at all, so yes, I do want to ask questions about it!"

The estate agent opened her mouth.

But Penelope held up her palm and pressed on. "Because there's something else. I went for a walk and almost got shot. There could very easily have been another dead body in St Merlot.

Everyone says it was the hunters. But what if it wasn't? Is anyone interested in that? And just yesterday my house was broken into, but nothing was taken. Why?"

"I am sorry to hear that, Penny. I am sure the police will do their best to find out who broke in."

Penelope gave a humph of disbelief. "I doubt it. A very young officer told me it was probably the wind!"

"Ah. That I cannot say. But let us think about the shots. Hunters go hunting at this time of year. They are overexcited to start their sport again. Maybe not so skilled, as they have not practised for months."

"I admire your sangfroid, but it was a bit bloody close for comfort." Penelope had old-fashioned notions about the repercussions of shots being fired at Englishwomen abroad. "What if someone was out to get me? The authorities really should do something about this. These people are . . . are . . . a danger to themselves and others!"

Clémence sat back throughout this outburst. Then she gave a little pout. "But the police . . ."

"The police know that what happened to Manuel Avore *was* murder—but what are they doing about it?"

"They are, how do you put it in English, chasing after the suspicions?"

"Pursuing leads? Clémence, pursuit involves the concept of motion. I do not see motion of any kind in this case! I think they just want it to go away."

"And would that be a bad thing? Avore was a very unpleasant man. His wife must be much happier now."

"Well, shall we find out?"

"What are you suggesting, Penny?"

"That you and I go and see her . . ."

"Mon dieu, we cannot do that!"

"Says who?"

"The mayor will not like it! And the police . . ."

Penelope decided it was time to play her trump card.

"But Clémence—you *must* be interested in what really happened!"

"I think that we should leave it to the experts."

"So, it was just chance that you went to the shop in Coustellet to ask about the axe?"

"How do you know that?"

"Because I did, too."

For a few moments the two women glared at each other. Then the Parisienne shrugged her elegant shoulders. "It seems, Penny, that we are both more interested than we should be."

"So was that why you kept coming over to see me?"

"It might have been."

"So, are we on the same side here? Two nosy parkers . . ."

"That means . . . Oh." Clémence tapped her pretty little nose. "I think I understand."

They both smiled.

"So," asked Penelope, "have you found out anything about the axe and who might have bought it?"

"No, not yet."

"It can't have given a good impression that we both went to the shop and asked the same questions. Maybe it would be better to work together. What do you think?"

Mme Valencourt shrugged.

"Yes?"

"It makes sense," the estate agent said at last.

Penelope raised her coffee cup. "To the Luberon ladies' detective agency!"

"L'entente cordiale investigative! But be careful," said her new partner slyly, looking around over her shoulder. "Laurent must never know."

"All right by me. Now, have you seen this?" Penelope pushed the newspaper across the table. "I spotted it just as you arrived. But I don't think we should talk about it here."

⁂

THEY DROVE down the hill in their respective cars. Penelope led in the Range Rover, like a mother duck keeping an excitable chick in line behind her.

"Don't you ever have work to do?" she asked as they got out at Le Chant d'Eau.

"It's a very quiet time from now until Christmas. But I want to check what M. Geret has done with your swimming pool."

On the kitchen terrace, Penelope pointed to an advertisement in the paper.

FÊTE VOTIVE DE SAINT MERLOT

2–3 septembre

Grand concours de Pétanque
Aioli—Place de la Mairie

Grand Bal avec L'Orchestre Echeverria
Grand Prix—Meilleur Tracteur du Luberon 2017

"Look who is sponsoring the competition to find the Best Tractor in the Luberon? It seems to be a shop in Coustellet—"

"Darrieux SARL!" read out Clémence.

"So what I want to know is, what on earth is a shop in Coustellet doing sponsoring an event in a small village miles away? Do they do this every year? Is it just a coincidence?"

Mme Valencourt shook her head. "I don't know."

"So where do we go from here?" Penelope couldn't wait to get started. "We are going to get to the bottom of this, even if no one else wants to."

"I wonder who is on the fête committee . . ."

"The mayor would know. But you say we can't ask him."

"I will ask M. Charpet," said Clémence. "He will know."

"What can I do then?"

"Perhaps you should pay Mme Avore a visit, simply as a courtesy from a new neighbour."

"I was going to, but then I thought, wouldn't that be odd, in the circumstances?"

"Normally, perhaps, yes. But I hear that she is now a very happy woman. Her situation is not a normal one. Why not walk over to the Avore house now? You know exactly where it is, don't you?"

"It's hard to miss."

"Should I take anything?"

"Not in the circumstances. Go to pay your respects, introduce yourself—and see if she tells you anything useful."

Penelope walked back up the unmade track to the ramshackle house on the main road. It still did not look inviting. Large cracks issued up one of the walls, and ivy had spread from the trees to cover most of the roof. Rusted farm implements lay in the driveway, almost hidden by the long grass. It radiated neglect, and Penelope found it hard to believe, even now, that Mme Avore had not gone long ago. There was police tape across the door, and no sign of life. She knocked—it was an old-fashioned lion's-paw knocker, much corroded—but got no answer.

She returned home to find Clémence sitting on the terrace, absorbed in the private property advertisements of *La Provence*.

"No good," said Penelope. "Mme Avore wasn't there. It looks like the police have been in."

"Maybe she is staying with a friend," said Clémence.

"Do you have someone in mind?" Penelope thought she could see where this was going, but she wanted to hear it.

"Your neighbour from the other end of the lane? M. Louchard . . . ?"

"Who has always loved her . . . and now there is no obstacle to them being together," supplied Penelope. She sat down on the stone wall. "Is that what you're saying, that Avore's wife and M. Louchard could have killed him?"

"I don't know. I suppose we have to consider it."

"I have heard that he has a dark side."

"Who told you that?"

"Oh—" Penelope stopped. She was being indiscreet. "You know, I can't remember. Someone told Frankie, I think. Said he was a bit volatile. Some of these ex-army types can be, can't they? They find it hard to adjust."

"A man with a passion, perhaps?"

We are in France, supposed Penelope. "But you can't put everything down to affairs of the heart, can you?" Or maybe they could.

"It is possible, that is all I have said."

"You're right, it is possible. But is it likely?"

"That is what we must find out."

Penelope was silent as she wondered how they were going to do that. "Did Louchard have any business dealings with Avore?"

"I wouldn't know."

"Nothing . . . that could have linked them contractually?"

"It's unlikely, but I can ask around. Now, there is good news, Penny. M. Geret has done an excellent job on the swimming pool, as I knew he would. It is *impeccable*! You must profit from it.

September is a marvellous month for swimming here. No wasps! You swim, you relax, and you try to enjoy being in Provence!"

"Wouldn't that be nice! Some peace and quiet at last."

They parted, having promised to keep each other posted with any developments. They also decided to go to the St Merlot fête that coming weekend.

⚜

PEACE AND quiet would have to wait, thought Penelope grimly. She watched for the sight of Clémence's red blur taking the bend down to Apt, and went back out to her car. She wondered whether the baguette and cake she'd deliberately left under the table at the boulangerie would still be there, or whether she'd have to buy another. It didn't much matter either way.

It was close to ten o'clock when she arrived, and the breakfast rush at the bakery had ended. There was no bag under the table where she had been sitting. Good, she thought.

She went inside.

The large woman smiled, dipped down, and held up her shopping bag.

"Merci beaucoup!" said Penelope, grinning as she tapped the side of her head in mock despair.

"Can I get you anything else—another coffee?"

Penelope was already buzzing, but it seemed her best chance for a chat. "Yes, please. But with lots of milk, a grand crème."

"I'll bring it to you outside."

"I can wait. I want another look at your wonderful pâtisserie. Is it all made here?"

"Everything. My husband gets up every morning at four to start baking. I make everything ready for him at midnight before I sleep. And I make the macarons and the petits gâteaux génoises, the mousse cakes. My specialities. The trick is in the precise consistency of the egg whites and sugar, and the very best chocolate. We met at bakery school, you know."

"Quite a partnership," said Penelope. She was just digging in before steering the conversation to less mouthwatering and more useful territory when Jacques Correa emerged from a fringed partition behind the counter. He had obviously started another batch of baking. Sweat trickled from his hairline, leaving rivulets in the flour dust on his temples.

"Second visit of the day—you are French already, madame!"

"Oh? Does everyone come here twice a day?"

"The French are very demanding. The bread must be absolutely fresh. The precise texture of crispness in the crust. The centre must be soft but still chewy. But the bread lives and changes. What is perfect at lunchtime will be no good at dinner." His dark eyes were intense as he spoke about his craft.

Then he changed the subject abruptly. "I am sorry to hear of your break-in, madame."

How on earth did he know about that? Penelope supposed it was the efficiency of the rumour mill in small French villages.

"It's not so bad, thank you. They didn't take anything," she said. Then almost to herself, "And I suppose it is one village crime that can't be blamed on Manuel Avore."

She didn't need to reply as he launched into a torrent of words, the name Manuel Avore prominent among them. How was she bearing up? What a terrible thing to happen on the first day in her new house. Oh, they all knew all about it all right. Of course they did. How could you keep a secret in a village like St Merlot?

"Did you dislike M. Avore too?" asked Penelope.

The baker pulled down the corners of his generously expressive mouth. "Me? No. With me, he was OK. I felt sorry for him. I would give him the stale bread for nothing. Huh, not really stale, just not up to the perfection that everyone else expects. Maybe some pâtisserie that was past its best."

"You're the first person I've met who has a good word to say about him." He was not the Jacques who wished Avore gone, she thought. That must be someone else.

"Bread is life. It has to be made and given with a good heart."

His wife nodded sagely. "How are you getting on with your surviving neighbour—Pierre Louchard?"

"Well . . . OK, I think."

"He has been polite, he hasn't tried to—Ah, Jean-Luc!"

Penelope turned round. A man stepped forward, and he and the baker clapped each other on the back. He nodded politely at her. She hoped he hadn't overheard too much of their chitchat.

"Welcome to St Merlot, madame," said Jean-Luc, affably enough. He was another good-looking man in his forties, not overly tall but with olive skin and lustrous dark hair. His jeans were patched with dust, but he was casually stylish. He too seemed to know without being told who she was.

"Thank you."

"How are you getting on? It was not good, what happened. We were all horrified."

"I'm doing well, in the circumstances."

"Glad to hear it." He extended his hand. "Jean-Luc. I own the garage over there, among other interests." He nodded in the direction of the picturesque little service station.

She shook it. "Penelope Kite."

"You've come for the peach and pistachio gâteau, I take it?" Correa addressed him. "Would you mind, Sylvie?"

"Ooh." Penelope gave an involuntary sigh. "That sounds lovely."

His wife fetched a large white box from the back. "Keep it in the fridge until six o'clock, then somewhere shady until around nine. You won't be eating it until nine, surely?"

"Perfect," said Jean-Luc. "By the way, did you hear about what's going on with the priest and his old friend?"

They were practised gossips. Penelope's ears were waggling, but they spoke so fast it was hard to understand, and they were careful not to drop too many actual names. She was longing to get on to the subject of the mayor, but then thought better of it. Whatever she said was bound to get back. She was going to have to play a long game here. Very possibly involving unwise quantities of pâtisserie.

AN INTERESTING morning, thought Penelope as she bit into the *puits d'amour*. The caramel on top cracked divinely on the tongue, rich with a hint of salt, while the redcurrant jelly filling was sharp against the sweetness of the spongy exterior. Jacques Correa was a baking genius.

He also heard and saw everything that went on in St Merlot, which could be very helpful. Had he been about to say something about Pierre Louchard when Jean-Luc came in? How had he found out about the break-in so quickly?

She entered the drive to find M. Charpet inspecting the repair of her front door. He smiled as she walked up.

"Madame, tout est bien!"

Penelope came close to shedding a little tear at the man's kindness.

"Ne t'inquiète pas. Don't worry. It will have been a few young idiots, nothing serious."

Penelope carried on smiling, and pumped his hand enthusiastically as he made ready to leave. But she did not share his optimism.

23

DIDIER THE ELECTRICIAN ROLLED UP with M at nine o'clock the next morning. Like the sun coming out from behind a dark cloud, he peeped round the back door, then held out a box of six speckled brown eggs. "Fresh from my hens. I heard about the break-in. I hope everything is all right. These are to cheer you up."

Before starting the rewiring of the ground floor, he had a look at a leaky pipe under the sink, fixing it with a monkey wrench, and recommended a bathroom supplier to ask for a quote. Then he set to work, whistling in tuneful bursts, while Penelope scraped Polyfilla into the cracks in the hall.

At eleven they had a tea break, with a bowl of water for M. She nuzzled Didier's hand, tail wagging joyously, as he produced some bone-shaped biscuits from his pocket. The dog had been so well behaved, you wouldn't have known she was there. Her black silky coat gleamed. She was obviously very content and well cared for.

They settled down for a spot of English conversation. It was a win-win situation. While they were speaking English, he told her what she wanted to know about St Merlot, like the weekend opening times at the shops and which bank in Apt had the most pleasant and helpful staff, and asked her all about herself and her life in England. None of it felt forced, despite his occasional awkwardness.

"Are you married, Didier?" She hadn't noticed a girl watching him play pétanque.

"Me? No."

"A girlfriend, partner?"

"No. I am not lucky yet."

He seemed quite happy about it. Penelope could imagine that he enjoyed being left alone to follow his own slightly nerdy interests, watching his Bond films and playing British music very loudly. He reminded her a bit of one of Justin's friends who worked in IT.

She was tempted to mention the bones in the chapel to find out whether there was any gossip in the village, and only just stopped herself in time. Instead she asked about Mme Avore. "Is she still living at the house at the end of the track here?"

"I haven't heard otherwise. Though she is often out all day. She drives a mobile library round the villages of the Luberon."

"Oh!" A memory from the day she arrived at St Merlot popped up in Penelope's mind, in full Technicolor. "Not the lavender-mauve Bibliobus? I think I saw it, my first day here, up at the square."

"Which day would that have been?"

"Let me think, it must have been . . . a Wednesday."

"Voilà! That is the day the Bibliobus stops in St Merlot for two hours before lunch."

"She sounds a very different character from her husband. It's hardly credible that they could be together," mused Penelope. "Why did she marry him in the first place?" She knew the answer, but didn't want to seem too well-informed.

"She was some kind of cousin. The family arranged it."

"That's grim," said Penelope. "And hard to get out of."

"Almost impossible," concurred the young electrician. "Families are very close around here."

They chatted a bit more about the village and its businesses. He agreed that Jacques Correa was a very fine baker, though he thought the *épicerie-fruiterie* could be more adventurous in its stock. Penelope learned nothing new.

He left for lunch at twelve on the dot, calling for M, and said he would be back soon to tackle the rest of the replacement wiring.

⁂

THE DOOR to the little stone barn that Penelope hoped one day to make into her music studio was warped. Its lavender paint was peeling off, and the latch was hard to shift. She had to wrestle with it before it gave way.

It creaked open to reveal a musty, dusty space. Cobwebs hung like fishing nets from the rafters. She stepped inside and picked her way across rusting farm implements, buckets, animal troughs, and other castoffs. More rickety kitchen chairs were pushed against the wall. She picked up a colander and a broken fly swat. If she was ever going to make it into a light, airy space, she would need to get a dumpster in to clear it.

As she made her way farther in, though, she noticed an old table in the corner. It had clearly seen better days, but a table could always be upcycled, if only for the garden. She went over and dragged it out. Not bad. It was old, but more of an antique than first impressions had suggested. In fact, she thought, cleaned up and polished, it might make a very nice piece for a music studio—or even the sitting room. It had drawers that would provide good storage space for her sheet music: Fauré's *Pavane*, the Rachmaninov sonata that she had daydreams about practising to perfection—or as close as she could get.

She pulled a tissue out of her pocket and wiped it across the top. Was it made of rosewood, or walnut, perhaps? A chessboard revealed itself. This was clearly some sort of games table. She studied it, and opened one flap, then another. The top transformed into a green baize card table.

There were two drawers, tricky to open, as if damp had swollen the wood, but she was rewarded by finding a jumble of chessmen in one, and a cribbage scorer. The other was particularly stiff. Penelope returned with a screwdriver to try to prise it open. After several heated tries, she was able to rock it free.

This drawer contained two objects—a set of playing cards and, lying underneath it, a piece of creased paper.

She drew it out carefully. It was a newspaper cutting, slightly crumpled. Intrigued, she took it outside to examine in the light.

A photograph showed a group of men at a gaming table in a casino—"Le Casino de Salon-de-Provence." The name of the establishment was clearly visible, as if the photographer had set up the shot to include it for promotional reasons.

She looked more closely at the faces. The man at the centre of the photo looked glum, while those around him were celebratory, in a formal kind of way. Infuriatingly, the caption had been snipped away, but there was a date at the top of the page: Monday, April 12, 2010.

It was clearly a gambling scene. Penelope was stumped. Was one of these men Manuel Avore? Did he still own the house in 2010? Why didn't he take this nice piece of furniture with him when he left?

She picked up the pack of cards.

The pattern on the back was of leaves and tendrils. Just like the one that she had found with the skeleton in the ruined chapel. She would check it against the photo she took, but she was pretty certain they were a match.

Heart pounding, she ran inside. She put on her rubber washing-up gloves and began to deal the cards at the kitchen table. Sure enough, as she finished and looked down at the piles of the four suits, arranged from two upwards, there was only one card missing—the ace of spades.

※

PENELOPE TRIED to call Clémence, but she was not in the office, and her mobile went straight to voice mail. She wondered whether she might try the mayor, then decided against it. She still didn't know what his game was. Besides, it was nearly lunchtime on a Wednesday, when the *mairie* closed for a half day.

"Lunchtime on Wednesday!" she said out loud.

She hurled herself into the hall, grabbed her car keys, and was driving up the hill into the village before she had time to think of a strategy. All she knew was that she couldn't miss her chance to meet Mariette Avore.

The lavender-mauve Bibliobus was parked at the edge of the square, exactly where it had been the first time Penelope had seen it. The old man was sitting on his usual bench, half asleep over *La Provence*. A couple of elderly folk were chatting nearby, books in hand. The door to the mobile library was in the middle of the bus, and it was still open.

Penelope parked the Range Rover and walked over. She looked up at the driver's seat, but it was empty, so she climbed the steps into the bus. The interior was cramped but welcoming. Shelves of books lined each side from floor to roof. Reference tomes took up stately position close to the back, and well-thumbed novels were within easy reach of the entrance. A purple and green carpet added a jaunty note.

Standing near the front, pushing books back into place, was a pretty woman in her mid-forties, humming to herself. A few strands of silver gleamed in her long dark hair, which was scrunched into a bun and held in place with a plastic grip jaw. She wore a linen tunic, of a design found in every market in Provence, over cropped trousers and sensible sandals, sturdy enough to wear to drive a bus. A pair of glasses hung on a chain necklace.

"Excusez-moi—Mme Avore?" ventured Penelope.

Mme Avore's dark eyes were tired, but the smile lit her face. Her teeth were very white. "Oui, madame."

"Bonjour! I am the new owner of Le Chant d'Eau. My name is Penelope Kite."

"Ah, l'anglaise! English!"

"Yes."

They looked, a fraction nervously, at each other. Perhaps they were both wondering whether to mention Penelope's swimming pool and its unfortunate significance. Neither found it necessary to do so.

"I am very sorry for your loss," said Penelope.

Mariette Avore accepted her condolences with a simple nod.

"Do you have a book about St Merlot?" asked Penelope, in accordance with the scratch plan she had formulated as she hurtled up the hill. A nice anodyne request to start the conversation rolling.

Mariette gave a wide smile. She certainly seemed happy in her bereavement. "Ah, yes, I have many. I love books about the old days in the Luberon. So much history. There is a whole row just behind you."

"May I borrow one, or do I need a library card?" The spectre of French bureaucracy was never far from Penelope's consciousness.

"*Pfff!* I know where you live. I think I will be able to make you return it."

It sounded like a joke, but was delivered without a smile. Mariette Avore was a serious woman, thought Penelope.

She got back on track. "Do you know a lot about the history of this village?"

"Plenty."

"And my house?"

Mariette inclined her head.

"I don't suppose there are any books that mention Le Chant d'Eau?"

"You want to find out about your house? That is normal. But I cannot think of any book here that will tell you much. Sorry."

"It doesn't really matter. I just thought I'd ask."

They exchanged another appraising look. Mariette was still an attractive woman. Was it the romance with Pierre Louchard that was responsible for the sparkle in the eyes? Or was it, as Penelope recognised all too well, the cautious optimism of a woman emerging from her old life into a new and potentially better future?

"You have lived here for a long time?" asked Penelope.

"A very long time."

Penelope hesitated. She recalled all the conversations with people who had confirmed that this was a good woman, kind and worthy of respect. Maybe this was the moment to take a gamble of her own.

She pulled the newspaper clipping out of her pocket and held it out. "I found this in my house. Do you recognise any of these men?"

Mariette took the piece of paper and solemnly reached for the reading glasses dangling from her neck. She studied the photo without comment.

The silence was eventually broken by the bleep of an alarm from the direction of the driver's seat.

"It is time for me to move on to Castellet," said the librarian, without raising her eyes from the clipping.

Penelope waited silently.

"I'm not sure. There is something . . . but I can't be certain. It's been a long time since I saw him."

"Which man?"

Mariette pointed at the glum-looking man.

"Who is he?"

"I can't be sure. I only saw him once."

"When did you see him—I mean, in what circumstances?"

"He came to the house to see my . . . late husband. Manuel told me to stay upstairs."

"Why?"

"It did not seem like a friendly visit."

"When was this?"

"Years ago. Around the time we moved into the house where I live now—so it must have been in 2010."

A pause. Penelope waited, hoping she would elaborate.

"Was it to do with gambling?" asked Penelope, pointing at the casino sign in the photo and hoping that Mariette wouldn't conclude that she had been gossiping about Manuel's difficulties.

"It could have been."

"A gambling debt?"

"Quite possibly."

"Did your husband frequent the Casino de Salon-de-Provence?"

"If he did, it was against my wishes—but that never stopped him." Mariette gave a sad shake of the head.

Another pause.

"How can I find a copy of the newspaper that this piece came from?" asked Penelope gently. "Is there a main library in Apt that keeps old editions?"

"Of course. Do you know the square behind the cathedral?

The main town library is there. You can just go in and ask. But can I ask a question now? What is your interest in this?"

"Oh . . . you know how it is when you move into a new place, you just get interested in who was there before." Penelope was well aware how feeble that sounded, but she couldn't admit the truth to the murdered man's widow. That would have been totally insensitive.

"I must go," said Mariette.

"Do you drive this around every day?"

"Wednesdays I visit Rustrel, Gignac, St Merlot, and Castellet. Thursdays, it's Gargas, Le Chêne, Murs, and Lioux. I just do two days a week."

They both said goodbye, and how pleased they were to meet. Penelope watched as Mariette started the Bibliobus's engine with a shaky rumble and took the road to Castellet.

⁂

THE RECORDS of old newspapers were to be found in a hot, airless room with no windows at the end of the corridor in the Bibliothèque d'Apt. Extraordinarily, the 2010 records were still stored on a microfiche reader so ancient that Penelope remembered using it at the Home Office before the system was upgraded. She lifted the dust sheet of the machine and turned it on.

Having located the microfiche with the correct paper and date, Penelope inserted the celluloid strip. On a large screen she had the Apt edition of *La Provence* for the date in question. Scrolling through various news stories about Easter pageants and cherry orchard blight, she at last found what she was looking for. There was no article attached, but underneath the photo on the screen, a legend read "Résident de St Merlot gagne 50,000 euros—Casino de Salon." A St Merlot resident wins 50,000 euros.

No name, Penelope thought, but a St Merlot resident. So why did Mariette not know who he was? And why did he look so wretchedly miserable?

He must have been the unhappiest winner in the history of gambling jackpots. Unless it was the publicity he was gloomy about.

Luckily, she knew how to make a copy of the page she was looking at. She checked for paper in the printer, and hit the button to make two. She folded one of these and put it in her bag. Then she took a piece of copy paper and wrote on it.

Next stop—there was nothing else for it—the police station.

At the front desk, Penelope handed over a small package addressed to Inspector Paul Gamelin. It contained the pack of fifty-one cards she had found, a note of explanation, the original newspaper clipping, and the second copy of the microfiche page. She made no suggestion of her own deductions, stating only that, in view of the card found in the ruined chapel, she could not in all conscience ignore the possibility that this might be evidence.

24

THE SEASON OF FESTIVALS IN the Luberon lasted all summer long. Every village had one. There was a traditional communal meal for all the villagers, a boules or pétanque contest, a *vide grenier*, and perhaps a show of some kind. On the Saturday night a dance band played in a central square or on a road lined with trees that could be cordoned off and strung with fairy lights.

Over the years it had become a point of honour and considerable competition amongst the various mayors to provide the most lavish of spectacles. There was little argument that Viens, with its incomparable band, had the best music. Lacoste mounted a complete opera funded by Pierre Cardin and other wealthy residents. Not to be outdone, Gordes produced a fireworks display that, it was said, caused a number of the older residents to recall the days they watched the Allied forces liberate Provence in 1944.

By the first weekend in September, it was St Merlot's turn.

Penelope was particularly looking forward to the *vide grenier*, the empty-the-attic sale on Sunday morning. Back in Surrey she would have called it a jumble sale, and steered well clear. But here it seemed exciting, and she was itching to see what glorious shabby-chic items she could pick up for a few euros. She intended to get there early to beat the professional *brocanteurs* to the best bargains. All those years of watching antiques programmes on the telly would not be wasted.

First, though, was the *aioli* on Saturday night, the gathering at which all the villagers sat down together at long tables outside and ate this traditional dish of garlic mayonnaise with local vegetables and bread.

Penelope decided to walk up rather than try to park the Range Rover. She also wanted to have a few glasses of wine if she felt like it. The events of the past few weeks were enough to turn anyone to drink. She put on some pretty but practical espadrille wedges and a long boho dress and was pleased enough with the reflection in her new mirror. A couple of days by the pool and working in the garden had given her a light golden tan that suited her. Not bad, she thought, not bad at all.

The village square had been decked overnight with garlands of flowers. Bunting of various vintages and flickering lights delineated the stage where the band would play. Tables had been covered with white paper and set with cutlery, glasses, and bottles of wine and water. *"Pa-dam, pa-dam, pa-dam!"* sang Edith Piaf over the PA system, and a sense of anticipation was palpable among the villagers.

Penelope smiled at everyone who looked her way, aware that they all knew who she was. She spotted the mayor, who raised his hand in greeting, then her new friends, the baker and his wife. This was the hardest part about being on your own, she thought: making an entrance. But then she imagined how awful it would be to have her ex-husband in tow, annoying her. That would have been infinitely worse. She went over to the bar that had been set out near the fountain and bought a glass of rosé.

A bell rang promptly at seven o'clock. Women wearing white aprons bustled out of the *épicerie-fruiterie* to place plates of cold meats on the tables. A queue of villagers, all chattering loudly, formed against the sun-blasted stone walls surrounding the square, perhaps the only orderly queue Penelope had seen since leaving England. Plates in hand, they were served the lightly boiled vegetables and potatoes that they would dip in the aioli. Just as well I like garlic, thought Penelope. It was exceedingly pungent.

She stood back, waiting for Clémence to appear, and watched as families and groups of friends started to take their seats. Before too long the tables had been all but filled, and Penelope was starting to worry whether there would be enough space for them.

The mayor was seated at a prominent table with a group of laughing people who looked tanned and sleek and wealthy, the women in chic, tight-fitting short dresses and the men in billowing white cotton shirts and well-cut trousers. She recognised one of them as the silver fox in the red Ferrari.

Penelope found it very hard not to keep staring over at the party. They were by far the most glamorous group at the event.

She joined the queue to buy tickets for the meal, one for herself and one for Clémence, though she was unsure whether it was a dish the native Parisienne would relish. She'll just nibble at the vegetables, predicted Penelope. As the line shuffled slowly forward, everyone chatting in celebratory mood, Penelope watched the mayor lay his arm over the silver fox's shoulders and exchange a few words that made them both laugh.

Eventually she saw Clémence arrive from the direction of the *mairie* and pick her way daintily across the rough surface of the square in the prettiest shoes Penelope had yet seen her wear: pale pink suede with a black bow around the ankle. An immaculate shell-pink fitted dress, cream pashmina, and black bag completed the ensemble. She would have been right at home in the mayor's party.

As it was, the two of them perched at the end of a table packed full of jolly, shouting locals. Penelope waved at Didier, who was in the thick of it at another table. He waved a cauliflower floret back. At least the noise meant that she and Clémence could have a chat without being overheard. Even so, Penelope kept her voice low as she reported her latest find, the meeting with Mariette Avore (carefully referring to her as "the wife") and the matching of the newspaper cutting. The Frenchwoman was clearly impressed, even if she was unconvinced about the wisdom of delivering the playing cards to the police.

"I had to. What if that pack really is material to the case? I couldn't ignore that. So, have you managed to find out anything?" Penelope crunched on a carrot, feeling very garlicky already.

"Nothing at the moment, Penny. Have you been shot at again over the last few days?"

"Very funny. So you haven't had any more thoughts about the connection between the Darrieux shop and this village?"

"We need to wait. To look carefully while being discreet." Clémence sipped delicately from her glass of white wine, glancing over the rim at the crowd. It was no surprise at all that her gaze lingered on the mayor and his friends. "What have you been doing since I saw you?" she asked, overbrightly, then lowered her voice. "Talk as if you haven't a care in the world. About something of no consequence. We need to be careful discussing these people here. The villagers are mainly farmers, and they will know the names."

"Those are very beautiful shoes you are wearing, Clémence," gushed Penelope. "You always wear lovely shoes. May I ask where you bought them?"

"They are pretty, are they not?" Clémence extended a slim, well-shaped calf.

"Chanel?"

"I bought them in Paris, but they are not by Chanel." Clémence lowered her voice. "That is most interesting, is it not,

Penny? It seems our friend from Coustellet is saying hello to Laurent."

"Ah, those shoes . . . from Paris but not by Chanel!" Penelope caught sight of the man from Darrieux shaking the mayor's hand. "The big man from the shop! Now that is fascinating!"

"I bought these shoes in a sale," said Clémence. "Interesting. They have clearly met before."

"I wish I could find sales like that. Is the big man Darrieux himself?"

"Yes, Paul Darrieux."

"What if he recognises us?"

"My goodness, the sun shines right into my eyes this time of evening," said Clémence, whipping out her enormous sunglasses.

"Mine too." Penelope followed her lead. "Did my new gardener have anything interesting to say about this Coustellet connection, by the way?"

"I did not manage to speak to him."

"So we don't know anything for certain, then. This could all be coincidence."

"He will surely be here tonight. Perhaps we could ask him. Keep looking, Penny. Can you see how M. Coustellet is handing over something?"

"So he is. And the mayor is putting whatever it is he's been given straight into the inside pocket of his jacket. As if he knows exactly what it is without looking."

"Keep watching what they do next."

The big man nodded to the mayor and walked away, belly rippling. The mayor sat down and was soon drinking and chatting away again with his friends.

"What do you think that was about?" whispered Penelope. "Surely our friend who took me to lunch the other day can't be involved in anything dubious?"

"I would like to think not." A large *but* hung over her response.

"By the way, did you ask him whether Avore and Louchard had any business dealing together?"

"I have not. Sorry."

"I think I need another glass of rosé," said Penelope.

"I am going to have a cigarette," said Clémence.

❧

PENELOPE AND Clémence stood watching under the trees as the support band took their places on the stage and began their sound checks. Some flashing lights revolved experimentally. Within minutes the show had started with a full-blast rendition of "Jumping Jack Flash." It was good to know that the French had lost none of their adoration of the Rolling Stones.

From their new vantage point, they had a better view of the tables, where most people were still eating. Penelope gave Clémence a nudge. "My gardener," she said.

M. Charpet, his beret on the table by his plate, beckoned to them.

"Go on," Clémence urged her. "I will join you when I have finished my cigarette."

Penelope marched over. M. Charpet wiped his mouth with a large paper napkin, pulled a chair out next to his, and ushered Penelope into it. There were handshakes all round and introductions to so many people; the only one Penelope remembered was his sister Valentine. She was a carbon copy of her brother (minus the moustache, of course), though he assured Penelope that they were not twins. She started talking the moment Penelope was seated, and showed little sign of letting up—all in an accent quite opaque to anyone not born and brought up in the region.

This table was still in thrall to the *aioli*, guzzling with gusto. A large golden gobbet was ladled onto a plate and shoved in front of Penelope, along with more vegetables and potatoes. Her glass was refilled, and she found herself keeping pace with some expert bottle-drainers. After a while she relaxed, and then began to enjoy herself. She could still only catch one word in ten from Valentine, but after yet another glass of wine, she felt she could understand everything through a strange osmosis. Afterwards she realised that her French companions were feeling much the same way about her efforts to join in, but in the garrulous and friendly atmosphere that pervaded the square, no one really minded.

Wiping the last smears from her plate with a large crust of bread, Penelope sat back in a mellow state of mind and surveyed the scene.

Clémence was speaking to the mayor—and behaving quite coquettishly, it had to be said. The mayor seemed perfectly relaxed to have her flirting with him in front of everyone, leaving her hand on his arm as she threw her head back, laughing at something he said. They did make a well-matched couple.

It might have been the wine, but Penelope suddenly found herself wondering whether Clémence had been annoyed that she had lunched with Laurent.

Laurent and Clémence's animated conversation was interrupted by a small man in a cream linen suit and hair that gleamed under the lights in the trees. Both stopped laughing. Even from where she was sitting, Penelope could see the mayor's face cloud over. Then the small man turned around. It was the chief of police.

When had the chief arrived at the fête? Was he a welcome guest, or was he using the occasion as a chance to make further inquiries? The next moment, the Coustellet shopkeeper reappeared, breaking away from a conversation with a group of back-slapping men. The mayor's face bore an unfathomable expression.

The band came to the end of a Beatles set and went off. There was a pause, and then, as if everyone realised that a momentous event was about to take place, conversation quietened, and the night grew still. The mayor reached into the pocket of his jacket. Penelope held her breath, then took a large gulp of rosé.

M. Charpet tapped her on the arm. "Maintenant, c'est le moment de l'annonce!"

The winner of the Best Tractor competition was about to be announced. From up the hill a rumble grew louder; at the corner of the square appeared a line of improbably shiny tractors, which came to rest—some belching smoke—in formation in front of the *mairie*.

Laurent Millais stood up and tapped the microphone in front of him in the self-important way of all civic officials.

"Mesdames, messieurs, bonsoir," he began.

There was a collective sound of cutlery being placed back on the table, chairs being rearranged for viewing, and sighs of either contentment or boredom, Penelope could not tell.

She turned to see that Mme Valencourt had rejoined her and was leaning forward to whisper in her ear. "Maybe we can get to meet M. Coustellet after the mayor has awarded the prize."

"What's the chief of police doing here?" hissed Penelope.

Clémence put a finger to her lips.

They turned to listen. The mayor was in the midst of thanking a long list of sponsors, organisers, and helpers for the fête, each name rapturously applauded. Then, shifting his papers, he moved to the competition, and the square grew silent.

"Le Prix du Meilleur Tracteur du Luberon pour cette année est . . ."

Surely he's not going to prolong the agony, thought Penelope crossly—did they have the X Factor in France as well? She had found Britain irritating in many ways, but none more so than the habit recently formed of pausing before announcing any winner in any sort of contest. It drove her demented.

"Get on with it, man!" she muttered under her breath, as the pause extended.

"M. Pierre Louchard!"

The crowd erupted as Penelope's neighbour jumped down from his pride and joy. A smiley woman with a sleek dark bob and bright red lipstick stood up and cheered wildly.

"The new widow has been to the hair salon," said Penelope.

"She is almost chic," said Clémence. "Well played, good for her!"

Penelope raised her hands high to clap as M. Louchard gave an exaggerated bow and went up to receive his prize, receiving pats on the back from those he passed.

The prize-giving ceremony was brief. A handshake from the mayor, the presentation of an envelope, and it was all over. The man from Coustellet and the chief of police had melted away into the crowd.

Almost immediately, the stage erupted with lights and sound. People rose from their seats as the tables were cleared of everything but the wine, and gathered in front of the musicians. This was the main act. Ingeniously positioned on and around several tons of amplification, eight singers and musicians, including a trombonist and saxophonist, launched into their opening number.

From the back of a lorry parked up behind the stage emerged dancing girls in skimpy costumes. The party had really started. The band was tight, with great rhythms. They were clearly used to being on the road. Maybe, thought Penelope, they made their living moving from fête to fête.

"Bonsoir, St Merlot!" bellowed the lead singer.

The reaction wasn't quite what he was hoping for, so he tried again.

"Bonsoir, St Merlot! Comment ça va?"

This brought a louder cheer, and in an instant the band were into their second number. Judging by the reaction, it was a favourite. Couples old and young, mostly either very old or very young, took to the floor, in the former case waltzing beautifully round the square, and in the latter jumping about and running in circles. As she watched the mayor smiling and clapping along, she saw her chance to go over and say hello.

Penelope had nearly made it through the crowd when she felt a hand on her arm. Forced to check her stride and turn around, she found herself staring straight at the slick dark hair of a very short man.

The chief of police was as pompous as ever. "Bonsoir, madame. You seem to be looking for someone. Can I be of help?"

Penelope smiled weakly. "Actually I was after the ladies' . . . You know . . . WC . . . toilette . . ."

Comprehension dawned, with some distaste, on the face of the chief.

"Always ask a policeman," said Penelope. "That's what we say in England."

He looked at her as if he could not decide whether she was being rude or unpleasantly foreign. "Ah, of course—it is over there." He pointed straight back in the direction from which Penelope had just come.

"Silly me, I must have missed it."

"Yes, madame. And when you are finished, I wonder if we could have a brief word. It is quite important."

"Have you found out who broke into my house?"

"No, madame."

Penelope backed away, flew into the *dames*, and stood in the cubicle thinking. There had been a hardness to the police chief's expression when he looked at her that she did not like at all. At length, she flushed the loo and lingered over washing her hands.

He was waiting for her outside. There was no escape from whatever he wanted to say to her, though she noted with a little satisfaction out of the corner of her eye that Clémence had found the man from Coustellet and engaged him in conversation.

25

THE CHIEF OF POLICE PULLED out two chairs from a nearby table and gestured to Penelope. "Please, madame."

They sat down. Perhaps remembering that they were not at the police station, he reached over to a bottle of rosé and poured her a glass. He had none himself.

Penelope took a gulp of wine and tried to look as if she was completely relaxed, but close up, those ratty eyes and moist lips were quite disconcerting.

"I am glad that I have seen you here, Mme Keet. It is better that I speak to you casually, I think."

None of this seemed very casual to her. She knew what he was going to do. He was going to warn her off asking questions. That bloke from the shop at Coustellet must surely have reported her for meddling in the investigation. Then there was the package she had left for Gamelin. Penelope braced herself, feeling like a schoolgirl hauled up before her headmistress for a misdemeanour.

Reyssens leaned closer, about to say something.

"Have you identified the bones yet?" Penelope said, deciding to defend by attacking first.

She had a nasty flashback of holding the skeleton's hand. Of pulling the arm farther out of the undergrowth.

The chief sighed. "Madame, we are still investigating. It is not easy. The body was almost completely decayed, and apart from the fibres of a suit he was wearing, there was no obvious identification."

"A dead man. With no obvious identification. Probably murder, then."

"It seems so."

"How did he die?"

"His skull was crushed. A heavy blow to the head."

Just like Manuel Avore.

"You must have some theories about what happened?"

"Indeed, madame."

Penelope was not used to being kept at arm's length in a police investigation. It made her quite cross, especially now that her inhibitions were drowning in rosé. "It seems, monsieur le chef de police, that the dream house I purchased in a quiet corner of the Luberon is in fact a home for murderous psychopaths! Am I going to discover a new body every time I go for a walk? The place is cursed."

"I must admit, Mme Keet, that I have thought the same. Especially since the previous owners of Le Chant d'Eau complained more than once about strange events."

Penelope suddenly felt very drunk. "What strange events, exactly?" she spluttered. "Strange enough to report them to you? Would you consider that I am a victim of strange events?"

"Mme Keet. You must listen to me. I know that you found the victim in the old chapel. But I must ask you again to keep this information confidential. It is of great importance that the precise location of the body is not widely known."

Penelope knew of the reporting rules on murders from her Home Office days but had always found the police generally keen to pass on information once verified—except in very unusual circumstances, usually involving personal safety. Her heart skipped a beat.

The chief of police rammed the point home. "In this case, it is better we do not say too much."

Good luck with keeping that quiet in this village. "Why is that?" Penelope asked.

"Because, madame, I think that the perpetrator was someone who lived in the village, and may still be here."

Penelope shivered. "Why can't you find them, then?"

"Mme Keet, you ask all the time questions. You are even doing it now. Making your own investigation. Bringing me axes from a garden hut. Sending Inspector Gamelin playing cards. Do you think this is a game? Will you bring me a piece of broken tombstone from the chapel next week? I hope not, for I do not find it amusing."

They glared at each other.

"All right," said Penelope. "I have a few final questions. If you will answer them now, I promise I will ask no more. Now," she went on doggedly to head off any objection, "have you found out any more about the murder of Manuel Avore?"

He regarded her with some distaste.

"Not so much. We have not found any serious motive to kill Manuel Avore. Oh, we know he was unpopular, but not that unpopular. He was not particularly wealthy. But he was a gambler. In fact the only lead we have involves his gambling—he had debts, and I am sure you can imagine how some of the gambling establishments deal with those who do not pay up! The card, the ace of spades—"

"Oh! So you do have the card from the pool, then?"

"Of course. My scene of crime team is most expert."

Penelope was relieved to hear it.

"As I was saying, the ace of spades has a significance."

"It's the Death Card!"

The chief of police brewed up an exasperated expression. "No!

It is a tradition in the criminal gangs of the Marseille area that those unfortunates who repeatedly do not pay their gambling debts face the consequences—they are beaten up, or worse, and this card is left."

"I've heard that. I wasn't sure how seriously to take it."

"The kind of people who leave these cards, they do not like it when their activities come to the attention of the police. When the beatings are so bad that they become murder, and bodies are found after a long time. They are ruthless, madame. They take revenge."

The evening air took on a sharper edge as the impact of these words sank in. It seemed far-fetched, but the chief appeared deadly serious.

"You think . . . I might be in danger now?"

Reyssens pulled a face. "When a dead body is found, you always seem to be there . . ."

"The break-in! The shots at the chapel! You all keep saying it was hunters, but what if— Do you think— I was thinking that, what if whoever was shooting at me was actually trying to make me go into the ruined chapel, so that—so that—" Penelope felt sick, losing track of what exactly it was she was thinking.

"There is another possibility. These criminals exist to make money, and it is very satisfying for them to be paid for a crime they want to commit for their own purposes. Do you know anyone who would wish you harm?"

"What? You mean anyone who wanted to get a hit squad to take me out?" Penelope squeaked, appalled. She honestly could not. "Well, my husband wasn't very happy after the divorce settlement, but I really truly could not see him doing anything remotely like this. He's far too wet to contemplate murder, and I am no longer there to clean the mess up after him. I have had to deal with a number of sensitive issues in my previous employment, but again, nothing springs to mind."

He held up his hand. "Then you must leave everything to us. No harm will come to you—unless you continue to involve yourself in this matter. I ask you again to be calm and wise. We, the police, are investigating. You can be vigilant, and please feel free to report anything out of the ordinary to me. As for the reckless hunters, the mayor will have to review the licences for their guns."

Reyssens stood to go, drew himself up to his full not-very-impressive height, and poured her another glass of rosé. If he meant it as an insulting gesture, it succeeded. She had not done well this evening in her quest to prove that she was not another wine-soaked expat, but surely these were extenuating circumstances.

Penelope watched him retreat into the whirling dancers and the flashing lights from the stage. She tried to think logically. Was Reyssens just trying to stop her asking questions? An awful one wriggled out from somewhere in her rosé-induced haze. What if *he* was the murderer? What if Avore was the prey that always eluded him, until he settled the matter for once and for all? Perhaps only that would explain why was he so unpleasant to her . . . what if . . . what if . . . Reyssens were a very dangerous adversary indeed?

It was highly unlikely that some murderous criminal gang was after her blood. But she drew no comfort from that. Did the more recent crime have anything at all to do with her, or the house, or Manuel Avore's gambling debts? What about Avore's merry widow and her possible recognition of the man in the newspaper cutting? The pack of cards missing the cardsharp's ace of spades? None of it felt remotely personal to her. In fact, the only focal point at which any of the stories intersected was her house. So what was the draw to Le Chant d'Eau?

She started to feel very worried indeed about returning to her dark and isolated house. There were whoops as the band's lead singer announced "Le Madison!" and the villagers began to move as one to perform a kind of line dance. As Penelope watched them jump and change direction, some smoothly practised, others hopping to keep up with the row, she tried to imagine one of them as a cold-hearted villain.

"Penny! I have some interesting news!"

Penelope jumped as Clémence sat down next to her. She seemed a little breathless.

"So do I."

Clémence stood up again, grabbed her arm, and guided her toward an empty bench just beyond the coloured lights in the trees.

"You first," said Penelope flatly.

"I spoke to M. Darrieux. He told me he is not allowed to give out any information about the bank card details to us. I cannot say I am surprised. When he saw us here tonight, he told the mayor that we had both been asking questions, and it is now entirely clear to him that we are not, and never have been, agents for the Strauss toolmaking company."

"He told the mayor? What a sneak!"

"However, it does mean that the mayor now knows that the axe was purchased at Coustellet. At the same shop that sponsored the prize for the best tractor."

"But where does that get us?" asked Penelope, struggling with the feeling that the axe had only led into a blind alley for a second time. It was very small beer indeed compared to the possibility of being the next dead person in the village.

Clémence shrugged. "I don't know." But she couldn't help smiling. A little bit smugly.

"What is it?"

"Nothing. Nothing to do with Coustellet. But I took the chance to have a nice conversation with the lovely mayor. And now I feel much better."

Penelope rolled her eyes. "Oh, well. That's all right then. You get kissy-kissy with the mayor, while the chief of police intimates that I might be next in line!"

"What?" Clémence's eyes widened in horror. "You—and Laurent?"

"No! The next victim!" Penelope had had far too much to drink. She burst into tears. "I'm scared, Clémence! And you know what? Reyssens wants me to be scared."

Clémence could not have been kinder. Getting her on-again, off-again relationship with the mayor back on track had obviously had a beneficial effect.

"I find it hard to believe that you could be in danger, but we must take every precaution," she told Penelope when her sobs subsided. "Mon dieu. I must go."

"Great," said Penelope. Mustn't keep the mayor waiting. The two lovebirds would soon be making fantastic French whoopee while she staggered back to an empty house of horrors. "That's all right. You leave me here. I'm sure I'll be safe from psychopaths for now because the not-so-nice policeman says so. Perhaps I need another drink."

Clémence shook her head. "No, Penny. I must go to collect my things, pack a suitcase—"

"Are you running away?"

"Precisely, Penny. I am leaving my house . . . to come and stay with you."

Penelope did not know what to say. "What about Laurent?" she managed eventually. "I thought you would be, you know . . ."

"We are not 'you know' at all. It is finished. Never again."

"Oh, no. What happened?"

"I shall not speak of it. Please do not ask."

Penelope did a double take, utterly confused.

"So, I will come to Le Chant d'Eau," said Clémence. "I stay, just for a day or so, while we think of what to do next."

It was a sweet offer, accepted gratefully.

Penelope sat on her own for the next hour, sipping fizzy water and politely declining requests from both the mayor and M. Charpet to dance. It was hard to know which was more upsetting—the dismissal of her fears by the chief of police, or his insinuation that she might really be the next victim if she didn't leave everything to the authorities. If it wasn't paranoia, this was where she was safest: in full view of the massed villagers of St Merlot as they danced under the stars. But what if one of them had her in his sights?

AS THE last slow dance drew to its overblown conclusion and the accordion's final chords drifted over the entwined couples, Clémence came to take her home.

"Where did you leave your car?"

"At home. I walked up."

Clémence shook a finger. "It is just as well you are not walking back in the night. Everyone is drunk. The road is very dangerous."

"Everything here is more dangerous than it looks," said Penelope. Her head was already starting to hurt from all the wine. "Urgh. Why did I drink all that gut-rot?"

An enormous suitcase took up all the space in the rear of the

Mini Cooper. Penelope squeezed into the passenger seat beside more bags.

"Exactly how long are you intending to stay, Clémence?"

"Just an overnight bag, Penny."

"I've seen expeditions to the North Pole that departed with less!"

Clémence crunched the car into gear, and they shot off down the hill. "In my job, it is important always to look good."

They screeched to a halt round the first bend. Just as well I wasn't too drunk to forget my seat belt, thought Penelope. Bang slap in front of them was M. Louchard on his prize-winning Best Tractor of the Year, weaving around the road in slow motion, the digger cradle held proudly aloft.

He looked around, smiling for practically the first time that Penelope could remember, when he heard the tyre burn behind him. "Bonne nuit, mesdames!"

Clémence opened her window and congratulated him on his win, then swerved violently and suddenly to overtake. They bumped along the grassy verge.

"That was close!" cried Penelope.

"We did not want to get stuck behind him on the track to your house. Or indeed at the entrance to the track by the Avore house. Did you see?"

"See what?"

"His passenger."

"Passenger?"

"I think we can assume that the romance of the fête has worked its magic. Mme Avore has finally found 'appeeness."

Penelope spluttered. "Wha-at? Oh, I see. Yes, happiness. I didn't see her on the tractor."

"She was riding in the cradle. And now, look, they are following behind us very slowly and carefully down the track."

At the front door Penelope fumbled for her keys, and then for the lock. She was finding it quite hard to concentrate—and she wished she could remember where the outside light switch was. Funny, she thought she'd left it on.

She finally managed to get the door unlocked and pushed it open. She stepped carefully into the hall, and was reaching for the light switch when from behind her came the sound of a gunshot and a scream. Another bang. Then the sound of glass shattering.

"Clémence! Oh my goodness . . . Clémence, are you OK?"

"Merde!"

"Are you hurt?"

The light flared and then fizzed as the bulb popped, leaving them in blackness. Penelope felt her way towards the kitchen and found the switch in the corridor. It revealed Clémence in mid-hop, holding her foot up. It was bleeding. The hall floor was covered in shards of broken glass. The window next to the door sported a large round hole from which further cracks emanated like a spiderweb.

"Your foot!" exclaimed Penelope.

"My beautiful shoes!" wailed Clémence. She hobbled to the stairs and sat down to examine the blood on the pale pink suede. "They are ruined!"

"What just happened? I mean . . . beyond the obvious . . ."

"Un coup de fusil," breathed Clémence. Her command of English seemed to have deserted her with the lateness of the hour and emotions running high.

Penelope shivered. "Oui."

Silence. It was broken by the squeal of a squirrel-like *loir* outside.

"Aimed at one of us," said Penelope.

"Of course not, Penny! Hunters . . ."

"Do the hunters go out in the evening?"

"The sangliers come out at night, certainly . . . so . . . ."

Penelope shook her head. "Should we call the police?"

"Hunters do stupid things. We all know that. Especially on the night of the fête. No one is allowed to shoot within four hundred metres of a house, but they don't care about that if they see the animal. They will have seen a sanglier and chased him too close. I think we will see tomorrow in the light that there are the tracks of an animal."

"Leave the glass and the shot where it is," said Penelope.

The two women tried to dismiss their fears over cups of chamomile tea. They did not entirely succeed. Clémence stuck stubbornly to her belief that crazy things happened on nights like these. It was not sporting to report local incidents.

Penelope felt stone cold sober as she went upstairs to make up the guest bed. As she shook out clean sheets, it occurred to her that Clémence was as reluctant as she was to call Reyssens.

26

THREE ANADIN EXTRA FAILED TO neutralise Penelope's
headache the next morning.

She had spent a fitful night, sensitive to the least sound from
outside. When she managed at last to drop off, she was pulled
abruptly from sleep by reruns of her conversation with the chief
of police. Clémence had had similar problems, judging from the
sound of movements in the spare room.

Penelope trudged wearily outside. There was a chill in the air,
and the grass glittered with the first dews of autumn. The stones
and dust of the driveway had been churned up. But was it done
by an animal? How was she supposed to know what a wild boar
track looked like?

Whatever it was, the scuffing on the ground did not seem significant. Most of it was accounted for by their own footprints and
the marks caused by dragging Clémence's enormous suitcase to
the front door.

Penelope rubbed her head. She went back into the kitchen,
where Clémence was preparing coffee. As the pot began to
steam and bubble on the stove, the women sat down and considered the situation.

"I'm not convinced, Clémence. There doesn't seem to be
much evidence of wild boar outside."

"It was just an idea."

Silence.

"I will call someone to repair the glass on Monday," said Clémence. Unlike Penelope, she looked fresh and smart and exuded efficiency, even on a Sunday morning.

"Thank you. I am very glad you are here! After what the chief of police said . . ." Penelope slumped as she realised something. "He wants me to stop asking questions and getting involved—but we have to tell him about this. Show the police the broken glass and the shot. Urgh. My head hurts. I could so do without this!"

Clémence pushed a cup of strong black coffee in front of her. "He's not going to like it."

"That is true." Penelope sipped. "Here's what else is bothering me. Apart from the possibility that I'm now on some gangland hit list, of course. This theory that Avore was killed by the Marseille underworld enforcers because he couldn't pay his gambling debts. Has the mayor mentioned that one to you?"

"He may have . . ."

"How likely do you think that is, honestly?"

"It is true that many bad things are blamed on gangsters from Marseille."

"Exactly. Every week *La Provence* carries stories about 'Le Chicago de Provence,' and you know what I think? That there are many crimes that are blamed on the bad people from Marseille because that is what the people who live in these lovely villages in the Luberon want to believe. If they can't blame the Avores or the hunters, of course. But that doesn't make the stories true."

Clémence considered this. "You could be right," she said at last. "So who are the real suspects in this case, then?"

Penelope went to get a sheet of paper and a pen. "OK, this is blue-sky thinking. We make a list of every person and every idea, even if we don't agree. First, let's put down the criminals from Marseille and Avore's gambling debts, because both the mayor and the chief of police have said that is a line of inquiry. Then we have all the people in St Merlot who had a reason to dislike Manuel Avore. There are plenty of them."

"Unhappily, that includes Mme Avore, who perhaps had most to gain from her husband's death."

"That's the spirit. Now, there is M. Louchard, who loves Mme Avore . . . and M. Charpet, but only because it looks as if someone tried, rather incompetently, to frame him by using his tool store here." Penelope drew a cartoon frame around his name as she saw the look of horror on Clémence's face.

"Now we come to the theory that it might be something to do with me and this house. Does some xenophobic Provençal hunter resent my purchase of the house and want to scare me off?" Penelope wrote down "Brit-hating local." She drew a wiggly line attaching that to Louchard's name.

"You don't really think that," said Clémence.

"We are ruling nothing out. I suspect the chief of police might have some sympathy for such a person."

"Write down: 'Person who bought the axe from the shop in Coustellet.' It might still be relevant."

Penelope nodded. "I agree."

"What about the shots last night? And the shots fired at me in the ruined chapel?"

"It really could just be the crazy hunters."

"OK, but I'm not convinced. Now let's think about this house. Is there any reason why anyone would want to scare me off?"

Clémence shook her head slowly. "I know these villages. Some here might resent foreigners buying up houses, but none of them would threaten you. The worst resentments are kept between themselves, the bad blood between families that has existed for generations."

The coffee and the conversation were starting to clear Penelope's head. Now she needed some sugar. She ripped into a bag of supermarket croissants bought for emergencies and slathered one with black cherry jam. Clémence, who visibly shuddered at the sight of this processed chemical pick-me-up, stuck to black coffee.

"So," said Penelope, munching, "we are left with one decent lead in the Avore case. The axe purchase in Coustellet. But the police have that and won't even discuss it now. There are Avore's enemies in the village, and his widow and M. Louchard. And there is one more thing I think we need to talk about. Why does the mayor always dismiss this case as if it's of no importance at all? Why does he do that?"

"Does he?"

"He does with me. It's as if he just wants it all to go away so we can pretend it never happened. He wants to leave everything to the police, almost because he dislikes the chief and knows how useless he is. And it has made me start to wonder whether there is anything more to it." She was on the point of coming clean about the mysterious draft contract she had found in the priory, but something inside stopped her. Clémence had too strong a relationship with Laurent to risk passing on this little nugget. She decided to dig a little further first.

"What are you saying? That you suspect the mayor? Penny, really!" Clémence gave a peal of laughter.

"Haven't you even considered that he might know more than he is telling us? Has he got other connections with Louchard and Avore that we do not know about?"

Clémence looked serious for a moment. "Laurent always knows more than he tells. But you cannot suspect him! Why would he do such a thing? What gain would there be for him? Next you will be asking if I have done this murder!" Clémence rocked back and laughed hard. This was clearly the funniest thing she had heard in months.

Penelope put her hands up. "We don't know that Laurent has nothing to gain. But I'm not saying I think he did it—of course not. It's just that I get the impression he might know more than he says he does, and he has some reason for not wanting the killer to be found locally. That's all I'm saying."

She fought against her better judgement, then added, "Also, there's the man in the red Ferrari. His friend."

"What about him?"

"I think I heard that car the night before we found Avore in the pool. It was just before I went to bed."

Just like Frankie, Clémence couldn't understand what was strange about that. "And you can't really believe it was strange, or you would have told the police when they asked if you had seen or heard anything that night. But you didn't, did you?"

Penelope had to admit it. "Who is that guy, anyway?"

"Benoît? They knew each other in Paris, years ago."

"So what is he doing here? Is there something between him and Laurent?" Benoît? The draft contract. BdeR. LM.

"They are friends! If there were more, I am sure it would be merely of the business nature."

"Anything to do with the priory here?"

"I cannot tell you. All I can say is that there are delicate negotiations there."

"Could Avore and Louchard have had any involvement with that?"

"I can assure you that Laurent has nothing to do with the death of Manuel Avore."

"I think if you had been broken into and shot at, your mind might become as suspicious as mine, Clémence," Penelope said. Every time she felt absolutely confident that she and her erstwhile estate agent were on the same side, another seed of doubt grew. She was grappling with this disturbing thought when they were interrupted by a knock on the kitchen door.

M. Louchard stood, beret in hand, looking both furtive and distinctly the worse for wear.

"Entrez, monsieur," said Penelope, getting up to usher him inside. He seated himself, still clearly ill at ease, and began an explanation for his visit, which lost her after the first few words.

Clémence heard the farmer out as he stumbled through his speech. Then she sat back with a relieved expression. "It was just as well we did not call the police."

"I didn't catch all of that. What did he say?"

"He has come to apologise about the window. On the way up the track last night, behind us, he saw a wild boar close to your house and the temptation was too much for him. He was showing off to Mariette and took a stupid shot. He missed. The boar ran up the track towards his house, and he shot it—eventually—but unfortunately some damage was caused in the battle. He cannot remember shooting in the direction of your house, but he had had a few celebratory drinks and he fears that he may have inadvertently broken your window. He has come round to say sorry and that he will repair it, and . . ."

Clémence glanced towards M. Louchard. He got up and went out.

"He has brought a gift by way of apology."

Louchard reentered, bearing a tray. On it sat what appeared to be a large snarling boar's head, giving them the evil eye from a mess of bloody fur. Almost worse was the brown-stained cloth tied around the neck, like some horrific cravat.

Penelope took one look and gagged. She dived for the sink. Just managing to hold down the contents of her stomach, she took a large gulp of water.

Pretending not to notice, Clémence continued, "He says maybe you can stuff it and put it over your mantelpiece." Was there a hint of a malicious smile on her lips? "Or of course, there is the tête de sanglier—that's quite a delicacy in this area. You must boil up the head until the eyes fall out, and then . . ."

"Enough, Clémence! Please." Penelope took a few deep breaths, composed herself, and returned to her chair, avoiding the penetrating gaze of the dead boar.

"Isn't it strange, Penny—wherever you are in the room, it always seems to be looking at you!"

"Mme Valencourt, you are not helping!" Penelope was beginning to lose her cool with her French companion.

In the ensuing silence, M. Louchard placed the head on the kitchen table and went outside to collect a tool kit and a sheet of glass. Without another word he went along to the hall, and they heard the sound of the remains of the broken glass pane being tapped from the window frame. Penelope flopped onto a kitchen chair. It creaked and groaned under the additional weight of *three* supermarket croissants and jam. She couldn't worry about that this morning. "Oh, golly. What a relief! I mean, at least we know what happened last night. Even if I'm not thrilled to know that my neighbour takes passing potshots at the house when he sees the ingredients for a casserole trotting around outside. Is it going to be like this all winter?"

Clémence wiggled her hand to imply that it might.

Penelope slumped. After a few moments she said uneasily, "He could have killed you. How can you be so sanguine about it? The only reason he has come round this morning to mend the window is because he doesn't want any trouble with the police. But what if he *is* trouble—big trouble?"

27

THE CENTRE OF THE VILLAGE had been transformed yet again for the *vide grenier*. Stalls had been set out under the plane trees and crowds were milling around, though the professional *brocanteurs* must surely have come early and taken all the best stuff.

Clémence dropped Penelope at the edge of the square. She clearly had no burning desire to rummage through other people's old tat. "See, nowhere to park. I will come back for you later. And I will speak to M. Louchard when he has finished his repairs. If he is hiding anything, I will find out, I promise."

She was probably hoping to run into the mayor.

Penelope had visited a few *brocantes* on her earlier trips to the region, and quickly realised that they fell into two categories. First, there was the true *brocante*, the *vide grenier*—"empty the attic." Anything and everything that the locals wanted to chuck out would be laid out on the trestle tables, in no particular order or price, to turn a quick euro. Prices were sensible, and bargains could be had, though Penelope reckoned a few hours boiling in disinfectant might be necessary for some of these items.

The second type of *brocante* was staffed by professionals, intent it seemed on getting their own back on all foreigners (and in this case "foreigners" meant anyone who hailed from beyond the valley's boundaries, particularly Parisians). Vastly overinflated prices were asked for unwanted paraphernalia of all sorts, from pots and pans and glassware to the distressed chest of drawers retailing at about the same price asked for a Chippendale in Christie's, which turned out to be so distressed that it fell apart with a moan and a death wish when the drawers were opened.

The St Merlot *vide grenier* had attracted a few professional *brocanteurs*, but it seemed to be a classic village event. Where table space was not available, patches of ground had been cleared and mats put down to display the items. The array of goods was bewildering.

Penelope stopped to admire a full-size fibreglass panda that stared glassily back at her from an open van.

"Trois cents euros, madame," quoted the stallholder, a young man with long hair and a silk waistcoat.

"Merci." Her accent was not yet good enough to pass muster, and the youth carried on in broken English.

"The black and white markings are one hundred percent accurate."

For a moment, Penelope considered whether or not it would be a good idea to purchase the panda, placing it in her mind's eye peering out of the bamboo thicket from which M. Avore had emerged a few months previously. But, unsure of exactly how M. Charpet might react to this surreal intrusion into his domain, she moved on to the next stall, in which were arrayed tablecloths, napkins, and laceware of intricate design—items that Penelope knew she actually needed rather than wished for. She sorted through the piles, hoping to find starched vintage sheets and tablecloths.

She made a purchase—a white embroidered bedspread, clearly freshly laundered, for twenty-five euros—and then moved on, hoping to find some colourful pottery to give her new home that authentic South of France vibe. Instead, she found an awful lot of old vases and terrible pictures, cutlery, scruffy books, and scratched vinyl records, along with kitchen devices bought in the 1970s which probably had never worked, even then.

She was still feeling rather under the weather, and the midday heat was not helping. But she perked up when she saw a smarter group of stalls. One had wrought-iron garden tables and chairs; another was selling mirrors and small pieces of bedroom furniture. She went up to a stall set out with lanterns. They were all shapes and sizes, mostly made of distressed metal. Some were painted white to give exactly the shabby-chic look Penelope was seeking.

She picked out two lanterns of the same design and asked the price. They weren't as cheap as she'd thought they'd be, but they were exactly what she wanted for her terrace.

"Votre meilleur prix?" she asked. She knew the phrase from watching all those thousands of British antiques programmes when the contestants went across the Channel to sniff out more interesting bargains.

"Soixante euros les deux, madame."

Penelope smiled at the stallholder, a pleasant-looking man in his forties wearing aviator glasses. He looked familiar, but she couldn't think where she had seen him before. Then she realised. He was the man who'd come into the bakery and interrupted the conversation about Louchard. Jean-Luc. So this was one of his other interests, apart from owning the garage. "Pas mal," she said, grinning. But what was really his best price? It always worked on the telly.

Sixty euros, he repeated. Clearly business was business, a chat in the bakery notwithstanding.

Penelope reacted casually. She moved away from the lanterns she liked and picked up an old oil lamp. It was a simple burner, the oil reservoir made of brass, rather battered, with a new wick and a glass bowl.

It looked very similar indeed to the one that she had found in the hall cupboard, though hers had not been polished. Perhaps they might make a pair on her dining table on a warm summer evening when she had guests.

"How was M. Correa's peach and pistachio gâteau—the one that was going to be perfect at nine o'clock?" she asked. "It's rather wonderful, how people here are so precise about food and how it should be served."

"It's how we live," he said.

"I will take both lanterns and this lamp for seventy euros," said Penelope firmly.

The deal was done.

"Don't believe everything you hear at the bakery, by the way," he said, warming up to a chat as he wrapped them and found a bag. "Correa is a terrible gossip. His wife is almost as bad, and the information is not always reliable."

"Oh?"

"For a start, they both loathed and detested Manuel Avore, despite what he told you, for a very good reason."

"Really?"

The stallholder shrugged. "Just like everyone else. Only it cut deeper with Jacques. He and Manuel had been friends since they were boys, then gambling partners. But one day, Manuel could not stop himself. He borrowed money, then cheated his friend. Jacques went back to the table to try to win it back—in Cavaillon, in Salon, in Marseille, in Nice—but he only went deeper into trouble. He almost lost everything, including his wife. It took him years to pay off his debts. But he stopped gambling and worked and worked to build his skills and his business."

"That doesn't mean he couldn't feel pity for Manuel," Penelope pointed out.

"Sure. Until Manuel gets out of prison and starts blackmailing him, saying he's found out that Jacques is still gambling, that he is starting to owe money again, and only buying the cheapest ingredients for the bakery. People can accept many things, but not that. Not where their daily bread is concerned."

"Is it true, though?"

"Who knows?"

Penelope took her purchases and thanked him. It was clear that, as ever, nothing was quite what it first appeared. The boulangerie-bar in the corner of the square was as busy as ever, so there was no chance of popping over for a quiet coffee and a gentle fact-finding chat. It was odd that Correa had been so effusive about not hating his old friend, when he hardly needed to say anything at all.

She couldn't see Clémence anywhere, so she went over to the boulangerie-bar and lingered. M. Charpet, with his diminutive sister Valentine, wandered over.

"Madame," began her gardener, haltingly. Then he hesitated. Valentine poked him and whispered a command.

"Madame," he began again, "my sister and I—what have you bought there?"

Penelope showed them.

M. Charpet made a face at the candle lanterns, but took the oil lamp and examined it carefully.

"It's pretty isn't it? And it could be useful," said Penelope.

"Where did you buy it?"

"Where? Over there at the stall near the garden tables and chairs."

M. Charpet continued turning it around in his hands.

"Have I made a good buy?"

"I think perhaps you have, madame." He handed it back. "Now, I must ask you. Valentine and I would be most honoured if you join us for lunch next Sunday."

Penelope was touched, and tried hard not to let it show. But she had a wide smile on her face as she answered. "Of course M. Charpet, I would be delighted to come. Thank you."

Another voice broke in. "Did you enjoy the first band last night, Penny?" Penelope turned round, in a good mood after M. Charpet's invitation. "And did you like the special effects with the stage lights?"

Didier wore a black AC/DC T-shirt, and his hair was wilder than ever.

"I did! The band was brilliant! I loved the Stones and the Beatles sets. And as for the stage lighting, you should be a professional!" Actually, Penelope didn't think it had been anything particularly spectacular, but she sensed Didier would relish the praise and recognition of his efforts. "Just promise me you won't go on a world tour before you've done my rewiring!"

He grinned widely. "Did I hear that you have been invited to a Sunday lunch chez Charpet?"

"You did."

"That is certainly an honour, madame. He is a famous man in this village, and his sister's cooking is excellent. Though if I may, I would like to give you some advice."

"All right."

"Eat nothing from now until Sunday. Nothing at all! They keep an excellent table."

"You mean the food is good?"

"That is exactly what he means." The mayor materialised by her side.

"Oh, hello," said Penelope. The electrician said a cheery goodbye and rubbed his stomach, telling her not to forget.

"Have you seen Clémence?" Penelope asked Laurent innocently.

"No, is she here?"

"She stayed with me last night. I got a bit . . . upset at the fête." She was not going to admit to being tipsy and letting her imagination run away with her. "The chief of police talked to me, and as usual, I did not find the conversation exactly *sympa*."

"Penny, you really must not take this personally. I am sure he is just trying to make his investigation."

"What can you tell me about the body in the ruined chapel, then?"

Laurent was smiling, but he shook his head and wagged an index finger. He did a passable impersonation of Reyssens. "No more questions, Mme Keet!"

They were interrupted by an old couple Penelope didn't know, who started twittering like excitable starlings about the success of the fête. Laurent did not introduce her to them.

Penelope backed away, left with the feeling that she had received a brush-off again, however charmingly delivered.

At home, she placed her new purchase on the terrace wall next to the oil lamp she already possessed—she had thought they were very similar, but she was astonished to find they were identical. Despite everything else on her mind, she felt immensely pleased with herself for spotting the item at the *brocante*.

Clémence came out to admire it, and she had some more good news. Pierre Louchard had finished the repair. He'd also been persuaded to take the boar's head away, to give to someone who would really appreciate it.

28

PENELOPE DID NOT FOLLOW DIDIER'S gastronomic advice over the course of the next week. Each morning she resolved to eat like a bird, and ended up stuffing herself like a goose being prepared for foie gras. It must have been stress.

There were no more strange incidents, though as a precaution she gave up the country walks. Clémence had returned to her luxurious house in Viens, imparting one pearl of wisdom before she went. "Frenchwomen do not eat croissants, Penny. And if one day the spirit is not strong enough to resist, we will never, *ever* have a second one. And afterwards, we will not eat lunch that day."

So now she knew. A chic woman with the body of a Chihuahua was a croissant-free zone. Penelope felt shamed. She took lots of exercise in her pool, delighting in the sparkling freshness of the unheated water. It was definitely not seeping out. At least that was a success, though she had to make a conscious effort to push thoughts of Manuel Avore and bones to the back of her mind. She also visited some furniture stores, arranged to have the bathroom refitted, and worked hard to make the house feel like a home. Her cello remained in its case.

Each day she expected Clémence, the mayor, or the police to call with further news of the investigation, at which point she would tell them what she had confirmed from a forensic perspective. But all remained quiet. She was left alone, hoping that the professionals were getting on with their jobs.

COME SUNDAY, she thought about driving up to the Charpet house, but decided to face her fears. Her gardener always
walked. The route was hardly off the beaten track. She set out
wearing a bright pink jacket she had found in Apt. This time, no
hunters could possibly mistake her for a wild boar.

From across the valley she could hear church bells. Her heart
rate quickened at a smattering of gunfire from the hillside below, but it sounded a long way off. With any luck the hunters
would stop soon for a legendary French Sunday lunch in the
country.

It was a clear sunny day, and over the hills the green of the
trees was edging imperceptibly into gold. Black grapes hung in
bunches from the vines along the way, and fig trees were dotted
with large, sticky ripe fruit.

Where the track met the path down to the ruined chapel, she
felt a frisson of fear. She quickly turned left and took the path in
the opposite direction up the hill towards the village, as M. Charpet had instructed. She climbed for some ten minutes, past crumbling stone walls and brambles, until she came out in the village at
the point beyond the main square.

The narrow streets of the old part of the village were quiet
and still deep in shadow, even though it was near midday. Large
tubs of red geraniums and lavender clustered at doors and windows. All seemed in various states of mild disrepair. Pink vale-
rian sprouted from every crack in the stone walls.

Penelope walked along looking for a house number or a name
on a postbox that would help her identify the Charpet house, but
the village, as always, seemed intent on keeping its secrets.

A rich aroma of roasting meat drew her to a house on the
corner. It had the blue shutters she had been told to look out for.

She went up to the door and pulled on the iron chain that hung to one side. Somewhere far away a bell sounded.

She readied herself. This lunch was going to be a real test of her French, but surely the important aspect was the goodwill on both sides. And she was certainly looking forward to sampling Valentine's fabled cooking.

The door was opened by a smartly dressed M. Charpet. She was touched to see him in a grey suit with a white shirt. As Penelope stepped over the threshold, she was struck by the cool freshness of the interior.

The ground floor of the house was effectively a cellar, with a vaulted stone ceiling. The flagstones on the floor had been polished by centuries of footfall, though they were only occasionally visible between the piles of potatoes, jars of preserved tomatoes, and tins of unnamed provenance that occupied most of the space. From the arches, long strings of onions, hams, salamis, and garlic in plaits hung on meat hooks. Along the back wall, shelves groaned under dusty bottles of wine.

If ever there is a nuclear holocaust, thought Penelope, this is where I'm heading.

M. Charpet ushered her up the old stairs in the corner. He proudly pointed out more produce arranged on shelves as they passed.

The first floor was one large room, with a kitchen along the side, leading onto a large verandah at the back that overlooked a strip of garden. It was the most perfectly designed allotment that she had ever seen. Apart from a pen in the corner from which a large brindle dog stared back at her, the whole space was given to lines of startlingly healthy vegetables, an artist's palette of colour. Not one inch was wasted, not a hint of any fertile area given over to a garden as Penelope and her English neighbours would imagine it. This was a garden for production, not show. But that did not stop it from being beautiful, as long as one liked things in straight lines.

Valentine was adding the finishing touches to lunch. She was such a tiny woman that she had to reach up like a child to the kitchen counter. Penelope handed her the flowers she had brought, and they exchanged three kisses.

"Can I help you to do anything?" asked Penelope, but Valentine waved her away. Her brother beckoned her to a table on the terrace that already groaned with aperitif bottles and slices of salami, no doubt from the cellar, large orange cubes of melon, plump black olives, radishes, crisps, nuts, and toasts covered in pâté of some sort. It would have been quite enough for an averagely hungry rugby team.

She had a sudden horror that more guests were expected, which would change the complexion of the relaxed gathering she'd been anticipating. But no, it was just the three of them. Penelope began to see what Didier had meant. If this was the ballast with a prelunch drink, what would the main course be like?

It was to be some time before Penelope found out. For between the aperitif and the main course were no less than three starters: a pork terrine, followed by prawns and mayonnaise, and aubergine caviar and Melba toast.

"Didier Picaud told me it was going to be good." Penelope sighed as she helped herself to a tiny extra spoonful of aubergine caviar. "But I never thought it would be this sublime."

The Charpet siblings exchanged a look.

"I keep a good table, madame," said Valentine with evident pride. "Like at your house. Le Chant d'Eau was once renowned in the village. My parents used to talk about how everyone wanted an invitation to dine."

Penelope loved the idea of owning a house that had been known for its hospitality. She allowed herself another little daydream about giving her own summer parties when all the work was finished. Then she shook herself. "You mean the Avores were once popular hosts?"

M. Charpet and his sister laughed derisorily.

"No, never! This was before, when it was owned by the Malpas family. Before they were forced out by the Avores."

"Forced out?"

M. Charpet glanced at his sister, whose almost imperceptible nod seemed to stiffen his resolve. "Madame, the history of the Avore and the Malpas families is not a happy one."

Penelope leaned forward unconciously as Charpet continued.

"Le Chant d'Eau was owned by the Malpas family for generations, but something happened during the war. No one knows what it was exactly, but we all knew that Gustave Avore, Manuel's grandfather, was a collaborator."

The old Frenchman paused to register his disgust. "There were four Malpas brothers, all strong Resistance men. It is rumoured that old Avore informed on them."

He spoke carefully so that Penelope would understand. "The occupying forces needed information about the Resistance—and they had plenty of collaborators in the town hall administrations willing to reward those who did the dirty work of informing on the patriots. Whatever happened, when Provence was liberated, the Avores were living at Le Chant d'Eau, and the two older Malpas brothers and their families had been shot. The younger two were still fighting farther north. Roger and Jean-Jacques were hotheads. They wanted to take the fight all the way to Germany. They did not return for many months."

"But surely the Malpas brothers got the house back when they reappeared?"

"Ah, madame, the end of the war was a difficult time. Many people wanted to forget that some among us were collaborators and traitors. Roger and Jean-Jacques Malpas were quietly given compensation, but they never managed to repossess Le Chant d'Eau. That would have required the opening of too many old wounds. Who knows which official had sanctioned the original transfer? Was he still there? Everyone preferred to keep the past closed. Especially some of our administrators who had cooperated with the Nazis."

"So that's why people hated the Avores."

"Collaborators can never be forgiven, not here in the Luberon. That was the cause of the feud between the Louchards and the Avores, too. The Louchards were brave Resistants. This Avore business is of course sad, but I cannot say that I am not pleased that he has finally met with justice." Charpet, who had been working himself up throughout the conversation, finished by bringing a fist down hard on the table and tossing back a nearly full glass of wine.

Penelope did not want to upset her host by pushing him now for more information. There would be other times. Grasping for a change in subject, she launched into the first optimistic thing that came into her head.

"When I first arrived, M. Louchard said there was a village rumour that there was hidden treasure somewhere on my land. Do you know anything about that?"

"That old story!" piped up Valentine.

"It's not true? Oh, now I'm disappointed!" joked Penelope.

"Actually, that's a wartime story, too," said Charpet, looking fierce. "The so-called treasure was supposed to be another reward old Avore received for helping the Nazis. It must have been a lot of help, because the word was that he was given looted jewellery and gold that was never processed into gold bars. Dirty gold, from terrible thefts. Jewish gold, you know."

Penelope nodded, feeling uncomfortable.

"It was kept hidden because he knew it would be taken from him if anyone found it. So he buried it. That was the story anyway."

"But surely he would have sold it, bit by bit, over the years?"

"He probably did. But the story persisted."

A pause lengthened as they considered the past.

"Mme Valencourt told me that there had been a few strange events at the house when the people from Lyon owned it."

M. Charpet exhaled deeply. "They were not here very much. And when they were, they did not seem very happy. They were always having problems with the water, the electricity supply, too much rain or too little rain. They came here less and less, though it was supposed to be their dream retirement home . . . and then, the fatal accident, poor souls."

"Then it was empty for, what—two years?"

"About that."

"Do you have a big family, Mme Keet?" asked Valentine, side-stepping the depressing turn the conversation had taken on the subject of Le Chant d'Eau and its previous owners.

"No, not really."

Under close questioning, Penelope told them a little about David, the children, and the "très amicable divorce." She didn't want them to think she was the slightest bit sad.

"David is a lawyer in London. He works very hard. Now I look back, I realise he was not at home very much, even when the children were very young. I married him and instantly had a family."

Valentine nodded slowly. "You did not have a child of your own?"

"No." Penelope paused. "I think of Lena and Justin as my own. And I am the only mother they remember. Though they have always known that their birth mother died—it was terribly sad, very sudden. She drowned, in the sea. Caught in the current on a weekend trip to the beach. David was devastated. When I met him, he was so tall and handsome, but he had the saddest eyes I had ever seen. All I wanted was to take some of the pain away."

She found she wanted to talk about this. "David used to tell me I was too hard on the children, discipline-wise, when they were growing up, but I could see problems ahead if I let him spoil them and do whatever they wanted when he was not there. I thought that was part of being a good mother. Sometimes I feel they still resent this, even now they are adults—and at others I know that the fact that we can have all the normal family disagreements and still love each other means that they consider that I really am their mother. Does that make sense?"

"Naturally!" said Valentine.

"That is life," said her brother.

Valentine busied herself with the many plates, and resisted forcefully all attempts by her guest to help. Soon she staggered back to the table with a *blanquette de veau* so delicately fragrant that it brought a tear to M. Charpet's eye.

"La pièce de résistance!" he cried.

They drank a gloriously deep red wine from a bottle with no label. It seemed to unfurl a rich fruitiness in the mouth, but somehow did not overpower the creamy veal dish. The combination was magnificent.

Penelope put down her glass in a concerted effort to pace her drinking. "What do you think about the murder of Manuel Avore?" she asked. Oh, dear. She probably had had far too much to drink again. It was making her bold. "Could it have been connected to the feud between the Avores and the Louchards?"

"Who knows?" asked M. Charpet.

Penelope turned to Valentine. "I saw M. Louchard with Mme Avore at the fête last weekend. They looked very friendly."

"I saw them too," said Valentine.

"What do you think, will there be a happy ending for them?"

"*Pfff!*" said her brother. "Who knows?"

"There is no chance that Mme Avore could have . . . helped herself to win her freedom?" It came out awkwardly in Penelope's French, apparently without the insinuation she had intended.

"You mean, why didn't Mariette Avore leave Manuel long ago?" Valentine shook her head. "He would have come after her. And she did not want to leave the village. She has many friends here. A kind woman, who is much respected."

"A bad marriage is hard to endure," said Penelope.

"That is certainly true, madame," M. Charpet joined in. "He was a difficult man with many enemies, but it was easy to blame Manuel Avore for any trouble in the village."

"It does seem so."

M. Charpet sat back in his chair and regarded her intently.

"Last Sunday I saw you buy the lanterns and the oil lamp from Jean-Luc Malpas at the vide grenier."

Penelope nodded. "Jean-Luc is a Malpas?"

"You were so happy to find the oil lamp because you thought it made a pair with the other one you found at Le Chant d'Eau. What a piece of luck! Can I ask you, madame, when you took it home, was it an exact pair?"

"It was!"

"What did you think about that?"

"I thought . . . it was, as you say, a piece of luck. And that probably it was mass-produced in this region."

M. Charpet shook his head sadly. "No. That oil lamp was stolen from Le Chant d'Eau. There were always two at the house, used in the garden in summer when the breeze would have puffed out the candles."

"You think that Jean-Luc stole it?"

"The Malpas family may have been Resistants, but they were no saints. It might have been Jean-Luc."

"Manuel Avore," said Valentine, firmly. "I bet it was him. He was always crawling over Le Chant d'Eau, and he would take anything that wasn't fixed in cement."

"You see? Avore was always getting the blame!" said her brother.

"Tell, me," said Penelope, thinking back to what Jean-Luc had said to her about the baker and his wife. "What is your opinion of Jacques Correa, the baker, and his wife?"

"He is an excellent baker."

"He is an artist," said Valentine.

"Oh, I know that. But apart from that . . . how does the village see them as people? Simply as a centre of information and gossip?"

"That, yes."

"How reliable are they as purveyors of information?" Then, when she saw her hosts look blank, Penelope said, "Correa told me he had no problem with Manuel Avore, but others say differently. What was the truth, as you saw it?"

"He's all right, Correa. He had a few problems a while ago, but all is well now. If he gets a bit creative with the chat, it's because he wants people to like him and come to his shop. And mostly they do."

Valentine concurred.

"What kind of problems?" asked Penelope.

"His gambling got out of hand for a while. Some violence. But all in the past now."

So Jean-Luc's story could be true. It was another gambling connection. Penelope could not help noting that the baker was used to hefting heavy trays of dough around in his strong arms. A nasty comparison between the dough and a lifeless body floated across her mind's eye. His wife Sylvie was strong, too. It occurred to Penelope that they were always up early in the morning, when most other people were asleep. She was going to have to find out a bit more about the loquacious baker and his wife.

Valentine served an oakleaf lettuce salad with tangy vinaigrette. Then a cheese board. A raspberry tart and Chantilly cream followed. As they progressed in stately manner through the menu, Penelope became full to bursting point, not only with wondrous delicacies but with new information that forced her to reevaluate all her impressions of St Merlot and its inhabitants.

❧

PENELOPE WALKED home very slowly. How long would it take to become truly part of St Merlot life? She had a wise friend in M. Charpet, and her confidence was growing as she became more determined to solve the crimes. She made her way down the path, pushing aside the gorse and bramble bushes now laden with blackberries, until the slope levelled and she found herself staring at M. Louchard's farm.

For a minute she stood catching her breath and staring at the distant hills of the Petit Luberon, hazy and brown. She was about to start off again when a flash of reflected sunlight from behind the wall of the farm caught her eye. It startled her. In a moment of pure reflex, she jumped towards a tree trunk. It was a fortunate move, as a split second later, the now familiar crack of a rifle sounded and a bullet whistled past. She hit the ground and rolled towards the scrub at the side of the path. She stayed down for at least fifteen minutes, shaking from head to foot. There were no more shots, just the sound of running feet from the direction of the farm. All became quiet.

That can't have been drunken hunters, she thought. It must

have been deliberate. If she had drunk less wine at lunch, she might have stayed down for longer. But she wasn't thinking straight. She eased herself out of the ditch and crawled along the path, as if she was on some military training exercise.

She arrived home dirty and tired, but still in one piece. This was distinctly unfunny. With trembling hands she stabbed out the number the chief of police had given her, but there was no reply. The same went for the mayor and Clémence. She tried repeatedly, with the same result.

29

AS DAWN TOUCHED THE TOP of the Luberon ridge, a sleep-deprived Penelope got dressed and went out on foot. She kept away from the track and took a route through the trees to Louchard's farm, keen that no one, least of all Louchard, should know where she was headed.

Once at the scene of the shooting, Penelope surveyed the landscape, trying to reimagine her way back to the previous afternoon. She was heartened by the fact that the farmer's car was not in the drive, and the farmhouse appeared empty. Was he already up and about—or could he have spent the night with Mme Avore at her house, maybe? She pulled out her camera, a large map, and some tape. Looking around to make sure she was not being observed, she began to take furtive photos from various angles.

Every few seconds she glanced anxiously towards the farmhouse and back down the track to check that nobody was coming. Then she stood where she had been when the shot was fired, trying to picture exactly the moment she'd seen the glint of reflected sunlight.

Carefully she pieced together the incident. The gunshot had whistled past her right ear as she was standing on the path next to the tree. She could imagine its general trajectory, which she marked on her map in pencil. Then she stumbled down into the ditch where she had lain hidden.

It was clear, even with a rough estimate, that the gunshot had come from the direction of the farmhouse. The glint of sunlight on metal had definitely been behind the farm wall. She felt sure that she had been targeted. Tracing the path of the bullet in her memory, she marked out a small area of trees and undergrowth, then pulled out her gardening gloves and secateurs and went to work sifting through the brambles.

It was a painstaking and sometimes painful task. The wild brambles, some bedecked with blackberries, had thorns that punctured the most resistant of materials. Penelope soon found herself sweating, arms shredded by scratches. Nature was conspiring to hinder her search, but she stuck to her task.

After several hours she was rewarded with the sight of something metallic burrowed into a tree root in the cleared area. She wormed it out. It was a bullet.

Penelope stared at the shiny piece of metal. It looked new. It was horrible to think that it could so easily have hit her the previous day—killed her, even.

That was it. She was going back to the police, even if the chief did think she was a figure of ridicule. She was just imagining the scene at the police station, and what she would say, when the unmistakable sound of a tractor intruded. It was getting closer.

Penelope scarcely had time to scramble upright before M. Louchard's prize-winning machine crested the horizon, taking up the whole width of the track. She was trapped.

The tractor rumbled towards her, then stopped abruptly. Louchard jumped down. Penelope adjusted her dress into some semblance of order and gripped the spent bullet tightly in her gloved hand. She took a deep breath as the farmer advanced on her with a questioning look.

"Bonjour, monsieur, comment allez-vous?" She tried hard to act as if nothing had happened. The shot had come from this man's land. Maybe even from an upper window of his farm-house. Was it possible that this was her adversary all along, even as he had pretended to befriend her?

"Très bien merci, Mme Keet, and how are you?"

He sounded amicable, but her veins ran to ice as she remem-bered how he had talked about hunters and their stray bullets when she was on her way down to that fateful encounter with the bones in the chapel. That was not long before the first incidence of gunfire. Almost as if he knew what she was about to encounter.

He took off his cap. "What are you doing, madame?"

"I was walking here yesterday, monsieur, and I seem to have lost an earring—I was looking for it in the undergrowth."

"I am glad that you have found it, then."

"Found it?"

"Well, you have two earrings on now, so you must have been successful."

"Er, yes. Jolly lucky." She touched her right earlobe, all the time silently thanking the Almighty that she had forgotten to take her earrings off the previous night. "I found it in the ditch just over there."

"Well, it seems that you needed to look very carefully. But that is good—you have done a job that I was not looking forward to, clearing all those brambles away! Please, come in and have a coffee—it is the least I can do to thank you."

"Oh, no, thank you."

"Why not?"

"Well, because I—"

"Come inside. I insist."

He caught hold of her arm and steered her firmly towards his house. For a second, Penelope wondered if she should scream. But no one would hear her. She had been unlucky—or plain stupid—and now she was going to pay the price.

M. Louchard led her into his kitchen and released her arm. Penelope was determined not to let him see how scared she was. If she was to be finished off, she was going to maintain a stiff British upper lip to the end.

He took a bottle of plum brandy from a cupboard and poured the dangerously smooth spirit into two glasses.

"Bit early for me," said Penelope, as he handed one to her. "But you go ahead."

"Drink!" he said in English. "All!"

She glanced at her watch. Nine thirty in the morning! She was on a very slippery slope. Though would alcohol prove to be a mercy, given whatever she was facing?

But the farmer did not show any sign that he was about to finish her off. In fact, he seemed to be in a remarkably jolly mood. Perhaps he wanted to have a civilised conversation about why he had found it necessary to attempt to shoot her, not once but twice.

"It's a beautiful morning, is it not?" he trilled.

Penelope agreed that it was. Wasn't that the kind of observation an executioner would make? She braced for the revelation of his evil intent. Why didn't he just shoot her from close range, now, instead of spinning it out?

She couldn't concentrate. Nothing quite made sense. Had he murdered Avore to free Mariette? Had they been seeing each other while her husband was in prison, and he could no longer bear to see her reluctantly accept him back? Perhaps Avore had found out and threatened him. Or worse, threatened to take his fury out on Mariette, thought Penelope; but what has that got to do with me?

Louchard smiled broadly at her.

"You are looking very happy, monsieur. Have you had some good news?" Penelope desperately tried to keep her voice light and even.

She looked around, subtly, for his rifle. Several people had told her he was an expert marksman. Was he so mad that he could no longer hit a large target? Emotional overload could affect physical coordination. But then she thought of the boar he had shot on the night of the fête, in the dark. No, there was nothing wrong with his marksmanship.

"Mme Keet, it has been a very good week for me. Yesterday I had my greatest success!"

"Yesterday?" squeaked Penelope, thinking about the whizz of the bullet that only just missed. And the one on the night of the fête. "What happened yesterday, monsieur?"

"Mariette won again, and at one of the most important contests in Provence."

"Mme Mariette Avore? It was a beauty contest?"

This time Louchard sat back and laughed properly, a deep raucous chuckle. "Mme Avore! Non, Mariette is the name I gave to my tractor. It was a . . . tribute. I had to leave before dawn to get her to Banon, but it was worth it. Best Tractor of Show at the Banon Agricultural Fair is worth a lot of money. I have nearly paid for this year's taxes."

"Were you in Banon for the whole day?"

"You have just seen me returning from there. There was a celebration after the show, you understand. And I had to drive back all the way at thirty kilometres per hour. Along the back roads. It takes some time!"

Penelope smiled. Surreptitiously slipping her glove and its contents into her bag, she took a sip of plum brandy and congratulated the proud tractor owner.

"For a success of this magnitude, a celebration!" He downed his glass and poured another, topping up her glass to the brim. "Drink! Drink!"

She did so, reluctantly.

"Jean-Luc Malpas won't be happy, though," chortled M. Louchard.

"Why do you say that?"

"Because he sold me the tractor. It was in a terrible state, too, so I got a very good deal. But I worked hard to restore it, to impress the real Mariette. As I polished its curves, I was thinking only of her."

Bit too much information, thought Penelope. The ferocious plum brandy was now burning its way through her system.

"You should have seen the look on Paul Darrieux's face at our fête when I won here!"

"Darrieux—the owner of the store at Coustellet?"

"That's him. Malpas acts as his representative for secondhand vehicles this end of the Luberon. Apparently he told Darrieux that my Mariette had been broken up for parts. He must have pocketed quite a margin on the quiet. Ha!"

Sharp practice, thought Penelope.

Louchard chortled and reached for the bottle again.

"Goodness, that reminds me—I must go! Thank you—and congratulations!" She dived for the door as Louchard had his hands full mid-pour, and made a run for it.

"Mme Keet!"

Penelope looked for cover, prepared for rifle shots, but none came.

The moment that Penelope got inside the house, out of breath and feeling quite tipsy from her neighbour's lethal brew, she called the estate agency in Ménerbes.

"Agence Hublot, bonjour."

"Clémence, it's me, Penny."

"Ah, comment ça va, Penny? Le repas avec M. Charpet, hier, c'était bon?"

"Sod lunch, Clémence. I was shot at again on my way home!"

"Oh, mon dieu! Are you OK?"

"I'm OK, for now. It happened about half past four, near Louchard's place."

"Louchard? Penny, calm down. I will come over—on second thought, no. Are you all right to drive?"

"I don't think I am. Plum brandy."

"I will come as soon as I can."

Clémence was as good as her word. In no time at all—goodness only knew how fast she had driven—the Mini Cooper drew up in the familiar flurry of screeching brakes and scattering gravel.

The estate agent was genuinely concerned. For the first time, she looked less than perfectly groomed, with smudged makeup and hair out of place. She looked around nervously behind her as she entered.

"I've made us some strong coffee," said Penelope.

They sat down at the kitchen table. With so much to discuss, it was hard to know where to start.

"That bullet was meant for me, I'm sure of it," Penelope blurted out. "The first time I was shot at, I could just about rationalise it as the hunters. But yesterday's shot could not have been a mistake. This morning I went back to the spot and found the bullet."

Clémence looked surprised. "A bullet, you say? That is unusual."

"How so?"

"Well, Penny, la chasse—the hunters—almost all use shotguns. They are a little bit safer—even in the hands of the wild men! Shot spreads out quickly once it has left the gun. Makes a flying or running target easier to hit. But shot are smaller and less deadly. Bullets need to be aimed precisely."

"I know all that! Look, I was standing on the track just below Louchard's farm, and I felt the wind as it went past my ear."

"Louchard's farm?"

"Yes, and that's where it came from. I'm sure of it. I checked the sight lines this morning—before M. Louchard caught me."

"What do you mean, Louchard caught you?"

"He chose that moment to come down the track—he was coming home on his tractor. I didn't show him the bullet—I just told him some story about losing an earring."

Clémence looked perturbed. "Did he believe you?"

"He seemed to."

The Frenchwoman shook her head, as if she were having some difficulty with the story. Penelope realised with some irritation that Clémence was staring at her dangly painted parrot earrings, bought from a highly reputable designer stall in Camden Passage some years previously. Her disdain was as ill-disguised as it was typical, even at a time of crisis.

Penelope ignored it. "He said that he was in Banon, at the Agricultural Fair, for all of yesterday. But that rifle shot definitely did come from his land, near his house."

"You are sure of that?"

"Yes, absolutely sure."

"And, the last time you were shot at, Penny, you met Louchard on your way back. I think you said he had his rifle then, yes?"

"He was cleaning it when I went past."

"Think back, Penny. Everything that you can remember. Every detail."

Penelope cast back to that afternoon. The lovely blue sky and the farmer's pessimism about the weather. The shots and the ruined chapel where she had taken cover. The sky clouding over, and then the first spots of rain as she sat outside with Louchard on her way home after the ordeal. The rain becoming more insistent, raindrops bouncing off the iron café table, and fizzing on the barrel of the rifle that still sat beside him.

Realisation hit.

"It was still hot."

"What was hot?"

"Louchard's rifle—I remember, when it was raining, how the drops fell on the barrel and boiled off straightaway."

The two women fell silent, and Penelope gave an involuntary shudder.

"I may have just had a narrow escape. If he is the one who has been shooting at me, he would have realised that I suspected him. Which is why he spun the tale about being at Banon and driving back through the night. So why didn't he try to do something this morning?"

"Perhaps he did."

"What do you mean?" asked Penelope feebly, even as she started to feel a bit sick. "The plum brandy? He was drinking it too, but what if he put some kind of drug in my glass?"

"How do you feel?"

"I've been better."

"Have some water. Lots of water, just in case."

Penelope opened the fridge and grabbed a large bottle of Evian.

"You still have the bullet you found?"

"Yes."

"We must take it down to the chief of police to get it matched."

⁂

PENELOPE WAS still feeling queasy when they arrived at the police station. The drive down, predictably, hadn't helped. But three large glasses of mineral water and a mini baguette with ham had toned down the effects of the plum brandy. It seemed possible that any malevolent physical symptoms attributed to M. Louchard's hospitality had been imaginary. This time, her queasiness was due to another rendezvous with the chief of police.

They were asked to wait in a bare room where a young gendarme took a brief statement.

"I bet Reyssens keeps us waiting for as long as possible. He's not going to be pleased to see me, is he?" hissed Penelope.

Clémence put her finger to her lips. "Don't say anything."

Clémence looked quite rattled herself for once, Penelope thought as she watched her texting from her phone as dexterously as a teenager. Perhaps she was feeling guilty about selling a property that had thrown up one unforeseen problem after another. Especially as she had been so sure that Le Chant d'Eau was the house for Penelope.

It was a full half hour before they were called up to the office of the chief of police. Inspector Gamelin, his smartly dressed sidekick, stood at his side, taciturn as ever. Greetings were polite but perfunctory.

Clémence wasted no time in telling them exactly why the situation had become urgent. Penelope handed over the plastic bag holding the bullet casing.

The chief took it, and the two policemen peered at it, exchanging a few muttered words.

Gamelin spoke in English. "Mme Keet. Monsieur le chef de police is very concerned."

"Thank you. That is a great relief."

"No, Mme Keet. He is concerned that you refuse to accept his advice to leave this case to the police investigators."

The man himself turned to meet her gaze with a look of intense annoyance.

"The chief thanks you for your help, but he requests that you cease your investigations from now on. This is not the first time he has asked you to desist."

"What?" cried Penelope, glaring at the sour-faced chief.

"He is concerned that you have compromised this bullet by touching it and bringing it here. Even if it *was* indeed fired in your direction, as you say."

Both Penelope and Clémence objected forcefully.

Penelope drew herself up and turned to face the police chief. "Monsieur, I wore gloves whilst I searched, and as you can see, the bullet is properly bagged and tagged. I have done this before, you know, in England."

Reyssens gave a dismissive snort. "Angleterre—oui, Agatha Christie, M. Poirot! Amateurs! Toujours les amateurs!"

"This is not one of your mystery novels, madame," interjected Gamelin. His contemptuous tone made the words sound almost profane.

The spectre of the axe rose before them.

Another nasty look from the chief of police made Penelope wonder whether they had any hope of solving these crimes.

"He feels that this is a specialist job best done by the police," went on Gamelin.

"But I have been shot at, at least twice!" protested Penelope. "At the fête, you said if you thought I was in danger, you would protect me. Well, I am in bloody danger!"

The chief of police narrowed his eyes. He sat back in his chair.

There was a long pause, during which Penelope remembered her drunken certainty that he was also a very real threat. She felt an aura of increasing menace around him.

"I will ask my men to look in each day," he said. "We will set up CCTV observation. Are you alone in the house?"

Penelope could not help feeling that the surveillance was as much to keep an eye on her as for her safety. "I'm alone," she said quietly. "Thank you for that, monsieur. It will be a great comfort to know that the security cameras will record the entrance of the killer before he strikes."

But the irony was lost on the chief, who rose from his seat and told her that was all he could do.

"And are you going to ask your ballistics and forensics experts to examine the bullet casing?"

"Naturellement, madame."

With that, they were dismissed.

30

EVEN CLÉMENCE THOUGHT THEY HAD been badly done by. They rocketed back up the hill to St Merlot in near silence.

"Thank you for coming with me," said Penelope. "I'm sorry that I've messed up your day—again."

"I could not leave you to deal with this alone."

Penelope was just about to say that what Clémence had done was surely above and beyond what was required of an estate agent when the house came into sight. Outside was a smart blue Mercedes. The mayor was waiting for them. He looked concerned.

"How did it go with the chief of police?"

"How did you know where we were?" asked Penelope.

"Clémence sent me a text."

"That rat Reyssens could hardly bear to listen to us," said Clémence. "He gave the impression we were keeping him from something much more important. Like a four-course lunch."

"You are probably right," said the mayor. "But don't forget, I am on your side. The bullet casing that you found, Penny—I suppose you have left it at the police station, but can you describe it for me, please? I know all there is to know about the guns kept in St Merlot. It is one of my duties to issue the licences."

"I can do better than that," said Penelope. "Come inside, and I'll show you."

In the kitchen, she reached into her bag for her phone. "There," she said.

She held out the photos she had taken of the bullet, all of them next to a tape measure.

"Well done, madame—well played!"

Clémence looked suitably impressed.

"Does that help?" asked Penelope. "Can you narrow it down to the weapon that fired it?"

"It does help," said the mayor cautiously. "But we have to be very careful before drawing any conclusions. We might be able to identify the gun, and the ammunition—but this alone will not tell us who fired it."

He was right, of course. They all looked at each other.

"You have some ideas, though," said Penelope.

"Make me some good strong coffee," said the mayor.

Clémence answered a phone call and walked back down the hall to take it.

The mayor paced around as Penelope attended to the coffee. "It is good that you came to this village, Mme Keet," he said, abruptly. "When all this is over, you will be happy here, I promise you."

"I hope you're right—if I survive long enough!"

He started to say something, then stopped. He closed the door. "There are a number of issues I would like to discuss with you."

Penelope felt a lecture coming on.

"If you want to tell me off, it really would be better to do it here and now," she said, furious at how prissy that sounded.

"Tell you off?"

"I've probably done something wrong, as usual, so you might as well tell me now and get it over with."

He gave her an odd look. "I did not mean—"

Clémence returned, tucking her phone back into her bag.

"Just in time," said Penelope. "Er, coffee's ready."

They sat down at the kitchen table.

"Right," said Penelope, recovering her composure. "Who is on your list of gun licencees who owns weapons that could potentially have fired this bullet?"

The mayor's handsome face clouded. "There are only two. One is M. Louchard."

Penelope and Clémence exchanged glances.

"And the other is M. Charpet."

"No!" they cried together.

"Impossible!" said Clémence.

"They both have old-fashioned rifles that they use for hunting. The bullet could have been fired by either one of these weapons."

"Did you manage to check with the organisers of the fair at Banon that Louchard was supposed to be at?" asked Clémence.

"I tried, as soon as you texted," said the mayor. "I'm still waiting for a response."

"It can't have been M. Charpet. For all sorts of reasons," said Penelope. "I was with him and Valentine for lunch. He likes me. I'm giving him work!"

"He could have followed you after you left his house," pointed out the mayor.

The two women shook their heads.

"But no," went on the mayor. "You are right. I do not think M. Charpet fired the gun. But as I said before, that does not mean that one of these guns was not the one that was used."

"We should get the police up here to visit Louchard and take his gun for testing. And to look, at the same time, for any evidence that his house was broken into," said Clémence, scrolling numbers on her phone. "I'm calling them now."

"I think we have to," he agreed.

Clémence spoke briefly and ended the call. "Right. They are on their way."

"I would like to warn Louchard, though," said the mayor.

"What?" shouted Penelope. She had forgotten, in the heat of the moment, how the mayor always looked out for his villagers. "Why would you do that?"

"He will appreciate being treated correctly and fairly, you will see. That is how we act in this village—most of us, anyway."

"It doesn't seem right. Surely . . ." Then she remembered the draft contract, and the times she had seen them together. Why did everything seem to come back to this piece of the puzzle—a piece that she couldn't admit to having seen?

The mayor raked his hand through his hair and gave her a stare that might have been smouldering in other circumstances. "This is the difference between us, Penny."

She felt herself overheating.

"Between the French and the English, I should say," he went on. "In your country, people are innocent until they are proved guilty. Here, we have the Code Napoléon. Guilty until proved innocent. If the police are lazy . . . I am sure you see the problem." He sighed. "By the way, did Reyssens tell you they have a potential identification of the bones in the chapel?"

"No, he bloody well did not!"

"Ah. Well, they only have a partial match using dental records, but the name I've been given is Michel Cailloux."

"Do you know who he was?"

The mayor thought for a while. "I cannot say I do. There are some who pass through the village quickly, before anyone has had a chance to get to know them. Maybe he was here for a short while. It would have been before I was mayor. Although I have had my house here for many years, I spent most of my time working in Paris until about seven years ago."

Despite her confusion over Louchard and the mayor, something snagged in Penelope's mind. Michel Cailloux. Was it possible she had heard that name before? "No more information at all?" she asked the mayor.

"Only the name, and there is no absolute confirmation."

THE MAYOR left swiftly to get along to the Louchard farmhouse before the gendarmes did. Clémence, too, made her excuses. "Something urgent has come up with the sale of one of our properties in Goult. I'm sorry. I need to go there immediately. I will call you later."

"That's OK. Thank you—again—for everything you've done." Penelope would have been more effusive, but Clémence had clickety-clacked on her high heels to the front door and run out to her car.

Penelope sank onto a kitchen chair, grimaced at the strong coffee, and got up again to make the only brew that would do. As she boiled the kettle to make a cup of brick-red builders' tea, she tried to look on the bright side.

It did seem as if matters were finally coming to a head. Was the person who tried to shoot her also embroiled in the murders of Manuel Avore and this Michel Cailloux?

She looked outside at her terrace. Though the sun was shining, she decided against taking her tea outside. She was not daft enough to present herself as a sitting duck until the police had resolved what was going on.

She sat back down at the kitchen table, sipped, and closed

her eyes. That was a mistake. All she could see were bullets and bodies. Bones. A skeletal hand. The ace of spades. She picked up a book but found she couldn't concentrate. Too much was still whirling around in her head.

Manuel Avore. Michel Cailloux. Like a roll call in a nightmare. The names being intoned. It worried her that this new one had a ring of familiarity about it. Cailloux.

She drummed her fingers on the table. Cailloux. Was it just that she'd heard the French occasionally refer affectionately to their beloved Rolling Stones by that name? *Cailloux*. Stones, in French. Michel, Mick . . . Jagger.

Suddenly Penelope raised her hand to her mouth. Then she rushed upstairs. She scrabbled for her locked suitcase, under her bed. She opened it with trembling hands and took out the folder containing the notary's documents, her title of ownership of Le Chant d'Eau.

That was when she had heard the name Cailloux. When the notary had read out the names of all the previous owners.

Penelope flipped through the pages, so many pages. She noticed the name of Malpas in the rather sketchy prewar notes, and that of Avore afterwards, just as M. Charpet had indicated. And then, there it was. Michel Cailloux. Owner of the property for only a few months, between March and July 2010, before selling to the Girards from Lyon. She pulled the newspaper microfiche copy from her bag to check, though she was certain of the date: April 12, 2010. Her instincts had told her there was a connection between the two deaths and Le Chant d'Eau, and it looked as if she was right.

The games and card table where she found the newspaper cutting and the pack of cards. If Cailloux had briefly owned her house, then the table could well have belonged to him. Which explained why Avore had not taken it when he moved out.

Piece by piece, it was all starting to fit. But that meant that whoever killed Michel Cailloux must have had access to this house and the pack of cards.

A scraping noise outside made her look up. She went over to the window and peered out. The courtyard and the garden slumbered in the heat, undisturbed. A lively breeze played in the leaves of the olive trees.

"Just the wind," said Penelope aloud. "That was dried leaves being blown across stone."

She had almost convinced herself that she was being paranoid when she heard the noise again. It sounded like the scraping of metal. Then a rattling that was definitely not dried leaves.

Penelope was alone again in the house. In all the comings and goings, that had been forgotten.

She crept down the passageway towards the front door.

The door was open. Had she not closed it properly after Clémence had left? Had the wind blown it open? Penelope felt her mouth go dry.

The next moment someone called her name.

31

PENELOPE ALMOST COLLAPSED WITH RELIEF when Didier's smiling face appeared around the door. The electrician stepped into the hall, carrying his tool kit, the very picture of reassurance. Today's T-shirt bore a retro image of The Avengers. Diana Rigg gave her a sultry wink.

"I have a free afternoon, so I can make a start on the rewiring upstairs now, if you like," he said.

"That's great, thank you! Come on in."

It was rather wonderful how people here often seemed to arrive at just the right time. She wondered how the mayor was getting on with M. Louchard, and whether the police were on their way up to St Merlot.

She turned to show Didier upstairs, and noticed that he was staring intently at the newly cleaned card table in the hall.

"Do you like it, Didier?"

He snapped out of his trance and looked back at her

"The card table. I found it in the barn. Pretty, isn't it?"

Didier looked back at the table. "Yes, very nice. I'll get started, shall I?"

"Cup of tea?"

But he said he wanted to get cracking.

Penelope stood in the cool air at the open kitchen door while she gathered her thoughts. Surely she should tell the chief of police what she had found in the house deeds?

How much had happened since that first day when she stood on this very spot, looking out into the overgrown courtyard. Her dream house in Provence. The heat. The cicadas, the annoying wasps. If only she had known what lay in store.

From above she heard sounds of the electrician at work, interspersed with the odd French swear word.

It was nice to know that she was not alone in the house. She made herself a soothing cuppa and sat at the kitchen table, trying to make sense of what she had discovered on the deeds to the house. She had left them in her bedroom, she realised. She stood to go upstairs to fetch them.

Her phone rang.

"Hello?"

It was Clémence, but not the perfectly controlled version that Penelope had come to recognise. This time the voice was urgent, worried. "Penny, where are you? Are you on your own?"

"Yes, in the kitchen."

"Thank God for that!"

"Well, apart from Didier Picaud, the electrician. He's upstairs, replacing the wiring."

"Mon dieu! Penny, you must listen carefully and say nothing. You have to get out of the house."

"What?"

"Get out of the house now, and start running down to the road. Go—and stay close to the trees!"

Still holding the phone to her ear, Penelope grabbed her bag in a daze and did as she was told.

The urgency in Clémence's voice stalled any more questions as she slipped out of the back door. "Penny, are you there? I just got a call from my police contact, who has been checking out the Coustellet connection. Thank goodness I took it before I arrived at Goult. I'm on my way back now. It all fits together: the axe, the tractor competition, the break-ins, the shop at Coustellet . . ."

"I'm listening." Penelope brushed past a pine tree, scraping her arm.

"The connection we were looking for—"

Two strong forearms grabbed Penelope from behind and gripped tightly around her waist. She gave a scream of shock as her phone was snatched from her hand. She kicked backwards, hoping to reach her assailant's shins. The arms were so powerful, she could see the sinews straining. Flecked with pale dust. Or was it flour? Baker's arms. Jacques Correa! But how could he possibly know that she had reluctantly added him to her list of suspects?

"Help! Didier! Help me!" she yelled up at the bedroom window.

"Don't be stupid," said the man. "Argh!"

One of her sharp kicks had hit home.

She wrested herself around. It was only then that she could see who her attacker was.

"Didier!" gasped Penelope. "What the—"

Her young friend was no longer smiling. Penelope was no match for him as he jettisoned her phone and pulled her arms tighter behind her back.

"What's going on? What are you doing?"

He was very strong and smelled of sweat. He frogmarched her round the house to his van.

"For goodness sake, Didier! This is no time to go all James Bond on me!" Penelope joked feebly, trying to remind him of all the friendly chats they'd had. "Besides, Bond was always very well mannered."

"Shut up! Get in the camionette! We are going somewhere quiet to have a conversation."

"What about?"

"Your house, madame."

"Well, talk to me then! Didier?"

Penelope dug her heels in and tried to get free.

"Do not do that! I am much stronger than you are, and you will get hurt, believe me. I can hurt you very badly, madame, but I would rather that we came to a suitable arrangement. I realise that you might take some time to come to the correct decision, so I have decided to look after you until you do."

"What? We're friends, aren't we, Didier? You're just not thinking straight. We need to talk this through over a nice cup of tea."

"One more thing, Penny. I hate your English tea with milk— *c'est dégueulasse*! Disgoosting! No French person can drink it."

Didier opened the van door at the back and bundled her in. She kicked out again, but he pushed her over onto her front, pulled her hands behind her, and tied them together with what felt like wire. It cut into her wrists. He closed the door on her and went round to the driving seat.

"And now we go on a little trip, Penny. I will show you some of the beautiful scenery of the Luberon."

"But Didier!"

"Shut up!"

Penelope whimpered as the van bumped along the cart track to the gate of the property, then stopped.

"Merde!"

She tried to get up to see what was happening, but slithered back painfully against the sharp edges of several pieces of electrical equipment.

Didier began shouting expletives to no one in particular, and then reversed the van round in a rapid turn, bumping down into the lower field and throwing Penelope from one side of the van to the other. As they headed back towards the house, Penelope caught a glimpse in the rearview mirror of the panic in her captor's eyes. They turned up the hill and crunched over rough terrain. Then they screeched to a halt. Penelope bumped her head.

The young man got out and wrenched open the back doors. The van was almost wedged between trees. "We will have to walk. Get out."

As soon as she managed to scramble upright, he pushed her into the trees that lined the upper side of the track. Branches scratched her face; with her hands tied, she could not clear them.

"This is stupid!" she whispered. "The police will be here any minute. They're on their way now."

"Sssh!"

He obviously didn't believe her. He pushed her again, even more roughly, as they penetrated deeper into the copse of holm oaks and pines.

"Oww, that hurt!"

Didier's profile was grim as he gripped her arm and marched deeper into the trees. They tramped in silence for a few minutes. When they stopped, it was in front of a large dog rose bush. With one hand he reached in and pulled some branches aside.

"Get in."

Penelope looked around, wondering if there was any way she could make a break for it. His grip tightened as he dragged her behind him into a structure within the large bush. A dim light filtered through a long rectangular slit at eye level.

She realised they must be in some kind of hunting hide on the hill above her land.

Didier was sweating profusely now, obviously nervous. Penelope thought that if she could only speak to him in a civilised manner, there might be a way out for both of them.

"This is all a misunderstanding," she said. "We're friends, aren't we? There's no need for any unpleasantness. Please, Didier, why—"

"Shut up."

He produced a large, slim-bladed knife. "Silence. Understand?"

Penelope nodded.

She couldn't understand what had happened to this previously pleasant young man. But the more she stared at him, the more she realised that his slightly geeky awkwardness was an indication of more serious problems.

"There is not much time, madame. I want you to listen to me. I have a proposition for you that will help us both. First, you need to understand the history of Le Chant d'Eau. You need to understand who the house belongs to, and—"

"But I do—"

"Be quiet and listen, madame! Your electrical wiring, it is very old. Very old and very dangerous. There could easily be a fire."

"What? But you said it was fine!"

"It is not fine, Mme Keet." All amity and first-name terms were disposed with. "The wiring is no good. It could spark a fire that would leave the house a wreck. No one will be surprised. And that is what is going to happen—a big fire. You will be OK, of course! The insurance will cover the costs—and we, the Malpas family, will make you an offer for the ruin, at a reasonable price."

"But if it's my house you want, why burn it down? And what do you mean—we, the Malpas family?"

His eyes blazed. "My mother was a Malpas. I told you right at the start that my family had a long association with the house. That JRM Électriciens had looked after it for years. As we look after so many homes in St Merlot."

She didn't understand.

"JRM. Jean-Jacques and Roger Malpas. It is now my business. I continue the tradition. And it was *our* house!" Didier shouted.

"The house *and the land* my family owned for generations before that bastard Avore and his Nazi friends took it!"

"What on earth do you mean?" said Penelope. This was the story M. Charpet had told her, but she knew how important it was to keep him talking. Could he possibly be referring to the treasure said to be hidden in the grounds? She wasn't going to let on that she had heard the story.

"My grandfather and his brother were in the hills with the Resistance. My two older great-uncles were shot after a sabotage raid. Their parents were caught helping the maquis fighters and taken by the Gestapo. No one ever saw them again. That filthy collaborator Gustave Avore, Manuel's father, had informed on them. All to get his grubby little hands on the house and its land."

"Why didn't you try to get it back after the war?"

"Aah, if only it were that easy, madame. But after the war no one wanted to speak of the treachery that ran through all the villages around here. It was all about forgiveness, a break with the past . . ." Didier spat on the floor. "So the Avores stayed in the house, and we had to start again with the pathetic reparations that they offered us."

"If it meant so much to you, why didn't you try to buy it back later? You've been successful—you could have afforded it."

"Why should we pay good money for a property that was rightfully ours? We decided to wait. Everyone knew that things always went wrong for the Avores. Sure enough, old Gustave died; Emile, his son, crashed his car while drunk in the 1970s. Manuel Avore started drinking and gambling his way through all his money. We knew he would need to sell up sooner or later. Then, a few years back, came the moment. Avore was up to his eyes in gambling debts."

"A few years back?"

"About seven years ago. My uncle Jean-Luc approached Manuel

with an offer to settle his debts in exchange for Le Chant d'Eau. He refused, but then we made him an offer no gambler could refuse. We would play for the house. If he won, we would pay off his debts. That's when we put our plan into action."

"Your plan?"

Didier's voice took on a hint of pride. He was a psychopath, thought Penelope. He wanted her to know how clever he was. She was furious with herself for not spotting the signs earlier—but had there actually been any, beyond his obsessions and slight awkwardness?

"It was a brilliant plan. We knew he could never resist a game of cards. But we had a secret weapon."

"What was that?"

"Not what—who. A friend of a friend who was known as the best gambler in the Luberon Valley."

"But you didn't win the game," said Penelope.

"Oh, but we did!" Didier examined the knife. It looked lethal. "Or at least we would have won, but for that cheat Michel."

Penelope felt the pieces of this jigsaw of malice begin to fall into place.

"Michel?" She affected a disingenuous tone. "Who's he?"

"Michel Cailloux, card shark and cheat. Cailloux joined the game. It was high stakes, set up to look as if he too was playing to win the house, or to settle Manuel's debt—Manuel was greedy and stupid enough to agree. But we had arranged with Cailloux to defeat Avore together in front of witnesses. A perfect solution. We get the house, Cailloux gets paid off, and Avore gets what was coming to him."

"So what happened?"

"I was winning, just about to clean up. And Cailloux tricked me! He took the game and the house. Before we could do anything, he had the deeds signed over to him, in front of the honest witnesses, and the house was on the market. Oh, we tried to reason with him, to buy it for a marked-down price, but he wouldn't listen. We were outbid."

"By the Girards from Lyon?"

"Yes."

"And Cailloux?"

"He paid for his sins."

Penelope visualised the skeletal hand clawing at her from the chapel floor. Her blood ran cold.

"Was he from St Merlot?"

Didier gave her a baffled look. "No, he was from miles away. The other end of the valley."

"But why did you not buy Le Chant d'Eau when it was for sale this year?"

"It was too expensive. You outbid us."

Had the Malpas family been the other interested party Clémence had mentioned?

"These days only those who come from outside have the money to buy and then restore these old houses. We should have started a fire, partly destroyed it. If it was a ruin, then we could have afforded it. Perhaps we should have done it then, but we did not. Not then."

Penelope grappled with this dark logic. The spectre of an electrical fire, the blackened walls.

"And why would you want to stay anyway," he asked aggressively, "after a body is found in your swimming pool? That would have been enough to make most women run away fast."

"I don't give up easily." Penelope sounded a lot braver than she felt. "Whatever this is about, it's just got a bit out of hand."

Make that a lot out of hand.

"It should have been enough." A tic was pulsing in his cheek. The knife glinted in a shaft of light. He moved closer.

"OK," said Penelope, trying not to upset him further. "We can talk about this." But she wondered what on earth she could possibly say.

She thought she heard the faint wail of a siren. Could it be the police, coming up to St Merlot to see Pierre Louchard?

Neither of them said a word. They listened as the sirens grew louder.

Didier moved closer. "Did you call the gendarmes? How did you manage to call them?"

"I didn't."

The sirens reached a crescendo and stopped.

Penelope tried to think clearly. The police had arrived, but no one knew where they were hidden. Didier was rattled. He could lash out at her with his blade in a second.

"I can understand," she said, in a wobbly voice. "I can understand why you felt so strongly that the house was morally yours . . ."

The knife trembled in his hand.

"It was an accident," he said. "Avore came to my uncle Jean-Luc's house. Making trouble as usual, taunting us with the news that the new owner of Le Chant d'Eau was moving in. Asking why we didn't have the money to buy it. Were we so unsuccessful that we couldn't even get the house back this time? We were cutting wood that morning. They had a fight, and Avore went down when I hit him."

"Hit—with an axe?"

"It might have been."

"It was an accident, then?" Penelope knew it was always better to disarm an assailant by offering sympathy.

"We put him in the back of my van to take him home. We

thought he was only knocked unconscious. But when we got to his house, and we opened the doors to get him out, he was . . . not breathing. We panicked. I wanted to call for an ambulance, but Jean-Luc disagreed. He had an idea that could make everything right. It was only justice for us."

"To scare me away from my house?" Penelope was incredulous.

Didier moved closer.

Penelope had to keep him talking. With any luck, someone might hear. "When was this—you said it was the morning?"

"Early, for Avore, before nine o'clock."

"The day I arrived at Le Chant d'Eau?"

"Jean-Luc was outside his garage later and saw you arrive in your big English car."

"But . . . then, Manuel Avore apparently came into my garden at about six o'clock that evening. But how could it have been him?"

Didier stared hard.

"Perhaps the blow didn't kill him. You didn't kill him," said Penelope.

"No," said Didier. "You did not see Avore that day."

"But I was supposed to think I had!"

"You saw Jean-Luc."

"Eh?"

Didier was regaining his poise. He began playing with the knife, looking at her and then at the blade. Penelope had worked on enough cases to know when a psychopathic perpetrator was needy for recognition. She shivered.

There was a rustle of branches behind him.

Abruptly, Didier's expression changed. It registered incomprehension, then fear. Penelope peered through the shadows of the hide, unable to make out what was going on.

The knife fell from Didier's hands. He slowly raised his arms.

"Do not move, Didier. I have my favourite rifle in your back. I am taking off the safety catch."

A loud click sounded. Pierre Louchard emerged from the darkness.

"Get on your knees, Picaud."

Didier dropped to the ground.

Penelope felt dizzy. The adrenaline that had buoyed her up to this point drained away. She felt herself swaying.

"Sit down, madame. All is now well. The police are on their way."

M. Louchard kept the rifle trained on Didier.

Didier let out a grunt of rage. Louchard dug deeper with the rifle. "Don't tempt me," he warned.

Penelope tried to thank him, but no words would come.

From outside came the sound of cracking twigs and boots on the ground. Several gendarmes pushed their way in behind M. Louchard. Didier flailed around in a hopeless bid to escape. He was removed by two large men in blue uniforms.

Penelope fainted.

32

WHEN SHE CAME TO, PENELOPE saw flashing blue lights through the trees but couldn't work out what they were. M. Louchard was leaning over her. Two gendarmes in blue uniforms moved swiftly to her side.

"What's happening?" she cried. "Did someone shoot me? I knew someone was trying to shoot me!"

"Is all right, madame. Everything is OK." Louchard smiled. "Only a few moments you have been sleeping."

"Sleeping?"

"You passed out," said a muscular policeman.

She was helped down the hill to her house, to find a reception committee outside comprising the chief of police, the lugubrious Inspector Gamelin, the mayor, and Clémence.

The diminutive Reyssens stepped forward. "You did well, madame."

Praise indeed.

"I will make you a cup of tea," said Clémence. "We will all have one!"

"I think I need a plum brandy," said Penelope.

"How do you feel now?" asked the mayor, sounding genuinely concerned. "Do you need to lie down?"

Penelope lowered herself onto a kitchen chair, helped by a gendarme. She felt a little shaky but not too bad, all things considered. "No, I'm fine."

The mayor sat down next to her and held her hand. That felt nice. "As soon as you feel ready, tell us what happened out there."

Everyone looked at her expectantly. The chief of police stood by the window. "There are two gendarmes standing guard outside the back door, and two more by the front entrance," he said. "You have no more worries."

The mayor took a nod from Gamelin and asked her gently, "What can you remember?"

"I don't really understand what happened," Penelope murmured. "I thought Didier was such a nice, helpful young man. I thought we were friends—and then he dragged me off in the back of his van!"

It was galling to think that her judgement had been so flawed. Had she taken leave of all her senses since moving here, or had hormonal confusion seen off the last of her brain cells? She closed her eyes.

"He had a knife." It was coming back to her, but everything still seemed a bit fuzzy. "He was going to set my house on fire . . . or something. He wanted my house."

Was that right? Penelope sat back in her chair and took a sip of plum brandy. Feeling sticky and hot, she picked up the nearest flat object from the table and started to fan herself. She put it down again quickly when she realised it was her copy of *The Menopause and You*.

"The Malpas family has been trying to take ownership of this property for many years. But legally their claim had no validity, and no one took them seriously," said the mayor.

Penelope was still feeling fuzzy, but she remembered something. "M. Charpet told me the Malpases *did* own it before the war."

"That may be true," said the mayor. "And there have always been questions about how the Avores came out of the war living here, rewarded for some act of treachery. Unfortunately, many of the official records were lost or destroyed in the months that followed the Liberation."

"How convenient," said Penelope weakly.

"After the war there was such confusion. Much was covered up, especially by the collaborators. Whatever we suspect about their misdeeds can never be proved."

"What happened then?"

"The Avores were useless farmers. They couldn't make this place work, and it was eventually sold by Manuel Avore to pay his debts."

"Except that it wasn't!" cried Penelope. She had a rush of clarity. "I need to fetch something!"

She climbed the stairs and returned, clutching her head and the title deeds to the house.

"Ooh, I don't think I should have done that. But look at this!"

She set the document on the table and found the relevant page. Her legs were so weak, she sat down again quickly. "Manuel Avore did not sell the house to the couple from Lyon in March 2010. By then, it wasn't his to sell. For only a matter of months, it was owned by . . ." She pointed to the name.

They all spoke at once.

"Michel Cailloux!" exclaimed the mayor.

"Sacré bleu!" said the chief of police.

"That changes everything," said Clémence. "The disputed land on the title deeds! The complication arose because a parcel of land had never been correctly transferred to the previous owners, the Girards. It remained registered to the Avores, though it is clearly part of this property. The notary thought it was a simple mistake, years ago. But perhaps Manuel Avore deliberately kept it back from Cailloux when he sold the house and land to him."

Inspector Gamelin made a measured note of the page number on the document. "May I take this to copy?" he asked.

Laurent Millais was nonplussed. "So why did no one know this Cailloux, then? Where did he come from?" He seemed quite cross not to know.

"I think I can answer that," said Penelope. "And tell you why Cailloux was killed. Cailloux was a professional gambler—a cheat and a card shark."

They all stared at her.

"Cailloux double-crossed Avore *and* Malpas at a game of cards. The prize was Le Chant d'Eau."

Penelope closed her eyes to marshal her thoughts. She explained about the game that was supposed to deliver justice and the house back to the Malpas family, and the way Michel Cailloux took his chance to outwit both parties and renege on his deal with the brothers, a piece of chicanery that resulted in his murder.

"So you suggest Cailloux was killed by a Malpas?" asked the chief of police.

The mayor whistled. "It would explain the ace of spades in his hand."

"What if the card was placed with Cailloux's remains to make it look like a sign from the Marseille underworld?" Penelope turned to the chief. "That was what you told me you thought it was, didn't you?"

He went puce.

"And what's more," said Penelope, "I think Didier must have seen these deeds this afternoon. I was reading them upstairs when he arrived. I left them out when I heard a noise and went to find out what it was. Didier went up there, supposedly to begin rewiring. He was up there alone. Come to think of it, he was acting a little strangely after he had seen the card table I found."

"Card table, madame?" asked the chief. "What was special about that??"

"I found a card table at the back of the barn. It had the deck of cards and the newspaper cuttings in it—the ones I sent to M. Gamelin. You remember, the deck without the ace of spades. Didier must have recognised the table before he went upstairs. He might even have put the cards in there himself, after . . . after . . ."

"After helping to bury the ace with the body of M. Cailloux!" supplied Clémence. "So, he would have known you had found the cards, and he saw that you were searching the deeds. Which was why he threatened you as he did! You were close to making the connections. And that is why . . ." She hesitated.

"Go on," commanded Reyssens.

"Before the sale to you could go through, we had to sort out a mistake in the land documents. You remember? A small section was still registered—wrongly—to the Avores. No one had noticed that in the quick sale to the previous owners."

Penelope's head whirred. "Goodness . . . I've just thought of something. You know the old story about treasure hidden on the property? What if it's in the parcel of land that caused the legal difficulty . . . that Manuel Avore tried to fudge when he lost Le Chant d'Eau in the game of cards?"

Clémence widened her eyes.

"What if that was what Jean-Luc Malpas and Didier were after, as well as the house? Didier admitted it—or I think he did."

"We will be investigating all of this," said Reyssens pompously.

Penelope glared at him. "Do you think the Malpas men are the ones who've been shooting at me? Breaking windows with hunting shotguns? Trying to kill me in cold blood with bullets?"

"We are already investigating this," said Reyssens.

"I should think so, too," said Penelope. She looked across at her neighbour. "And don't forget that one of them could well have fired the shot from M. Louchard's farm with the express purpose of framing M. Louchard, making it look as if he was the gunman."

"C'est vrai—les salauds!" said Louchard.

Gamelin nodded. "I have no doubt that we will find that the rifle used was that of Louchard. My detectives will be taking it for examination."

"How did he get his hands on Louchard's rifle?"

The mayor interjected. "Oh, that is easy to explain. You see, Jean-Luc Malpas is a representative of a tool and machinery shop—a business that also supplies locks. Sometimes Jean-Luc fits these locks if there is no one else to do it. For him, it would be the work of moments to get into M. Louchard's farm and his rifle cupboard. He can open any house or outbuilding without damage. Without leaving any evidence that the door has been opened."

Penelope silently digested this news. "This tool and machinery shop—Darrieux SARL, at Coustellet?"

"Yes."

"And of course, Jean-Luc Malpas knew Louchard would be away that day at the tractor competition in Banon," added Clémence.

"And Didier knew I would be having lunch with M. Charpet and his sister!" Penelope realised. "He was right there, at the vide grenier, when M. Charpet invited me, and I accepted!"

"There you are, then."

"It's so hard to believe . . ."

Reyssens puffed up his chest like a cockerel. "As I have said, it is clear that the Malpas family wanted to scare you off. It was a horrible act of intimidation against you, the new owner of Le Chant d'Eau. I have no doubt that the murder of Manuel Avore and the planting of his body in the pool, perhaps even the shoot-ings . . . it was all intended to scare and confuse you. To make you leave almost as soon as you had arrived."

"And to make the property almost unsaleable," added Clé-mence. "Who wants to buy a house associated with a murder? The Malpases could then have bought it for very little."

"It nearly succeeded," said Penelope.

"Ah, but you are British, madame. We can all see that you have the famous stiff upper lip and courage," said the mayor warmly.

Penelope managed a smile, feeling—it was true—a certain stiffness around the mouth. She sat up a little straighter.

"So Didier was talking to you?" asked the mayor.

"He would hardly shut up. He's a chatterbox under the best of circumstances."

Gamelin listened intently, pen poised above his notebook.

Penelope rubbed her right temple. "It was something to do with his uncle. He said I saw Jean-Luc the day I arrived. I'm not sure I'm thinking straight. A minute ago everything was clear, and now I'm just getting a headache."

"No, I think you are right, and we are beginning to see the answer," said the mayor. He squeezed Penelope's hand and then stood up, as if he were giving a speech.

"It was the bad luck of the Malpases that you, Penny, had no fear of dead bodies—and also that you understood them and what forensic science can tell us. For it was you who first disputed the idea that Manuel Avore had met with a simple drowning accident or was a suicide, was it not?"

She nodded. "It was the floppiness of the body when it was brought out of the pool. I couldn't help noticing."

"Exactly."

"The timing didn't add up. M. Avore couldn't have been that

dead, if you see what I mean, if indeed it was him, I'd seen him around six thirty the previous evening. Judging from the lack of rigor mortis, the body that came out of the pool at midday the next day had been dead for more than twenty-six hours." She turned to the chief of police and Gamelin. "I tried to tell you that. The man I met on that first evening and the body in the pool could not have been the same person."

Reyssens nodded, expressionless.

The mayor held up a palm. "And you were right, Penny. My theory is this. You were supposed to think that you met Manuel Avore in your garden on the day of your arrival at Le Chant d'Eau. I think you met Jean-Luc Malpas—dressed as Manuel Avore!"

"You're right. Didier admitted it."

The mayor smiled at each of them in turn. "A clever idea, was it not? Jean-Luc is a skilled trickster. He is about the same height and build as Manuel Avore. He could do a good job of impersonating Manuel—especially to someone who has never met Manuel Avore before. He put on the man's cap and suit. He would have made sure you noticed all his characteristics. If you would give them in a description, it would seem obvious that this person you saw was Manuel Avore. You, newly arrived in the village, who knew no one here yet!"

The chief of police reached into a pocket and brought out a notebook and pen.

"They killed Avore earlier, and in the evening, when you had only been here for a few hours, Jean-Luc Malpas dressed in the dead man's clothes and came down the track into your garden, pretending to be him. Everything he did and said was calculated to sound like Avore, from the description you would give when the body was found."

"When I was in that . . . that hide," she started haltingly, "Didier said that Avore came to Jean-Luc's house to make trouble and taunt them about me moving into Le Chant d'Eau. There was a fight, and Jean-Luc hit Avore with an axe. I'm guessing it's the axe I found in the borie. So what was the point of this whole charade, of pretending to be Manuel Avore, of meeting me? Was it to try to give themselves an alibi for the supposed time of death?"

Suddenly she was feeling much better, as if she was back at work with dear Professor Fletcher at the Home Office forensic department.

"I think it must have been," said the chief of police, making a note. "We will know for sure when they are interviewed."

"Do they know nothing about forensics—how quickly that trick would be exposed?" Penelope shook her head. The lack of proper planning and attention to detail among the criminal fraternity never ceased to amaze her. "And . . . though I did meet Jean-Luc Malpas at his brocante stall at the vide grenier, and he did look familiar, naturally I never connected him with the man I thought was Manuel Avore. He was wearing nice clothes and sunglasses, too."

"Exactly."

Many of the villagers had the same shortish, wiry stature and suntanned faces, Penelope thought, but it might be rude, if not un-PC, to say so. One had to be so careful these days. Not that that stopped anyone from commenting on British upper lips.

"Do you think Jean-Luc heard M. Charpet saying that the oil lamp I bought looked familiar? I found out later that I'd probably bought back the outside lantern that he'd stolen. How mean is that? I expect he thought it was funny. How easy was I to rip off! But I never could have imagined that—"

"Tell her about the Coustellet connection," prompted Clémence.

"I was coming to that," said the mayor. "That was what we discovered today. You were quite right to link the Darrieux store at Coustellet to the perpetrators of this crime. It was an important observation that may not have been given due credit."

Reyssens shifted uncomfortably.

"It was Jean-Luc Malpas who bought the Strauss axe. I exerted some . . . pressure on M. Darrieux to reveal the credit card details of purchasers. His name was not among those, but he found himself remembering that Malpas had bought that make, and had first tried to get it for free because it was faulty and its head was loose. Darrieux wanted to send it back to the manufacturer, but Jean-Luc persuaded him to let him have it at cost price. It was very lucky for you that we did go to the shop. That was when Clémence phoned you, only to find that Didier Picaud was with you. We came straight back up—only just in time, as it turned out."

Penelope shuddered. "When they dumped Manuel Avore's body in the pool that night, they planted the axe in M. Charpet's hut. They must have thought they had solved all their problems at once."

Mention of the axe seemed to have made the chief aware that he ought to be scuttling back to the police station. He stood up and said goodbye, shaking hands solemnly, this time with a noticeable modicum of respect.

Slumped at her kitchen table, Penelope found she couldn't stop talking now. "Didier! I had no idea! How on earth did you know? I feel like such an idiot—but how could I have known?"

Then she raised her hand to her mouth. Everyone looked startled.

"What is it?" asked Gamelin urgently.

"It must have been either Jean-Luc or Didier who cut the brake cable on my car, too! What if I'd got in it to drive down the hill?"

The horror seemed worse now that she really was safe.

In the end there was only one more question. "Why didn't Didier drive farther away after he had bundled me into his van? Why stop at the hide?"

"I can answer that, madame," said M. Louchard proudly. "There was nowhere else to go. When I get the call from Clémence that Didier is at Le Chant d'Eau, I drive my prize-winning Mariette to the end of the track, and I park her there to block the exit!"

33

TWO DAYS LATER, AFTER COUNTLESS cups of tea and acts of kindness from her new friends and neighbours, Penelope was invited to present herself at the *mairie*.

Gentle wind in the trees sounded like running water as she walked briskly along in the autumn morning sun. In the woods above, the hunters' hide where she had spent such an agonising half hour with Didier was so skilfully masked by holm oaks that it was invisible. She moved on swiftly.

No cars passed her on the road up to St Merlot. When she arrived at the square, the stock-still old man reading the newspaper under the trees looked up as she passed, and raised his hand in salute. The unexpected movement almost gave her a heart attack.

"Bonjour, Mme Keet!"

"Er, bonjour, monsieur!"

Penelope gave him a wide smile as he tipped his beret and resumed reading.

Next, she passed a few people milling around the shop, who smiled at her. Penelope felt as if a door had finally opened. She would still be a foreigner here—but a welcome foreigner, who was part of village life.

At the *mairie*, she was ushered quickly by Nicole into the inner sanctum. Laurent was standing in front of his desk with the chief of police and Clémence.

The mayor flashed her one of his most devastating smiles. "Ah, Mme Keet, Penny, I am glad you are here. Now we can start."

"Start what?" Penelope was still reeling from the after-effects of his greeting.

"Monsieur le chef de police has some new information for us. I think you will find it very interesting. Come through to the meeting room."

They all sat at one end of a long table. Nicole brought in coffee and lingered, obviously hoping to hear the latest at first hand.

"Thank you, Nicole," said the mayor.

The door closed, and the chief of police began.

"I wanted to update you on our progress since we arrested Didier Picaud, and also Jean-Luc Malpas. Although Didier's confession to you gave us new information, and there is enough evidence to charge him with a number of crimes, including attempted abduction, we were still unable to find proof of his part in Avore's murder."

Penelope frowned as she remembered back to her brief incarceration. "He told me it was an accident, monsieur."

"Yes, and he is sticking to that story. However, we have been examining Manuel Avore's house and we believe he is lying."

"Really?"

"We have taken forensic samples from the house, and they tell a different story."

Penelope listened carefully as the chief continued.

"In the kitchen of the Avore house, we found traces of blood in the mortar cracks between the floor tiles. The blood was that of Manuel Avore. Normally this would not be conclusive—he was living there, after all. But then we discovered something else. Something very interesting."

He puffed out his chest.

Penelope was getting impatient. "And this something else was . . ."

"We discovered some flecks of blood that did not belong to Avore."

"Do you know whose they were?"

"Well, madame, this is the strange thing. They did not belong to anyone . . ." The chief of police smiled, as if at a happy memory. Penelope felt her temper begin to fray. Did the man do this on purpose?

"Blood but no donor?" she asked.

Was this what she'd been summoned to hear? The mayor and Clémence were listening respectfully, but she was unimpressed.

"Patience, madame, I am about to explain. The blood did not belong to anyone . . . human. They belonged to a very special animal."

The glimmerings of a snigger on his ridiculous face only served to infuriate Penelope further.

"As I say, a special animal. A . . . rabbit. Your rabbit."

Penelope was lost. "But I don't have a rabbit!"

"The rabbit whose blood you found on the axe, under the faulty head. In Avore's house, it was on flakes of varnish from the axe shaft that we think must have been dislodged—microscopic! Very, very leettle!"

She managed to stop herself from retorting that she knew perfectly well what microscopic meant. In fact, that she probably understood forensic pathology better than he did.

"These flakes that carried the blood of the rabbit fell like the dust when the axe was used to attack Manuel Avore."

"And conclusively place the axe in Avore's house, along with his own blood, at the time of death!" Penelope couldn't restrain herself this time.

"Exactly," said Reyssens. "He was killed by being hit on the

front and the side of the head by the blunt side of the axe. Probably so that there would not be any blood to clean up. But the
blade must have caught Avore's hand when he raised it to defend
himself, and caused him to bleed."

"His hand . . ." Penelope pictured the body bag and the limp
hand. "It was gashed. I saw it."

"So it was not an accident, as Didier told Penny," said Clémence. "The axe! We always knew it."

"No, that was a lie," Reyssens reiterated, as if he was pleased to
be able to lord it over one of them. "The perpetrators were very
careful to make a plan and to cover their own traces. They tried
to confuse the time of death. They took the axe that had been
used to kill rabbits. They cleaned the axe head and the blunt
side used to kill Avore. Then, before they put it in M. Charpet's
shed, they used it to kill another rabbit, cleaned the axe again—
but not perfectly, to make sure to leave a few traces of the blood
of this last rabbit. Our more detailed tests show that it has been
on the axe for approximately the same time that Avore is dead.

"But they did not clean the traces of the axe's previous rabbit
victim under the faulty head. We have charged both men with
the murder of Manuel Avore. They will spend a long time in
prison."

Penelope sat back in amazement. The blood on the axe
had been material to the case after all. Her instincts had been
proved right. "So Manuel Avore was killed in his own kitchen.
But where was Mariette, his wife—was there no danger that she
would come home and interrupt them? Oh!"

She clapped her hand to her mouth. "The day I arrived was a
Wednesday. Mariette Avore was in the Bibliobus in the square.
She was out all day, driving the mobile library!"

"That's right!" said the mayor. "She must have been."

"But why was Manuel killed now—why not long before?"

asked Penelope, glad of a chance to ask the question that had been bothering her.

"Didier Picaud has provided a very full account," said Reyssens. "He has hardly stopped talking, in fact. By the way, he was the intruder who broke into your house. He was eliminated from the inquiry on the grounds that his fingerprints were already legitimately inside.

"Anyway, it seems that when Manuel Avore was released from prison, he started drinking immediately. He told various locals in a bar down in Apt that he had some very interesting information about the Malpas family, but not what that was. He liked the power of knowing he was a threat to them.

"Bad news travels fast. The Malpas men were ready for trouble, even before they saw Avore in the village. When they did, Avore taunted Jean-Luc and Didier that he knew that they had murdered Michel Cailloux, and he was considering what to do about it.

"He told them that his information had come from an old thief he had met in prison. This man had known Michel Cailloux well; Cailloux had told him he was selling the house he'd won as soon as possible, and that he'd double-crossed the Malpases. It wasn't safe for him to be anywhere near St Merlot, and he'd feared for his life. Cailloux told his friend, who told Avore when he met him in jail that he'd used the house a couple of times for high-stakes card games.

"Cailloux then had to leave quickly, after threats from the Malpases. It seemed he had moved to a different region, perhaps under a different name. In any case, his friend never heard from him again."

"Which would explain—sorry," said Penelope.

"No, go on," said Reyssens with heavy forebearance.

"The newspaper cutting I found in the card table. The unhappiest jackpot winner in the world. Cailloux didn't want the publicity, and he certainly didn't want to be identified as a 'St Merlot resident,' which might lead to questions about how he came to be the owner of a house there. All he wanted was a quick sale, and out."

"But the Casino de Salon always names the winner of its big Easter poker competition," said the mayor. "It's good publicity for them. Cailloux shouldn't have won if he didn't want to be in the newspaper."

"Maybe he couldn't help himself," said Penelope. "He always had to win, maybe even when he'd agreed not to. He was addicted to his winning streak."

"Or cheating streak," said Reyssens. "Anyway, Manuel Avore was now out of prison, and talking. Jean-Luc and Didier knew they had to act quickly."

"But they had to wait for the next Wednesday or Thursday, when Mariette Avore would be out all day driving the mobile library!" cried Penelope. "That Wednesday was the earliest they could get rid of Avore—the day I moved in. But they didn't think it all through properly. They didn't have time. Perhaps"— she turned to Reyssens—"you could ask Didier how the ace of spades got into Cailloux's dead hand. Did they break into the house and take it from the card table, or was the marked card already being carried by Cailloux? It has to be one or the other. I'm sure if you flatter him, he will keep talking."

The chief of police exhaled through his wet, red lips. "It seems that maybe I should have taken more seriously your understanding of murder, Mme Keet." He didn't actually apologise for making fun of her, but he was the type who never would.

Penelope smiled graciously. "Perhaps les amateurs have something to offer, after all."

She was going to enjoy telling Camrose that.

34

IT WAS A SATURDAY IN late September. The day dawned bright and clear over the Luberon. At eight o'clock in the morning the air was crisp with the first intimations of autumn.

Penelope dived into her swimming pool, relishing the delicious tingle of the cold water.

M. Charpet and his lad had finished restoring order to the chaos of the garden. The swimming pool looked splendid. At each of the four corners stood a brand-new cypress tree next to a large terra-cotta urn. Penelope had particularly enjoyed searching through the multitudes of reclamation yards to find those. In a moment of reckless daftness she had also acquired a fibreglass panda, surprisingly similar to the one she'd seen at the *brocante*, but for half the price; it gazed ruminatively out from the thicket of bamboo in the garden. It was really quite lifelike, she thought, and it confirmed a certain English eccentricity that was no bad thing. The locals already thought she was mad for continuing to swim in her unheated pool, but she found the cool freshness of the water just glorious.

Forty lengths of breaststroke and front crawl, and she was invigorated. She dried herself off quickly and pulled on her dressing gown before wandering back to the house.

This was going to be a day of treats, she had decided. A day for a two-croissant breakfast. She hardly ever ate them these days, and her figure was definitely benefitting. Balancing a cup of fragrant coffee and a plate, she wandered out onto the terrace, still in her dressing gown. Yes, it would be a day of treats at her dream house in Provence.

By nine thirty, it was miraculously warm again, one of those days when it might still be summer. She would play her cello for an hour or two later. Now the interruptions had ceased, she had finally been able to give herself over to her music. Sometimes she played outside, thrilling to the progress she was making and the increasingly assured richness of the notes she released into the air, floating off towards the blue hills.

She felt safe and among friends here now. Later on, she was having dinner with Laurent Millais. At his house, no less—her curiosity was in overdrive, and she was looking forward to seeing it. He had promised champagne to raise a toast to new beginnings.

Didier Picaud and Jean-Luc Malpas were in the Avignon jail, awaiting trial for the murders of Manuel Avore and Michel Cailloux, and the harassment and attempted kidnap of an Englishwoman. As part of some complex plea bargaining, Jean-Luc had admitted forcing entry to M. Louchard's gun cupboard and breaking into Le Chant d'Eau to get the symbolic ace of spades—simulating a gangland calling card—on the night they killed Cailloux in April 2010, not long after he appeared in the newspaper. Didier had admitted that he had fired the shots at her. He swore that he had never aimed to injure her, and Penelope desperately wanted to believe that. According to the mayor, the chief of police was finally doing a reasonable job, and there was every sign that justice would be done.

The village was a happier place, too. The murders seemed to have brought everyone together. Any minor quarrels were being settled over a game of pétanque or in the bar.

"You have been a force for good at St Merlot!" the mayor told her when he issued his invitation. "Though it was very unpleasant for you, I know."

"It's over now," she said.

The following week, builders and decorators were scheduled to start repairing, replastering, and repainting. Le Chant d'Eau would be watertight and cosy by the time winter came.

The second buttery, flaky croissant was raised to her lips when she heard the sound of a vehicle arriving. Acutely aware of the suburban English style of her dressing gown, Penelope was about to withdraw discreetly when a taxi screeched to a stop on the track. Stones rattled.

As the dust cloud subsided, a voluptuous figure in shocking pink emerged from a passenger door, hollering, "Surprise!"

"Frankie!"

"Hello, darling!"

"What the hell is that?" Frankie left the taxi driver staggering under the weight of an enormous suitcase. "That dressing gown is disgusting, Pen—it's got to go!"

Penelope bustled up to her friend. "And why didn't you tell me you were coming?"

"Clémence phoned me and told me about the celebration dinner at the mayor's house, and I just had to come! You don't mind, do you?" Frankie gave her a big hug. "I couldn't bear to miss the party, and I want to hear all about everything face to face."

"No, of course, I don't mind, but—" Penelope stared as another huge suitcase appeared from the boot of the taxi.

"Just a short stay, darling."

Penelope did not know whether to be pleased or exasperated. So much for her quiet day of self-indulgence and pampering before her big night with Laurent. Not that it wasn't always fun to have Frankie around. They sat out on the terrace gossiping, and Penelope spared no detail of her mini-abduction by the young man who had apparently been so keen to be her friend and speak English.

"Got that one wrong, didn't we, Pen, eh? Nasty business."

"I feel sick that I fell for it."

"You were only being nice, Pen. Thinking the best of people."

"Still feel stupid. That knife he was holding . . . still makes me shudder."

"When's the trial?"

"In a few months' time."

"You going to go to court?"

"I don't know yet. I might be needed as a witness."

"They can't be pleading not guilty!"

"I'm trying to put it all out of my mind. But have to say it was very satisfying when Laurent made the chief of police come to the mairie to tell us in person about the final pieces of evidence against them in the Avore case. He's an odd character, though— Reyssens, I mean."

A car beeped as it came down the track, heading for the Louchard farm.

Penelope waved, and then turned to Frankie. "It's nice to know that Pierre's not too far away. He's a nice man. That was another thing. Didier tried to make me suspicious of lovely M. Louchard."

"They've stopped. They're getting out."

Penelope resolved to stay off the plum brandy if that became an issue. She wanted to be on top form for the evening to come.

Pierre Louchard and Mariette Avore bounded through the garden gate, holding hands.

"Ah, bonjour, bonjour! Mme Frankie!" said Louchard. Everyone kissed everyone else three times.

"It seems a good moment to tell you all that we are getting married! At our age there is no point waiting when we know each other so well, and we should have wed when we were nine-teen!"

Mariette beamed.

Cheers and congratulations erupted. Everyone kissed every-one else three times more.

The sound of churning grit on the track, followed by a squeal of brakes, announced yet another visitor. Clémence arrived, bearing gifts from Apt market—white nectarines and olive oil. "Bonjour, Penny! Bonjour, Frankie! Une bonne surprise, n'est-ce pas?"

⁂

NATURALLY, FRANKIE wanted to go out for lunch. Clémence suggested that they try out a new restaurant in Saignon, ensured that Frankie was salivating at the prospect of a slap-up meal, and then left them to it.

Bet she's eating an apple for lunch and going to the hairdress-ers this afternoon, thought Penelope. There was no getting away from it, she did feel a bit put out that what she had thought was dinner à deux with the mayor had somehow metamorphosed into a dinner party. But perhaps she had misunderstood. Too much wishful thinking.

The restaurant in Saignon was very good, and it was always a pleasure to visit the village, with its main street that looked like the perfect location for a French film set in the 1950s. Penelope stuck to Perrier and just had a light main course, while Frankie drank rosé and worked her way through the three-course menu.

"I did get up at an unearthly hour to get on a plane this morn-ing, Pen!"

"You carry on, Frankie. I'm keeping to the Frenchwoman Diet."

"I must say, you're looking good on it, too."

"I think we should both have a siesta when we get back. Here, have the rest of the carafe."

The wine did knock Frankie out for a few hours—long enough for Penelope to relax in the garden, have another swim, and do everything else she had planned to do at leisure, like painting her nails and taking her time washing and styling her hair. It hardly mattered now. Laurent wouldn't pay her any more attention than any of the other guests. Not that he ever would have done, she reminded herself. It was just as well Frankie and Clémence and whoever else was going to be there. They had stopped her from making a complete fool of herself.

At seven o'clock, Penelope put on a slinky deep-violet dress that flattered her curves, and grinned at her reflection in the mirror.

Through the open window she could hear Frankie outside, chatting nineteen to the dozen with Johnny on her mobile.

"It's all coming together, the house is going to be amazing, and you wouldn't believe the change in Pen since she left Esher. . . . She looks years younger. . . . Yes, really . . ."

⊰❧

"ARE YOU driving, Pen?"

"I booked a cab. I know it's hardly any distance, but better safe than sorry. I don't want to drink and drive."

"Well done. Now we can really enjoy ourselves." Frankie was resplendent in a silvery tunic that showed off her legs. Wearing false eyelashes, too.

"That was the idea."

"Have you been to Laurent's house before?"

"No. Can't wait to see it."

The taxi ride only took about five minutes. The driver knew exactly where to go: through the centre of St Merlot and out the other side towards Les Garrigues.

They passed the old priory and turned into a drive lined with olive trees and oleanders. The grounds were extensive but beautifully maintained. The grass was like a bowling green. He must have a team of gardeners working round the clock, thought Penelope.

The mayor's home was an eighteenth-century manor house with elegantly faded grey shutters. Frankie was impressed. "All very chi-chi. The roof's new, and it's top quality," she hissed. All the windows along the ground floor were French doors. The setting sun gilded the exquisite pale stucco exterior. A line of plane trees shaded a substantial gravel terrace where a table was set with candle lamps and flowers. Close by, at either end, were patio heaters for when the evening temperature dropped. It was like a photograph in a lifestyle magazine.

From this perfect picture stepped Laurent Millais, carrying three bottles of Dom Pérignon. He placed them in a silver cooler filled with ice and raised his hand in greeting.

"Bonsoir, mesdames!"

Laurent looked heart-stoppingly gorgeous in a cream shirt and burgundy jeans. Penelope suppressed a retort as Frankie launched herself at him, to be first in with the three kisses.

"Thank you so much for inviting us," she said when it was her turn. "What a stunning house!"

"I could not live anywhere else! Now, let us open the champagne."

A waiter brought crystal glasses on a tray, and then opened one of the bottles and poured.

Visible through the open door to the kitchen, caterers dashed around, and a young waitress brought out canapés.

They all raised their glasses.

"To Penny, and her new life in St Merlot!" said the mayor.

"Thank you!"

Penelope felt shy all of a sudden. Goodness, it was just as well she hadn't arrived to find she was the only guest. That would have been rather overwhelming.

"You haven't cooked for us yourself, then?" teased Frankie.

"I do cook, but not tonight. It is a special occasion."

"So how long have you had this place?" she went on, giving the pale stone façade a professional evaluation.

Laurent did not have a chance to answer, as the red Mini Cooper made it down the drive in a matter of seconds, stopping abruptly in front of the terrace.

Clémence emerged alone, hair immaculate and subtly blonder. She looked like a miniature Catherine Deneuve in a designer black dress that nipped in her tiny waist. Her high shoes fastened around the ankle with soft leather bows.

"Love those shoes," gushed Frankie. "Yves Saint Laurent?"

The Frenchwoman winked at Penelope. "My special place in Paris." She kissed Laurent and accepted a flute of champagne.

"No M. Valencourt this evening?" asked Frankie. From anyone else, it would have sounded too blunt.

Penelope had still not discovered anything about the elusive Monsieur V.

"Oh, non. Malheureusement pas. He sends his regrets."

"So he's busy, then, this Saturday night?"

"Hélas, it could not be avoided."

"What's he doing?" Frankie bulldozed on.

"He is not here, he is away on business."

Anyone else would have left it there, but Frankie persisted. "Where is he?"

In spite of her own curiosity, Penelope cringed.

"He is abroad."

"He's very mysterious, your husband!" Frankie laughed, to show she didn't mean any harm. "Does he get home much?"

"No, not very often."

Politeness was restored with the arrival of a glamorous couple in a black Mercedes. Penelope was pretty sure that she recognised them from the mayor's party at the St Merlot fête.

A round of introductions was made. They were Claudine and Nicolas, and they lived in Roussillon. She was a museum director, elegant in silky draped blue. He was an artist and wore a black linen suit with a black shirt. There was an air about him that suggested his art sold very well.

Penelope started speaking to Claudine—she had a wide smile that made her very approachable—while trying to hear Frankie interrogate Clémence. "Does that mean you and Laurent are still . . ."

Penelope found she was holding her breath. Frankie's directness could be embarrassing. She hoped Clémence wouldn't be offended.

But surprisingly, she didn't seem to be. "That has all cooled off," said Clémence. "It was fun while it lasted, but you know, there is a time . . . and then it passes."

The waiter refilled glasses.

"How are you finding St Merlot?" Claudine asked Penelope. "Not too quiet?"

"It's wonderful," said Penelope, deciding to gloss over the body in the swimming pool and the shock of shaking hands with a skeleton while under fire. "Not nearly as busy as Roussillon, though. Tell me which museum you work at?"

Claudine hadn't got very far into her explanation of where the

Ochre and Paint Museum was and what her role there was when another car came up the drive. Penelope felt the champagne go to her head when she heard its engine.

The red Ferrari growled towards them and parked in front of the terrace.

Penelope glanced at Frankie, who raised an eyebrow in return.

Laurent stepped forward and enveloped his friend in a bear hug. They obviously knew each other well. The silver fox was introduced as Benoît de Reillane. He kept hold of Penelope's hand slightly too long after shaking it and her first thought was that he was of the type that needed watching. He was attractive, though, no doubt about it.

"I heard you wanted to meet the priest," said Laurent, mischievously.

"What?"

"Benoît is my friend the priest."

"You're the priest?" said Penelope. "Crumbs."

Benoît smiled gnomically. "And you are the neighbour of my business partner Pierre Louchard? He is a lucky man."

Penelope's mouth dropped open a little. She was about to ask him what he meant when other voices broke in. More guests were arriving.

As guest of honour, Penelope was seated next to Laurent. Under the warming glow of candlelight, the wine flowed, delicious food was placed in front of them, and interesting conversation was interspersed with lots of laughter. Penelope was toasted again, and the story of her difficulties retold. She felt happier than she had in ages.

"I have one more toast," said Laurent, standing at the head of the table. "Let us drink to the success of Le Prieuré des Gentilles Merlotiennes and its new purpose." He sounded excited.

Penelope saw him smile at Clémence.

"As some of you will know, we heard yesterday that the deal has gone through, and the consortium is in place to develop the priory as a holistic retreat and natural healing spa. Thanks indeed to Father Benoît and the Agence Hublot for making it all possible. They are tough negotiators, and I couldn't have done it without them."

Everyone raised their glasses.

"A retreat and spa! That sounds wonderful," said Penelope, when Laurent sat down.

"I hope it will be. If we get it right—and we have been taking advice from all different sources—it could bring the priory back to life in a way that is good for all of us. I want to grow lavender there—"

"Like they do at the Abbaye de Sénanque," said Penelope, understanding at last.

"Exactly. But also to use lavender and herbs grown locally in a range of organic creams and soaps and natural remedies. Pierre Louchard's lavender is excellent, and he will be able to expand his business."

"It's a great idea. Wait a moment, M. Louchard is in this scheme as well?"

"He is a partner, leasing part of his land and providing the lavender."

"And were there any other partners—like Manuel Avore, for example?"

"How do you know that? We needed a small strip of land from none other than Manuel Avore. We were willing to agree to a decent sum of money, but he always refused to sell—it was the last tiny parcel he owned—but said he would consider leasing it. In the end we dealt with his wife after his death. She was much more amenable."

Laurent refilled her glass. "If you wanted to plant the higher part of your land with lavender, or thyme, for that matter, you could be part of this too."

Penelope thought of the scent that would produce. "Mmm . . . I like that idea."

"It's going to be a good project."

"I've never met a Ferrari-driving priest before."

"My friend Benoît is unlike anyone else. And he has always loved Italian sports cars. Though it's really not very practical for our terrain. Every time he wants to see Pierre, he has to park and walk down that track you share—the rocks and bumps would destroy the suspension on that car."

He must have been visiting Louchard, that first night when she heard the roar of the engine! And that was why he stopped at the end of the track. She kept those thoughts to herself, glad it was all over.

"How did you meet?" she asked

"In another life, when I was making a television documentary. He was running the monastery over at Reillane, though as no abbot had ever done before."

"Oh?"

"In order to assume charge of this ancient institution, he was obliged to take holy orders. Luckily, he was allowed to choose the seminary that would supply his religious education. So his ordination comes courtesy of an online church in Nevada."

"He's not really a priest, then?"

"Do not ever say that in front of lawyers for the Church of the True Believers of Christ on a Burnt Taco, founded in 1983."

Penelope giggled. "No!"

"Something like that, anyway. Benoît once had a rather successful career as an actor in French cinema. Benoît Berger?"

She shook her head, making a mental note to look him up online.

"Much loved by female film fans of a certain age. But his great achievement at Reillane is the conversion of the monastery into a beautiful theatre and arts centre that benefits the whole community—and beyond, for that matter. I want to achieve a project here that will be equally good for this village."

Penelope looked over at the former film star. He was chatting animatedly to Frankie. No doubt she would hear all about him when they got home. "How did your documentary turn out?"

Laurent pulled a mock-modest expression. "It won a national award."

"Congratulations."

"It was a long time ago."

"It's a perfect evening," she said. "A lovely celebration."

"I didn't intend for quite so many people to join us. But the priory deal was signed, and Clémence insisted we should mark the event with Claudine and Nicolas, who are big investors. They are leaving in a few days to set up an exhibition in Berlin—and she was sure that you would want Frankie to be invited to the party."

That was interesting. It chimed with her feeling about Clémence's machinations that morning.

"We must have that dinner together sometime," said Laurent.

Penelope's mobile whistled. She ignored it. Then it went off again.

"Have a look. It might be important."

The first text was from Justin: Hi Mum, hope you're well. All fine here. Send word sometime if you are still alive.

Penelope smiled. If only they knew. She had spared the children the details, not wanting to worry them. The barest details of her neighbour's death had sufficed.

The other was from Lena: We haven't talked properly for ages, it said. We all miss you, and Zack says he wants his Gan-ma to play football with him soon. Hope everything is going well and no news lately is good news. Xxxx from all of us.

She smiled.

Absolutely fine, darling, she texted back to each of them. Lovely—everything I hoped it would be. Sorry, been very busy. Lots to tell you, but let's wait till you come out.

She switched off her phone and turned back to Laurent.

"Now, what were you saying about dinner?" asked Penelope.

Acknowledgments

Huge thanks to Stephanie Cabot and Araminta Whitley for loving the characters in this book immediately and laughing a lot, as well as for brokering the deals that meant readers would have a chance to meet Penelope Kite and friends. Also to Ellen Coughtrey at the Gernert Company in New York, who gave us a brilliant critical edit at a crucial stage.

At HarperCollins in New York, the incomparable Jennifer Barth took the change of direction from previous books in her stride and made everything happen. In London, Harriet Bourton at Orion pushed us further with her enthusiasm and the strength of her vision for future adventures with Penelope.

We are extremely grateful for all their hard work to everyone at Harper, especially Jonathan Burnham, copy editor Miranda Ottewell, assistant editor Sarah Ried, Joanne O'Neill, who designed the fabulous cover, marketing director Jennifer Murphy, publicist Emily Vanderwerken, and interior designer Bonni Leon-Berman.

Croissants all round in London for Marina De Pass, Olivia Barber, copy editor Francine Brody, Alainna Hadjigeorgiou, Brittany Sankey, and everyone at Orion who launched Penelope with such aplomb.

And a great big *pain au chocolat* for Maddy Rees, who spent sultry afternoons reading detective novels in the garden in Provence and offered her own inimitable comic insights.

About the Author

Serena Kent is the nom de plume of Deborah Lawrenson and her husband, Robert Rees. They met at Cambridge University and pursued completely different careers, she in journalism and fiction; he in banking and music. They live in a house full of books in England, and an old hamlet in Provence, which is also in dire need of more bookshelves.